MW01489635

The Epicureans

A novel by Charles McNair

Illustrations by
Robert Altbauer
& Ollie Hoff

Art direction by
Andrew P Hind

TUNE & FAIRWEATHER
DUBLIN, IRELAND

Tune & Fairweather, 2021
First published online in serial installments across 2017-2018, in a slightly different form, by *The Bitter Southerner*. Graphical textures applied to illustrations and pull quotes sourced from TextureFabrik.com.

Visit us online:
tuneandfairweather.com @tuneandfair
facebook.com/tuneandfairweather instagram.com/tuneandfairweather

ISBN 978-1-91-627991-9

First Edition

The Epicureans is a work of fiction. Unless otherwise indicated, all the names, characters, businesses, places, events and incidents in this book are either the product of the author's imagination or used in a fictitious manner. Any resemblance to actual persons, living or dead, or actual events is purely coincidental.

Art direction by Andrew P Hind
@andrewphind instagram.com/andrewphind

Contents

—1—

The Black Forest

A pretty postcard.

Snow settles over the Black Forest.
The dark trees put on robes, arms raised like obedient children. Their sleeves slowly whiten.

Here's a stone cottage, hidden from any traveler. In the derelict, ice-glazed front garden, a weathered wooden statue greets visitors.

A boy.

Clean snow collects atop his walnut cap.
One of the child's eyes wears a cataract of ice.

His rosy cheeks and red smile look happy.

This evening, the painted figure silently welcomed twenty-five people, arriving in a whitening storm. The distinguished visitors creaked through a dusted iron gate and churned the snow on the stone path to the cottage door.

Inside, thirteen tables waited, candles dancing. Against old stone walls, the colossal shadows of these guests flickered and jerked like projections from old movies. A phonograph played Wagner, the soaring Rings. Aromas sang from the kitchen, breads and spices and soup and sauces. Truffle. Citrus and sweets and roasting potatoes.

Potatoes go with anything.

The Epicureans have gathered. This is their night.

This solstice, they chose a secret place in the forest near Baden-Württemberg. Next December 21 will be in Alabama, home to a solitary gentleman in a white Stetson and fringed white western jacket seated against a far wall.

In two years, the group will gather secretly near Rio (for tropical sun with their feast) or maybe Buenos Aires. Votes on the next venue will be tallied at the end of the evening.

Tonight, the gifted chef chosen to prepare this year's feast will weep in front of his twenty-five guests, his white toque blazed in firelight. The Epicureans will reassure him, pat his back, murmur *there, there, delicious, you've outdone yourself, it was the meal of a lifetime ... two lifetimes!*

Indeed, the annual feast will be sensational, the best so far in a quarter-century of December meetings.

After two dozen courses and a fine dessert, the chef will roll out Persian plums, quince, pomegranates and apricots. He will offer an exquisite rare coffee, an astronomically expensive French cheese board, and a two-hundred-year-old grappa salvaged from a Roman wreck at the bottom of the Aegean.

With their final toast, The Epicureans will watch as the chef is strangled to death before their eyes. He will eventually quit his silly twitching, slump in his white apron to the floor, his face purple as crushed grapes.

Secrets must stay secret.

Outside, lacy snow gathers along the window mullions.

For now, The Epicureans wait patiently at their places.

A lion-headed English duke and his fiercely rouged duchess, these from their famous old Albemarle estate, hold hands atop the Burano tablecloth.

The Duke comes from old British Empire tea-trade money, enough wealth to buy and sell Prince Charles and the boys. The Duchess – magnificent, bejeweled, once insanely beautiful – will never in her life be photographed alongside the Queen.

This is the Queen's decision. Even in royal finery, Her Majesty appears diminished, made most plain, posed beside the Duchess. A photograph reveals the monarch as a commoner. Queen Betty.

The next table seats equally remarkable guests.

An industrialist from Nagasaki and his handsome partner light a private brand of opium-laced tobacco. They lift glistening twenty-karat lighters to cigarettes rolled in papers of gold leaf. A sweet, heady smell lingers at their table.

The elegant, entwined fingers of both the Japanese businessmen bear permanent gold stains. One shows off a streak of gold dyed into his jet-black hair.

The Japanese gentlemen have fasted two days, preparing for the solstice feast. Imperially slim, they watch the kitchen door of the cottage the way hawks watch a field for baby rabbits.

Outside the windows, snow falls, hypnotic, fast as rain.

The spear tips of the black iron fence turn white.

A lone bare bulb burns over the cottage door, and the heavy flakes swarm crazily around it like midsummer moths.

Tables, of course, must be served.

A bald, blocky waiter, thick through the shoulders as an ox, moves quietly from couple to couple. His thin fingers, long and delicate, don't match his enormous body. The hands might belong to a young girl, a harpist.

His name is Stefan, and he places antique Dresden plates and four-hundred-year-old Colombian silverware on snow-white tablecloths. He carries the settings casually, like workman's tools, at the end of massive arms. His black tuxedo is the style with a split tail – the tail of a tern.

Terns wear black and white, travel island to island.

A second servant, Ronaldo, has very black skin and a white tuxedo. He serves The Epicureans a rare Reims champagne, stopping at each table to display in white-gloved hands the faded labels of the last bottles known to the world. He deftly pours the chilled bubbly into ancient flutes, Venetian, with seven-hundred unbroken years of service.

The Epicureans raise their toasts with this shell-thin glassware every year – two dozen solstice feasts and counting.

At the finale of every meal, through the uneven glass of the upraised stems, The Epicureans have seen:

The huge bald waiter, Stefan, garrote in hand, approaches the weeping chef from behind. He pauses to raise the chef's chin just so with one finger before a final, nearly tender, embrace.

The red-faced Duke and Duchess, the taciturn Japanese partners, the ten other couples, plus the lone man from Alabama, all merrily sated, all impossibly wealthy, applaud the great chef's final act of service.

Who are they, The Epicureans?

The Duke and Duchess, of course. The men from Nagasaki.

The other characters are as colorful.

The two Danes started out stealing jewels. These lovely, aging sisters from a wealthy shipping family in Copenhagen used connections through their father and rich uncles to meet fugitive Nazis in Argentina after the world war.

The sisters were very beautiful then.

They picked the rings and earrings and necklaces off their male corpses, off the corpses of their families too, and emptied safes and bank accounts. From one of the victims, the sisters learned of a hiding place, an Alpine cave used by the Third Reich to store art pieces raided from French manses. That trove made the sisters shamelessly wealthy. They sold … they sell … one canvas or statue at a time to secretive buyers wanting to cap off a private collection with a missing masterpiece.

The sisters have giggled, naked as worms, on antique rugs with priapic clients above them and moving, circling, in the radiance of a Rembrandt, the cool marble glow of a Praxiteles.

Ronaldo quietly makes his rounds.

Clos d'Ambonnay now sparkles in the delicate flutes, the champagne bubbles spiraling upwards in the glass as fast as the snow swirls outside.

A cuckoo clock, ornately carved from Bavarian silver fir, thrusts out its bird-shaped tongue and cries midnight.

It's officially the solstice.

The room catches its breath.

Now. It's time.

On cue, far out in the storm, headlights appear. A vehicle approaches. Its beams bounce once or twice wildly among the inked-in branches of the deep woods.

The vintage Mercedes makes its way down a long white path toward the cottage.

A small African man rises from his table, leaves his swan-necked black bride, steps to the cottage window.

The diminutive Tutsi rules a large sub-Saharan nation. *The New York Times* calls him "a ruthless warlord". His wizened face shows no emotion.

A white ghost of vapor appears on the window pane beneath his broad nostrils. An unholy spirit.

A taller man joins him.

"This sort of holiday meal is a tradition among you African people, isn't it, Mr. Okar?"

The jest, spoken in English with a French accent, turns the African's head. A wide smile reveals teeth filed to sharp points.

"You surely know." Mr. Okar answers the taunt with a perfect Oxford accent.

"Know what?"

"That your comment is deeply racist. Bigoted and insensitive. My wife and I find this French humor most deeply offensive."

The statement hangs in the air, then Mr. Okar adds, "Monsieur Grenouille."

Mister Frog.

A shriek of laughter, the Frenchman's included, shakes the room.

"*Touche!*" cries the billionaire shipping magnate from Marseilles. "I shall give your black princess a string of black pearls as my act of contrition!"

Thus merriment rules.

For eleven months a year, The Epicureans lie awake in the dark, eyes shining, dreaming of solstice night. They will not waste these few precious hours in quarrels.

Headlights jounce once more into view, twin pencils of illumination sketching snowy branches, dark evergreen trunks.

The delivery grows closer to the cottage.

A heavy log shifts. The fire in the huge stone hearth at one end of the cottage flares furiously, flings gold coins.

Through a frost-lined kitchen window, the chef watches a white Mercedes approach through the snowstorm.

He turns even more pale, if that were possible, under the dazzling spotlights of a lavishly appointed kitchen. The kitchen of a lifetime.

Every surface gleams – carefully customized Viking stove and counters of Carrera marble, burled maple cabinetry, rows of steel knives, a hanging rack of seasoned pots and pans. Enough herbs for a botanical garden. Spices heard of, read of, but never before used on any table of his.

The chef tests a blade he's sharpened against an ancient whetstone – a Sumerian relic. The knife flashes when he holds it up, and he catches his reflection in bright steel, the worried face, the little brown moustache, the eyes black, mortal, so afraid.

A thought crosses the chef's mind – he will plunge the knife into his own thin chest now, to avoid the horror of what he must do, what he must be part of.

The knife will slip in so quickly, a surprise to himself, to everyone. His heart will sob to a halt. He will die as innocently as any man who has lived fifty years working hard and caring for his craft with all his might.

But then the chef thinks of little sweet Marie, of his brave boys, Jean-Louis and Ricard. His wife, Celeste. He knows what will become of them if he does not consummate this night, create the perfect solstice feast.

In that event, The Epicureans have made his family's fate crystal clear.

He has been chosen. His bad luck. He knew good luck most of his wonderful days.

Now this.

At least the rewards will flow to Celeste forever. She and the children will never want. The Epicureans have made that perfectly clear too. If this kitchen delights The Epicureans on this one unique night, this night of nights, his family, when he is gone, will never know want.

All is prepared.

The chef constructed his kitchen for six days, secretly, at unlimited expense.

How curious, that he will cook just once here – just once more *ever*, one last meal. The Feast of the Solstice, this single night.

How curious that back in Paris, where he made his name, where he earned the Michelin stars, he lacked for nothing, yet had nothing even *close* to the extravagant culinary equipment in this small stone cottage on this black night in this secret place at the end of the world.

Rrrrrrrrr. Rrrrrmmmmm.

Now not even heavy snow can muffle the rumbling diesel of the approaching Mercedes.

The African warlord has been joined at the window by the Arabs, two men and two stunning women, unveiled, modern. Oil billionaires. Royal family.

Other tables empty too.

Eager faces crowd the glass, patrons welcoming their special guests. The Shanghai realtor and his tiny bride. The stunning fashionista from Milan and her scandalous, bad-boy Spanish soccer star. The Jews from Tel Aviv in the jewelry they designed. The bearish Russian arms merchant and his sultry, red-lipped Ukrainian call-girl.

A low chatter runs among The Epicureans, a kind of voltage.

Just one remains seated. Next year's host, the man from the American South, the Alabamian, supports his jowly bald head on a thick fist and stares without blinking at the door.

His country-western jacket is white as the snow. The man's looming head and cowboy hat seem somehow even larger by candlelight.

His eyes wear hoods. His mouth takes up much of his face. As he waits, two thick fingers lightly tap heavy lips. Another place, another night, somewhere warm with crackling music from an antique radio, he might be blowing kisses.

Voices pierce the storm. German. One higher, childlike.

The *whump* of a car door quietens them.

The Epicureans jostle to see.

"Now, here are our gifts!" breathes one of the Arab women. Diamonds brilliant as Venus on a summer night glitter in her ears.

Voices near. Cold hands fumble with a heavy iron latch.

"Kommen!"

Coming in!

An Epicurean near the door, the white-curled Russian in his heavy black coat, thrusts an arm out like a policeman. The gorgeous, high-heeled escort of the Frenchman from Marseille falls back. She's annoyed, her thick blonde hair a little wild, her lips tight.

She has no time to curse.

The heavy cottage door swings open wide. Shards of ice tumble from its corners.

Through the opening gusts a big bluff German in a heavy coat. Dieter Felty is the Epicurean host of this year's feast. He picked this year's private venue. He selected the chef. He set up the kitchen. He made all the … arrangements.

Dieter's ice-blue eyes water with cold, but his smile beams.

"*Gute nacht! Gute nacht!* Good to see you, my friends, so good! Sorry about the weather! I prayed for better, but no one listened!"

"Dieter! Dieter!" they answer, delighted.

The German unbuttons his long black overcoat, and snow avalanches down his shoulders. His hand grips something curious.

A length of rope. It stretches through the door behind him out into the snowy yard.

"Welcome to my Germany!" Dieter exclaims, stamping his feet to shake off more snow. "And now ... an introduction!"

He jerks the rope, and pulls something into the room.

Two children, noosed at the neck like geese, stumble over the threshold. Snow swirls in around them, stinging, cold as North Sea spray. The boy is no more than six. The girl can't be older than four. They are completely naked, except for gags of bright yellow silk. They tremble violently, stare with terrified eyes.

"Here, my friends ... welcome our Hansel *und* Gretel!"

Ahhh!

The Epicureans sigh.

The Duchess reaches out red-nailed fingers, takes the bare flesh of the little girl's upper arm. She gives a sharp pinch.

"Very nice work, Dieter," she hisses to the German host, ghastly mouth smiling. "This feast will be most special."

The little boy manages to yell out in terror around his yellow scarf.

"*Hilfe! HILFE! Mama! Ich habe Angst! ...*"

Dieter's big jolly hand smothers the cry, and this year's Epicurean host lifts the boy and his sister, carries them upside down, heads nearly bumping the stone floor, away to the kitchen.

The chef furtively falls to his knees in front of the hot steel stove. He prays the most furious prayer of his life.

He hears them. He senses them.

The Epicureans enter the kitchen.

The chef rises, wipes his knees.

The knives are very sharp. They will not hurt the children.

Not much.

God please forgive me. Please save my black damned soul.

—2—

Lafayette

Elmore Rogers stared in disbelief.

Was any shock worse than a thumb brutally clubbed with a hammer? In freezing weather. On a steeply pitched roof. On a Friday. One hour before quitting time. Two days before Christmas.

Funny. It didn't hurt yet.

The bloody mess at the end of Elmore's left hand made his heart hammer. He closed his eyes and exhaled into the cold afternoon. White vapor gusted away like a soul.

Blood suddenly welled, fast, from the top and bottom of Elmore's thumbnail. Bright red drops spattered the sticky black tar paper under Elmore's work boots.

Jesus!

Elmore squeezed the bludgeoned thumb, held it tight against his belly like a caught little bird. Stinging tears rose. Roofing tacks spilled from his carpenter's apron, wobbled drunkenly down the tar paper to the roof edge. They fell three stories. Streaks of blood chased them.

Now. Here it came. Mister Pain.

Oh JESUS! Now it hurt!

A hiss like frying bacon rose in Elmore's ears. His thumb pulsed lightning.

Who knew? This hurt might last all the rest of his life.

Some hurts did.

"You! Slacker! Up there!"

A bull-necked man, far below on the ground, glared fiercely up at Elmore. His square shadow fell before him over a sand pile, a mortar mixer, a puddle of rainwater. The man wore a white hat. His heavy white fringed jacket made him look something like a football player in shoulder pads. He clamped a short cigar. The man's head was enormous, disproportionate, the head of a pit bull. Too big for the body.

"Plum! Over here! What's that slacker's name? Up on the gable?"

"That's Elmore Rogers, Mr. Wood."

"He's stopped working? Sucking his thumb? Did you yell quittin' time?"

Mr. Plum, the construction foreman, appeared meek, cowed.

"Elmore does real good work for us up on the high places, Mr. Wood ..."

"Good work? The HELL!"

Mr. Wood's angry voice flew to the roof. Elmore somehow *heard* the shouts in his throbbing thumb.

"ROGERS! House ain't gonna build itself! You want to leave here this afternoon with a check? Get a move on!"

Mr. Wood rarely appeared at a job site, even for the construction of his own vast mansion. Today, though, he had shown up in person. He ostentatiously carried a two-inch-thick stack of pay envelopes, holiday red, bound with a fat green rubber band. He'd come to play Santa Claus, two afternoons before Christmas.

Just back from Europe, somebody told Elmore at lunch break, between chews of potted meat. *Bet that booger went over there just to eat at some fancy restaurant. What you reckon they eat in Europe, anyway? Snails and shit ...*

Mr. Wood was Mr. Big Shot.

Elmore Rogers didn't care for people like that. Mr. Wood could have been satisfied with being a tycoon and flying around in a fancy jet. But now he'd decided to flaunt his fortune, build a castle. That's what people called the rising mansion: Wood Castle.

Richest man in the whole South, folks said.

Tightest man in the whole world, another construction worker had grumbled to Elmore that very morning as they monkeyed up a scaffold onto the icy roof. *Ass squeaks when he walks.*

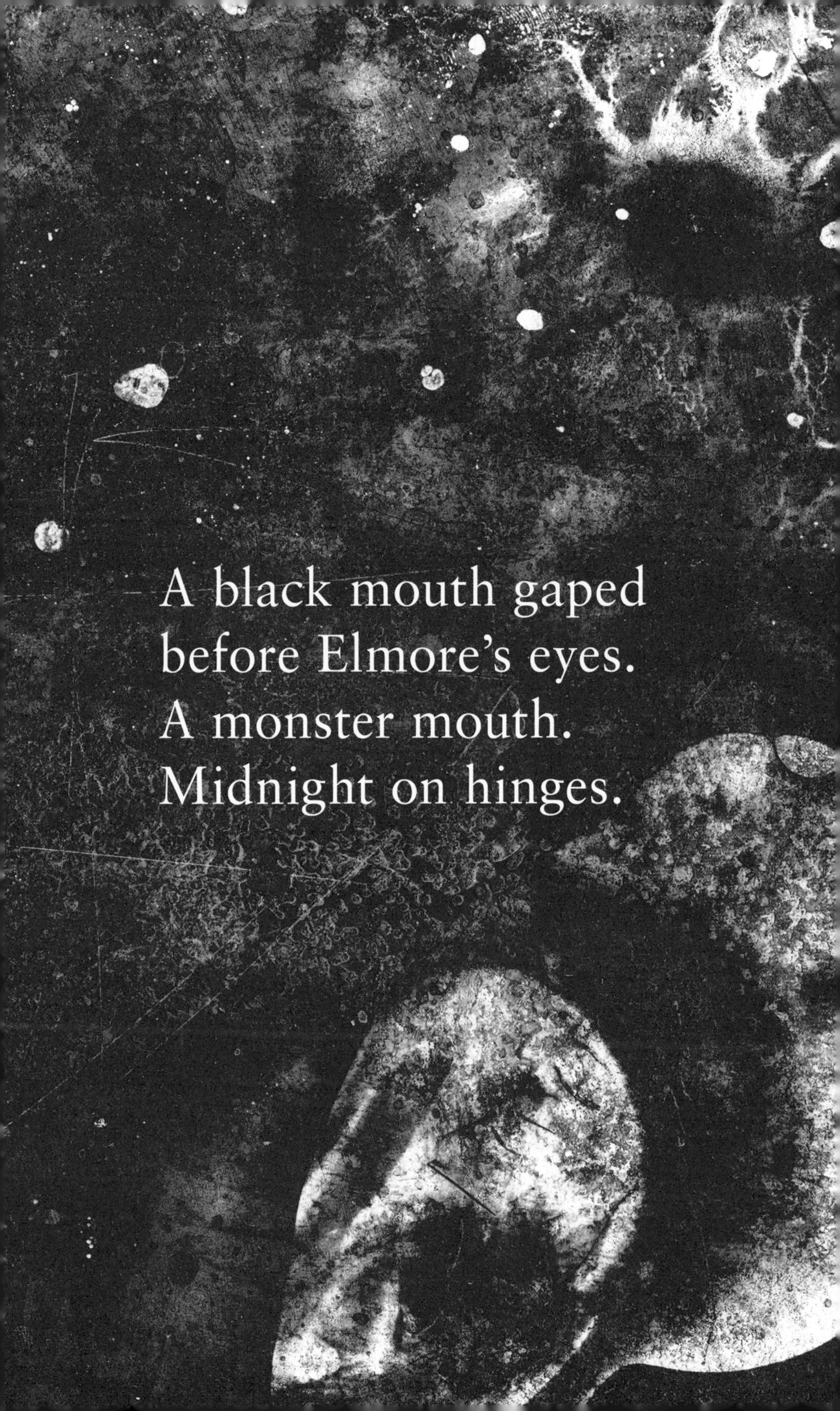

A black mouth gaped
before Elmore's eyes.
A monster mouth.
Midnight on hinges.

Elmore rocked unconsciously in pain, thumb clutched to his body.

House ain't gonna build itself … well, Mr. Big Shot, least I'm up here in the freezing cold earning a paycheck. I never stepped on somebody else's head to get where I am …

Elmore's spite boiled over. He hated that preposterous white hat and leather coat, all that silly fringe.

A coat with *fringe*? What was that? Fat Elvis meets Dan'l Boone?

With winter wind and a bleeding wound and a violently running nose, Elmore shouldn't have raised from astraddle the house gable to yell something defiant.

But he did.

A black mouth gaped before Elmore's eyes. A monster mouth. Midnight on hinges.

It opened to swallow him whole.

Elmore had battled a problem all his life – something about seeing blood leave his own body left him helpless. Shaky.

The midnight mouth laughed wickedly. Elmore teetered, struggled not to tumble down its black maw.

"Hey! You down there!" Elmore yelled, fighting vertigo. "Hey, Mr. Big …"

His legs wobbled. He turned to Gumby.

The roof rushed up, tarpaper black, blacker.

Elmore's face banged. He rolled down the roof through spilled roofing tacks.

Elmore fell.

A silver rainfall of nails showered after him.

Elmore's cloth nail apron snagged on an eave and ripped away. It dangled like a bloody flag in the Christmas wind.

The broken fall might have killed another man.

It didn't kill Elmore Rogers.

But he did, briefly, wish he'd died. And not for the first time.

Elmore again felt an explosion. Fire and flame. Desert sun. A white hand reaching down from a blue sky. His old friend Dan Neeley, a violent sun flaring over his helmet.

Iraq.

But now, this winter day in Alabama, Elmore stared up grimly from flat on his back. He blinked at the gray afternoon. Stars out early. They burst among migrating blackbirds and dirty nimbus clouds.

Would he ever breathe again?

Would he?

Elmore beheld a vision.

Two beautiful kids, Mary and Will.

His twins. His reasons to live.

Elmore took a deep, magnificent gasp of air.

His ribs nearly killed him, but Elmore breathed.

He would choose pain, if he had nothing else to feel.

Shouts rose, the heavy, scary sounds of grown men running. Grown men only run when something bad happens.

He somehow rolled onto his stunned left side …
but then flopped back again.

So many things hurt.

He closed his eyes.

Safe. Safe in there.

Two black brick masons, Dawsy and Oscar, stood over him. Oscar held a dripping galvanized bucket.

Elmore felt numb, but vividly awake.

Magically, Mr. Wood reappeared. As the blocky figure stalked up, gusting wind cocked his Stetson at a silly angle.

Mr. Wood pushed his head into the open window of a pick-up. The boss fixed a scalding eye on Plum, the rabbit-faced foreman, who shrank back of the wheel.

"Looks like they might be starting the holidays a little early here, Plum!"

"Sir?"

"I said," Mr. Wood hollered, "that when your crew is so drunk they're falling off the roof at four in the afternoon, you got a quality control problem. Think you got a quality control problem, Mr. Plum?"

All fifty or so construction workers looked on, some high on the roof, others from unfinished house windows, still more at jobs far out in the lot. They would later talk about how mild Mr. Plum, a church-going National Guardsman who rarely raised his voice, showed Mr. Wood a little backbone.

"Elmore Rogers ain't a drunk, sir. He can't drink a lick. He got his insides messed up in Iraq. His liver don't tolerate ..."

"You don't contradict ME!" yelled Mr. Wood. "I just saw a drunk fall off a roof!"

Mr. Wood's wide face had blackened. His strange shark eyes did not blink.

"Plum," Mr. Wood blustered, "you get this Elway, or whatever the hell his name is, off this job. His Christmas check pays for the emergency room. AND tell him not to bother showing back up here Monday or any other day. I don't hire drunkards."

A few of the construction workers stared sheepishly down at their work boots.

Dawsy and Oscar gingerly rolled Elmore onto a sheet of plywood. They lifted it like a stretcher into the bed of Plum's pick-up. If he ran the lights, it was a ten-minute drive to the emergency room at Lafayette General.

The two men crouched silently on either side of Elmore.

Plum wheeled the Dodge away fast, bouncing it over the plowed rows of an old field. The truck's bumper snagged a nest of rusted barbed wire and noisily dragged it. In the flatbed, Elmore rattled like an epileptic.

"Yah! Giddyup!"

Elmore watched Mr. Wood wave his white hat in the air, receding, his voice fading.

"Git that drunk the hell outta here!"

Dozens of workers, black and white and brown, all male, all grim, stared on. They watched from the unfinished skeleton of the vast 100,000-square-foot antebellum-styled main house. From the sides and roof of a gigantic carriage house and a huge garage rising behind the main structure, even more men watched.

Wood Castle.

Mr. Wood's new residence would be the largest private home built in Alabama state history. It would dwarf Biltmore Mansion in North Carolina. It would cost more than San Simeon in California.

"Listen up!" yelled Mr. Wood. "Clown show's over!"

Clown show's over!

An eerie echo rang back from the soaring surfaces of Mr. Wood's future home.

"Drunk's on his way to get pumped out! Now get back to work. You'll hear from me, when it's quittin' time. *Hop to it!*"

The crews hopped to it.

A shrill of skill saws and gunshot tattoos of air guns and the staccato blows of framing hammers drowned out any other commands Mr. Wood might have shouted.

One hour to Christmas break.

A working man could endure anything for an hour.

Minutes later, like a movie miracle, snow began to descend from fleecy gray clouds over Alabama.

Flat on his back in the cruelly bouncing bed of Mr. Plum's pick-up, Elmore Rogers stared up without blinking. The sky was gray cotton. Gray cotton with a flashlight behind it where a puny sun burned.

Elmore tasted blood.

He licked. His tongue found a broken tooth and a red crumb of Anglian Rustic brick.

What were his two young'uns gonna think about their daddy now? What kind of snaggle-toothed, busted-up, flat-broke Santa Claus is Elmore Rogers going to be for Christmas?

The truck slowed at an intersection in downtown Lafayette. Light snow blessed Elmore's bruised face. He heard – or imagined – the ringing of Salvation Army bells.

Cool white flakes, soft as bandages, soft as angel feathers, settled over his bloody clothes.

I love you, Will and Mary, Elmore whispered to himself.

I'll give you a merry Christmas. Even like this.

—3—

Will and Mary

The twins pressed nearly identical faces to icy window panes. Snow would be general over Alabama. But for Will and Mary Rogers, the only snow in the world fell oh so tantalizingly near – just beyond the windows of Mrs. Mock's stuffy house.

The storm hit hard and fast, a shock to Lafayette people who only witnessed such a white miracle every five years or so.

Who knew what to do?

Public schools shut down early. Kids ran crazy on playgrounds among white flurries. Furious school bus drivers honked horns and harried teachers flailed arms and red-faced coaches blew whistles.

Shelves in Mr. Stevenson's Piggly Wiggly and Mr. Woodham's Independent Grocery took on waves of panicked shoppers. In a few hours, bread, batteries, bottled water, candles, milk and beer disappeared. Gray puddles filled the empty aisles from snow melted off overcoats and tracked in on shoes.

Elderly motorists slowly crept along ruttled road shoulders toward their homes, watching with apprehension as streets slickened and the world turned white as their hair. When these seniors finally left their cars, they skated their feet, trying not to fall.

No death in Lafayette, Alabama, would ever be stranger than a person breaking a hip and freezing to death in a driveway.

The grandfather clock in Mrs. Mock's living room loudly tolled 5 p.m. Will and Mary wanted only one thing in the whole universe – to romp in snow like Santa's reindeer.

"When is Daddy coming?" sniffled Mary.

She had a cold. In winter, Mary always had a cold, maybe more from the parched dry air of space heaters in drafty rooms than from rhinovirus. Her blue-green eyes glowed moistly, a sure fever. No one had washed her hair today. Normally pretty strands hung like red spaghetti.

"*When id dada cubbing?*"

Will loudly mocked his sister in a baby voice.

"*When da baby get her pacifier? Goo goo waa waa!*"

Will scowled. Will never got a cold. Born impatient, the first one out of Kelly Rogers' womb, he too was long past ready for Elmore to drive up and spring him from the strict after-care of Mrs. Mock.

Will reckoned he would already be merrily playing out of doors if his snotty-nosed sister didn't have the sniffles. Even better, if Daddy had picked them up on time today, he'd already be back at the Rogers' rental out in the country, throwing snowballs at bewildered feral cats creeping out of the woods, shaking snow off their paws.

Will itched to escape. He only needed six inches of cracked doorway to be gone, out, vamoosed. For all he cared, Mary could stay in, blowing her nose till it came off in her hand.

Will and Mary! Except for their faces, no twins – redheads, freckled as cowbird eggs, blue-eyed or green-eyed depending on the sunlight – were ever born less identical.

Mary was a thin sharp shadow of her brother. She acted like a shadow too, waiting for bold Will to take the initiative, following as he blazed the trails. (Will first! Will always first!)

Will came into the world a solid chunk, deep-chested at birth, now at age seven a 'husky' size. He heard this humiliating word from a gaunt bifocaled sales witch at J.C. Penney who measured him, straight pins in her mouth, each September for back-to-school clothes.

Will had front teeth missing, shed before Mary's. He was a good little second baseman for his age. He could put two fingers in his mouth and blow, and dogs lifted ears a half mile away. To Elmore's surprise, his son behaved like a miniature grown-up from the moment he could stand and point a stubborn finger the direction he wanted to go.

"Daddy's gonna get here any minute."

Will breathed, nicer to his sister now, face so close to Mrs. Mock's window that his breath ghosted the glass.

"Any minute, Mary! Then we'll have a snowball fight!"

"I want to do a snowball fight!" she answered.

But it was already dark.

Too late? Too late to enjoy snow, to be outside? It almost surely wouldn't snow one flake tomorrow. This was Alabama. White stuff fell once in a blue moon.

Will only remembered one day of snow in his whole life before. The single thing he recalled was a line of animal tracks through the perfect white front yard in front of their house. Blotchy blue scars left by ... something strange.

It thrilled Will to think some kind of monster made them. A monster had walked through the snow close to their house!

That was then.

Now ... today ... when would Daddy's old lumbering panel truck roll up, big as a friendly woolly mammoth, its wipers beating *left, right, left, right?* When would Daddy's cheerful hand appear out the truck window, snow falling from his fingers like a magic trick?

"William Rainer Rogers!"

Mrs. Mock's voice cracked like a whip. Both children jumped.

"Yes'm?" Mary answered too, though she hadn't been addressed.

"Did I invite you two children to stay in the parlor?"

"Yes'm. But it's *snowing*, Mrs. Mock. We can't see it snow from the parlor ..."

"WILLIAM!"

The tone of Mrs. Mock's voice made more words unnecessary, but she spoke anyway.

"I would truly hate to tell your father that either of you two children disobeyed me."

Mary drew a brave breath, her eyes luminous.

"Daddy would be happy we got to see it snow! He would be happy if we *played* in it!"

Will wheeled on his sister, furious.

"Shut up, igmo! It's your fault we can't go out and play. You had to get ..." Will sneered these last two words, "... *a cold*. You're a baby!"

Mary barked helplessly. The sharp cough hurt Will's chest a little. But he didn't relent.

"I bet Mrs. Mock thinks just watchin' the snow out a window will give you a double whooping cough. And you know what? I wish it WOULD!"

Will jumped from his window seat and stormed past his sister, ripping himself away from his strange shadow, so different, so much the same. He thumped into the formal parlor of Mrs. Mock's hot, airless house and flopped heavily onto a red loveseat. China rattled in glass-and-cherry cabinets.

The voice cracked again. "Young man, do I see your street shoes on my velvet settee?"

Mrs. Mock entered, marching Mary ahead of her.

Down plunged Will's feet, fast and hard. The china cabinets chattered a second time.

Do I see those shoes on my velvet settee, young man? Will's mouth silently mocked the admonition. Tears of frustration all at once gleamed in his eyes. The stingy aluminum Christmas tree that Mrs. Mock kept in the parlor blurred and went out of focus. A revolving color wheel changed the tree tinsel to watery red, then watery yellow, watery blue.

Mary took a seat on the sofa by her brother. She was an extraordinarily beautiful child, fair and delicate. She stared plaintively at Will, her oversized eyes and ridiculously long lashes exaggerated by fever. She seemed thinner, wispier, in winter, if it were possible, just as Will seemed more chunky and square. A sea-spray of freckles dotted Mary's cheeks.

Mary's beauty was utterly lost on her brother. But Mary noticed his sadness as she settled by him, quiet as a snowflake. Will's face reminded her of a wild kitten's. She had tried to coax one from the crawl space under their house last year with a raw weenie.

It snarled and spit, savagely unhappy.

"You children tell one another stories," Mrs. Mock said. "Stories stimulate imagination."

Will used his imagination. He vividly pictured what he would do if Mrs. Mock were a poison snake, and he had a pocket full of rocks.

Mrs. Mock kept the Rogers children on Friday, the day after-care at Lafayette Elementary shut down early. Elmore worked till five to earn every possible penny.

Mrs. Mock was Will and Mary's step-grandmother. She'd been the second wife of Elmore's father, who now slept in a VA Hospital in Mobile and rarely woke. Elmore Rogers Sr. had grown really good at sleeping, and really old.

The children had heard many times from Mrs. Mock how their "real grandmother" died of a massive stroke one afternoon two days before Elmore's twelfth birthday.

"Weak blood," she insisted to the children, with a meaningful purse of the lips and a nod at pale Mary. "They say it was weak blood. It runs in families, you know."

After Iraq and after his divorce from Kelly, Elmore knew of no one else in Lafayette who would keep Will and Mary for free, even for one afternoon. Still, Mrs. Mock's after-care came with a risk – she had a reputation for canasta-with-sherry parties. She was proud of her looks too. She'd been a beauty once … and in the right light, still was.

Elmore didn't like the idea of drinking around the kids. But did Mrs. Mock's social inclinations matter for two hours after school each Friday?

The snow storm closed the school early, of course. The moment the school bus pulled up, Mrs. Mock's 1:30 p.m. canasta date with garden club friends flew out the window.

She had glanced at her hallway mirror, a fancy maple thing. *Mirror, mirror on the wall*, she whispered aloud. *This'll go better with alcohol …*

She quickly poured a glass of sherry.

Long ago, she mothered her way through a frustrating first marriage. Will and Mary only reminded Mrs. Mock uncomfortably of how much she disliked children. Even her own, long scattered.

Then there was this ...

The spoiled canasta party didn't hold a candle to her second well-laid plan for the evening. Mrs. Mock's middle-aged body tingled to think of it.

If Elmore didn't show up at a reasonable hour, that plan might get scuttled too.

Mrs. Mock didn't like the thought one bit.

Now the grandfather clock in the hallway made a *sproinging* noise and chimed six times.

Elmore never picked them up so late!

Mrs. Mock stared sullenly at the clock. Time did not fly.

The Mock house held down a corner lot in a grand old neighborhood, finest in Lafayette ... at least the finest until Mr. Wood finished his castle. Lafayette Heights proudly showed off to the world its collection of two-story homes of uniform whiteness, wooden, porched, balustraded, landscaped-to-death. A lot of work went into keeping up the looks of "Lafayette Garden District", as well-to-do residents sniffingly referred to their few special blocks.

Who could blame them? Lafayette wasn't much to speak of. This part of Alabama either, truth to tell. Pride always fought for a grip.

Will, calmer now, considered that snow might look better on the roofs and lawns here than on the mobile homes and cheap houses that made up a lot of Lafayette. He thought about snow on barns and chicken houses out in the country where he and his sister and his daddy lived.

Mary coughed. The noise in her lungs sounded like ripping cloth. Mrs. Mock clucked from her nearby rocker.

"Weak blood."

Mrs. Mock rearranged her magazine. She read about movie stars and the British royals. She kept scissors by the rocker to cut out pages she liked.

Sometimes she cut out photos of the handsome men.

The heat in the parlor stifled. So did the silence. Worse, the floor furnace terrified Mary. Under its black grille glowed a blue light. Mary thought it looked like a hot eye watching from the bottom of a grave. It scared her, that devil waiting under the house. It never blinked – you could always see it, it could always see you. The grille felt scorching hot even through shoes.

Brave Will asked a brave question.

"Can we watch TV, Mrs. Mock?"

"*May* we watch TV?" the older woman corrected, flipping a glossy page.

"Yes'm. May we watch TV?"

"No you may not. Television is extremely bad for the eyes at your age. And your father will be here any time. And your sister has a cold. You two need to be ready to leave here the minute he drives up. I have my own important plans later on."

Mrs. Mock then, out of nowhere, raised a chocolate-chip cookie to her mouth and took a bite. She did it slowly and deliberately, so both children could see. A pair of gold-rimmed bifocals with what could have been real diamonds magnified her defiant stare. She chewed the cookie slowly, as if it were the best one ever baked.

"A TV ruins the eyes," she mumbled, through falling crumbs. "And stifles imagination."

Hours later, Elmore Rogers rattled up. Both children lay fast asleep, uncovered, on the sofa. The grandfather clock tunelessly rang eleven times.

Mrs. Mock fumed.

At suppertime, she had actually been forced to scrounge up a can of tomato soup for two ungrateful children. As she served it, somewhere down deep she wondered how her life might have turned out if she'd paid further attention to that handsome friend of Elmore's dad, the one who always looked at her *that way*. Mrs. Mock remembered how the man sat on the groom's side of the aisle and forever held his peace on their wedding day.

He could have disturbed the peace. He knew her secrets. She shared them with him two nights before the wedding. In his town car.

That gentleman got rich and retired in Panama City. He belonged to the yacht club. She heard that he won regattas and spent nights at the Ebro greyhound track.

Eleven p.m.

What a careless father, Elmore Rogers! Mrs. Mock vowed she would absolutely, positively, make sure this never happened again.

When Elmore rang the doorbell, she had her tongue sharpened, her blessing-out speech rehearsed.

Mrs. Mock noisily yanked open the frozen door.

She stepped back without a word.

She barely recognized her stepson under the porch light.

One side of Elmore's bruised face had completely changed color, to purple. A gruesome black caterpillar crawled his swollen mouth. The stitches marred Elmore's top and bottom lips. A front tooth was broken.

"Hey, Mitheth Mock," Elmore managed to mumble, sheepishly. Painfully.

She caught a glimpse of black stitches in Elmore's tongue too, the reason he pronounced his words oh-so-carefully. A foolishly oversized bandage, like something made for a Halloween costume, covered his left thumb.

Mrs. Mock couldn't see, under Elmore's clothes, the mummy swath of bandages that tightly wrapped a broken rib. He also concealed a sprained wrist, a dislocated shoulder, and a broken toe on one foot. He reeked of hospital alcohol.

As Elmore waited on the porch, snowflakes turned to water droplets over his baseball cap and shoulders. Awkwardly, even on a night like this, Mrs. Mock would not let Elmore enter her house without formality.

I have a wicked stepmother, Elmore thought to himself.

"Mitheth Mock," he managed. "It lookth nithe and wom inthide. May I thome in ...?"

She stared ridiculously. It occurred to Elmore that perhaps she hadn't understood a single garbled word.

"One minnith?"

He waited. He tried again.

"Thorry I'm tho late ... I hath a litthle troubba ath work ..."

Boom!

Will and Mary burst past their grim-lipped gatekeeper. They charged barefoot onto the snowy porch to hug their daddy.

Their tight little hugs nearly killed him.

With happiness. With shocking pain.

Without a parting word, the trio limped and hopped and staggered down the snowy walk to a big panel truck idling at the street. Before Will got in the cab, he hurled a couple of wild snowballs.

Elmore climbed in slowly. The panel truck rolled away into the white Alabama night.

Mrs. Mock firmly shut the door.

She bustled to the kitchen, glancing at the big mirror on the way, tugging a bra strap beneath her red holiday blouse. She lifted her telephone, briskly spinning the old-fashioned rotary dial. She felt something inside like she did in her younger, girlish days.

She let the phone ring once, quickly hung up.

Their signal. For a rendezvous.

Mrs. Mock only waited seconds. The phone rang under her palm.

She glanced self-consciously at another mirror, a small one on her kitchen wall. She slipped a loose strand of silvery-gold hair behind one ear. *Not bad*, she thought. *Thank you for those special soaps from Germany.*

She lifted the receiver in the middle of the third ring.

Why ..." she breathed coquettishly. "*Mr. Wood! The celebrated ... notorious ... handsome ... manly ... Mr. Wood! What a nice surprise on this cold, snowy evening ...*"

—4—

Kelly

Kelly Rogers kept Elmore's name after both of her break-ups. She didn't feel herself without it.

This strange, snowy night she squinted through wipers, her freezing hands guiding a green VW Beetle foot by slippery foot up her driveway. What an ugly noise the engine made.

When she crested out onto the county road, the VW wheels slurred and lost purchase. Kelly stamped the accelerator sharply. For a tricky moment, the little vehicle wagged side to side, then it valiantly eased onto the blacktop.

Tonight, it was whitetop. Snow completely covered County Road 11.

It crossed Kelly's mind to just reverse down the drive, kill the engine, climb back up slick cement-block steps into her aging mobile home. That would be easy, safe.

She could put something in the toaster. She'd listen to the record player. She'd take a pill. She'd go to sleep.

Again. Another little death.

Tonight, though, she wanted the river.

She looked her best. She wore a long beautiful river of a black dress that showed off her long beautiful river of black hair.

She dressed to kill every time she visited the Black Warrior.

In four inches of snow, the trip might take thirty minutes instead of ten, but her loyal little VW would get there.

Kelly clicked on the radio. Ghost music, then ghost voices, spoke.

Snow falling on central Alabama. Temps below freezing. Wind from the north.

The snowflakes that rushed the headlights fascinated Kelly. She got a fright when an owl unexpectedly lunged toward the windshield, then another owl. Mates. They flumed big and scary, then quickly disappeared, like a memory.

Some memories, anyway.

The snowy woods and fields ended.

Even with billions of white flakes falling into it, the Black Warrior ran catastrophically dark, too black to even reflect light.

Halfway across a derelict wooden train trestle, abandoned for years now to cane-pole fishermen and beer-drinking college students, Kelly Rogers stopped.

An inky plunge lay off both sides.

Her dark obsession crossed Kelly's mind again, that needle stuck in one place on the phonograph in her head.

Get out of the car.

Walk to the edge in your Sunday best.

Stand on the rail.

Walk one more step.

Let go of guilt. Let go of pain. Let go of twins, postpartum, hot car. Elmore.

Slam down hard into that by-god blackness once and for all and forever.

Since the split with Elmore, five years and counting, Kelly went to the Black Warrior at least once a week, rain or shine.

She did so for many reasons, but mostly ... so far ... simply to stare the black lethal water in the face and say *no*.

When Kelly first came, she sat in the car and wept and ruined her careful makeup. More than once, she banged her forehead in mortification against the steering wheel. Pain never hurt enough. In August, she left windows up and sweltered in the black interior, imagining what her twins went through that terrible afternoon.

She endured worse nights, many, including a few when she almost said *yes* to the black water.

Kelly climbed out of the car those nights. She stood at the guard rail and bit her bottom lip. The wind tossed her skirt and tossed her hair.

She tried to decide what took more courage.

Falling.

Or not falling.

It might have always been the same. But then, one night, something happened.

She had never been a believer. In much of anything. Church. Marriage. Her mothering. Herself.

But a voice spoke to her on the trestle that night.

Kelly heard it plainly. It spoke near her left ear. It was one of those jump-or-stay nights. She arrived high on good stuff, a little dark rum and the pills that made her Kelly.

She distinctly heard words.

It's not what you did. It's what you will do.

Amazed and frightened, Kelly Rogers stumbled back from the rusted trestle rail, then broke down and wept on the hood of her VW. She fell like a soggy magnolia blossom plopped onto black water.

She *did* drop and plunge under that night – she drowned in a rushing flood of grief, old wrongs, guilt, black regret.

Poor Will and Mary, Mary and Will. Poor Elmore.

She had to make her way back to the kids. Someone would need to tell them the *why*. Someone would need to love them.

She could *want* her children now. The postpartum demon had passed. Maybe the children would want her too.

Maybe.

They wanted her at the start, coming into this world, so close together.

Beautiful babies. Beautiful children made from her own body, her own spirit.

They chose *her* to grow inside. They chose *her* to be born.

It's what happened *after* that crushed Kelly.

Almost too terrible for memory.

She tried to forget. She tried and tried.

That night, after she heard the voice on the trestle, she tried and tried to remember.

That fateful night, she waited a long, long time, her tears cried out, the weeping ducts so empty they ached. A little gray bird sang somewhere high on the iron trestle, out of tune in the moonless night, but mocking grief with all its crazy heart.

It's what you will do. It's what you will do.

Was it God? Did God speak to her?

To Kelly Rogers, so lost, so screwed-up inside?

She watched the snowflakes fall in the dark. After a time, the wind above the Black Warrior picked up briskly, and it grew too cold to stand on the trestle.

The Volkswagen puttered Kelly safely back to the trailer home.

She made it. Again.

When she climbed out of the car, Kelly could see her precious breath in the night.

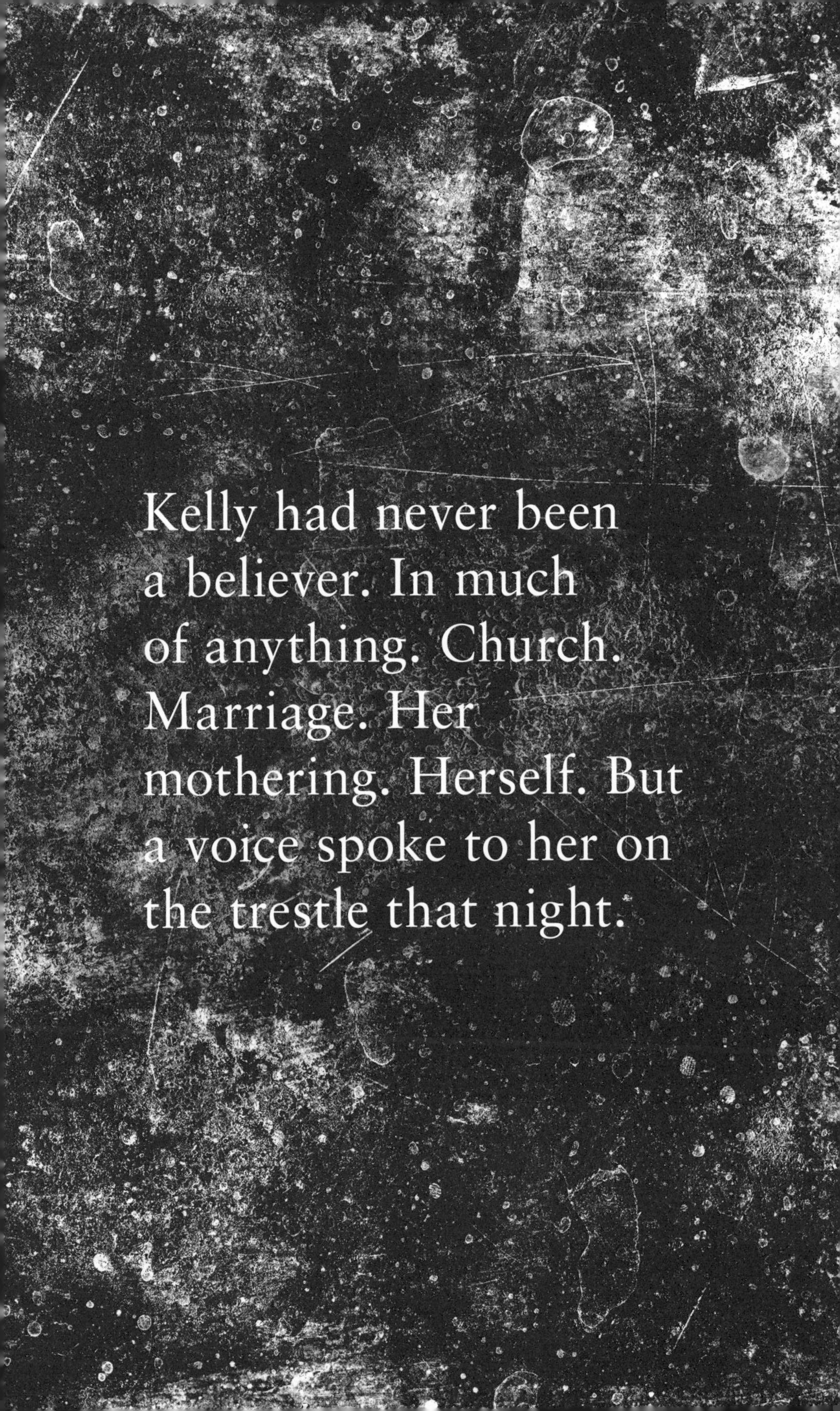
Kelly had never been
a believer. In much
of anything. Church.
Marriage. Her
mothering. Herself. But
a voice spoke to her on
the trestle that night.

—5—

Mr. Wood

The desk phone rang. Once.

Mr. Wood knew the signal. He'd waited hours. He never liked waiting.

The fringed arm of his jacket stretched across a vast executive desk, its surface a polished mirror. The reflection of a gold-nugget button on his sleeve flashed in the dark walnut.

She sounded odd, distant, on this snowy night. A wasp trapped in a bottle.

Why ... Mr. Wood! The celebrated ... notorious ... (he stopped listening to look at his clock) *... Mr. Wood! What a nice surprise on this cold, snowy evening ...*

Mr. Wood gave instructions, no small talk.

The phone clattered onto the cradle, gave a little wounded sound.

Mr. Wood's fingers drummed. Thick fingers. Sticks of butter. They left smudges on the fine wood.

For twenty minutes, Mr. Wood thought of things, and of nothing.

Finally, a soft knock.

"You know it ain't locked."

Mr. Wood's voice was Cracker South. Distinct.

Perfume entered before the woman.

Mrs. Mock wore a long mink coat, buttoned to the top – a gift from Mr. Wood a year ago, back when they started, those first autumn nights. She shimmered into the room, changing it with femininity. Her hair was bunched with a yellow silk scarf, another of his gifts, this one arriving early today in a box from Germany, no return address.

He liked her hair back – remarkable hair for a woman of a certain age, thick as a mare's mane. It gleamed in the soft office lights, revealing every lovely color in chestnut. Mrs. Mock's bare legs showed under mink. On her feet she wore – oddly – white athletic shoes. Mr. Wood took note. Her lipstick looked moist, a cheery holiday red. She wore the rest of her makeup a little heavy, but Mr. Wood understood.

She looked make-believe pretty this time of night.

If Mrs. Mock were nervous, Mr. Wood could not tell. He gave away absolutely nothing in the tell-tale spots where a skilled dealmaker can read the emotions of other people. The color in her high cheeks held the steady pink one sees in rose marble, no blush of nerves or embarrassment. Or shame.

She was eager, he realized.

She liked a rendezvous.

Mr. Wood had grown accustomed through the long years in this office to tremblers, beggars, snivelers. Occasional weepers, the pleaders.

Mrs. Mock seemed ... what was the word?

Pert.

"Do you mind if I smoke?"

Her voice always surprised him. She drawled like he did. A husky smoker's alto. She had the tone of a pure country girl who knew how to use what she has to get places. *She got status with her brain-dead husband*, Mr. Wood thought. And money ... though like her looks, money wouldn't last forever.

Mr. Wood shifted heavily in his big leather chair. The Throne, he overheard a cleaner call it a few months back. He allowed himself a good chuckle. After he fired the woman.

"Light one for me too," he ordered.

Mr. Wood reached into his desk. He showily flourished a mother-of-pearl ashtray.

He expected Benson & Hedges. But Mrs. Mock tapped out two Camels, no filter. He knew her red plastic lighter cost a buck at some 7-Eleven. She offered it with the cigarette.

"I'll light my own, thank you."

The snap of his 18-karat lighter was loud in the small room. Like a small bone breaking.

The glowing tip of her Camel briefly lit Mrs. Mock's face.

Once upon a time, those cheekbones could have gutted a man, thought Mr. Wood. He noted the way Mrs. Mock's red lips nearly disappeared as she took a drag. She showily exhaled, waving the smoke, red claws on full display.

Mr. Wood's corporate office sat in a far corner of the sprawling central lumber yard of Wood Industries. Snow still fell, and a train moaned under a heavy holiday load in the night.

Through a one-way office window, Mr. Wood could see mountains of raw logs waiting to be milled. Outside the woodlot, 30 square miles of land belonged to him. Every tree. Every acre. Every animal and stream and stone. He owned lands beyond these too, and buildings, networks, factories, franchises, on and on.

"So." She breathed a plume. "Merry Christmas. Woody."

"Merry Christmas," he answered. "All that."

She kissed the cigarette again, stared hard at him through the smoke.

"Mr. Wood ..." She became a coquette. "I brought you a little Christmas present."

"I've got you one too."

She smiled slightly at that, picked tobacco from the tip of her tongue with a sculpted nail. Mr. Wood thought those nails must be troublesome around the Rogers twins. Or when she poured sherry.

Mr. Wood knew everything about Mrs. Mock.

Everything.

"I'm Jennifer for you tonight, Mr. Wood."
She gave a quick wink.

"Jennifer?"

"Jennifer. Cheerleader Jennifer. Wearing the school colors."

Mrs. Mock stood. She reached for the soft buttons of the mink.

Blue-and-white Lafayette High School colors appeared underneath. Pom-poms. A play-toy blue cardboard megaphone on a strap. The little white shoes. A cheerleader smile.

Her body looked petite.

The words came from deep in Mr. Wood's throat.

"I'm impressed. You'll show me what's under that skirt?"

She maintained eye contact. A strand of loose chestnut now dangled onto her forehead. Her chin rose slightly, enough to cast her face at a surprising, sensual angle in the track lighting.

"I'll show you all the colors of the rainbow, big boy."

Mr. Wood shifted. The leather seat complained.
He felt unusual excitement.

He rose with some effort. He was an enormous man.
He had enormous appetites.

"Ahh ... Jennifer?"

Her narrowed eyes answered without words.

"Place both palms on the desk."

She took one last drag of her cigarette, stabbed out its fire in the lustrous tray. Her heavy fur tumbled. She slipped off her shoes too, and flexed her toes in soft Persian carpet – a rare indulgence Mr. Wood allowed himself, special carpet, for times like this.

Mrs. Mock reached both hands high, removed the yellow ribbon. Her breasts rose under the cheerleader outfit, hidden and tempting. Down fell her hair.

She leaned forward, palms flat on the varnished walnut.

Mr. Wood eased his bulk through a narrow space by the paneled wall.

Over her shoulder, through newly loosened lustrous brown, Mrs. Mock watched him approach.

Her bottom wagged ever so slightly.

Mr. Wood flipped up the sass of blue skirt.

No underwear.

He eyed the white curves of her bottom, on full display for him. He also noted deep lines, her age vividly mapped, on the back of Mrs. Mock's neck, in the loose skin of both arms. Her face reflected in his desk – rough lines of her skin blended with rough wood grain.

She'll do anything for money, Mr. Wood thought. *She'll deliver the twins when I need them, no questions asked.*

From his hip pocket, he pulled one of the Christmas-red envelopes that paid his construction team that afternoon. He tossed it onto the desk between Mrs. Mock's hands.

"One thousand little green elves," he told her. "Yours in sixty minutes."

She seemed tiny now, submitted to him. He caught her giving one quick glance through tangled chestnut back over her shoulder.

No other woman in this room ever gave him that look.

Jennifer.

Mr. Wood had learned one sure thing about the world.

Any and every man he matched himself against in business had a price. He could always seal a deal.

Every woman had a price too.

The wife of the famous evangelist from North Carolina. The hot girlfriend of the professional football player from Dallas. The community-pillar wife of the principal at Lafayette High School. The fashion model from Los Angeles. The pretty woman passing through town on her way home from a relative's funeral, encountered as she gassed up the family station wagon. The wife or daughter of any man Mr. Wood happened to meet and want.

All had their price.

When he roughly pushed himself into her, Mrs. Mock abruptly stood straight. One hand raised from the desk and involuntarily went to her forehead.

Mr. Wood trapped the hand, tiny as a sparrow, in his huge one.

"Did I tell you to take your hands off the desk?" he asked. He twisted a finger hard enough to make Mrs. Mock catch her breath.

She placed the hand down quickly, dropped her face.

"I want your hair just like this every time," he said deep in his throat, taking himself out of her, pushing roughly in again.

"Always tie it up with that yellow ribbon ... Jennifer."

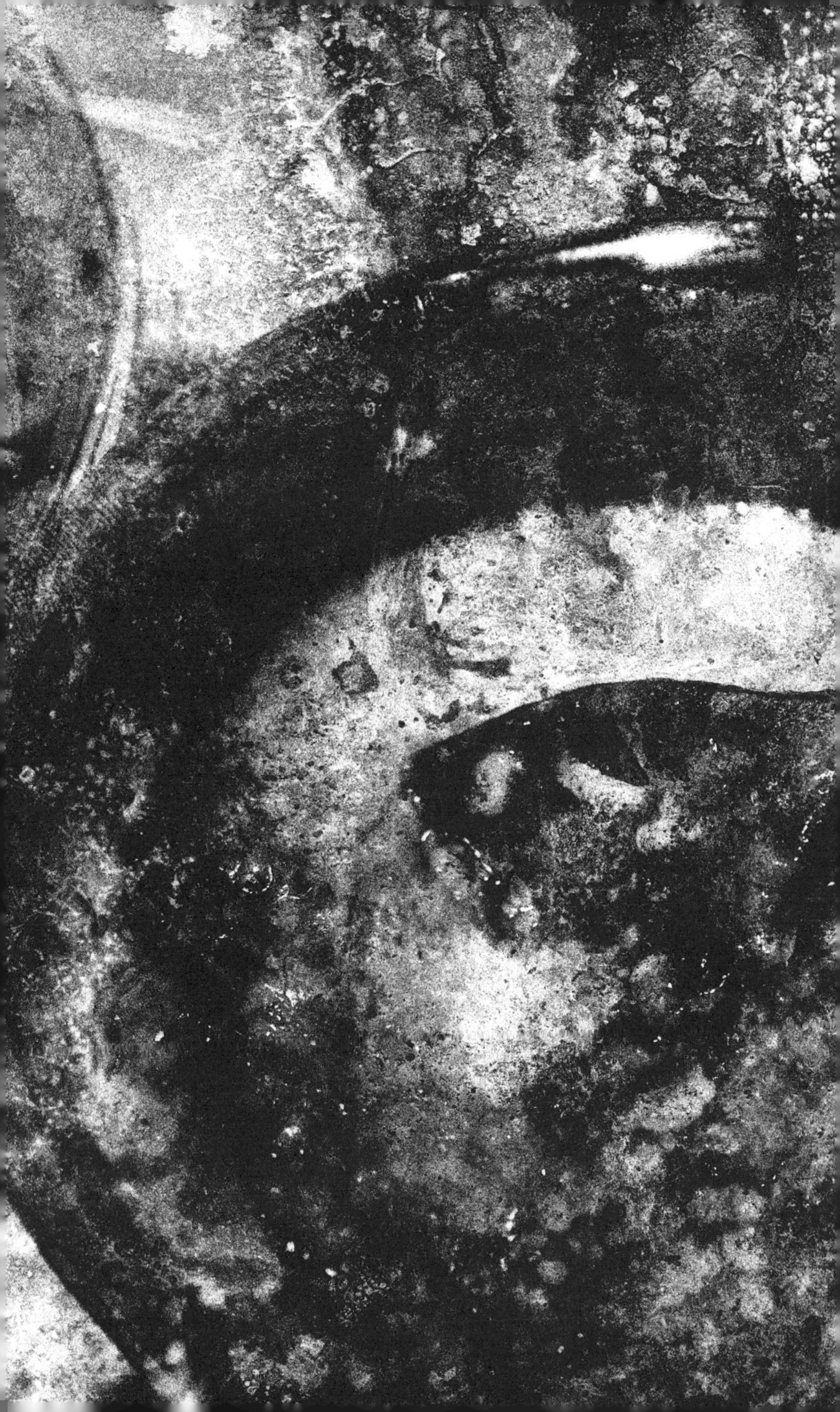

—6—

The Morning After

Bang! Bangbangbang!

Morning.

Loud morning.

Blows on the plywood front door woke Elmore. Cruelly, he relived his rooftop tumble, his long fall, the moment his body slammed frozen ground. All night, he'd fallen from that roof and broken, over and over.

Now … this wake-up noise.

Bang! Bang!

The two-bedroom Rogers rental, cold and still, amplified every knock.

Elmore pushed up from the bedsheets with a weary grimace.

Mistake.

The pillow case stuck to his ruined mouth. It ripped away with a moist noise. Two stitches opened, stinging. Fresh blood trickled down Elmore's chin.

He didn't remember hurting this bad even with fever burning up his brain in Iraq, his temperature as high as the desert around the hospital tent. Mosul had been bad, but at least he slept through the wounds. Thank God for morphine. Thank God for delirium.

In Lafayette, with the weaker hospital meds, every muscle and bone hurt when Elmore breathed. When he didn't breathe too.

At least his liver wasn't damaged any worse. Those X-rays haunted Elmore. It was bad.

Now, Christmas Eve morning of his twenty-ninth year, he struggled from bed still dressed in yesterday's dirty jeans and jacket.

The banging grew louder.

The floor felt like maple-colored ice. Shoeless, shirtless, at the door, gripping the jamb, Elmore caught his reflection in a mirror. Torso taped and bandaged, he looked like a mummy in a horror movie. Ugly little flashbulbs seltzered his vision.

Bang! Bang!

Behind the door's frosted window, a large indistinct figure raised a fist.

Bang! Bang! Bang!

"Daddy?"

Mary's tiny, still-asleep voice floated from the bedroom. Elmore frowned. With this damned fool pounding, both kids would be up and begging for early breakfast.

He yanked the knob with his good hand, noisily unstuck the door.

Dick Wragg, his neighbor, leered, mid-knock. His six-year-old son, Timmy, stood in back of him. Both wore green hunting coats. They looked like a big pea and a little pea.

Wragg whistled, eyes widening.

"Holy crap, Rogers. Mr. Wood must throw one helluva Christmas party for roofers."

So Wragg knew. Word got around. Ugh.

"You look like what the cat dragged in, Rogers. After the cat shit it out."

Elmore flinched at Wragg's raw language in front of his son. He worked swollen lips. The open stitches stung.

"Mewwy Crithmath, Thimmy."

Wragg issued a laugh.

"See that face?" Wragg told his son. "See what happens when you lose a fight? It's a whole lot better to win, ain't it?"

"Yes sir."

Timmy looked horrified at the sight of Elmore. And Elmore felt embarrassed to appear this way, tongue-tied, unwashed, bleeding, scaring the daylights out of a six-year-old.

"Whath you bithneth, Wagg?"

Every word hurt.

"Well, Elmo Wogers," Wragg mocked. "It snowed all over yesterday. Don't tell me you ain't noticed."

It took Elmore a second. Oh yeah. Snow on Alabama.

"Timmy wants your young'uns to help make a big-ass snowman. We already got one started in the front yard. Hell, we might make a whole *army* of big-ass snowmen."

Snowmen? Elmore suddenly felt disoriented.

"Rogers," Wragg went on, elbowing Timmy, "here I am, thirty-three, the age of Jesus Christ his own self ... and no doubt better lookin'. And you know what? It ain't snowed on Christmas Eve for my whole long lifetime. Just look at it now, Rogers! Snow! Godalmighty!"

The world did amaze. Jeweled and beautiful. By night, an ice storm had come in after the snow. Elmore's panel truck was a big white ice cube on wheels. A pecan tree fanned out jeweled branches, peacock style, against a sky that couldn't decide on a color. In the pines across the road, snow tumbled like feathers from a busted pillow. Three confused crows flapped, cawing.

Otherwise, it sounded ... quiet. Like earth had gone deaf.

Snow! A white Christmas ... Christmas Eve, anyway ... in Alabama!

For Elmore, last night had been a blur of pain and ineffective medication. He could barely remember driving Will and Mary home. *Should I go in the house and check on them?*

No need. Elmore felt warmth against his leg. The top of a little ginger head bobbed. Mary, wide-eyed, snot-nosed, gawked past him. Beckoning winter wonderland transfixed her.

Harder footsteps thumped down the hallway. That would be Will, charging the door with the stealth of a small rhino.

Did children ever just walk?

"Can we go play in it, Daddy?"

Mary's innocent face pierced Elmore. In a certain light, Mary looked like her mother so much. She had ginger hair instead of Kelly's summer-night black. But still …

"Daddy," Mary pleaded again, "can we make a snowman?"

"An ARMY of snowmans!" Will yelled, among them now, leaping, boisterous. He wore an oversized Marshall Tucker Band T-shirt. Nothing else, not a stitch.

Mary's green eyes stayed on her dad, beseeching. Elmore didn't like to say no to those eyes. He didn't see that weird fever light in them now. He might be wrong, but Mary looked fine … if you didn't count that runny Rudolph nose.

He flattened his unbandaged palm against Mary's forehead. Her expression changed, a worried look. A drop of blood had fallen from Elmore's split lip onto her blue nightgown.

"Cool!" Will flashed a broad smile missing top teeth. "Daddy, you blooded on Mary."

She seemed unfazed.

"I feel gooder, Daddy. I won't get back the fever. I promise."

Elmore nodded yes, okay to snow. Go play.

It hurt his neck. And another ruby of blood fell, this time from his chin.

"Good God, Rogers. You're a messed-up man."

Elmore knew Wragg couldn't care less. A boastful ex-Navy SEAL, Wragg loved telling Iraq war stories in gory detail over a bar table crowded with what he called "dead sand monkeys" – empty Pabst Blue Ribbon bottles.

Elmore wiped his chin on the thumb bandage. A bloody little face laughed up from the gauze. Elmore shuddered.

His *blood*.

"Awight, Wagg. Juth leth me geth food in 'em. I'll thend 'em out."

Elmore addressed his kids.

"Go geth all your clotheth on. Play clotheth. And firth we eath bweakfath."

"Bweakfath!" snorted Wragg, punching his son's shoulder.

Timmy Wragg. Timmy for *timid*, Elmore thought. Tiny Timmy. A kid scared mute by his ass of an old man.

Or maybe by blood syruping down a grown man's chin.

Go ahead and hide back there behind your papa, son.

I'm scared of blood too.

Elmore boiled water in an aluminum pot with a broken handle. He poured in a snowfall of grits from the box's clever metal spout. He added salt and thumbed in squares of butter left over from a meal weeks ago at Lafayette Waffle House.

Mary and Will, bundled up like little snowmen themselves, charged into the kitchen.

Breakfast looked good. To Will and Mary, anyway. Elmore didn't want hot grits anywhere near his stitched-up mouth. He'd search the cabinet later for a can of cold peaches.

The children clanged down empty bowls. Elmore then pulled a surprise – cinnamon toast from the oven. The charred white bread smoked, but only a little, and each slice held a melted sun of butter. Cinnamon fragrance filled the kitchen.

"Here's your MRE," Elmore said. "Meal ready to eat. So eat."

Will snatched up a slice of cinnamon toast in each hand and bounded for the door.

Elmore had a flash, out of nowhere, of his own boyhood. He ate all day, non-stop. He ate more after dark, then he begged for a snack at midnight. His mom would boil and peel an egg, and Elmore would chew it happily, salted and peppered, head on his soft pillow.

Next morning, he'd wake to ruins of fragmented egg shell on a cracked white saucer. Humpty Dumpty. A fatal fall.

These days, they'd chopper old Humpty out to a field hospital.

They could save that old egg, Elmore thought. *Maybe put Humpty Dumpty back together.*

Where was that medivac this morning? Elmore hurt everywhere.

"Now, Daddy?" Will shook the house jumping up and down at the door. "You said!"

"PLEASE, Daddy?" pleaded Mary. "You said!"

Mary really did appear to be wearing every stitch of clothing she owned. An outside pink sweater made her look like a ball of yarn.

"Noth yeth. Buth go geth on your pig coatth!"

"Pig coats! Daddy said put on our pig coats!" yelled Will, crazy with delight.

"Pig coats!" echoed Mary, her little face bright.

Elmore gave a grunt and made a pig squeal (it hurt his tongue like everything) and set off on a short hobbling run to chase the children.

"Whoth afwaid ob da Pig Pad PIG?" he yelled.

The kids ran for their big coats. They acted like they understood Alabama snow would quickly disappear, a miracle gone in the blink of a golden sunny eye.

They reappeared, bundled, bigger. Will turned the doorknob.

"Whoa! Waith! Juth one more thecond ..."

Elmore brought the last piece of cinnamon toast, dripping butter, down the hall.

He suddenly heard the ear-splitting whistle of a tea kettle.

He didn't own a tea kettle.

The house roared, hot as the oven. He tottered, clenched his eyes to stop the room spinning.

The swoon passed. Elmore tried to act normal.

"Take thith thinnamon thoath to Thimmy."

"Thoath! Thimmy! Thoath!"

Will imitated him gleefully, bouncing in the doorway. Mary trampolined beside him.

"Toads! Thimmy! Toads!" She laughed hysterically at her own joke.

Elmore smiled wearily. "Y'all come inthide ifth you geth cold. And do whath Mr. Wagg tellth you."

Will lived for moments like this. He cocked his shrewd little head.

"What if Mr. Wragg tells us to throw up?"

Mary shrieked with excitement.

"Or *blow* up? Or *grow* up?" Rhyme was Mary's thing right now.

"Well," considered Elmore Rogers, "I gueth you phetter throw up and gwow up."

"You sound funny, Daddy. I love you!"

Beautiful little Mary!

How did he live without his kids those long months after the judge gave them to Kelly in the divorce? How did any parent ever get out of bed after something like that?

The truth? Sometimes he hadn't ...

The twins exploded from the house and dove into the first snowdrift. Will and Mary rolled over and over in the light two inches, laughing their heads off.

They scrambled up dusted in white. Sugar-cookie children.

"Mary! Will! Y'all hurry!"

Timmy Wragg waved quilted green arms from the Wragg house, through a wooded lot.

"We got world-class big-ass snowmen under construction!" Mr. Wragg yelled.

Where the hell did Wragg get snowsuits? Elmore wondered. *Is it fire department gear?*

He briefly second-guessed himself about leaving the twins with a jerk like Wragg.

Then wind whipped snow through the door, and Elmore grimly shut himself in and limped through melting flakes that dusted his floor.

He reached his still-warm bed and fell in.

He lay there – how long? Hours? Months? A second painful convalescence?

He dreamed he fell from a high roof. Landed hard. Dreamed it again.

Things broke. Inside.

Where was his helicopter?

Bang! Bangbangbang!

Elmore woke. That wasn't the front door.

Those were gunshots.

For a dazed moment, Elmore flashed back.

—7—

Hot Day in Iraq

A Big Boom.

Wind moaned. Rain spattered Elmore's face.

Not rain.

Falling dirt.

Elmore heard men scream, the middle of the day a midnight. The reek of gasoline.

Dan Neeley? Where? His Bama buddy had been riding shotgun in the transport ...

Broken glass crunched under Elmore's boots. He looked down. His femur, shocking white, jutted through his desert fatigues. His arm dangled. Elmore's liver, lung, pierced kidney, everything inside, screamed. Blood bubbled out when he breathed.

Soldiers ran past his shattered driver-side window. Elmore heard shouts, male, rough. A radio crackled.

Cold seeped into Elmore's bones even in this blast furnace of a cab in this blast furnace of a blown-up transport truck in this blast-furnace of a desert.

He clenched his eyes.

He saw a glow. It flickered and beckoned.

He heard singing. A choir. Words he did not understand.

He wanted that light, that music.

Roughly, from nowhere, a bleeding hand grabbed Elmore's arm. The hand dragged him out the cab, through coarse sand. Something plastic settled onto his face, and strange cool air rushed up his nose, into his lungs.

What was happening?

He saw a metal vehicle of some sort, smoking, torn like tinfoil. It lay on one side under a merciless sun. Three of its tires burned, roiling black clouds.

Overhead, a gigantic machine appeared, shuddering down. It rocked side to side in black smoke as it settled. Whirling blades flung sun-blasted stones and sand. A red cross on its side.

Elmore heard choral voices again. They sang *his name! Elmore Rogers!*

He stood before an enormous bonfire in the woods, firelight climbing up and up into dazzling clouds. Elmore perceived that those were not clouds at all. They were stars – stars brilliant and densely packed like clouds. A cloud heaven.

Around the bonfire stood a host of beautiful, shining animals. Some looked vaguely like people, and some looked like deer, and some looked like wildcats and foxes and quail and opossums, and some looked like snakes. All of them stared into the fire. One tiny deer opened its mouth. The creature's tongue was a miniature flame.

What did the beasts see in the bonfire?

Then Elmore saw too.

In the brightest flames, a figure motioned to Elmore. *Come, come on.*

Square. Masculine. Slightly bowed legs. Ruddy face and red hair. Bunched, solid athletic shoulders.

His buddy, Dan Neeley.

His old friend and platoon leader ... high-school football teammate ... long-forgiven rival for Kelly's love.

Neeley led two small children by their hands.

Will. Mary.

They had the same shining eyes as the animals. They held Neeley's hand and called.

Daddy! Daddy!

In the desert, Elmore opened his eyes, furious to live.

The real Dan Neeley knelt over him, sweating, cursing. Wounded too, Neeley knotted bandages, compressed wounds. He toiled with all his might to save Elmore's flickering life.

Medics from the helicopter rushed toward them.

"Damn it, Elmore!" Neeley yelled, right into his face. "Live! *Live,* goddamnit!"

Elmore lived.

One tiny deer opened
its mouth. The
creature's tongue was
a miniature flame.
What did the beasts
see in the bonfire?

8

Frosty

Will and Mary charged through ragged nandina at the Wragg lot line, scattering red berries in the snow. Crimson dots filled their footprints.

"We got a carrot to make the nose!" yelled Timmy Wragg.

Timmy played Sisyphus, pushing a snowball half his height around the long sloping lawn of the Wragg place. The meandering trail around the yard might have spelled something, a phrase in cursive, but Will couldn't figure it out. His and Mary's second-grade class had barely started 'real writing', as Mrs. Alexander, his teacher, called it.

"Let's make a snow angel!" cried Mary.

"Snow angels are for girls!" yelled Will, galloping ahead.

He muscled in beside Timmy. Their snowball wobbled, then picked up speed. White clots dropped off, but the round mound slowly swelled to the size of a cartoon boulder as they pushed it, laughing and panting.

Mary picked a spot where snow shone clean and undisturbed. She carefully sat down – even with all her layers, the cold against her bottom briefly knocked the breath out of her. Then she settled onto her back and moved her arms and legs up and back like windshield wipers. She had seen people make snow angels on TV. Her face glowed with joy.

The boys pushed their giant snowball until they finally ran out of strength. They flopped down, puffing smoke from bright cheeks.

"Perfect! The perfect spot!"

Wragg loomed. He carried a handful of gravel from the CSX railroad track across the road. Beyond that stretched a tract of Mr. Wood's vast properties.

"Here! Y'all take these!"

Will and Timmy took cold slag from the man's gloves. Mary, the back of her jacket white and fluffy as a rabbit, held out a hand too, but Will quickly snatched the last stone.

"Use the rocks for buttons!" Wragg instructed. "And snaggle teeth!"

Wragg seemed not to notice Mary's pair of snow angels, twins like she and her brother. He turned again to the boys.

"Y'all roll up another snowball now, big as that first one," he ordered. "We'll make the top part of old Frosty with it ..."

Will wondered if people named every snowman Frosty. Always Frosty. He wondered if he could make a T-Rex or some other cool dinosaur out of snow, or if anybody ever made anything except round men.

He'd like to make a monster. Maybe the Abominable Snowman!

"Daddy!" Timmy said. "Help start us the other snowball like you done the first one?"

Wragg looked like he'd give a lecture. Instead, he stopped and pointed.

"I ain't got to start one, son. Looka there! Look at that pretty young lady!"

On her hands and knees, Mary collected snow. A strand of her red hair dangled. Her nose glistened, running faster than she could sleeve it away. She rolled a little football-shaped snowball, fattening it with snow.

"You boys gonna let that little girl make the snowman?" Wragg jeered. "You go, Mary! Show these sissies how it's done!"

Sissies!

Oh, the snow that flew! The boys hustled and packed and pushed. Their second snowball was an egg too, at first. Then Will took over, muscled it, flopped it end-over-end, by himself. Ten flips added enough fresh snow to make a roundish ball.

Wragg squatted in front of Mary, both knees popping. His bright eyes shone. He had a funny top lip like a goat's. Mary saw it twitch when he spoke. One twitch per word.

"Sweetheart," he said, "that snowball's big enough just like you got it."

With blazing determination, Mary looked at the boys then back at Wragg.

"But I want mine *big!*" she insisted. "Big like theirs!"

"No," corrected Wragg, "no you don't."

Mary felt odd. Why was Mr. Wragg staring at her that way?

"Know why, you pretty thing?"

"No sir."

Wragg's grin split his red face. His goat lip twitched.

"Cause we're gonna use yours – just this size here – for old Frosty's HEAD!"

He rose to help the boys. Mary's delighted smile chased Wragg across the yard.

After a minute, the male trio, yelling mightily, hoisted the second fat snowball. They shakily balanced it, then squashed it down atop the first one. Now Frosty's torso stood taller than either boy and reached to Wragg's shoulders.

Frosty lived.

Lafayette's newest snowman wore railroad gravel down his front like buttons on a vest. Mary found a serendipitous piece of Christmas tinsel magically dangling from a bare limb. (Mr. Wragg suggested a crow draped it there, since crows loved to steal shiny objects.)

That tinsel became Frosty's scarf.

The children jabbed two garden rakes into Frosty to make long skinny arms. The splayed tines dripped snow off trembling fingertips.

Mary's snowball made an excellent head. It turned out to be a little proportionally small – Frosty was Lafayette's first pinhead snowman. But when Wragg set a real fireman's hat atop the noggin, Frosty rocked. The hat belonged to Chief Wragg himself, proud captain of the Lafayette Fire Department.

Frosty's nose fell off twice before Mr. Wragg finally got the fat carrot frozen into place. For eyes, the boys went for an Asian look – broken sticks, angled. Pine needle eyebrows.

The boys also made a shouting mouth, over Mary's protests, from a Vienna sausage can.

Frosty looked to Mary like a Halloween creation – a snowman with steel teeth waving strange arms, hollering at the whole world.

"He looks scary."

"Scary! Good!" The two boys danced around Frosty, joyfully kicking up snow. Stray snowflakes drifted out of the trees.

"He'll scare away monsters!"

Will actually yelled those words, his handsome little face set, sure.

He couldn't have been more wrong.

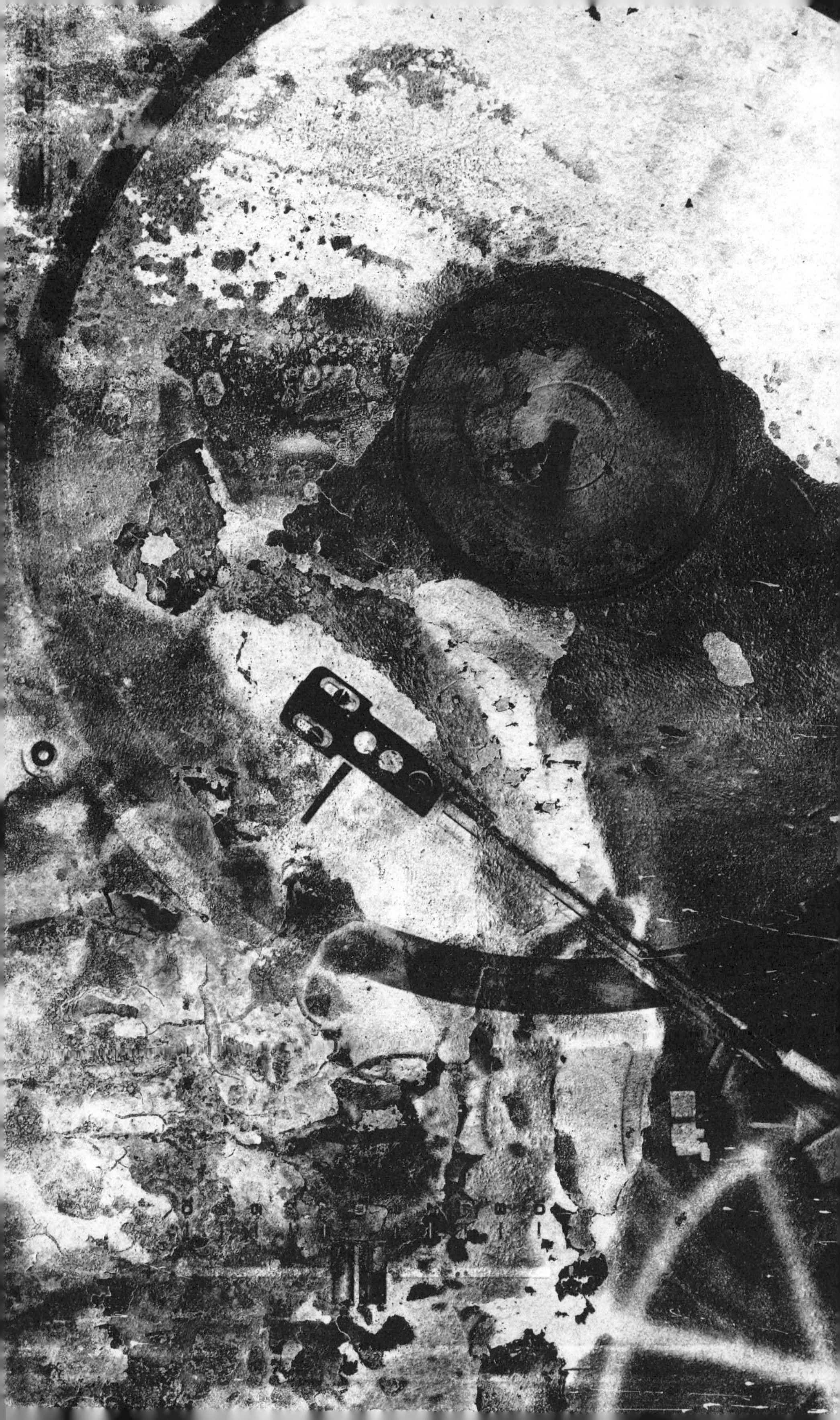

—9—

Night Shift

Kelly carefully taped a nickel to the cheap plastic stylus of her twenty-year-old turntable.

Now. Play.

Without the added weight, the stereo stylus drifted free of grooves on the 33 1/3 RPM Firestone Christmas album. The diamond-tipped needle randomly skipped from song to song. Perry Como unexpectedly joined the Mormon Tabernacle Choir. Rudolph the Red-Nosed Reindeer jumped gracelessly into The Hallelujah Chorus.

Joy to the world … the Lord is come …

Kelly's black cat, Chessie, stirred in the wicker seat of the only chair in the drafty trailer. Chessie looked like a charcoal sketch of an old cat. Ancient. An accident by the refrigerator earlier in the evening left Kelly wondering if this might be their last Christmas together.

It would be hard to say goodbye to a faithful friend of seventeen years.

Kelly didn't have so many friends now.

Chestnuts roasting … on an open fire …

The mobile home's electric heating hadn't worked since Kelly moved in two years ago, but she'd found a space heater at a garage sale, and it blazed tonight near her mattress. It didn't always get so cold at holiday time. Christmas Eve last year, the afternoon hit 71 degrees. Kelly saw people in Bermuda shorts grilling chicken outdoors.

Not now. Not this white Christmas. Thank goodness for the little heater. The orange of the sun glowed inside it, and it warmed half of the trailer.

Kelly wore heavy sweat pants and three sweaters, the outer one thick black wool with red snowflakes. She sat cross-legged on the bed … the mattress, really … near the front door. No bed frame, no box springs. A Dixie cup of grape juice aged on the floor. A scrap of fried egg, left from some past breakfast, hardened on a paper plate.

The other lady of the house purred loudly, and something about Chessie's contentment and the faint burning smell from the phonograph made Kelly nostalgic.

She remembered a little girl a long time ago.

But that made her remember her own little girl, Mary, and her little Will.

Kelly's mind switched off the memory like a bad TV show.

She wanted a tool to scrape out the gray putty of brain that remembered … things.

I'm dreaming … of a white Christmas …

Bing Crosby's voice annoyed Chessie.

The black shape in the wicker chair lifted a head from two outstretched paws, then rose and arched her back, the high trembling stretch of a classic Halloween cat. After a glare at the record player, Chessie thumped down onto the trailer's faded yellow carpet.

She padded directly to her litter box.

Kelly reached for the knob on the little plastic phonograph and turned up the volume.

"Just till you're finished, sweetie," she called out. "That's what volume knobs are for."

And may all your Christmases … be white …

What could Kelly do? How could she defend herself from memories?

Christmas.

She had a vision of Mary and Will as they might be tonight. Snuggled in bed, tired from throwing snowballs. Little Will with his boy movie-star face. Mary with her skin like a peach and the smell of ginger in her hair.

So much for memory control.

So much for a life that might have been.

Every Christmas made Kelly suffer. She considered the Black Warrior. On nights like this, the river called. But could even a black river drown her black memories?

It's not what you did. It's what you will do.

Chessie hopped onto her mattress, purring. Some gray pebbles of litter fell from the cat's rickety hindquarters. Kelly gently brushed those away as Chessie settled on a white chenille bedspread Kelly's parents had given her and Elmore for their wedding.

Kelly wore white.

Why? Why had she?

She kept no wedding photographs, no reminders. Kelly wanted no memories.

The trailer had no paintings, not even those generic ones of a wave breaking on big rocks at sunset. No European scenes where a barefoot maiden with a stick walks cows, heads nodding *yeah, yeah* on a muddy road.

On the first day of Christmas … my true love gave to me …

Kelly felt it anew, the black wave approaching, high and hard, out of her control like so many times before.

Four calling birds … three French hens …

Oh sweet God, no no no not now …

Two babies roasting ... two babies left in a hot car to die ...

She heard nothing but crying for a few minutes.

Could even God forgive her?

Could Will and Mary?

And a partridge in a ...

Kelly violently kicked the stereo. It went airborne and banged the trailer wall. The stylus arm pinged off, clattered away, taped-on nickel and all. Barbra Streisand squawked once like her throat was cut, and the black record shattered where it hit.

Shattered.

Somebody cried, and kept crying.

Chessie, tail three times normal size, glared from the distant safety of the bathroom.

Kelly sobbed so hard, so broken down on the bare mattress, that she never heard the heavy car roll up in the soft snow outside.

Sheriff Dan Neeley opened the door.

He didn't knock. He knew Kelly was in the trailer.

Somehow, upside down, the turntable still made a slow rhythmic noise.

Neeley entered and stood silently, his back to the door.

He let Kelly cry a long, long time.

Neeley furtively moved out of sight a small Christmas gift. He'd wrapped it himself in merry paper. He hid it under his police jacket.

The phonograph made an aching noise and finally stopped.

Neely waited before clearing his throat.

"They're okay, Kelly."

Neeley took a deep cold-weather breath.

"I'll see 'em tonight. Elmore too."

Her sobs rose.

"Will and Mary love you, Kelly. No matter what you think. No matter what."

Kelly's mind switched off the memory like a bad TV show. She wanted a tool to scrape out the gray putty of brain that remembered ... things.

10

Abominable

The kids had a snowman to worship. They paid little attention to Wragg.

Several times, he mysteriously disappeared into his house through the open garage. Each return, he weaved a bit more across the snowy yard.

"Wheeee!" he stumbled up, like a human fire engine. "Wheeeeeee!!!"

Some grown-up glee animated him. Mary thought Mr. Wragg might be freezing, his face was so red. He smelled like mouthwash.

Wragg squealed again, and he chased Timmy and Will round and round the snowman. His squeals changed to loud monkey noises, grunts and growls. Wragg made a snatch for the boys, but tripped and fell, bellowing.

"Run as fast as you can," taunted Will, "you can't catch us, Mr. Gingerbread Man!"

Will and Timmy counted coup, dashing forward to tag the fallen grown-up then bound away in happy terror.

Wragg struggled to his elbows. Clumps of snow fell from his hair. He stared for a long, strange moment at Frosty then yelled, a sudden terrific excitement lighting his face.

"Aight! Aiiiiight! I got it! Now we'll have some fun!"

Timmy looked confused.

"Daddy? Where you goin'? You just went inside!"

"Right back!" Wragg barked, humping it through the snow. "Stay right where y'all are!"

The door slammed. Too hard. Maybe the Christmas Eve wind blew it shut.

"He might be getting hot chocolate," Will speculated. "Hot chocolate would be great."

Timmy wiped his nose on a green nylon sleeve. Without his dad, he looked younger than a six-year-old. "We ain't got hot chocolate. Mama can't eat nothin' chocolate."

Mary had to ask why.

"Cause chocolate gives her the squirts. She don't eat nothing sweet but fruitcake."

"Ewwww!" said Mary. "Fruitcake don't taste like fruit *or* cake."

"You're stupid," Will barked at her. "It tastes like *fruitcake*."

Timmy gave Mary a sympathetic glance. "If Daddy brings us some fruitcake," he said, "I'm gonna spit mine in the snow."

Mary and Timmy laughed.

Will fantasized again. "Maybe he'll bring doughnuts!"

"Frosty could have doughnut ears!" Mary said.

"That's dumb," groused Will. "Snowmen don't have ears."

The house door slammed. Wragg swayed back across the lawn. He carried a stick. And Sunny, the Wraggs' little orange-and-white rat terrier, romped alongside, skittering like a dwarf antelope over the snow, barking and bounding, jubilant and confused all at once. Sunny leaped in the air to snap at windblown flakes.

"He's bringin' a BB gun," Mary announced.

Face even redder, Wragg huffed up. He cradled across his breast, sure enough, a gun.

But not a BB gun. Mary didn't recognize a double-barreled Remington 20-gauge.

Mr. Wragg's coat pockets bulged with shells. Two spilled as he clambered down the hill. They lay in the snow, one red, one green. Holiday colors.

Breathing hard, Wragg exhaled what could have been gunsmoke.

"You ... two ... Timmy and Will ... y'all come ... *whew* ... here. Get by me."

Mary watched the trio of males trudge up the hill. Sunny stayed with her, and she stroked the little dog. It trembled violently, and made noises in the back of its throat.

Wragg and the boys stopped thirty feet up the lawn, on a slope overlooking their newly built snowman.

"Can I shoot first, Daddy?"

"The grown-up always shoots first, Timmy."

Wragg sounded serious, the holly jolly Christmas gone right out of him.

"Can I shoot too, Mr. Wragg?" Will's face implored.

Wragg's index finger tapped the gun's cold blue barrels. His odd lip twitched.

"My boy goes first, Will. After me, I mean. When Timmy hits his shot, you'll get a turn. But Timmy's gonna let old Frosty feel some love first."

Mary stood off from this business. Her arms hugged her chest, the squirming terrier clutched tight. She felt very cold just that moment, and very hot at the same time. Confused.

Were they going to shoot Frosty? They'd just taken all this time and energy to *make* him.

That instant, with frightening speed, Wragg pivoted, snapped the shotgun to his shoulder, aimed, and pulled both triggers in succession.

Boom! BOOM!

It scared the hell out of all three children. And Sunny.

Mary tumbled back onto her bottom, hands over her ears. Sunny streaked for the house, struggling through a snowdrift halfway. The two boys simply jumped up and down, helpless with adrenaline, their faces bright as jack o' lanterns.

Look at Frosty!

Wragg had performed a magic trick. *Abracadabra!*

Seconds ago, the snowman's head sat right there, his steel mouth shining and his big red fireman's hat tipped back. The clown-white face, orange carrot nose, and twig eyes beamed holiday happiness to the whole wide world.

Now Frosty's head was gone.

The fireman's hat lopsidedly rolled away down the hill, half its long bill shot away.

Mary jumped to her feet and ran for the Rogers house. Her shoes sank in snow. Little Sunny returned suddenly, barking and bounding beside her in wild flight.

Yayyyy!

The boys screamed, out of their minds with excitement, flinging arms in the air, dancing every which way.

"Me!" yelled Timmy. "Now me, Daddy!"

Mr. Wragg loaded fresh shells – holiday colors – and handed the gun over to his son.

Mary tumbled, running too fast. She fell in snow, and the little terrier pushed its wide-eyed face to hers, black lips curled in fear. Sunny tunneled under her body to hide.

Boom!

"Dammit! Timmy, hear that?"

A metallic rattle.

"You missed the whole snowman, son! You missed the snowman and hit the mailboxes! You done gone and shot our Christmas cards! Baby Jesus got buckshot in his ass now!"

The shotgun had knocked Timmy down in the snow. He looked humiliated, his jacket and hat too big, the gun oversized.

"Git up from there, boy. Here. Put in a new shell. Now this time you line up that sight square in the middle of old Frosty's back! Do like I showed you – draw your bead, take a deep breath, let it out slow, squeeze the trigger. Don't jerk it ..."

Boom!

Mary kept hands clapped over her ears. The snow made things too loud. And in the snowdrift, she could no longer feel her hands or ears.

Or believe her eyes.

A bright scrap of the tinsel scarf she had knotted around Frosty's neck slowly drifted down from the sky onto her legs.

The spot where the garland hung – Frosty's neck – no longer existed. Timmy's shotgun blast had blown a huge round hole clear through the snowman. Mary could have pushed her whole head through.

Her nose burned from blue smoke and gunpowder.

Mary couldn't believe what happened next.

Wragg handed Will the shotgun. Her brother Will.

Will had a shotgun!

It waggled dangerously until Wragg caught the barrel in a big hand and held it steady.

Wragg loaded a shell, blood red, into a breech. He helped Will snap the barrel shut.

Click!

Wragg stood behind Will, supporting the barrel. The grown-up stopped for a coughing fit, spit a yolky glob into the snow.

He wiped his mouth and issued orders like a true SEAL, a true fire chief, clamping the wooden stock tight to Will's shoulder.

"Just like this ... or it will knock you flat on your ass like it did Timmy!"

Mary heard Wragg, but she closed her eyes tight.

"... or knock your shoulder out of joint. Now. That's it. Ready, son?"

Will's face intensely concentrated.

"... line up that little silver bead there between these two notches ... and put that bead on the spot to hit ..."

Boom!

Mary plunged her face into cold snow. Poor little gun-shy Sunny trembled under her.

"Damn! Looka yonder, ladies!

Mary had trouble seeing. A clump of snow stuck to her face.

Will's shot had ripped through Frosty at the exact spot the torso and base joined. A gaping round wound glistened. The snowman leaned to the right. It hesitated as if fighting for its life, leaned a little more, dropped one of its rakes.

"Timberrrrrrrr ...!"

Frosty the Snowman toppled. Shot dead.

"You got 'im, Will!" cheered Timmy. "Hooray!"

Over at the Rogers' house, a door slammed hard. It sounded as angry as the shotgun blast.

"Hey!" Elmore's voice. "What the ... HEY!"

Mary saw her daddy limp painfully toward them. He wore his work boots, untied, and he winced, hurrying at a hobble. His huge bandaged thumb waved like a crab claw.

"Wagg? Whath the heck you doin' with a shotgun aroundth my kidths?"

Mary hated when her daddy yelled.

"Cat got your eyes, Elmore? We're shooting a snowman in the ass!"

Daddy don't allow that word, Mary thought.

Sunny, poor baby, trembled like somebody had shot at her instead of Frosty. Mary snuggled the terrier. It lifted its noble little face to hers, scared by the guns, now the men shouting. Mary stared away too, across the road, into the woods.

She saw something.

Past the mailboxes, beyond the road and railroad track. In the woods.

Somebody moved. A man stood back in the trees. Watching.

He wore a white coat, color of the snow. He wore a white cowboy hat. Snowy undergrowth hid the rest of him.

Sunglasses made the man look weird. Like a white praying mantis.

Sunny whined, pushed her black nose under Mary again. Elmore and Mr. Wragg yelled. Mary couldn't understand half the words. Her daddy's mouth bled again.

The man in the woods stared squarely at Mary, then at the two boys, then at the quarreling men, now nose to nose.

The man in the woods wore no expression. His posture did not change. No vapor of breath came out of him.

Mary turned to her daddy and Wragg, faces red, fists balled.

"That man!" she announced. "Who's he?"

Mary pointed.

Everyone seemed relieved at the distraction. They all looked.

"Whath man, honey?" her dad asked, his voice tight.

"It ain't nobody," growled Will. "It's your imagination."

Maybe. The man in the woods had vanished. He was gone.

Like their snowman.

Except for one tell-tale glimpse. Elmore saw it too.

Strange. He remembered TV shows where people saw that thing ... what was it called?

Bigfoot. Whatever.

Elmore glimpsed a heavy shape in white. Moving fast until it vanished completely in the blue shadows of the woods.

A limb quivered up and down where it passed, spilling snow.

That was all.

"You missed the snowman and hit the mailboxes! You done gone and shot our Christmas cards. Baby Jesus got buckshot in his ass now!"

—11—

Say-More

Two summers past, Elmore and the twins spent a Saturday afternoon with heads bowed and necks burning.

Elmore owned a pick-up then, a clunker paid off with the IV trickle of green the army gives a wounded warrior. He drove out to a hard red field off Wood Road where arrowheads washed up after big rains, gleaming like bone among scabs of grass. Sometimes an actual human bone, brown as honeycomb after centuries in cakey clay, rose to the surface of Alabama.

Mary and Will had seemed hardly more than toddlers to Elmore before that day. But he discerned, that Saturday, for the first time a young lady and young man somewhere in the headlong ginger blurs that leaped from the truck. Will was a hot colt. Mary didn't yet have asthma, or weak lungs, or whatever kept her nose running all the time now.

It made Elmore happy when Mary found a quartz bird point, her very first arrowhead. She found two other broken points too. The boys scared up a few pottery shards the color of graham crackers, one with tiny bird-peck designs, but no arrowheads. Then Will trumped them all by kicking up a nasty-looking spearhead the size of Elmore's hand. Will declared that a deep brown stain in the flint must be dry bear blood.

"I bet this sharp point went right in that old bear's *heart*," Will proclaimed, and his eyes burned with conviction.

Elmore never had to look hard to see the man Will would one day be. He'd been like a little adult – willful, bluff, cocksure, decisive – since the day he came into the world.

They sunburned in the field until it started to rain. Fat cold drops and a scary clap of thunder chased them back to the pick-up in a thrilling, hilarious sprint.

Now Christmas Eve two and one-half years later, a gigantic new Sav-More Superstore covered the arrowhead field ... and snow covered its parking lot. The only Indian artifacts here would be the rubber tomahawks in Aisle 9.

The Sav-More drew more people Christmas week than Lafayette's churches drew in a year. Shopping had a hold on people like religion, Elmore reckoned. They streamed into Sav-More all day, all night, emerging with rattletrap buggies full of plastic bags. The 90,000-square-foot Sav-More building was the biggest structure in the county prior to Wood Castle.

Something occurred to Elmore, stitched and bandaged on a faded-white Christmas Eve.

How nice if a shopper could find even one thing in Sav-More actually made in Alabama.

He imagined a special section way in back: Aisle Alabama. The aisle where you bought moonshine and marijuana.

Mr. Sav-More would ring up a fortune in that department.

Elmore herded the kids past a friendly old greeter with skin cancers on the back of his neck, dark little spots clustered like ticks.

They pushed into a crowd. A farmer in a new pair of bib overalls, likely an early Christmas present, shuffled ahead. The farmer's little guinea-hen of a wife suddenly ruffled and darted off.

The farmer stopped Elmore.

"Sonny, do you work here?"

Elmore waited, his eye dark purple, his lips stitched, his thumb in a huge bandage. He would not be a typical Sav-More employee.

"Where can a feller find flea powder? My dog's got 'em, and Ann lets him in the bed."

"Well, sir, don't buy what they sell here," Elmore said. His tongue felt more sure, healing fast. "You and the missus go get a bag of lemons and squeeze 'em and make a paste with the juice and some baking soda and salt. Your dog won't like it. But the fleas won't like it even worse."

Will and Mary gawked at their daddy like he was the smartest man on earth.

Elmore liked that feeling. He wanted the spell to last.

Then he felt light pressure on his bandaged arm.

"Don't I know you, young man?"

A little woman with blue hair looked at Elmore through bifocals that magically magnified her eyes. Elmore felt a memory unhappily wake.

"I used to fit your pants at the J.C. Penney store," she said. "Your name is Elmore Rogers. You wore a husky size."

Elmore glanced at the kids in embarrassment. A husky himself, Will listened wide-eyed.

"Yes'm," Elmore confessed, through his stitches. "I remember you. You stuck pins in the cuffs of my pants when I tried them on."

You stabbed my ankles! his irritated memory yelled. *Every year! It hurt worse than back-to-school vaccinations ...*

"I'm Mrs. Ard. And these are your sweet little children? My, aren't they just *beautiful?*"

"Yes'm. Mine. Sweet. Beautiful. Mary and Will, y'all say hello to Mrs. Ard."

The twins mumbled.

"Where'd they get that pretty red hair? They don't favor you much, do they Elmore?" Mrs. Ard arched her eyebrows. "Well, maybe the boy. He's a husky size, isn't he?"

Elmore felt Will's stout little body bristle.

"I thank the Lord every day," Elmore said, "they got their mama's good looks."

"I look like Daddy," Mary protested. "Everybody says."

"You look like a *monkey*," Will snapped.

"Oh my!" said Mrs. Ard. "This child certainly has a temper like his daddy. You used to holler and cry when I tape-measured your middle, Elmore Rogers. You wore a husky size, you know ..."

"Will," Elmore said strictly. "Tell your sister you're sorry. She doesn't look one bit like a monkey. Do it now. Santa Claus has elves watching."

Will grumbled something apologetic. It nearly killed him.

"That's a fine, responsible young man," said Mrs. Ard. "This country certainly needs fine, responsible young men."

"It was mighty nice to see you," Elmore politely told Mrs. Ard. "Merry Christmas!"

Merry Christmas! sang Mrs. Ard, like a caroler.

Elmore shuffled the kids out of range, then cut the leashes.

"Last one to the toys is a rotten egg!" Will yelled, and he sprinted. Mary too.

Elmore all at once saw his children, now far up the aisle, through fatherly eyes.

Age seven, going on eight. Still innocent. Just how Elmore wanted it right now. Even without a job and all busted up, spending his last wounded-warrior money, Elmore would make sure the twins woke up tomorrow morning with gifts under their scraggly tree.

When the kids had visions of sugar plums dancing in their heads, Elmore would slip from bed. He'd roll the panel truck out of gear down the driveway, then fire it up. He'd run back up to Sav-More to buy presents.

Elmore saw Will stop up ahead.

The aisle to the toys passed through Sav-More's gun section.

Will's fascinated face swiveled left and right like the searching flashlight beam of a young explorer in a magic cave. Did he want to fill a shopping cart with shotguns and pistols?

Elmore winced.

This afternoon, Will fired his first gun. He now knew that lifelike kick of a stock, the heart-starting boom, the smell of gunpowder. Will experienced the strange power of doing something here that made something way over there fly in the air, or fall to pieces.

Or die.

The goddamn genie was out of the bottle.

Dick Wragg, you got what you deserve.

Elmore had felt a little guilt ... though not much ... about knocking Wragg down in front of his own boy. Out in that snowy yard, cold anger swept Elmore away.

He felt righteous. What right did the drunk next door have to wave a double-barreled shotgun around Mary and Will? Any daddy would kick some ass over that.

It took one push to topple Wragg into the snow. He hadn't gotten up for a long time.

"Keep moving, Will. This is not the toy section."

Will scooted. And now Elmore came up on Mary. She had stopped in the housewares beside a mountain of foam rubber pillows. How many pillows? Five hundred?

"Where are the pillow cases, Daddy?"

Mary looked up at Elmore. Those innocent eyes. She forever made him feel like the wisest man.

"Honey, I'm thinking they stuffed all the pillowcases with toys and threw 'em on the sleigh for Santa to deliver. I bet there's a couple for you and Will. Now c'mon!"

"Daddy, Will said he could *smell* the toys. I wish I could." Mary dragged the sleeve of her pink sweater across her face. "I only smell my nose."

Elmore reached into a jacket pocket stuffed with Dairy Queen napkins. Mary's cold just wouldn't get well. Her pale skin couldn't quite hide the blue veins in her arms.

Elmore wiped her nose. He remembered Mary lying in the snow, scared to death of the shotgun, protecting a little dog. Elmore felt his blood boil all over again.

Mary ran ahead. Elmore, in fact, watched dozens of Marys. In the housewares aisle, a heaven of mirrors – ovals, rectangles, hexagons, all shapes, all sizes – twinkled and flashed flying versions of the little girl.

For Elmore, the mirror department was a house of horrors.

I'm one to fuss about Mary's health. Look at that fellow.

A wild and lonesome thing stared from scores of mirrors. The man in every reflection looked like a ruin.

A loser.

Elmore studied his swollen shiner. He stuck out a tongue – the soft organ looked something like a pink whale bristling with old black harpoons. Elmore waved a bandaged hand, and a hundred bandaged hands waved back.

The mirrors didn't even show the hurt places *inside*.

There he was, Elmore Rogers. Twenty-nine years old. A mess. Shopping late for two kids at Sav-More on Christmas Eve with $57 in wadded bills, plus some quarters and pennies. His credit card might not work.

Less than 48 hours ago, he'd lost his job. He owed the emergency room. He owed house bills. Cold weather was here, with heating bills. And he looked and felt like a man dragged a dozen miles down a stony road behind a mule.

"All the bicycles are sold, Daddy!"

Mary again. Those blue-green eyes. They held a new expression.

Troubled. Disappointed.

"Sweetie! This is Sav-More! No way a Sav-More is sold out of bikes at Christmas ..."

Elmore's sentence trailed off.

The racks where bicycles normally hung, shiny and bright, smelling of tire rubber, festive with handlebar tassels ... those racks were absolutely empty twenty feet in both directions.

Will looked like a kid who'd just seen his dog run over.

"It snowed for Christmas, anyway," Mary chirped. "Didn't it, Daddy?"

"Sweetie! This is Sav-More! No way a Sav-More is sold out of bikes at Christmas ..." Elmore's sentence trailed off.

—12—

Champions

Mr. Wood left the engine running.

The big white Chevy king cab rumbled in front of a wooden shack not much bigger than an outhouse. Orange coals glowed inside the splintery thing, and smoke puffed from a tin stack. Like dirty cotton, unmelted snow lay on the ground.

A plank over a service window displayed faded letters, drizzled on in something like barbecue sauce:

CHAMPIONS

Neville Champion watched from the window. After pushing out his famous pork plates all day, the big Cajun looked like he'd rather be somewhere else at 8 p.m. on Christmas Eve.

Still, when Mr. Wood sent word, Champion kept the light on. His light was a burning lantern, swinging from a hook.

The man in the cowboy hat approached. Mr. Wood grunted, set down a red cooler.

"Champion," Mr. Wood said, his hat brim nodding slightly.

Why does the dude wear a hat at night? Champion wondered. *The top of that head must be some ugly.*

The smell of hickory and roasting pork filled the air.

"Merry Christmas, Mr. Wood. Santa Claus gonna be good to you?"

Champion's voice didn't match his big body, the pipefitter forearms and bulging belly. He fluted when he spoke, a surprising tenor that got him teased in his school days. The teasing stopped after he beat the living daylights out of a few boys. At the same time.

"Santa's always good to me, Champion. He's gonna be good to you this year too."

Like a magic trick, Mr. Wood conjured three $100 bills from a fringed sleeve. He laid them face up in the service window, Ben Franklins with Mona Lisa mystery smiles.

Champion smiled too. "Well I thank you, Mr. Wood. Santa Claus got them elves all over. They must know how good I been."

Mr. Wood didn't seem to listen.

"So, Champion, here's what I want."

He pointed at the cooler, the fringe on his jacket sleeve shaking.

"I got fresh meat," he said. "Six pork-rib slabs and two butts and four different legs. A hog leg. A beef leg. A deer leg. And a goat leg."

Champion gave a whistle.

"That was one strange critter, Mr. Wood. I believe you'll get on TV if you catch another of them things."

Mr. Wood stuck to business.

"I want you to grill up all that meat and have it ready first thing in the morning," Mr. Wood said. "Seven o'clock. Christmas Day."

"Yes sir. I'll start right now. It'll be ready when the sun comes up."

Neville Champion didn't see $300 many full weeks. He would cook and sing Christmas carols all Christmas Eve for that kind of money.

"I know you didn't plan to spend your Christmas Eve barbecuing," Mr. Wood said. "But something's come up. I want to see how you handle a ... special order."

"I'll get goin'."

"Got sauces and rubs?"

"Yes sir. I'm set."

Champion's soft voice almost sounded like singing. Mr. Wood had never met the pit man before, knew him only by reputation as the best barbecue cook in Lafayette.

"Surprise me, Champion."

The grill man blinked under the bright lantern. Champion looked tired after his long day over the coals. The whites of his eyes showed streaks of red, like the sign over his window.

"Exactly what kind of surprise, Mr. Wood?"

Mr. Wood had clearly put some thought into it.

"I want to see all the different ways you can make them meats taste. How many different flavors you can give 'em."

"Yes sir. I got my tricks, Mr. Wood."

"Tricks? What kind of tricks?"

Now Neville Champion smiled for the first time. His pride-and-joy gold front tooth flashed lantern light.

"Well, Mr. Wood, if I go and tell my tricks," Champion said, "they won't be no surprise."

Mr. Wood didn't smile.

"I'm a curious man, Champion. I'm interested in how things work. How tricks work."

Out in the cold, a whippoorwill went off. Champion thought how weird it sounded, like some kind of kids toy.

"I do stuff with vinegar. Make it taste different on the different meats. I blend up the peppers different ways, make the sauces mild or sissy or hot. I can ..."

"How hot?"

Mr. Wood made eye contact for the very first time. Champion thought the man's pupils looked like nail heads.

"Hot enough to make a grown man beg for his mama, Mr. Wood."

"Okay. Make some of it that hot."

"Yes sir. I sure will."

Now Mr. Wood smiled.

"What happens if you get that hot stuff on your pecker?"

Mr. Wood laughed at his own joke, but Champion didn't. The Cajun had indeed once accidentally gotten special-blend hot sauce on his penis. He didn't pee for two days.

Champion glanced at a shelf. Yes, he kept magic potions in unmarked canisters and bags. Only Champion knew what each held. Only Champion knew the mystery blends that made his shack a Lafayette legend.

When Champion looked again, Mr. Wood was halfway to his truck, chuckling.

"Seven o'clock, Champion. Show me what you can do on short notice."

"Seven o'clock, Mr. Wood."

Then a thought came to Champion.

"Mr. Wood, where you want it delivered?"

The white-suited man stopped. Unexpectedly, he pointed a warning finger.

"Champion, don't you or nobody else show up at my place. This is secret. Tonight. And forever. Leave it in your window there. I'll pick it up."

The king cab disappeared in a white flash.

ERGENCY 9-1-1
LAFAYETTE
POLICE

—13—

Blue Christmas

Blue lights ablaze, the squad car cracked crusted snow up the Rogers' driveway.

Two policemen in heavy jackets got out. They trudged through the snowy yard like mountain climbers to the front door.

Bangbangbangbangbang!

"Come out, Elmore! Everybody out! Do it now!"

Shapes flitted between rooms in the dark house.

Bangbangbang!

"Outside NOW!"

Surprised, two small faces and a big unshaven one, bruised and almost unrecognizable, blinked through the diamond-shaped door pane.

Sheriff Neeley trained a long flashlight on them. All three faces winced and drew back.

"Come out, Elmore. You heard me. You young'uns. Do it now."

Sheriff Neeley leaned toward his partner, Jessie Turnipseed. The hulking deputy's chew bulged in a cheek. The gut of an offensive lineman bulged over his belt.

"Jess, go keep an eye on the back door," Neeley ordered.

The deputy eased off, slipping once on an icy spot. His silhouette blocked one headlight, then the second. The trunk opened. Turnipseed fumbled there, hoisted out something metallic, jangling. The trunk slammed. Turnipseed headed for the back of the house.

The Rogers family emerged from the front door, shivering. The blue police light swept over them like a beam from a frozen lighthouse. Blue. Blue-and-white. Blue. Blue-and-white.

Neeley's flashlight seared their retinas again. Elmore felt a rising annoyance.

"What the hell you mean, Dan, comin' out here this late on Christmas Eve ..."

"Elmore," Neeley said, "don't cuss around little children. It ain't Christian." The sheriff flicked off his beam. "That's exactly how kids grow up to be juvenile delinquents."

A soft question interrupted.

"You ain't gonna hurt Daddy are you?"

Mary glanced up at her father's damaged face.

"You better not!" blustered Will. "Or we'll hurt *you!*"

Neeley fought back a smile. That boy was like Elmore, for sure.

"Listen," Neeley said. "You young'uns go back in there and get your shoes and coats. Hurry up. Me and your daddy will wait right here."

The children stuck to Elmore Rogers like sandspurs.

"GO!" the sheriff growled. "Scat! Unless y'all want to spend Christmas Day in jail."

Neither child moved a muscle.

Sheriff Neeley detected a potential problem with authority here.

Elmore squatted between the children. Neeley heard him wince.

"Y'all do like Dan says. Go put on coats. Get your shoes." Elmore used his no-nonsense voice. "Go quick. And bring my jacket."

They vanished through the crack of the door like cats.

When the twins got out of earshot, Elmore turned. He could shoot straight with his old running buddy and platoon mate.

"What the hell, Dan?"

Neeley flared the flashlight back on Elmore's face.

"Civic duty," Neeley said simply. "Got a call to check out a ... what did he call it? Oh, yeah. A fracas. A fracas with a neighbor."

"Wragg's a crybaby. You got a warrant?"

Neeley laughed.

"Elmore, you kiddin' me? You think this is a TV show?"

"Well, Dan, you ought to have a warrant to get a family out of bed on Christmas Eve."

"Elmore, how 'bout you call me 'Sheriff Neeley' this visit?"

Now it was Elmore's turn to laugh.

"How about *Private* Neeley?"

The blue police light flashed in a moment of silence.

"Sheriff Neeley, Elmore. This visit, I'm Sheriff Neeley."

His tone was flat. The flashlight shone straight into Elmore's eyes. Neeley made official note of the bruises, cuts and stitches.

"Your mug suggests a civil disturbance, El. About three magnitudes up from a fracas."

Mary's face popped back into view. She'd put on the same sweater, pink as a camellia. Will had stuffed his chunky body into sweats and a Crimson Tide jacket with a torn cuff.

Probably got those clothes from the church,
Neeley thought.

"Let's all go sit in the squad car, folks."

The kids turned to Elmore.

"Good idea, Sheriff Neeley. This little girl's had a bad cold. She'll get pneumonia standing out here."

Neeley led the way, barely ahead of Will, who seemed quite excited about sitting in a police car. Elmore hoisted Mary, light as a paper doll, up to his waist. It hurt his hand and ribs, but he gingerly limped along to the squad car, barefoot himself.

The Rogers gang, desperados, settled in the detention cage in the back seat, shivering.

"Are we under arrest?" demanded Will in a fierce voice.

"Will," Elmore said. "Sheriff Neeley is out here making sure the countryside is safe for old Santa Claus tonight. Ain't that right ... Sheriff?"

The police light splashed the house blue.

"Partly for the jolly old elf, yes," Neeley answered. "But I'm also here to ask all three of you some important questions."

"Is it a test?" Mary sounded scared. The roaring heater in the squad car almost drowned her out.

"Mary and Will," Elmore said emphatically, "your daddy will do the talkin'. Hear me?"

A monster's voice crackled unexpectedly from the car radio:

"SHERIFF NEELEY!"

Elmore and the children jumped.

Neeley keyed the receiver. "Turnip. Whatcha got?"

"Checked out the back yard."

"And?"

"A big ole possum. That's about it."

"Any signs of a ... fracas?"

"Negatory."

"Give it one more look, Turnip."

Neeley keyed the receiver, turned to the huddled family. Will wore a sour look. The caged back seat of the squad car disappointed him. He hadn't expected urine, sweat and vomit smells. Blood. The old squad car held a lot of stories.

"Takes a while to get this vehicle warm," Neeley apologized. "The heater's old."

"Where's the hot chocolate?" Elmore cracked.

Will looked up hopefully.

"All I got is hard candy," Neeley offered. "And it's sour. Gives me lockjaw. I don't know how Turnip eats it like he does."

The children snatched the brightly colored sweets Neeley dropped through a special slot and noisily tore off the cellophane.

"So, Sheriff Neeley. You got us out of bed on Christmas Eve. All tucked in. Visions of sugarplums. Why's that?"

"Visions of sugar plums?"

"Come on, Dan."

Neeley frowned, but answered. "Okay. I told you, Elmore. Questions about a civil disturbance. Somebody called it in. Anonymous. Families at blows. Claimed a gun fired. Know anything about that?"

Elmore theatrically raised both hands. Will and Mary sucked candy, listening with all their might.

"Elmore Rogers, if those lips won't talk, why not sew 'em up the rest of the way?"

No reaction.

"How many stitches?" Neeley asked. "I know about your work accident."

Silent night.

Suck suck.

"OK, then," Neeley breathed. "Maybe a more *specific* question. Did anything unusual happen this afternoon with Dick Wragg, your next-door neighbor?"

Will's mouth opened. A big adult arm levered down fast to shut it.

"I'm asking *you*, Elmore."

"I won't lie to you, Sheriff Neeley. Something did happen."

"What?"

"We made a snowman!" piped up Mary.

"Shut up!" Will snapped, jerking forward to glare at his sister around their father's middle. "Daddy *said!*"

"A snowman?"

Elmore saw Neeley's fine smile. Kelly had sure been crazy about that Neeley smile in high school. Those damned teeth. That red hair.

"Well, a snowman ain't too unusual this white Christmas. But how would a snowman cause a civic disturbance serious enough for somebody to call the police?"

A star fell, over the snowy field. Mary saw it, pointed without a word.

"We shot it!" Will confessed, unable to endure investigation any longer. "But Daddy didn't. He don't shoot a gun, *ever*. Mary neither. It was Mr. Wragg and me and Timmy ..."

"Will, enough."

Elmore's arms clamped down again on the twins.

"Say that again, little Will?" Neeley clicked the flashlight now and shone it back in Will's wide-eyed face. "Y'all *shot* a snowman? What ... was he robbing you?"

Elmore felt Neeley enjoying himself a little too much.

"You got some idiot law in Lafayette," Elmore snapped, "against shooting a snowman?"

The flashlight again, this time between Elmore's eyes.

"Neeley, I swear, it was a showdown. Will or that evil snowman. Good versus evil. Armageddon. For a minute there, I thought my boy was a goner ..."

The flashlight dropped. A look passed between the two men.

"Don't get too smart, civilian."

Elmore's bottom lip had burst open in the cold. He tasted salty blood when he talked.

"Smart ain't never been one of my problems, Dan."

Finally, the squad car had grown warm. Absent the cold metal cage, it now might actually have been cozy.

"So, Will. You shot an evil snowman?" Neeley said. "You win a medal for bravery."

He waited a beat.

"But ... did anything *else* unusual happen? Some sort of disagreement between two grown men? See, we had this complaint. We were even asked to make an arrest. But we don't arrest folks on Christmas Eve, unless it's pretty close to murder."

Neeley tapped the steering wheel, waited.

"You young'uns want more candy?"

It stayed quiet enough to hear crickets, had crickets been alive in December.

ZZSCSSSSSSHHHHH!

Shocking static, like water dashed on a red-hot skillet, leaped from the radio again.

"Chief?"

"Here, Turnip."

"Looked under ever bush," Officer Turnipseed reported. "No damn sign of a fracas."

"*Darn* sign, Jess. We got two minors in the car out here."

"Damn! Sorry, sir."

"Turnip? You messing with me?"

"No sir, Sheriff Neeley. I meant 'darn' ... sorry, sir."

Silence.

"Turnip, let's take it on home. Give these folks back their Christmas Eve."

"Yessir."

Will turned to Elmore. "Where are some miners, Daddy?"

"Mi-NORS," Elmore said, rubbing Will's head. "A minor is a young'un."

"Can a girl be a miner?" Mary looked up, her daddy looked down. A drop of blood fell on her pink camellia coat.

"Sorry, sweetie." Elmore slurred, wiping. "I got this bad habit here lately ..."

"You need stitches on them stitches, El."

Neeley sounded different suddenly.

"I do need some things, Dan. But not more stitches."

The blue light swirled.

"Listen," Neeley ordered, "y'all jump out of the car. I'll write up a report that says ain't nobody here but decent, law-abiding, peace-keeping, God-fearing folks who love their mamas and daddies and wouldn't hurt even a *mean* flea."

Elmore muscled open the back door.

"You've helped the good people of Lafayette to sleep tonight, Sheriff Neeley. Mr. Wood has it covered. Ace police chief and an ass fire chief."

"Ten-four, good buddy," Neeley answered.

"Merry Christmas, Danny," Elmore said. "Merry Christmas, Turnip."

Will and Mary sat mesmerized as Deputy Turnipseed approached. He loomed in the headlights. Turnip topped 400 pounds. He was huge as Frankenstein in the movies. His colossal shadow followed him down the white clapboard side of the Rogers' house.

Elmore found Dan Neeley standing by him as the children dashed for the house.

He spoke in a conspiratorial voice.

"Send 'em straight on to bed, El. Don't let 'em go in the kitchen. Not till morning."

Elmore drew back. He and Dan Neeley stood in the cold of Christmas Eve, inches apart, physically as close as they'd once sat in a dugout in high school. Or in a smoking IED crater in Mosul. A million changes ago.

"What the hell you playin' at, Dan?"

"*Sheriff* Dan."

A crease of a smile softened Neeley's face.

Blue smile. Blue-and-white smile. Blue smile.

Those damned Neeley teeth.

"Well, Danny, I reckon ..."

But Neeley was back in the squad car, window up.

Deputy Turnipseed heaved into the shotgun seat. The police car sank desperately to starboard, and the radio antenna on the roof wagged side to side.

Elmore limped, barefoot, back into the house. He spoke solemnly to the twins.

"Y'all go straight to bed. You're up way too late, and Santa Claus is coming to town ..."

"Daddy, we had candy," protested a sensible young girl. "We got to brush our teeth."

"No teeth brushing. Straight to bed. If you're awake when Santa comes, and you see that sapsucker ... he doesn't come see you again. *Ever.*"

Elmore waited a beat. "I know ... 'cause that's what happened to *me.*"

He spoke with conviction, and Will and Mary dashed like snowshoe rabbits for their single bed. Bigger and faster, Will shouldered his sister to one side at the bedroom door.

"I get the good pillow!" Will yelled.

"Noooo! Daddy, he cheated!"

"I'm comin' in there," Elmore called. "And if anybody's awake, I'm puttin' *both* of you in a sack and leavin' it out on the porch for Santa Claus to take back to the North Pole. You'll spend the rest of your lives being bossed around by mean little green elves!"

Through the front-door pane, Elmore watched the squad car back down the drive, bucking snowy ruts. In reverse, the transmission strained.

Did Sheriff Dan Neeley ... his boyhood friend, his teammate, his rival in love, the soldier who once had his girl, then had his back ... did Neeley wave one finger goodbye from the wheel as the police car chirred away on snow-chained tires?

Or did he shoot a bird?

Too dark to tell.

"Y'all quit your bickering! Get to sleep!" Elmore barked. "Not another peep."

Most nights, an imp would have chirped a single almost-silent ... *peep!*

Not Christmas Eve.

Elmore limped to his room and pulled out a squeaky drawer. He sat on the bed and clumsily rolled four socks onto each frozen foot. With the big thumb bandage, it took time. His teeth chattered. The room felt like a beer cooler.

He padded to the kids' room. He'd settle them down with a story about Santa Claus, how he brought switches and coal to the wicked, how he rewarded good little boys and girls with treasures beyond their wildest fantasies.

He wouldn't mention bicycles.

Once they slept, he'd hurry back to Sav-More for $57 worth of ... last-minute Christmas. Whatever.

Elmore lit a kitchen match and peeked into the bedroom.

Impossibly, his two beautiful twins slept.

Elmore felt like a hypocrite.

He'd been about to turn Santa Claus into the Old Testament god he grew up hearing about in church. The god that sent you to hell, not the god that forgave. The god that dropped you in a lake of fire instead of putting loving arms around you and asking you to try again to be good, to be better than before. The god who made you believe you really *could* be better.

Elmore kissed two untroubled foreheads.

He himself could use a long winter's nap.

But not just yet.

He dressed, slowly and painfully, and picked up his truck keys. He'd sneak out through the kitchen door, farthest from the bedrooms.

He tiptoed. For the first time in forever, he wanted a drink. His liver, missing a chunk, couldn't handle alcohol. But tonight he had that thirst.

Somewhere out there, a hound dog would not go to sleep. *Bow wow wooow*. Or maybe it was an owl. Elmore realized he was too tired and banged-up to tell the difference.

He reached the hall pantry. For some reason, he glanced inside. He had a can of Spam and two round furry blue things that used to be lemons.

But something glittered. In the kitchen.

Elmore turned in surprise.

What the devil?

He clawed clumsily at a light switch with his unbandaged hand. The overhead fluorescent tube took its sweet time, clicking, making a buzz.

It illuminated ... a miracle.

Twin bicycles.

One for a boy, blue. And a pink one. Schwinns. Tassels on the hand grips.

Brand new bikes.

How?

Elmore stared at the fluorescent kitchen light, not nearly as bright as a flashlight in his face.

Dan Neeley.

And red-nosed Jess Turnipseed ...

Santa Claus had come to town.

Something glittered. In the kitchen. Elmore turned in surprise. What the devil? He clawed clumsily at a light switch with his unbandaged hand.

June

—14—

That Friday Feeling

Hot Friday.

Elmore muscled the panel truck onto County Road 5. He worked through all five gears. Sweetgums and pines drooped limbs over the lonely stretch of two-lane.

Lafayette looked good in the rear-view mirror.

It was 5 p.m. The sun would still fume for four hours yet, furious at the world. A man on the radio announced June 21 as the longest day of the year. How in the world could summer days get any longer? Every workday seemed to last twenty-five hours.

Elmore flipped back the sweaty brim of his baseball cap and let the wind blow his hair.

The road reached home in seven miles. The drive gave Elmore some thinking time.

He had hired on with Rankin Cabinets in February, after five days training in Columbus, Mississippi. He learned how to install kitchen cabinets.

God knows why the Rankins hired him, still in stitches and a thumb cast and stooped with a broken rib. But the woodworking company had construction projects all over The New South. Rankin needed warm bodies. They liked veterans.

Elmore didn't complain. Thank goodness for work.

During Elmore's training, Johnny and Junie Rogers took care of the twins. The cousins, an unmarried brother and sister, lived in a brick ranch country house with pecan trees. Their acre held a catfish pond and an orchid greenhouse swarming with frisky, bright-green tree frogs. Will and Mary caught them by the cupful.

At 18, Johnny lost both legs in Vietnam. Junie, forsaking all others, took care of her brother when he came home. Not marching, but home.

Rogers people didn't complain. Why? The Lord laid out His plan. If it didn't make sense to anybody but Him, that's just how it was.

Elmore started work back in Lafayette on Groundhog Day. His first paycheck came in the nick of time – in one more week, eviction bulls would have bum-rushed him and the twins out the front door of the rental. Elmore had worked his new job without missing a single hour, Saturdays included, twenty straight weeks. The work paid $3.65 an hour. It added up.

On rough days, when his insides hurt and he just felt like lying down to die, Elmore opened his billfold and peeked at two elementary-school class pictures.

Then he got back to work.

The biggest tree in western Alabama, the Mayhew, threw deep shade up ahead. Elmore heard somewhere that the tulip poplar might be three-hundred years old. In its deep shade, the temperature would drop twenty degrees.

Elmore checked his odometer. He'd hit his driveway in exactly two miles.

The home stretch.

Elmore sniffed the air.

The fading afternoon held not even a high cloud. Still, some kind of faint blue smoke hazed the landscape. It smelled … peculiar.

Were woods burning?

An old wooden fire tower rose over the western treeline. It always made Elmore think of an abandoned lighthouse – with its eye put out.

Fellow National Guard mate Billy Cameron worked that fire tower years ago. Another Guard buddy told Elmore that lightning had struck the old tower seven different times with Billy inside. Elmore believed it. The forest ranger always talked a little faster than he needed to. He got nervous when it thundered.

Blue haze thickened.

An old wooden fire
tower rose over the
western treeline.
It always made
Elmore think of an
abandoned lighthouse
with its eye put out.

Elmore watched the woods – yes, smoke definitely clouded the air. Still, it didn't *smell* like a forest fire.

Maybe some old plantation house had gone up in flames. The fire traps still stood all over this part of Alabama.

A wicked thought entered Elmore's head.

A ringing fire bell would mobilize Dick Wragg and the Lafayette Fire Department. They would howl to the scene in that shiny red truck Mr. Wood donated.

With any luck, Elmore mused, today Dick Wragg will get his hair burned off ...

The strange, pungent haze suddenly thickened, clouding the windshield. Elmore heard chugging ahead.

He couldn't help laughing.

The county's slow-moving mosquito-control truck glowed ghostly yellow through a thick blue fog of DDT vapor. The chemical boiled from some contraption in back.

A cloud machine.

What Elmore saw next overflowed his heart.

Two beautiful children swerved in and out of the DDT fog on still-shiny Christmas bikes.

Pedaling with all their might, Will and Mary chased a cloud. They whooped like banshees. Will's bike sped ahead, but Mary gamely gave chase, pedaling hard, her pink-tasseled handlebars jerking side to side.

No mosquito would draw blood from a Rogers child this night.

Elmore honked, motioned out the window – *move over, stop!* He dropped the tires of the truck onto the shoulder, exploding a colony of Queen Anne's lace. The surprised twins panted like puppies.

The mosquito truck puffed off into the distance.

Elmore grinned out the window. Payday felt fine.

"Who wants to go to the picture show?"

Yay! Hurray!

God bless their little cherry-cheeked souls! Will had probably gained a pound of freckles this summer. Mary's sweaty red hair stuck to her forehead, and she chewed gum.

Elmore had never seen anything more beautiful. He roared the Mack engine, yelled at the top of his lungs.

"A'ight, then! I'll go wash off the sawdust! Y'all ride and tell Mrs. Yona I made it home. Let's leave in thirty minutes."

The children no longer stayed Fridays with Mrs. Mock. The way she treated Elmore, injured that snowy night, ended her childcare. This summer vacation, Elmore paid a Latina neighbor for daycare, a piece of paycheck he didn't mind sharing.

He wrestled the balky stick shift in the floorboard. The panel truck rocked onto the blacktop, clattering tools in the cargo.

The kids chased Elmore now.

Will and Mary grew smaller and smaller in the rear-view mirror. When Elmore reached the house, they were tiny, shiny specks.

The steaming tub was nearly full.

From the refrigerator, Elmore took the week's last banana. It was black as a finger with gangrene.

Most Lafayette folks didn't keep bananas in the icebox. But if Elmore left a bunch out on the counter on Monday, fruit flies filled the house on Friday.

The hot bath turned Elmore's hand lobster pink.
Just the way he liked it.

He eased in.

Jesus. How could hot water feel so good, even on hot days?

He enjoyed the best banana in history. Frozen and sweet. Elmore ate it in two bites. He flung the black peel, and it octopused through the air into the commode. *Two points!* The perfect shot made Elmore unreasonably happy.

He stretched a dripping leg, flushed the commode with a big toe.

Elmore savored a moment of peace.

Outside, the summer solstice throbbed like a pulse.

Thank goodness, Elmore thought, *Will and Mary don't remember that hot car.*

That memory ended the peace.

—15—

Skaters Away

Mr. Wood loved figure skaters.

The morning he moved into Sweet Comb, Mr. Wood programmed six satellite dishes to find and record skating broadcasts from anywhere in the world. Ice events funneled steadily out of the sky from Norway, Steamboat Springs, Japan. Unlike Alabama, those distant places always had snow.

Mr. Wood liked to stop the skaters with a remote control.

He could play God at the top of a quadruple spin, or a flying camel, or midway through a lift. He could stop time itself. He could make the figures on-screen skate faster, or backwards. If they tumbled to the hard ice and lay stunned, he could make them leap up again, like rag dolls, then fly away in reverse like the fall never happened, like they would never fall at all.

Mr. Wood glanced away from a young female skater in Moscow. The clock said 5:52 p.m. Neeley and Wragg, the police and fire departments, would arrive in eight minutes.

Mr. Wood noted the blurred features of his reflection in the brilliant finish of his walnut desk. Not the best-looking man.

He grew thoughtful.

A special pride came with being a self-made man. Mr. Wood grew up an only child in a modest middle-class home. (Rumors of inherited wealth came from jealous types.) He turned out to simply be better than other people at doing one important thing – making money. He did it mostly by working harder. And he never allowed even the most astronomical possibility of failure to corrupt his confidence. He could outcompete anybody.

His parents doted on him.

"He'll be a fighter pilot one day," his dad bragged to teachers on parent nights at every level of school – elementary, junior high, and even in the troubled years away, at the special school. The fact that young Mr. Wood had no intention of being a fighter pilot, that back then he *hated* airplanes and flying and anything military, did not discourage his father's daydreams.

Nelson Wood might have been right. His square-set son was rigid. Military. He looked and acted nothing like his old man, a modest, yellow-haired enthusiast prone to asthma attacks and flamboyant gestures. The senior Mr. Wood sold brass and reed instruments to high-school bands, then made extra money teaching kids to play. He prided himself on his potato salad and deviled eggs. He wrote poems about the color photographs that moved him so in *National Geographic*.

Nelson Wood went to Lafayette Pentecostal, alone, every Sunday except Easter, when he unexpectedly disappeared into his room for three days and got too drunk to even make it to the bathroom. Easter was the only time Mr. Wood ever saw his father take a thimbleful of spirits.

But Nelson Wood took a great number of thimblefuls on Good Friday, and he made a habit of going to bed early that day, just at dark, with tears streaming down his face.

"Poor, sweet Jesus," he sobbed, disappearing into a lightless storage shed behind the family's brick home.

Then, dawn on Monday morning, like Jesus rising one day late, Nelson Wood reentered the world. Instead of a shroud, he sported a spotless white blazer and a white tie, white shoes, a pair of black slacks, a black shirt. He tottered off to the music shop slightly worse for wear, but ready with all his might to sell clarinets. From the look of him, nothing unusual had happened the past few days.

Mr. Wood's mother, Betty Fay, never spoke of it. She couldn't. Betty Fay's own mother had contracted measles in pregnancy, and Betty Fay was born deaf. Her entire vocabulary consisted of "mom" and "pop" and "om" – short words with "o" in them. She spent life in a safe domestic bubble guarded by her band-leader husband from any sharp thorn.

Betty Fay's affliction had a side-effect. Mr. Wood learned to talk much later than other children, and he stuttered in early grades at school. A speech pathologist in Birmingham said the stutter had nothing at all to do with his mother, that the boy had "emotional problems." Nelson Wood didn't like the specialist ... and he especially didn't like that he charged the family $100 for the one hour it took for such a callous diagnosis. Mr. Wood began to understand money this way, hearing his father complain about "a little squirt of nothing for a big wad of cash."

Little Mr. Wood didn't like the doctor for another reason. Near the end of their session, the speech pathologist reached down to touch the boy's private parts. Little Mr. Wood froze and let him.

The session ended.

A few minutes later, as Nelson Wood and his blank-faced son exited the office, the youngster abruptly spun. Fast as a striking snake, he plunged an uncapped Sheaffer ink pen into the speech pathologist's right eye.

Little Mr. Wood was nine years old at the time.

That incident, forty years past, changed Mr. Wood's life forever.

He pulled a stretch in reform school, then four more years at Marion Military Institute.

He never went home when he received news from the headmaster that his mother had run off a bridge, alone, in a west Alabama rainstorm. But he often – vividly – imagined the car as it sank, his mother flailing hands for help, her eyes and mouth wide open, *OM OM OM*.

Little Mr. Wood got out of Marion and joined the Army.

He went to Vietnam. He stayed four tours.

He was very good at soldiering. He excelled in basic training, applied for Special Forces. He learned to turn green and disappear in a jungle.

Between deployments, Mr. Wood trained to parachute at Fort Benning. He developed a taste for being airborne after all, paying a private instructor to teach him to fly a plane. He mastered solitaire. He studied anatomy on his own, late at night. He learned martial arts.

In Vietnam, Mr. Wood mostly lived behind enemy lines, long-range reconnaissance, one of those daunting fighters with a thousand-yard stare. He learned to use most every weapon of the age, and to employ nearly any object he picked up with deadly force.

Things happened, deep in the jungles of Laos and Cambodia. For months at a time, he hunted alone in green solitary confinement, living off the land.

Mr. Wood developed ... unusual tastes.

It took him less than two months to deplete a Hmong hamlet. When he started, the population had been thirteen unlucky men, women and children.

He tossed their bones to the monkeys.

He returned from Asia, lean and quiet as his mother, with some military pay and $1,200 inherited from a shoebox some honest neighbors found under Nelson Wood's bed after that man's sad demise. Those neighbors, Elmer and Sam – Elmer was a woman, and Sam was a woman too – kept the cash under their own mattress until Mr. Wood reappeared.

The assets bought enough concrete block and two-by-fours to build an 800-square-foot box. The lot came cheap – it sat by a ditch running four inches deep with dirty feathers and slurry from Estes Chicken Processing. On a hot summer day, the creek surface glistened as black as tar with blow flies.

Mr. Wood meant to live in the new house himself, since the bank had repossessed his birthplace. With his own two hands, he dug ditches and pier holes. He set concrete block. He hammered 16-penny nails into floor joists, then rafters, with a $1 garage-sale hammer. He worked past dark for months, after a day job turning wrenches at Lathem's Rambler Repair.

In Vietnam, Mr. Wood mostly lived behind enemy lines. Things happened, deep in the jungle. He developed … unusual tastes.

He reached the house site at 6 p.m. every evening, riding a little Yamaha scooter. At top speed, it sounded like an angry mosquito.

Mr. Wood tied on a cloth nail belt and worked deep into the screech-owl hours, toiling alone, ghostly in the beam of the motorcycle's headlamp.

Mr. Wood glanced at his clock. Again.

He hated clocks. He hated time. Every tick made him think of an ax chopping a tree.

His life.

He clicked off the video screen. A skating couple flew into the void.

Neeley and Wragg had three minutes. They better be on time.

Mr. Wood had plans.

This was Friday. Jennifer the Cheerleader would visit.

Mrs. Mock no longer had the Rogers children in her care. But Mr. Wood still had her in his.

He'd still get the two things he wanted.

Mr. Wood let his mind drift as he raised that first house in summer 1970.

He remembered how Nelson Wood had been taken, one year after Betty Fay's accident. He went to sleep in his chair watching *Citizen Kane*. Two high-school students showed up for lessons and found him slumped, hands clasped.

Those summer nights under indifferent stars, Mr. Wood also recalled how his deaf mother took movie magazines to the beauty parlor and pointed to hairdos, nodding her pretty head like a cow, smiling hopefully.

Home, she ritually charged through the front door and to the bathroom. She attacked her newest hairdo with a brush. She howled like a lost hound. Tears streamed her pretty face.

On a hot August night, construction well along, Mr. Wood ran electrical wire in the attic. Next came drywall, tape and mud.

On break, Mr. Wood sat in a window frame, legs dangling. He smoked a hand-rolled cigarette, smoking it down to the finger-burn. A rooster crowed, confused by a full moon.

A couple in a Camaro pulled up. Two strangers.

The driver bore a scar on his forehead and a prosthetic eye. He was a fellow serviceman, a discharged Marine. Yes, Vietnam. His pretty young wife held a steady job at the county health clinic, immunizing children against measles, polio and other diseases.

To Mr. Wood's great surprise – the surprise of his life – the couple made a little small talk about weather, then extended an offer, on the spot, to buy Mr. Wood's unfinished home. Just as it was, $3,500 in cash.

It took Mr. Wood two seconds to decide.

They shook hands. They met the next morning at Beeline Café in downtown Lafayette. Good as his word, the Marine paid cash, twenties, touching his thumb to sticky syrup on the edge of his pancake plate to count out slick new bills.

After one polite cup of coffee, Mr. Wood walked straight to Lafayette Savings and Loan – a bank he would own in six years, along with Estes's Chicken Processing and the hardware company where he'd bought his first construction materials. Soon after that, he'd also own every lumber yard and a good number of timber tracts in five counties. He would then own radio stations, and manufacturing plants that made metal storage bins and double-wide trailer homes.

And Mr. Wood would own more than that.

He opened a checking account with the $3,500 cash. He set up a $10,000 line of credit.

The next day, he bought the remaining property along the foul creek – six cheap, tiny lots. He invested $1,200 in concrete block and bargain-basement lumber. He visited the part of town where black men and alcoholic whites hired on for day work, and he picked the ones who swore they didn't drink, most of them liars, and put them to work.

In fifteen years, Mr. Wood's crews had hammered together more than five thousand houses all over the South. He owned a real-estate and development operation in Dallas, an insurance company in Atlanta, an import business in Miami. Media. A casino in the Bahamas.

And he owned even more than that.

His pattern never varied. Mr. Wood first purchased land and buildings in a run-down neighborhood, then rehabilitated them. He plowed sale profits into more modern and more lucrative ventures – especially timberlands and mills.

He bought a dozen daily newspapers in second-tier towns all over the South – Rome, Tuscaloosa, Houma, Dothan. He bought banks and utilities like a man playing Monopoly. He developed a whole island off the coast of Georgia. His wealth rose like a thermometer on an August day in the Black Belt. He was worth a billion dollars by age 40, and he made several rankings of the nation's richest men ... to his great annoyance. Mr. Wood came from the school that a man's worth should be the most private thing about him, nobody's business but his own.

When Mr. Wood turned 45, he met a figure skater.

He'd flown his own plane to Brussels to close a deal. He'd then gone, reluctantly, to an ice skating competition as a special guest of a very rich epicurean who'd just sold him 50,000 hectares of vineyards in the south of France.

The two gentlemen had a long private talk in a suite high above the ice. Mr. Wood heard things that intrigued him.

The featured skater that day, Jeannette Benedictis, went by her performance name – Tatiana. She was 15 years old. Vietnamese. An orphan of France's bitter conflict in Southeast Asia. She'd been adopted by kindly bourgeoisie parents and raised in Paris.

Tatiana's beauty ... and the beauty of skating ... bewitched Mr. Wood. He negotiated with her parents to bring the young skater to the USA for development. He left money, jokingly called "a deposit". He refused to bring her coach, a former Swiss Olympian who had developed the young girl's uncanny natural talent since age five. Mr. Wood explained to the girl's parents that Tatiana deserved "a real coach" – Dorothy Hamill's, maybe – to replace her tired old one.

She would be a star.

Their PanAm jet landed in New York, and Mr. Wood took Tatiana on a long drive into the Adirondacks to meet her new coach at Lake Placid. On the road, they chatted in a friendly, formal way – Tatiana's command of English was excellent – and they stopped once to watch early October snow sift down through brilliant sugar maples on the granite slopes.

Mr. Wood took Tatiana to a tiny remote cabin with a kitchenette.

They settled in. Mr. Wood spent a long minute staring out the window. Then he strangled the girl in that little kitchen space with his bare hands, squeezing so hard her windpipe cracked, then the bones in her tiny neck. Mr. Wood lifted the skater clear off the floor. Her legs swung without touching.

Mr. Wood then carved, cooked and consumed Tatiana. In solitude, he prepared a series of lavish meals over a period of days. He used a recipe book from the Belgian epicurean.

Mr. Wood wrote a letter to Tatiana's parents and told them she'd run away with a salesman in New York City without even the courtesy of leaving a note. He explained that the New York City police promised to leave no stone unturned until they brought her back.

He scrawled another letter, this one to the epicurean in Paris, thanking him for his limited-edition book of recipes and accepting his invitation to meet in Bangkok on December 21 for a very fine meal with a few close friends.

16

A Little Dead Thing

Will materialized, a jumping jack, in front of Elmore. "Daddy! Come look! It's something *horrible!*"

Elmore, just out of the bathtub, wore a wilted white towel. He made sure the ratty old Cannon covered his worst scars, the ones on the right side, the right thigh.

Chunky little Will looked like his mother that moment. Then an identical Mary popped into view. Both were wild-eyed.

"It's *horrible!*" Mary shrieked, delighted by her own hysteria.

Down the dirt driveway, Elmore admitted the kids had it right.

The thing *was* horrible.

A baby mockingbird lay still, fallen from its nest. It sprawled in hideous pink saurian helplessness, gaping mouth frozen with no sound, eyes forever blind. Rapacious fire ants covered the tiny, already-stiffening body under a shining coat of deadly red-black armor.

"Daddy, what *is* it?"

Will's eyes bugged with fear and excitement, and Mary danced a little mad jig.

Will stepped forward, bravely, and spread his arms protectively. For show? Did Will think the tiny awful corpse might leap up from the ground and get his sister?

And ... look. Timmy Wragg watched from the wooded lot. His fancy Spyder bicycle lay hastily thrown down, front wheel spinning. Everything about Timmy's little body looked ready to run. He couldn't take his eyes off the baby bird.

"Daddy! What *is* that dang thang?" Will's voice had a roostery note of young manhood.

"Is she alive?" Mary wondered.

Elmore toed the tiny corpse with his bare toe. A furious eruption of fire ants made all four onlookers step back.

"It's just a baby," Elmore told the children, minding his words carefully. "No feathers yet. It would have been a mockingbird when it got big."

Will's eyes widened even more.

"Daddy, that ain't no bird!" He was incredulous. "That don't look one bit like a bird!"

"Yeah, Will. It's a baby bird," Elmore said solemnly. "It fell out of its nest."

Mary, of course, wanted more.

"It fell? Why, Daddy?"

Elmore thought.

"Maybe the storm, sugar. It got pretty bad last night. Remember how the wind blew?"

The kids gaped.

"Mr. Elmore, do birds get graves?"

Timmy Wragg asked it.

"Timmy, that's a real nice idea. Y'all go get the shovel. We'll give this little bird a decent burial."

Elmore limped inside for shoes and clothes. When he returned, Will had scraped a shallow hole. The shovel made a ringing sound each time it struck the hard red clay.

Out of some hiding place girls always have, Mary produced a paper napkin. Elmore folded it carefully around the bird.

Shrouded and as clean of fire ants as they could get it, the little bird disappeared under three shovelfuls of red dirt.

"Y'all want to say a prayer?" Elmore asked. "Think of something nice."

Will held the shovel straight.

"Lord, even if it was so horrible ugly, please let that bird go to heaven," he prayed.

"Amen," said Mary.

"Double amen," added Timmy Wragg. "Bird heaven."

"Triple amen," said Elmore.

They all stood a minute in the late afternoon of the summer solstice.

"Now let's go to the picture show."

The sun bloodied the sky as the Rogers family set off for town.

They rolled down the windows – the panel truck had no air conditioning – and Will made his hand play dolphin in the breeze.

They passed the Mayhew Poplar.

Lafayette General Hospital, a giant red brick, reflected sunset, windows blazing all four stories. Will pointed out a bright orange windsock on top, knowledgeably explaining how it helped medical helicopter pilots land safely.

Elmore knew a thing or two about a medical helicopter.

He clicked on the radio.

The Allman Brothers played "Ramblin' Man". Elmore held the steering wheel with his knees and played air guitar.

He had that Friday feeling.

They reached Lafayette's franchises for burgers and chicken and pizza. A giant neon catfish with stylish Hollywood-villain whiskers and a shiny top hat winked its eye from Robin's Fish Camp. (*Fresh from the Black Warrior! All you care to eat!*) Across the highway, cars jammed Kenny-San's Chinese, with its gold dragon on top. Elmore showed the twins twin Mexican restaurants, each named Los Hermanos, run by brothers.

The name "Wood" appeared. Wood Savings & Loan. Wood Commercial. Wood Realty.

Welcome to Wood World.

"Daddy?"

"What, darling?"

Elmore leaned and kissed the top of the gingery little head in the middle seat. Riding shotgun, Will hung out the window like a dog.

"Why do they hang little colored flags over car lots?"

Mary pointed to merry pennants fluttering over Hoke's Used Motors.

"You're dumb!" groused Will. "It's to make people *look*, igmo!"

"Will ..."

Elmore did tire of Will's constant hectoring. Why did Mary deserve scorn?

Little twin showed her pluck, though.

"YOU'RE dumb!" she said. "That's not why!"

"Well, why then, smarty pants?"

Elmore stopped at a light. He could hear Mary's brain shift little gears.

"Well, they could put up a flag for every car they sell," she said. "And the more cars they sell, the more flags they fly."

"That's dumb!" Will snorted. "I told you the reason."

"Well, I told YOU the reason."

"You're a space alien!" Will announced.

"Well ... you're a space alien TWIN!"

Elmore laughed out loud.

"Daddy, why do we have to be twins?" Will demanded. "She's a *girl!*"

Will said it like spitting sour milk.

"Well ... you're both right. Will, you're right. The pennants do make people look to see what's for sale. And Mary, sweetie, you're right too. They hang up a new one every time a car drives off the sales lot."

Will looked like his head might explode. Mary had a smug twinkle.

Lafayette Courthouse appeared, its historic dome rising over trees and low buildings.

Downtown Lafayette!

"Okay ... milkshakes before the movie? Or after?"

"Both!" yelled Will, and Mary giggled.

That Friday feeling was highly contagious.

Elmore pulled into The Milky Way, the best ice cream spot in Lafayette. The Milky Way had served cones and milkshakes since they were invented. Elmore's own daddy and mama, going and gone, bless 'em, brought him here for cones after baseball games.

Now Elmore brought Will and Mary.

The kids scrambled out behind Elmore. Twilight had come, and the ice cream shop twinkled. Like The Milky Way.

Elmore happily vowed to take the twins outside later on and study the summer night above the house. He would declare that he could actually count one million stars. A million! *Study your arithmetic*, he'd tell them, *and you can count to a million too.*

Elmore held little hands crossing the parking lot, a family, happy communion.

A dark dress pushed open the front door, colliding with them.

Kelly Bellisle Rogers.

Her face was so beautiful.

So haunted.

Kelly held a chocolate cone with red sprinkles. She simply stared at Mary and Will.

She bent closer to their upturned faces. So like hers.

"Hey, babies."

She whispered, words barely spoken, closer to thoughts.

"Mary? Will? Remember ... your mama?"

Silence.

Elmore felt something hurt so bad inside.

Kelly tried again.

"Sweet Mary? Sweet little Will? Give mama a hug?"

They did it.

The little twin bodies welded themselves to Kelly.

Elmore turned away. He looked down. Up. A million bright stars over the parking lot blurred.

"My little sweet babies," Kelly whispered, her voice breaking this time. "My twins ..."

Kelly's thin arms squeezed, changed positions, squeezed harder. She desperately embraced the two little bodies. Elmore could only see black and red hair tangled in hugs.

"We came for milkshakes," Elmore said lamely, after a time.

"Have my cone!" Kelly burst out, pleading. She offered it ... empty.

Her scoop of red-sprinkled chocolate lay in the parking lot by Mary's tennis shoe. It had fallen among the fierce hugs.

Elmore remembered a little dead bird.

Then he remembered something else.

The car. The roasting goddamned car. Little Will and Mary inside.

They pulled out all their hair in agony.

His children.

Bitterness flooded Elmore. He felt a black rush.

He said a cruel, terrible thing.

"Look at 'em, Kelly. Alive and well."

A joyous light in Kelly's face went out. Instantly.

Elmore felt misery surge through him. He wished to the core of his soul he could take back his words.

"Mama?"

Mary, her sweet face lifted.

"Will and Daddy take good care of me. But I miss you."

Will, stout little Will, burst into tears at that. He blubbered something nobody could understand. Elmore believed he heard the words *night time* and *some time* and *every time*.

Elmore needed – right now – to get this *one thing right* in his whole goddamned life.

"Kelly ..."

He had waited too long.

She walked away, fast. Her heels made a clicking noise. She didn't glance back.

Elmore felt the world ending. Again.

Kelly reached the green VW and got in. The brake lights blazed.

"Y'all stay right here," Elmore ordered, no-nonsense. "Do not move from this spot."

He ran for the VW as if his life depended on it.

He waited too long. Again.

The little green car sputtered into the streets of Lafayette.

Elmore didn't stop. He sprinted as fast as he was able. He felt the old sharp pain of the broken bone in his thigh. He felt the terrible pain of everything that happened.

"KELLY! Wait!"

Elmore stood in the street and waved his arms and cried her name.

"Kelly! Come back! Please!"

Kelly didn't.

She was gone. Lost in the dark.

—17—

Special Request

A surveillance camera recorded the arrival of Sheriff Neeley and Chief Wragg at the lumber yard. Mr. Wood watched the video wall. He saw Neeley check his wrist watch. Wragg leaned against his car door and lit a Marlboro.

The two men didn't speak.

Neeley climbed the stairs first. He knocked, waited for Mr. Wood's voice. Wragg came slowly behind.

Two chairs sat conspicuously empty at the desk. Mr. Wood didn't offer them.

He cleared his throat.

"I know everything. I'm everywhere."

He let the words sink in.

"I have some questions."

Mr. Wood studied the men. Wragg breathed heavily, shuffled his feet. Some SEAL. He played buff and tough, but Mr. Wood learned as a lurp to smell insecurity rising off men the way a dog smells fear.

Dan Neeley's ruddy features never flickered.

He's a harder one, Mr. Wood thought to himself.

"Wragg?"

"Sir?"

Mr. Wood let him squirm.

"Do you feel it represents the values of the Lafayette Fire Chief and his community in the best possible way for your paramedics to dump an accident victim off a Greene County Fire Department stretcher and load him onto one of yours?"

Wragg turned fire-engine red.

"Mr. Wood, sir! The Greene County unit reached the wreck first, but those two cars collided in Lafayette. This side of the county line. Those EMTs were poaching our patient, sir."

Mr. Wood's hooded eyes did not blink.

"Sir," Wragg stammered on, "we make money toting patients. We're running the fire department like a business. As you instructed, sir."

Mr. Wood's chair squeaked slightly.

"Remember our county values, Mr. Wragg."

Mr. Wood swiveled his chair slightly.

"And Sheriff Neeley?"

"Sir."

A fly had entered the office with the two men. It gave Neeley's red crew cut a green halo.

"Two days ago, you and Officer Turnipseed confiscated some unusual contraband from Hutchinson's Print Shop."

"Yes sir, we did."

Neeley somehow kept his face from showing what flashed into his mind: *How the devil does Mr. Wood know that?*

"Turnip seized a three-ounce square of red hashish," Sheriff Neeley reported. "We think it came from Atlanta. Mr. Hutchinson claimed it fell out of a shipment of fine press printing papers. I believe him, sir. Hutch reported it himself. The man's a teetotalling Boy Scout."

"And what happened to a confiscated block of red hashish from Atlanta?"

A short silence confirmed something: Each man knew the truth.

Neeley spoke up.

"Sir, the police department donated it to the fire department. At Chief Wragg's request. To be incinerated, sir, with other seized contraband items they possess. At his *personal* request."

Wragg said nothing.

"So," said Mr. Wood, swiveling his chair again, "was this red hashish from Atlanta incinerated, Chief Wragg?"

"Sir, it certainly was," said Wragg. "Absolutely incinerated, sir."

"Good. As it should be."

Mr. Wood turned to Neeley.

"Sheriff Neeley," he said in a measured tone, "tell me why you visit Kelly Rogers. Used to be Kelly Bellisle?"

Neeley showed no outward surprise.

"She's an old friend, sir."

"Romantic friend?"

"In high school, sir."

Mr. Wood drummed thick fingers on the fine walnut desk.

"That was then," Neeley replied.

Mr. Wood waited.

"She preferred Elmore Rogers," Neeley said simply.

"Elmore Rogers," Mr. Wood repeated.

"Yes sir. Baseball player. Wounded warrior. We went to Iraq together. Worked on your construction crew last year ..."

"Fell off the roof," Mr. Wood finished. "Drunk. Loser. Works for Rankin now. Yeah, I know all about him."

Neeley started to speak, decided better.

"I'm everywhere," Mr. Wood emphasized. "I see everything."

"Yes sir. I understand."

Mr. Wood leaned back in his chair. His gigantic head looked bigger than his chest. He put on a smile.

"And you visit Mr. Rogers' wife ... why?"

"*Ex*-wife, sir."

"Ex-wife. And ...?"

Neeley finally looked uncomfortable.

"Kelly's in a county recovery program, sir. She had that terrible thing with the twins. We check to make sure she's following judge's orders. Official business. Only."

Mr. Wood drummed his fingers again.

"My … uh … sources tell me," he finally said, "that Elmore Rogers has recently taken up an activity with controlled substances that isn't legal in Lafayette County."

Sheriff Neeley somehow controlled his surprise. Elmore? Controlled substances? Not a chance. Especially since Iraq …

"Am I right, Chief Wragg?"

Wragg grinned, greedily. He looked like a balloon about to burst.

"We needn't say more at this time," Mr. Wood finished. "But if Elmore Rogers keeps up his illicit activity, the day will come when Lafayette County Law Enforcement will need to run him in. Sheriff Neeley, do you understand?"

"Yes sir … but, sir …"

"You wouldn't let a personal friendship stand in the way of doing your duty for our good citizens in Lafayette, would you, Sheriff? Or an old romantic sentiment?"

Neeley stood ramrod straight.

"No sir. I would not."

"Even if you once saved the man's life in that Iraq mess?"

"No sir. The law is the law, sir."

The tone of that answer satisfied Mr. Wood.

"And … this is very, very important," Mr. Wood said, swiveling his huge head first toward Wragg then back to Neeley.

"You men are not to mention one word of tonight's conversation … or take any action into your own hands … or conduct any sort of investigation AT ALL … against Elmore Rogers, your fellow veteran of foreign wars and your next-door neighbor. Do you understand this?"

"Yes sir!" barked Wragg first.

"Sheriff Neeley? I want this crystal clear. You do NOTHING on your own in any regard for your buddy, Elmore Rogers. I know what he's up to. I'll tell you if … and how … I want it stopped."

"Yes sir."

The ticking clock grew audible.

"Now," Mr. Wood announced. "Today's business."

He reached into his desk and produced a sheet of paper. It held a short hand-written list.

“You wouldn’t let a personal friendship stand in the way of doing your duty for our good citizens in Lafayette, would you, Sheriff?”

"I want something special downtown next Christmas," Mr. Wood announced.

He gave a frightening smile.

"Lafayette's first-ever Jolly Holiday celebration."

He switched the paper around for Neeley and Wragg. He'd written the five main points in simple block letters, like first-grade writing:

- ☐ ALL MERCHANTS OPEN TILL MIDNIGHT. SPECIAL SALES
- ☐ COUNTY SCHOOL BANDS / CHURCH CHOIRS, COURTHOUSE SQUARE
- ☐ DRESS-UP CONTEST. SANTA, MRS. SANTA. PRIZES
- ☐ HERO CEREMONY FOR VETERANS / ACTIVE MILITARY
- ☐ GIANT NIGHT PARADE

"Questions?"

No questions.

"This will happen on December 21. Saturday night. The winter solstice."

Wragg looked like he wanted to ask what on earth a winter solstice was.

"Wood Inc. will underwrite all costs," said Mr. Wood. "But ... and this is important ... I do not want my name mentioned in any way, at any time, not once, in association with this celebration. The city of Lafayette pays for this. We will spend one-million dollars. Clear?"

"Yes sir." Neeley and Wragg answered simultaneously.

"Good. Sheriff Neeley, you let Mayor Baker know tomorrow. He'll be very happy to take credit. Tell him he has exactly six months to get this done right."

Mr. Wood pulled out a desk drawer again, this time producing three envelopes. He laid them on the shining desk.

"This is for you, Sheriff Neeley."

Mr. Wood pushed over the envelope, then one to Wragg.

"And you too."

The two men waited.

"Open 'em. Go ahead."

Mr. Wood looked pleased, leaned back, big fingers laced behind his big head. The white fringe trembled on his jacket.

Each officer pulled out five $100 bills.

Fire Chief Wragg gave a lopsided grin. Sheriff Neeley remained a poised professional.

"Thank you, Mr. Wood," Neeley said. "That's very generous."

"Yes, SIR! Thank you, SIR!" Wragg echoed. "Five hundred times, sir!"

"Christmas came early this year for y'all," Wood said. "Lafayette appreciates the work you're doing ... and will do. Dismissed."

Their footsteps died away. Mr. Wood flicked on the camera over the door.

Two black-and-white figures parted without speaking, headed to their cars. Sheriff Neeley moved briskly. Chief Wragg weaved, counting his hundred-dollar bills more than once.

Cars cranked, backed, disappeared from view.

Mr. Wood switched off the surveillance camera.

He now lifted the third envelope and carefully opened it. He drew out a special check ... written "*cheque*" ... from a special bank.

Swiss. Exclusive.

In fact, this institution only managed the accounts of ten people in the whole world. All anonymous. Not even the top bank leadership had access or privilege to these secret accounts.

Mr. Wood counted nine zeros after the first number, a slender "3".

Three-billion dollars. Thirty-million Ben Franklins.

Mr. Wood now had a large portion of his wealth hidden, buried like pirate treasure, but legally, institutionally. Only two people on planet Earth knew where and how much.

After the next winter solstice, three-billion dollars should be plenty.

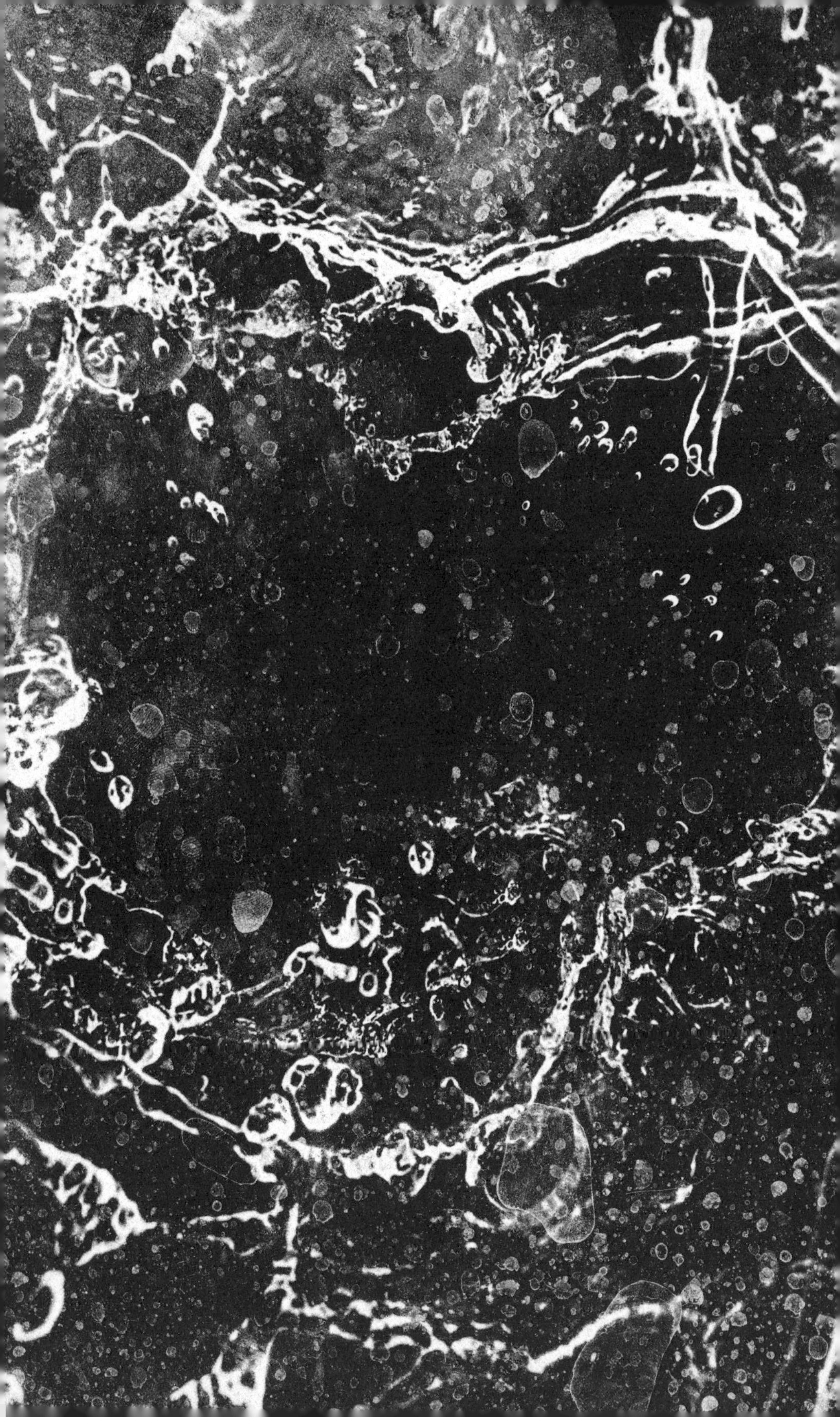

—18—

The Black Warrior

A light rain fell. A green Beetle appeared, bouncing along bumpy cross-ties.

When Kelly opened her door, rain and creosote odors flooded the car.

She got out. A gusting wind seemed determined to strip away her long black dress. Long black hair whipped her face.

Someone watching from the riverbank could have sworn Kelly slipped.

She didn't slip.

Will and Mary pushed you!

An old demon tortured her.

Kelly took three steps to the edge of the trestle. She said goodbye to the twins, to Elmore. To Lafayette. Then she took one more step.

Falling, she remembered, absurdly, a poem.

The year she attended the university in Tuscaloosa, James Dickey came to read. A professor told Kelly that Dickey was a great poet.

Kelly didn't like him. He used vulgarity. He leered. He stared straight at Kelly from the podium all through his poetry reading, a lamp under-lighting his face.

He looked ... hungry.

Still, Dickey read something memorable – a long poem called "Falling" about a stewardess sucked from a jet door by accident at 30,000 feet one night. It described the woman's ecstatic tumble from heaven to Kansas.

What utter bullshit, Kelly had thought.

Now ... she fell from the sky too.

Kelly kept her eyes open.

Diamond stars shone in a black river. Diamond stars shone in a black sky.

Kelly's hair streamed toward the sky.

Someone watching from the shoreline would have sworn she'd become a black arrow – that Sagittarius had drawn a brilliant starry bow and shot her straight down into the Black Warrior.

Scenes from her life unfolded.

Second grade

Kelly wore black bangs cut straight across her forehead. She sat by the door to the cafeteria with a Barbie lunchbox. She ate a peach. The warm sun made it smell wonderful.

A boy on a stick horse galloped by, wild and fast. Elmore wore a white T-shirt with Fudgsicle stains. He looked like he cut his own hair. In class, he and Kelly sat on the same row. They belonged to the Redbirds, the best reading group.

Elmore drew rein, turned to Kelly, and spoke, the first words he ever said directly:

You ain't as smart as you think.

Another schoolmate, Danny, the red-haired boy, galloped up on another broom handle.

Come on, Elmore! Them by-god Yankees are burnin' the train depot!

Off the boys thundered in a cloud of stick dust.

They left twin smoking furrows in the playground.

Church choir

The choir director chose Kelly to sing a solo – "Count Your Blessings Instead of Sheep" – on live radio at the Lafayette Street Methodist Church service on Sunday night.

Nothing had ever frightened Kelly so much. An hour before the broadcast, tears trickled down her pretty face, and her nose ran. Kelly's daddy soothed her in the car while her mother bustled ahead into the sanctuary to reserve a front pew.

Sweetie, just pretend you're singing to Catfish. Dad snuggled her with a strong arm. *Singing on the radio's not one bit different from singing to Catfish.*

Kelly took heart.

Catfish was the Bellisle's weird little orange mama cat. Kelly made up songs for Catfish after she unexpectedly gave birth to two orange-and-white kittens. The very practical, very sensible Bellisles gave the kittens away. Catfish seemed so sad, except when Kelly sang to her. She purred every time.

Kelly straightened her dress, bright yellow ... *canary yellow*, her mom insisted, *so you'll sing like one!* She took a deep breath, shuddering only a little. She blew her nose on a special lace handkerchief her mom insisted she carry to clutch *like an opera singer* between verses.

Catfish listened on the radio at home. Kelly would sing to Catfish.

Kelly's cue came when the deacons, serious men, rose from their special place in the second pew to pass big brass offering plates. She nervously stood before a big, intimidating microphone. It smelled peculiar, like metal, old breath.

The organist pumped pedals and swelled an introduction to "Count Your Blessings". In the congregation, fifty people, mostly gray and hard of hearing, leaned forward to catch the words of the lovely young woman in yellow with the handkerchief.

Kelly visualized Catfish, her sweet best friend.

But she spotted a young man, far in back. He wore a dark suit he had mostly outgrown. Unruly hair fell down into his blazing eyes, and he looked uncomfortable on the hard wooden pew, ready to jump on a stick horse ... or maybe a motorcycle ... and get out of there.

Kelly opened her mouth ... but she didn't sing to Catfish.

She sang to Elmore.

Behind the skating rink

Kelly gasped.

She had never heard human fists strike meat, the savage animal noises of boys in combat.

Under weak lights behind the Bob-A-Lu, a ring of cheering, jeering onlookers closed around two warriors like the iris of an eye. The crowd jostled Kelly forward.

Two sweating, shirtless young bucks separated. Both bled. Both breathed hard. They squared off, then they charged one another again.

Get 'im, Danny!

That yell came from a skinny country boy Kelly didn't know. One eye strayed, and his lank hair scraggled down in back like a mud flap.

Go, Elmore! Go, man!

A kid beside Kelly in a sleeveless T-shirt sported a badly discolored tattoo on the hard muscle of his upper arm – an ornate double L.

LL for Lafayette Lions.

The fighters grappled, delivered quick, nasty blows. They parted, sporting fresh blood and new purple knots. Both gasped for breath.

Kelly felt ... sick.

Why was this happening? How did things go from skating in the rink ... to a fistfight in the back lot? It all happened so fast.

Kelly still wore her high-top roller skates with the lavender tassels.

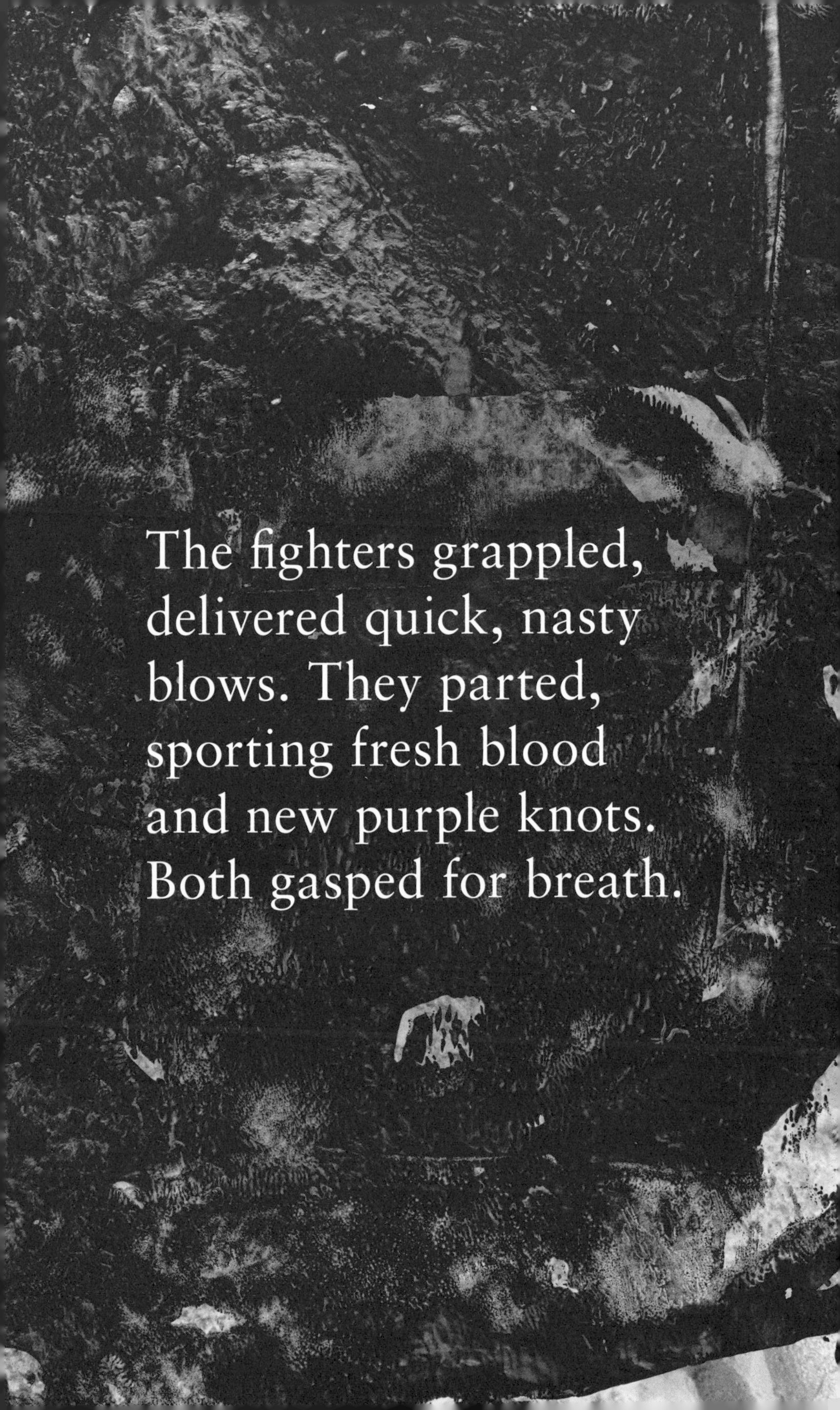

The fighters grappled, delivered quick, nasty blows. They parted, sporting fresh blood and new purple knots. Both gasped for breath.

Why are they fighting?

Kelly practically screamed. Her cry was lost in the mob's oaths and urgings. Onlookers crowded closer as the high-schoolers went whirling to the ground in a hard knot of headlocks.

Why are they fighting?

Kelly yelled it again, helplessly looking around the faces for an answer.

Poor, overweight, badly named Daisy Lay spun to face Kelly.

Why are they fighting? she hissed.

They're fighting over YOU, you stupid cow!

Junior prom

Kelly met red-haired Dan Neeley at the door. He wore a big smile, a white tuxedo, white shoes. He gave Kelly a rose. The crimson petals made his hair, for once, look pale.

Kelly admired Danny under the porch light.

A spatter of brown freckles adorned a handsome youngster with clear, intelligent eyes and ruddy cheeks and twin dimples like parentheses. Danny had a great smile. He looked very much like the Irish kid he role-played sometimes, especially on St. Patrick's Day.

Most girls at Lafayette High found Danny Boy irresistible.

Kelly did.

Parents appeared in the doorway.

"Good evening, Mr. and Mrs. Bellisle," greeted Dan, a perfect gentleman. "Thank you for letting me escort Kelly to the prom."

Kelly's dad craned his neck, staring beyond the young man.

"You're not driving a lime-green Gremlin, are you son? The last kid that came here pulled up in a lime-green Gremlin. Kelly wouldn't get in the car."

"Oh, Daddy! That's not true!" Kelly swatted her father.

They all chuckled.

Dan Neeley spoke up. Kelly liked that he wasn't shy.

"I'm driving Daddy's pickup, sir. Nothing but the finest for Miss Bellisle."

Kelly's dad kissed her forehead, and her mother turned her by the shoulders and appraised her one more time, eyes up, eyes down, beaming. Kelly wore a floor-length gown the pink of Lafayette azaleas. It had spaghetti straps and billowy short sleeves and a womanly neckline, though Kelly's bosom was modestly veiled with feather-pink chiffon. She and her mom had picked the dress out together.

"You look beautiful, Kelly."

"Why, thank you, Danny! So bold!" Kelly blushed in front of her parents.

Dan may have seemed smooth, but he had trouble pinning Kelly's rose. He jabbed himself. Mrs. Bellisle stepped in.

"There, sweetie," she approved, her breath of mints. "Go have fun now."

"Mr. Neeley, have her back at ... let's say ... midnight?" Mr. Bellisle used his man-to-man voice.

"Yes SIR! Not a minute past, Mr. Bellisle."

Danny Neeley tried to contain himself. All week, he'd expected to be returning to the Bellisle driveway with his date at 10 p.m., latest.

An extra two hours with Kelly? Dan thought of a song by old Alabama Hank: *Tonight we're setting the woods on fire!*

Neeley politely took Kelly's hand.

Mr. and Mrs. Bellisle closed the front door.

"I can't wait," Neeley told Kelly in a stage whisper.

"Me either, Danny." She squeezed his fingers.

Thirty minutes later, Neeley and Kelly lay naked and flushed in the flatbed of the pickup. A wild pavilion of stars gleamed over Lake Nicole.

Thrown to one side of an inflatable mattress, Kelly's pink prom gown looked like the fantastic shed skin of a nymph. Dan Neeley's white tux lay strewn, and two sticky condoms wilted against the side of the truck.

Neeley held Kelly desperately, his pale freckled arm across her breasts.

They would officially be late to the prom.

Their reputations would be okay. Kelly wasn't that kind of girl.

But then again ... she was.

She hit the river hard. The water cracked like concrete.

Her impact broke Kelly into bubbles ... a billion black bubbles, swirling, whirling and noiseless.

Was she alive?

The curious question crossed Kelly's mind. Then she reasoned that if her mind posed such a question, she must be alive ...

Somehow, she remained conscious. No breath in her lungs. No bubbles to rise as she opened and closed her mouth, fishlike, paralyzed from slamming onto water from a hundred feet high.

Kelly grew aware of the river's current. Its life.

She felt a river in her fingers.

She moved her right hand, and it obeyed, haltingly. She moved her left hand.

One foot moved in a circle, stirring.

Kelly could feel her wet gown bunched uncomfortably at her waist. The river water around her flowed cold and warm at the same time.

She wished she were home.

She did not know if she would ever breathe again.

Kelly heard burbles and squeaks and whispers. The whine of boat motors and haunted wailings of twin children. Old animals with fins and scales and shells. She heard a splash somewhere, heavy, muffled.

Kelly once read about the recovery of river drownings in the days of paddle-wheel steamboats. To jar a victim from mud and muck, a boat pilot cruised over the drowning site and fired a powder-loaded cannon. *Boom!* The report of the weapon shivered timbers, vibrated waters. *Boom!* In a few minutes, some member of a search party on the steamer would point a long finger toward an object floating to the surface.

There she is!

The deep black river didn't feel so very different from deep black sleep.

Until something touched Kelly.

A hand grabbed her.

She felt a jerk, and her body rose through water involuntarily.

It would be The Devil. Kelly knew with all her heart. She deserved it. She should have been a different Kelly. She should have found a way to be better. She should have adored her children, god knows she did adore them, god knows she tried to fight the postpartum that made her fear them, feel that way ...

The hand tugged her upward in urgent, spasmodic jerks.

The Devil pulled her.

Up.

To air.

Kelly heard The Devil break the Black Warrior with a barking painful gasp.

Ayyyy! Ayyyy!

Her body gasped too, breaths so starved and enormous they gobbled stars and clouds and moon and ... the trestle, wooden ties, steel tracks, the single light on the power pole, the undercarriage of her green VW in plain sight overhead ...

The Devil heaved forward – Kelly saw a silhouette as big as a whale – and all at once her head bumped terrifically hard against the hull of a small boat. A loud hollow thump echoed clearly from the riverbank.

The blow stunned Kelly a second time.

She gave up trying to make her legs work.

A big dripping head rose from the water beside her. It took a huge breath. A giant fist grabbed a rope dangling from an aluminum flatboat.

Even in the dark, Kelly recognized Deputy Jess Turnipseed.

"Miz Rogers," Turnip panted. "This ain't no way to have fun."

19
Fort Rogers

The children worked all Saturday to build a fort in the woods. Will and Mary and Timmy passed up TV cartoons to strike out early down a path into the woods behind the Rogers house. They carried sandwiches they made the night before and a jug of water. Timmy brought a hatchet from his daddy's shop.

They chose a clearing under loblolly pines.

After some intense architectural work on a scrap of notebook paper, Will marked the fort's corners with four white chunks of limestone. The old stones they kicked out of the pine needles had likely been the foundation settings of a long-ago cabin.

"We'll build it ... here!" announced Will, flourishing his arm. "Fort Rogers!"

The children cleared pine cones and old beer cans left by hunters, and they yanked up a few chin-high poke plants. The pulpy stalks stained their hands purple.

Timmy didn't touch the poke.

"Daddy says them berries are deadly poison," he warned. "They can kill a mama cow ... and her milk will turn purple and kill the baby cow too."

Will usually didn't pay much attention to Timmy. He worried about everything – dirt on his hands, dark sky, forest noises. A scratch with a single drop of blood freaked him out. But this time, Will's manly little forehead wrinkled.

"Know what? I heard about poke berries too," Will said. "You can eat the leaves if you boil 'em a bunch of times. But them purple berries ... *no way*."

He checked his palms. Red-handed.

"Mary, we gotta go wash this juice off. It might accidentally get in our mouths."

If Will showed concern, Mary showed alarm. Her two purple hands looked like a hog butcher's.

"We might accidentally get it in our eyes!" Mary said. "We might go blind!"

"Snake Creek!" Will cried. "Let's wash it off!"

They took a path through thickets of Chinese privet and a spot where kudzu climbed the trees. The trio in strange purple gloves emerged in a little sedge field.

As it always happened in that spot, no matter how they braced for the shock, a covey of quail burst from hiding and scared the daylights out of them.

"Damn!" said Will, practicing his cussing. "Damn bobwhites! Every damn time!"

"They're the scariest things in the world!" Mary answered, a thrill in her voice.

One last quail took off, late, wings whistling.
The children ducked and yelled – *yeii! yeii!*

"Next time they scare us like that," Will boasted, "I'm gonna throw our hatchet and split one right down the middle!"

Timmy looked at Will like he stood before a young god.

Not Mary.

"What if there's a baby?" she asked.

Mary hadn't been able to forget the little dead mockingbird.

"What if there's a baby?" Will didn't understand.

"A baby bobwhite."

Will still stared.

Mary blew hair out of her face. "When you throw the hatchet. What if you cut a mama bobwhite one in two, and she has a baby?"

Timmy Wragg piped up.

"We could save it! We could put the baby bobwhite in a shoebox with a hot-water bottle and feed it bread crumbs. And give it milk out of an eye dropper."

Mary chimed in. "I know where we can dig up worms, too! There's a million under the rabbit cage at school."

Will suddenly felt something, like the others.

"Well," he admitted, "I don't think I can hit a bobwhite with a hatchet. Not when it's flying, anyway."

They rounded a leafy turn in the path.

Snake Creek, ten feet wide, frothed between fern-covered limestone banks. Black water snails covered the creek bottom. A swarm of gnats twinkled over the water like a ghost.

They waded in. The cold creek made the backs of their heads ache.

Mary got up to her ankles, then stooped to wash her hands. The clear water magnified her fingers. A crawfish, quick as a flash, fled beneath a limestone shelf. Mary scrubbed the poke juice aggressively on loose sand in the creek bottom. Stains colored the water.

A dragonfly paid a visit, helicoptering for a moment in mid-air to take a close look at these strange creatures. Will had sunk to his knees in the creek, peering down.

"Wow!" he announced.

He'd found something.

He lifted an ornament on a muddy ribbon. Though discolored, it still gleamed in the sun as it spun, dripping. The thing had been at the bottom of the creek for a long time. The metal had a snail stuck to it.

"Treasure!" Mary declared.

"Maybe for sure!" Will agreed, excited.

Timmy jumped up and down on the bank. "That ain't treasure! It's a Army medal. My daddy's got one. On his uniform."

Will stood, water dripping off his elbows. The bright metal thing swung before his eyes in the sunlight.

"That's the one called a Purple Heart," Timmy insisted. "See the shiny part hangin' down? That's a heart."

Will wiped mud off the medal with his thumb. The snail dropped in the creek.

"Who's the lady?"

"That's George Washington." Timmy sounded, for once, authoritative. "Men wore their hair funny back then."

"Whoa!" Will mused. "A Purple Heart!"

Timmy, proud now, spoke with confidence. "The generals give you one if you get shot. My daddy got shot."

Will took his eyes off the medal for the first time.

"Our daddy got shot. In Iraq." He pronounced it *Eye-Wrack*.

Mary corrected him.

"Daddy got *blowed up*. He got in a bomb, and it broke his leg right *there* ..." she pointed to her thigh "... and hurt his insides. He's got lots of scars. And he don't talk about it, *ever*."

"Maybe your daddy got a Purple Heart too," Timmy said.

Timmy loved Mary. His face looked tormented with the effort of logic he made to agree with her.

Will separated strands of muddy ribbon – purple too – and slipped the medal over his head. It dangled to his waist.

"It's a million times better than finding an arrowhead," he said pointedly to Mary.

Mary tried not to feel jealous. *Well* ... she thought to herself. *I'll find something better than a Purple Heart one day.*

Will sloshed from the creek.

"Let's go build a fort!" he cried. "Let's build Fort Rogers!"

They sprinted up the path. Will's medal bounced crazily in the sun.

Will and Timmy placed pine and sweetgum poles for the long walls, one boy at each end. They held the poles steady while Mary lashed them together. She used tough smilax vines stripped off tree trunks. Will shaved thorns from the vines with Timmy's hatchet.

By noon, the walls of Fort Rogers stood above their heads – even Will's, the tallest. They made a window looking out at a natural clearing under the pines.

"Windows are to shoot out of," Will explained. "Wildcats and wolves might come."

As the sun passed its high mark in the sky, they added a roof of leafy branches.

It looked like a professional fort.

They finally rested happily inside Fort Rogers and ate peanut-butter-and-grape-jelly sandwiches. Mary had brought one for Timmy.

"This fort," Will predicted, "will be here till Doomsday."

"Longer," Mary said. "Cause that's just Doomsday."

Mary said something with her mouth full that made Timmy laugh. Will threw a bite of chewed sandwich into his open mouth.

Timmy spit, but he laughed. "Gross!"

"Yukkk!" screamed Mary, but laughed like crazy.

They rolled all over one another, helpless with mirth. Each time they thought the fit had passed, one repeated *yukkk!* again and away they went, hooting and beating the ground with their palms in a little hideout in the woods.

After a long time, things got still. They might even have taken naps.

Shadows fell across Fort Rogers.

Finally, Timmy sat up.

"My mama went to the hospital last night," he said out of nowhere.

Mary's head popped up.

"Did she eat chocolate?" Her voice was full of concern. Her red hair had leaves in it.

"She didn't get sick," Timmy said. "She woke up in the middle of the night with bad bruises. She don't remember how it happened. She got in the car and drove right by herself to the hospital and left me and Daddy asleep."

"Wow," Will whispered. He sat up too, sleepy but paying attention. The tarnished medal and the muddy purple ribbon stuck to his bare chest.

"She's okay now," Timmy insisted. "She got back this morning. She has medicine. But she's got bad bruises."

Timmy waited, like he'd say something else important.

"She told Daddy something," he went on. "I heard it, but I wasn't supposed to."

The twins waited.

"Well then?" Will buried the hatchet to the hilt in soft dirt by his bare foot. "What?"

Timmy turned to Mary, not Will.

"My mama saw *your* mama at the hospital," Timmy said. "A police car brought her."

Mary and Will traded glances. They only talked about their mama in private.

"It was Deputy Turnipseed," Timmy continued. "The big fat one. My mama said your mama was wrapped up in a white blanket, like she was freezing. But she was asleep."

The night before, after The Milky Way, Will and Mary had secretly climbed into bed together and whispered for a long time. They talked about how beautiful their mama looked. How hard she hugged them. How sad her eyes seemed. How she recognized them right off the bat.

They talked about how their daddy ran down the street calling her, waving his hands. And they both cried some before they went back to sleep.

The whistle of a bobwhite sounded out in the woods.

"Well," Will told Timmy, "our mama has spells. That's what Daddy says."

"She had a spell," Mary echoed. "Probably."

Timmy took a breath.

"Mama didn't talk to the deputy," he said. "But she said your mama was probably going to be alright."

Nobody spoke.

"My mama told me something about your mama," Timmy confided. He then breathed like he was about to run through a fire.

"What did your mama say?" Mary demanded. "About our mama."

A deep voice growled outside the fort wall.

Will! Mary!

It scared them to death.

"Y'all turned wild? Decided to live out in the woods now?"

It was Elmore. Daddy.

The three children melted with relief.

"You scared us, Daddy!" Mary actually scolded Elmore.

"Y'all come on home now," Elmore said. "We're serving hot dogs with melted cheese on top. And potato chips on top of that."

"No onions!" Will yelled. "Can Timmy come too?"

"No onions. You come too, Timmy. Everything's ready, and there's plenty."

The trio stumbled out of Fort Rogers. Lightning bugs seltzered the woods.

Mary hugged her daddy hard, and so did Will.

Breaking the embrace, Elmore held his son at arm's length.

"What's that, son? Around your neck."

Will, proud and excited, held up the medal up for his dad to see.

"It's a Purple Heart, Daddy. Timmy says so ..."

Elmore cut him off sharply. "Where'd you get it?"

Will looked surprised.

"Snake Creek," he stammered. "In sand at the bottom."

Elmore's grip tightened hard, and Will squirmed.

"Oww, Daddy ..."

Elmore released him.

"Son, you take that piece of cheap jewelry ... right now ... and go throw it back in the creek where you found it. Right now."

Will and Mary didn't remember hearing such a tone in Elmore's voice.

"Go on. Why you standing here, son?"

Will frantically yanked the medal and ribbon over his head as he raced down the path to the creek. He disappeared around a curve.

"We'll wait right here, Will!" Elmore called. His voice now sounded more fatherly.

Mary searched her dad's face. Timmy Wragg stared at the ground. For some reason, he kept the hatchet hidden behind his back.

All at once, from the direction Will had gone, came a weird thrumming sound ... and a piercing scream.

Elmore started to run in that direction ... but drew up short at Will's furious, faint, exasperated voice.

"Damn! Damn bobwhites! Damn!"

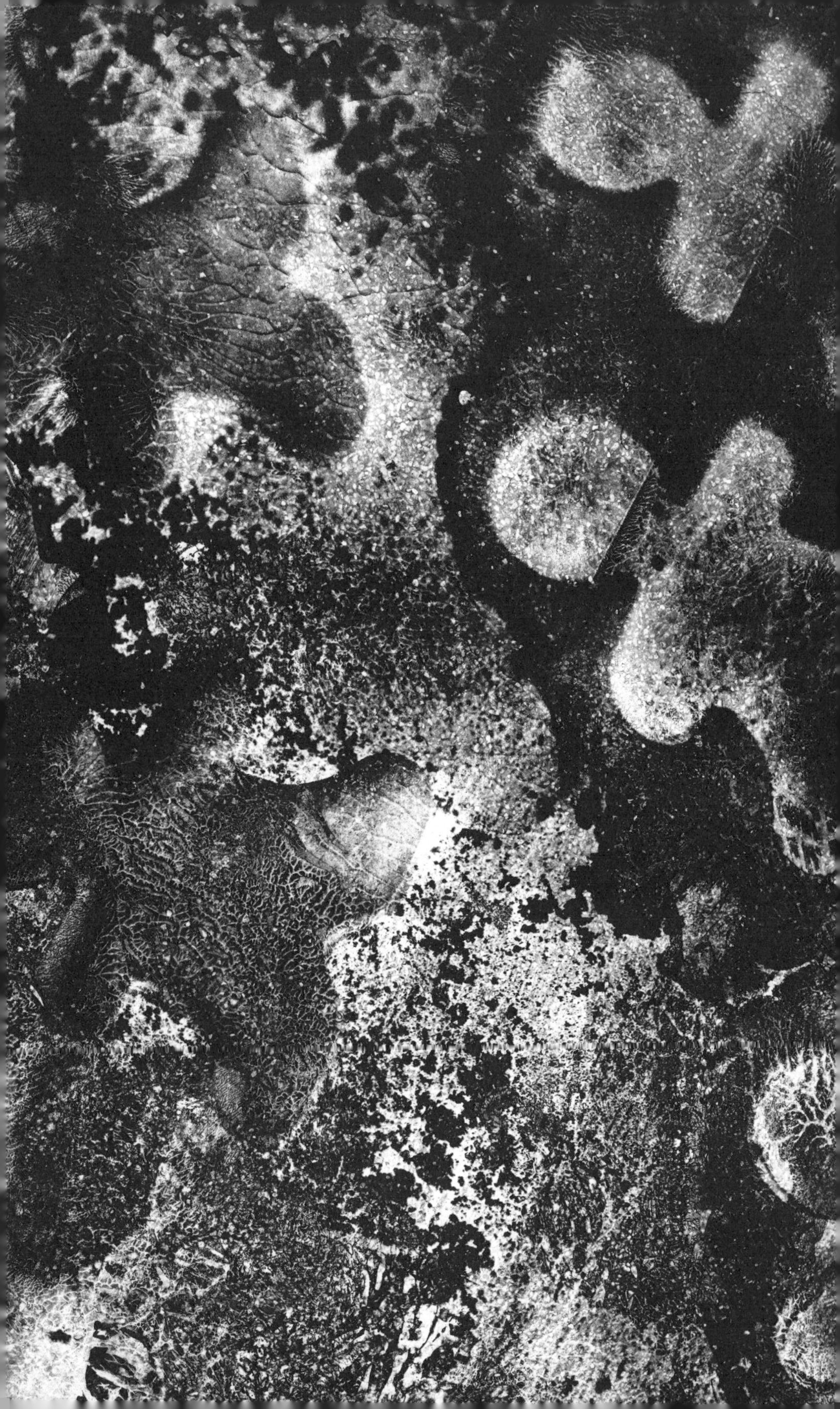

—20—

The Gingerbread Men

Mr. Wood saw Mrs. Mock to the door, patted her on the bottom.

She'd had a big time. She'd had a big reward.

Now she had a big assignment.

Mr. Wood pulled out his lap drawer. He withdrew a black remote. He pressed a red button.

A wall of polished wood smoothly parted. A glowing panel displayed a dozen surveillance screens, some static, some filled with moving figures, vehicles, time codes.

Mr. Wood didn't care for television or periodicals. He got all the information he needed here – his own personal worldwide web.

He watched Mrs. Mock's car cruise away.

On other screens, he could monitor his factories in Camden and Verona and Minsk. He could watch the staff in corporate offices in Bonn and London and Shanghai. He could study the faces of ship captains and airplane pilots and shift workers. He could watch total strangers, anonymous vehicles, private sanctuaries.

Mr. Wood was everywhere. He knew everything.

He pressed a new button. A screen filled, the quality of the video so exquisitely sharp that Mr. Wood could count sticks the Rogers twins and that little Wragg brat used to build their fort in the woods. If he zoomed in, Mr. Wood could count every single leaf in the thatching the pretty little girl, Mary, had reverently placed on its roof.

That video camera suddenly flickered, went blank.

Mr. Wood reversed the woodland video recording, finding a number of blank spaces and lapses. Something was wrong. He would send a technician to fix the camera ASAP.

Mr. Wood dealt with his annoyance by pulling a cigar from his western jacket. He broke the band, cut the end, blazed a gold lighter.

The smell of rich burning Cuban tobacco mingled now with the smells Mrs. Mock had left behind.

Mr. Wood explored the video. He found a viewable section and stopped it at exactly the instant Mary Rogers stretched on tiptoes to carefully position a branch atop that little stick house. He watched with interest as Will, that fine young man, abruptly muscled her aside to rearrange the bough in a way he preferred.

Mr. Wood paused the video and studied the two youngsters.

Then he reversed the video in time, fast speed, to magically watch the children deconstruct the fort, pole by pole, its sides coming down like pick-up sticks, the small figures moving in ghostly blurs, backward, always backward, speeding toward the past.

Toward that hot goddamned car.

Of course, Mr. Wood knew about the car. Everybody in Lafayette knew about the car. Mr. Wood also knew about Kelly Rogers, the struggles.

Mr. Wood hit another button.

This camera scanned directly down onto a wooden train trestle.

A green Volkswagen Bug magically puttered onto the screen. Mr. Wood watched as the Rogers woman, dressed for a night on the town, showed a lot of leg stepping out of the automobile. She stepped to the edge of the trestle in a light rain.

Then she took another step.

Mr. Wood clicked another camera.

A rain-speckled lens showed Deputy Jess Turnipseed yanking the cord of a Mercury outboard. His boat sped to a black whirlpool in the night where Mrs. Rogers had disappeared.

Mr. Wood reversed the woodland video recording, finding a number of blank spaces and lapses. He would send a technician to fix the camera ASAP.

Very good.

As Mr. Wood ordered, Sheriff Neeley assigned Deputy Turnipseed night watch on the river. His vigilance was rewarded.

Mr. Wood watched the fat policeman dive into the river.

He felt a kind of sensual thrill when Turnipseed appeared above water again, towing a limp woman by her black hair.

Deputy Turnipseed hoisted Kelly Rogers on his back, dumped her ungracefully into the boat, her dress to her waist.

Mr. Wood saw her pale hand clasp and unclasp, searching for something solid to grasp.

The Intensive Care Unit camera was a guilty pleasure. Mr. Wood would watch paramedics bring in the Saturday night miserables.

Last weekend, they lugged in a blood-soaked stretcher with a would-be convenience store shoplifter, shotgunned by the night teller. Later, Mr. Wood saw Sheriff Neeley himself deliver two heavy-duty black plastic bags filled with body parts of a crack addict who passed out on the railroad tracks after lighting up a pipe.

Mr. Wood scanned the hospital-room video, found the footage he wanted.

Nurses, two male and two female, cut off Kelly Rogers' clothes. Mr. Wood watched the livid skin of the legendary beauty burst out of a tight sheath of evening gown.

Mr. Wood studied a still frame. Kelly Rogers lay nude on a metal gurney.

Oh yes.

They would keep her alive in Lafayette General. Then she would go back to living a quiet life.

Mr. Wood would know Kelly Rogers' exact location on the winter solstice.

Her delicious kids too.

He pleasured himself, alone at his desk.

He waited for a thick drumbeat inside him to slow.

With a sticky hand, he clicked another surveillance view.

Elmore Rogers' driveway off Highway 11.

A car slowly bounced up the rutted driveway, then cut its lights. The old silver Chrysler might have been elegant at one time. It had a gleam on a moonlit summer night.

Mrs. Mock stepped out.

Mr. Wood zoomed in with deep interest.

She wore the same provocative red dress she had teased off for him just an hour ago. Her money-maker.

The lady in red lifted out an oversized picnic basket with a checkered cloth.

Mr. Wood turned up the audio.

He watched ... and heard ... Mrs. Mock attempt to ring the front doorbell. Of course, the doorbell on Elmore Rogers' rental house didn't work. She finally knocked, her tough little knuckles bunched.

Elmore Rogers opened the door, surprised. The tasty twins peeked around him.

The world's best spy camera, tiny as a dragonfly, and a listening device that could hear ants quarrel, observed from the splintery top of the telephone pole by Elmore's driveway.

Mrs. Mock, all in red with her cookie basket, looked like an adult Red Riding Hood.

"Good evening, Elmore! Will! Mary!"

"Why ... uh ... hey, Mrs. Mock."

She smiled so big.

Elmore's surprise dissolved. He remembered the last time he and Mrs. Mock stood in a doorway. Last Christmas. He had stitches and a broken rib. She didn't let him in.

"What's your business, Mrs. Mock?" Elmore asked.

"Why, Elmore, I've been missing these adorable children. Toodles, Will! Hey, Mary!"

Her voice trilled.

Mr. Wood could not believe how much he despised the woman.

Still, she would get him what he needed.

Clearly, Elmore didn't buy the act. He didn't crack the door an inch wider. Neither kid spoke.

"You miss ... Will and Mary?"

"I certainly do," Mrs. Mock insisted. "I brought them over some things I baked. Just this afternoon!" She pointedly looked at each child, and added, "Goodies! Plus a surprise or two!"

"Well, Mrs. Mock ..."

"Y'all keep the basket!" She smiled, extending the bulky thing. "I have lots."

Elmore didn't reach.

Mrs. Mock went on talking.

"Please, Elmore? When school starts back in September, bring the kids back to stay on Friday afternoons again? I want to be a better grandmother. The grandmother they never had."

Good god, thought Mr. Wood.

Elmore rubbed his nose.

"I mean it, Elmore. It's what your daddy would want. Let Will and Mary come after school on Fridays while you work. I'll get them off the school bus, and we'll have tea and cookies and play games."

Elmore didn't move a muscle. But young Will spoke up. Headstrong little fool.

"What *kind* of cookies?"

Mrs. Mock raised her painted eyebrows. She flipped the cover on the picnic basket so the twins could see.

"Why, there's ... peanut butter ... oatmeal ... chocolate chip ... and ... homemade gingerbread men!"

Like a magic trick – *shazam!* – Mrs. Mock lifted those oversized gingerbread treats. Cookies in the shape of tiny humans.

She waved one in front of Will, one in front of Mary.

"Have you children ever tasted real gingerbread men?"

Mary, looking up at Elmore, imploring. "I never tasted a gingerbread man. Did I?"

Elmore wavered.

Will chimed in. "Can we eat a gingerbread man, daddy?"

Mrs. Mock smoothed the front of her dress. The gingerbread men moved up, down, their little raisin eyes wide.

"Gingerbread is your daddy's very favorite, Elmore Rogers ..."

Mrs. Mock danced the gingerbread men side to side like silly cartoon characters.

"Daddy! *Please*, Daddy!"

Elmore took the picnic basket.

"I guess I'll say thanks, Mrs. Mock. We'll get the basket back to you in a couple of days."

"Don't worry a fig about that. Like I said, I've got lots of baskets. Or ... what about this? You just send it with the kids the first Friday after school starts. Yes?"

Mr. Wood could read absolutely nothing in Elmore's poker face.

"They'll have the most fun. I promise."

Elmore started to speak, but Mrs. Mock went on.

"You believe in forgiveness, don't you, Elmore? And kindness? I want to be a better step-grandmother. I know I can do better."

A big black moth hit the light over the porch, circled it.

"We appreciate the offer. The kids will enjoy the cookies."

Elmore firmly closed the door.

The listening device on the utility pole picked up a few excited words from the Rogers house: *gingerbread ... me first ... lots of 'em ...*

Then the little girl's voice rose. Surprised and thrilled.

"Look, Daddy!"

"What, sweetie?" Elmore's voice sounded tired.

"A cheerleader outfit!"

Will's little-man voice yelled too.

"And a snow dome, Daddy! A giant one with a snowman inside!"

Mr. Wood clicked off the surveillance devices.

Mission accomplished!

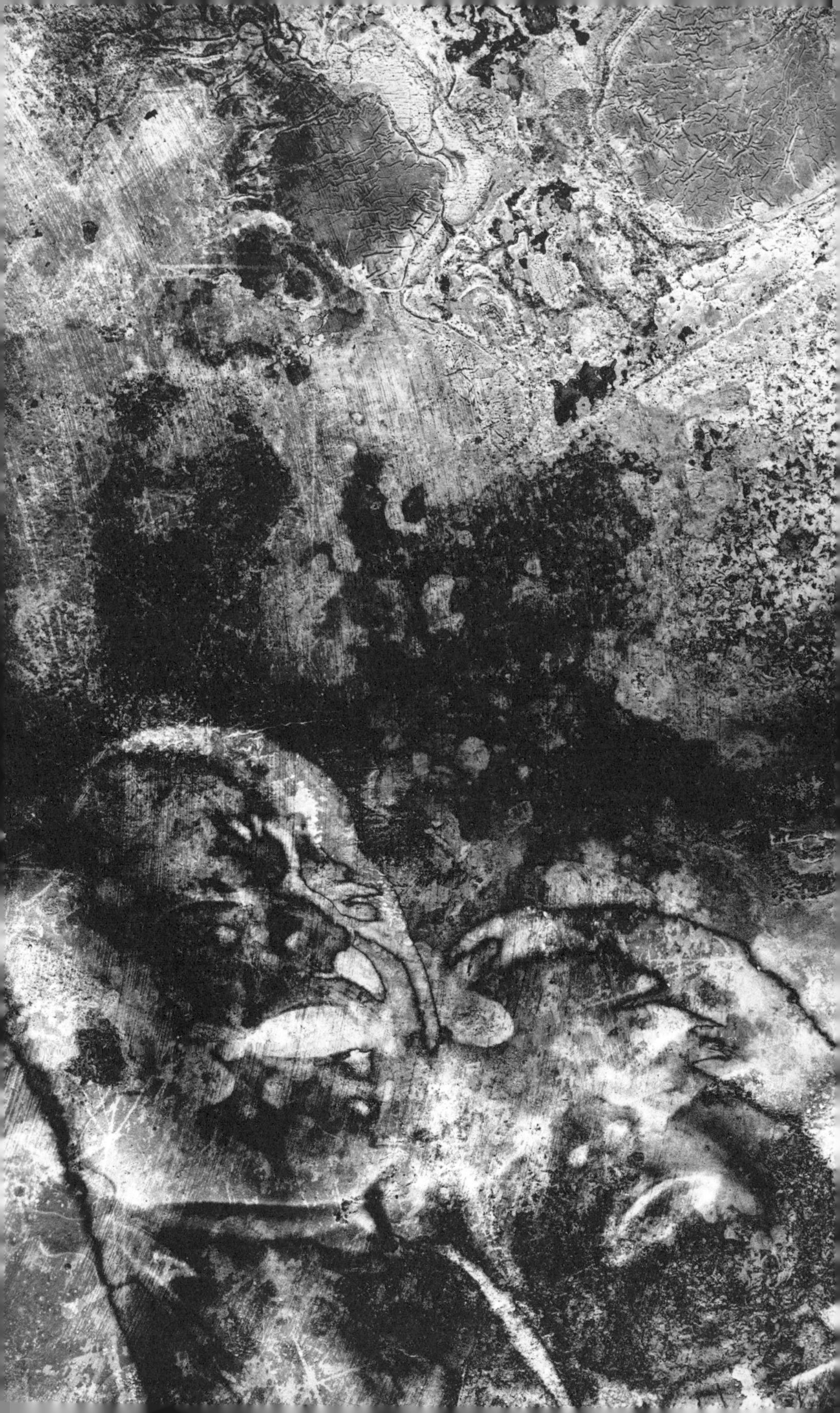

—21—

The Far Shore

Kelly opened her eyes.

Ahhh. Her old friend.

Lithium.

She didn't recognize all the other drugs jacked into her, but she did know this one.

With the twins and her troubles, the VA Hospital doctors in Tuscaloosa first prescribed it. Kelly got VA treatment free, a benefit of Elmore's National Guard service. The Army may have sent her new husband halfway around the world with a twice-over pregnant wife, but at least Uncle Sam had a generous compensation plan.

Snow-white pills. Discount prices.

Lithium. It sounded to Kelly like something they put in a needle to execute serial killers.

Oh, and if the lithium doesn't work, we have one other option, the VA doctor advised.

The greasy-haired physician left his stethoscope on Kelly's unbuttoned breast far too long. *Let's listen to your heart*, he explained. Dr. Hays wore aftershave that lingered on Kelly's clothes. Moist flakes of dandruff in his scalp looked like coconut.

For especially severe cases like yours, Dr. Swift tut-tutted, *we sometimes see positive results with … electroshock.*

So Kelly faced electrocution … or little white pills. And no matter how desperate she felt for a cure from the dark feelings about her own babies, Kelly didn't want electric shock.

Lithium.

She took it. One pill every morning. Like that wafer they served with grape juice at Methodist communion.

They gave her a pill to sleep too. She took a lot of them … and slept, but never rested.

Kelly made her eyes focus in the dark. Shapes shifted on the ceiling. She thought of oak trees blowing at night.

Why were mysterious sections of darkness slowly moving above the hospital bed?

Lithium devils. Her old friends.

Their eyes glowed in the shadows. They stared without blinking.

Kelly groaned.

Why hadn't she drowned?

The doctors called it postpartum psychosis.

Psychosis.

They spoke that word almost reverently, tapping nervous pens on clipboard charts.

Weeks passed, then months. And along with the unrelieved guilt of looking at her own twin babies and *despising* them, feeling *revulsion* for them, feeling a morbid, irrational *fear* of them, Kelly's daily dose of lithium rewarded her with terrible nausea, diarrhea and a constant dazed disorientation.

She saw devil eyes. Everywhere.

They ogled Kelly from tree shadows and the dark insides of closets. They stared up at her out of standing water.

Threatening. Sinister.

Over and over, Kelly lay her colicky twins in the same crib, bawling. Then she sat on the bed, bawling too. She cried even when Will and Mary didn't cry.

Kelly barely ate, couldn't hold anything down or in. Yet her weight ballooned, hips and thighs swollen so blue jeans no longer fit, feet unable to slip into old shoes. Kelly's body rebelled even worse than it had in pregnancy, when all sorts of things happened beyond control or comprehension. Leaks from body openings. Vivid fears. Sharp pains … or else just numb, dumb emptiness where a carefree spirit once lived.

Where was Kelly Bellisle?

Where was the high-school beauty queen who once cruised twice around the football field at Wood Stadium atop a convertible Mercedes? The Kelly who waved a hand in a downtown parade and blew kisses to friends and balanced a bouquet of red roses on her lap?

What happened to that beautiful, innocent girl?

She had hideously transformed and gone away. Forever. Kelly knew it down inside every aching 29-year-old bone.

Darling Kelly. Lost and gone forever. Dreadful sorry.

The devil eyes narrowed as she dwindled, body and mind.

Twins. Conceived in headlong passion.

Yes, it surely had been love. Mad love. Truly.

Love. The opposite of lithium, and even deadlier.

Kelly's first time with Elmore Rogers felt like nothing she'd ever experienced.

Her orgasm came with shocking speed, fast and careening, and it lasted and lasted and lasted. Then Elmore's hard, yearning body made her come again, and it lasted still longer. Kelly couldn't remember whether she passed out from pleasure.

After that, Elmore filled every thought. Day and night, night and day. Kelly craved animal passion with Elmore Rogers more than pride or propriety or practicality.

What had Elmore *done* to her?

In junior and senior year at Lafayette High, Kelly had her fun with Danny Neeley. She would always remember Danny, her first. So sweet and good to her.

Danny made her laugh. Goofy, farty old Danny. He would make some girl a wonderful companion and father. But Danny Neeley wanted just one thing in the whole wide world – to be a hometown cop and wear a badge and keep the good citizens of Lafayette safe and happy.

Kelly? She dreamed of Paris and Rome, the moon over Manhattan.

In her one year at college, Kelly dated a bleached-blonde mess of a California kid who wanted to be a writer (*like Faulkner*, he earnestly told her, *or Brautigan*). Flint wrote violent short stories about surfing and sharks. Kelly let him touch her, and she even let Silver Surfer slip himself inside her once after a raucous Jimmy Buffett concert.

Kelly returned to Lafayette to spend the summer. She hung out some with Danny again, mostly for old time's sake. Danny actually studied – real books – those days. He had started course work in law enforcement at Wood Junior College. He still adored Kelly, and the old redhead was always good for movie and a pizza. A kiss. Kelly appreciated his cheerful companionship. She remained deeply in 'like' with Danny.

Midsummer, Danny received an official letter from the City of Lafayette asking him to join its small police force. They would send him off to train in Montgomery for three months.

Kelly gave him a fond farewell. They met in his apartment behind a new Denny's franchise. Kelly found it an improvement in every way from the flatbed of his pick-up truck.

I'll miss you, Danny. She whispered like a close friend, a confidant, as they rested after love-making. *But I want to be honest. I met someone I really like.*

In fact, she added, her words surprising her, *Danny, I think I love him.*

Dan Neeley slowly rebuttoned his shirt, his head newly shaved, his big blue eyes wide and honest. He told Kelly he understood.

"I love you, Danny," Kelly told him. "As a friend forever. You are good as gold."

But Kelly had discovered something better than gold.

She'd run into Elmore again, as fate would have it, at the high school. Their old stomping grounds.

Kelly had driven over after a piano lesson to deliver a birthday present to her favorite old English teacher, Mrs. Lois Baker. Mrs. Baker taught remedial summer school. And why was Elmore there? The rangy center fielder's scholarship hadn't worked out – Elmore got in a little grade trouble, as he later explained it.

Kelly heard through the grapevine that Elmore partied his scholarship away. A coach's zero-tolerance policy interfered with Elmore's social life. So he returned home to Lafayette to figure out his future.

Elmore joined the local National Guard unit for a little weekend warrior money each month, and his old baseball coach helped him land a job keeping infields in shape for summer church-league softball.

Kelly had just left Mrs. Baker's classroom with a big goodbye hug. On a walk back to her faithful green VW, the blazing August afternoon popped out sweat beads on her lower back.

She had every intention of returning to her parents' home in Wood Forest for bacon, lettuce and tomato sandwiches and Golden Flake potato chips. Her family would watch the Atlanta Braves play baseball again ... and win again ... then click off the remote. Another Friday night would funnel into nowhere.

A mighty uproar turned Kelly's head.

Elmore Rogers chugged up next to the VW on a riding lawn mower. Gasoline reek filled the air.

Kelly had no clue that her life had just changed.

Elmore cut the engine, tipped back his Braves cap. He picked something off the tip of his tongue. A piece of grass. Newly mowed bits covered him. His Lafayette Lions T-shirt had sweated through.

It occurred to Kelly that Elmore might just sit there till the end of days and never speak.

"Well hey," Kelly said cheerfully. "You look hot, Elmore."

He grinned. What strapping young man wouldn't relish that compliment?

"You look hot too, Kelly."

She realized the double-entendre. She deeply blushed.

"I mean, you look ... *healthy*, Elmore." She changed the subject. "Tan and all."

Elmore *did* look healthy.

Kelly couldn't take her eyes off his handsome, sun-bronzed face. Shocks of light hair wisped from the edges of his baseball cap. Elmore's steady eyes held hers.

"Well, Kelly ... you look healthy too." She felt herself being teased. "Super healthy. Bursting with health."

Kelly leaned against the VW. Thinking back, she would wonder if it kept her from swooning.

They told a story, then two. They remembered teachers and baseball games and the time Kelly sang in church. They talked about Danny Neeley. *Nanny Deeley*, Elmore called him. So stupid. But it made Kelly laugh, and then Elmore laughed too, a way Kelly hadn't remembered. The brooding, unreadable loner of their school years ... laughing with his head thrown back?

Kelly felt something she couldn't control.

She folded her arms over her chest, almost in self-defense. She squinted straight at the setting sun. Elmore got off the mower. The silhouette of a tall, golden young man blocked her view.

A memory from high school flashed into Kelly's mind.

She'd kissed Elmore. Once.

It happened after cheerleading and football practices, a hot day like this.

An experiment. A joke. Kelly hung with Danny then. She couldn't even remember how she and Elmore had run into one another. She did recall how hard his chest felt, how big his hands seemed. Kelly had smelled something grown-up, forbidden, on his breath. His kiss surprised her. She had opened her mouth to taste his tongue.

Now, in an August-hot high-school parking lot, Kelly kept her lips tightly closed. She fought to keep her tongue from speaking without her permission.

She didn't need to speak.

Elmore left the reeking mower where it sat in the parking lot. Without a word, he took Kelly's hand.

"Come on," he said. And she did.

They walked toward the gymnasium. They might have been two dates on prom night.

Elmore carried keys for the school's athletic facilities. He unlocked a big metal door. Kelly would remember how he moved as quietly as possible for some reason ... that and the size of his hands.

Elmore took her down on a wrestling mat in a dark, smelly equipment room.

She wore a daisy-yellow summer dress, and Elmore wore sweaty jeans.

Until they didn't.

Elmore fit her perfectly. His key unlocked something.

She completely lost control.

Kelly Bellisle never, ever, got it back.

Oh my god! Elmore! Elmore!

Kelly heard words escape her without permission, her voice yearning, breathless.

He kept killing her. An assassin, one little death mounting the next, then another.

After a time, over pounding hearts and gasping breaths, they heard a voice.

"Hey!" someone called. "Hello? Somebody in there? You locked in?"

Keys rattled.

The equipment room door cautiously swung wide. A hand fumbled for the light switch. Shocking, buzzing fluorescence suddenly filled the equipment room.

Mr. Dove, the ancient janitor, peaked in. His black face seemed a little frightened.

"If somebody in there now, you say," he ordered. "I'm gonna lock this door back for the weekend. Ain't nothin' to eat in there but baseballs."

The wrestling mats and a big messy pile of football shoulder pads, like a heap of strange skeletons in a cave, gave no answers.

"Okay then," Mr. Dove announced. "Ghosts, y'all go back to sleep. Don't mind me."

The janitor closed the door and loudly locked it. His keys jingled off into the distance.

Laughter burst out under a mound of shoulder pads. A bare male foot poked from the pile. A smaller foot followed, toenails summer pink.

Two heads and bare shoulders surfaced. The heads looked at one another and giggled, then snorted.

Kelly and Elmore didn't get it together again for five long minutes.

Then they got it together. Again.

After that afternoon, Kelly had one purpose in life – to physically join her soft body to Elmore Rogers' hard one.

She woke in the morning and lay down at night desiring him. She wanted Elmore to fill her, complete her, dominate her, exalt her.

All the rest of her life ... and all of her lives after this one.

The janitor closed the door and loudly locked it. His keys jingled off into the distance. Laughter burst out under a mound of shoulder pads.

They connived ways to meet. They snuck through windows at their families' houses. They offered to run errands, then met behind Scarborough drug store or in the sedge field back of Burger Master or under the bleachers at Wood Stadium.

Anywhere.

Sometimes, on fire, Elmore and Kelly didn't talk or kiss. They simply tore off clothes and locked like wild animals. They snarled and mated. They coupled standing and sitting and on all-fours.

Each and every time, Kelly lost control and flew from the world. She learned how not to scream, though she wanted to always, every position, change of position. When her passion didn't need restraint, Kelly Bellisle's joy sounded like screaming, bloody murder.

Afterward, when the last delicious thrills had thundered through and Kelly's hair covered Elmore's chest, she felt his strong male heart beating like a tribal drum calling the world to war.

Dr. Castillo straightened up on a little black rolling stool. She lifted the stethoscope from her ears, untangled it from chestnut hair.

"Well," the doctor said gently. "You've got company, Kelly."

Dr. Castillo carefully fitted the stethoscope's arms into Kelly's ears. She lay perfectly still on crisp white paper that covered the examination room table.

Kelly heard a rhythmic murmur.

It was the strangest moment of her life.

Then she heard another beat, blended, then distinct, then blended again with the first.

Two heartbeats, said Dr. Castillo. *Two!*

Kelly wore such an incredulous expression.

Twins! The doctor smiled.

"They'll be born. They'll be my babies," Kelly announced without hesitation. "I won't go back to school."

Dr. Castillo nodded, her eyes on Kelly's. It seemed the pregnancy was no big surprise. The young woman had already made some decisions.

"Elmore?" Dr. Castillo asked cautiously.

If Kelly seemed surprised by the doctor's guess, she didn't let on.

"Yes ma'am. Sweet Elmore. We're going to have wonderful babies."

They married at Lafayette Methodist, the bride in white and Elmore in the first suit he ever bought with his own money. Their friends pelted them with rice like buckshot blasts as they made a getaway to the Gulf Coast in Kelly's VW. Danny Neeley slipped a bottle of champagne into the glove compartment ... and put an open, rancid can of cat food under the hood.

On their honeymoon, Kelly felt too sick to eat. But Elmore feasted on oysters – raw, baked, fried, roasted, stewed. He gave that delicious smile when Kelly leaned her tummy against him, full of life, and whispered that he didn't really need oysters. He couldn't be more fertile.

Ninety days later, a war started in Iraq. Elmore got mobilized, and so did Danny Neeley and twenty other Lafayette Lions in the National Guard.

Elmore and Kelly went together to the guard center, an aging Quonset hut. They explained about the twins and the due date, just four months ahead.

Nothing could be done, the Guard explained without even trying. Elmore and the transportation unit from west Alabama would deploy.

Their last night, Kelly and Elmore stayed up late, talking and slow-dancing in a little garage apartment the Bellisles fitted out for them. Elmore drank some whiskey. The newlyweds took turns putting 33s on Kelly's turntable. The Band. Johnny Cash. Rosanne.

They played with Chessie, Kelly's oldest friend, and Elmore purred goodbye in cat language. It made Kelly laugh.

At dawn, Dan Neeley's horn blew.

Elmore smiled that rare smile, and he walked out the door.

Kelly cried till her face hurt, and then she cried more.

She finally put the box of tissues away.

She would be strong for the twins.

Strong as steel.

Will and Mary came in April, a month early.

Spring hung around. Tired red and pink and white azaleas clung to green bushes.

The moment Will and Mary left her body, Kelly felt worthless. Scared. And *guilty*.

When the babies cried, she cried too – heartbroken, snot-running, helpless-to-stop sobbing. Sometimes, she couldn't stay in the room with the raging monsters. Who had squeezed these ugly E.T.s out into the world? How many different ways could newborns torture a mother?

Were they trying to kill her?

Where was Elmore? Where was Daddy?

He was with people he didn't even know. He talked on the phone about driving heavy trucks through some god-forsaken desert. He said he was fighting for his country.

Why couldn't Elmore be here to help *her* fight?

Kelly needed help. Wouldn't Elmore stop the screaming voices in her head? Drive her places she needed to go. Bring supplies and weapons to defend her *sanity*. Her panicked *mind*.

She hurt constantly, inside and out. Kelly was *losing*.

Didn't she matter to Elmore more than a desert? A country?

One morning, Kelly didn't recognize the shapeless, stringy-haired, haunted image staring from the mirror.

She opened her mouth. She hallucinated that her tongue was the meat of her own twins.

Postpartum.

The doctors gave it that fancy name. Postpartum depression. The baby blues. Just two medical words, like that.

Baby blues. Tra-la.

Kelly despised the way these men – always men in that VA place – clucked sympathetically with their open notebooks and said, in so many words, *It happens. Your case is more severe than most. Most mothers don't go through this. Short term. It will pass. Take these meds. Make healthy lifestyle choices. Let friends help. Talk to your minister.*

She gobbled lithium. She devoured her little white friends.

And?

The twins latched to Kelly's breasts and sucked her life out, glancing up with their slitted eyes and crying like dying cats each time one spit out a nipple to puke.

They woke Kelly any time she tried to sleep, any time she dreamed. They crapped their little diapers constantly, bowels active as birds in berry season. The smell of urine and feces filled Kelly's sinuses so completely that it never really went away. She smelled colic and crap and pee and newborns on her skin, day and night. Her deodorant and mouthwash and perfume smelled like babies with colic.

When she delivered at Lafayette General, Kelly's doctor had been a stranger, a substitute for Dr. Castillo. She'd been deployed too. The Middle East needed physicians.

So Dr. Kakade caught Kelly's babies, and handed them over. For life. Just like that.

What could Kelly do? An anonymous doctor put two gray lumps of meat on her breast, Will first, then Mary, their blood and ooze everywhere.

Her head swam in terror.

For a shocking moment, Kelly distinctly saw the newly severed heads of baboons on top of her, leering, barking, growling gruffly at one another. Tiny Mary still had placenta over her face, and big-shouldered Will worked greedy little fingers on both hands like a farmer milking a cow in some shit-covered stall.

Everyone had told Kelly how sublime childbirth would be. She had heard her own mother and a dozen other mothers give warm advice on the blessed event.

Kelly burst into tears with her babies on her chest. Her arms embraced Will and Mary, but she felt nothing – *nothing* – just terrible dread. Terrible fear.

Plus sweat-soaked guilt.

What mother ever felt this way about her own little babies? What's the matter with you, Kelly Rogers? Why can't you feel love ... or feel *anything* but throbbing pain between your legs and a vast emptiness?

Oh god! What kind of monster mother was she?

Kelly brought the babies home. She talked to Elmore on a sputtering connection a couple of times a week. He passed out cigars to all the soldiers.

Kelly couldn't be sure with the connection, but she thought Elmore cried once.

A few days later, Kelly arranged with a high-school friend who had a reliable internet connection, to show him the babies on video.

She put on lipstick and make-up for the first time in weeks and pulled her hair back in the ponytail Elmore liked. Kelly held Will and Mary up and tried to wear a big happy smile. Not fifteen seconds into the video call, both twins puked on her Sunday dress. Will first, violently. Like a little gargoyle.

You might have baby blues for a couple of weeks, Kelly's doctors chanted, like a chorus. *Then the sun will come out and the clouds will burn away, and the world will be shiny and beautiful forever and ever, amen, for you and your precious, God-given twins.*

Tra-la.

Will and Mary woke all night, crying, hysterical. Kelly woke, crying, hysterical.

She didn't want to see her parents. She never, ever, wanted to go inside their house again. Their worried faces scared her.

Still, she made herself go. Both babies cried and screamed until an evil bomb went off inside Kelly's brain.

The Bellisles sat around the fireplace. Her father had a camera on a tripod to take baby pictures for next year's Christmas cards. In May.

They lit a merry fire and tacked candy canes and red-and-green stockings to the mantel.

Kelly, the demons, and her mom and dad all posed.

God forgive Kelly for what she imagined, dandling screaming twins and faking a smile.

Kelly prayed, *God, never, ever, let such a thought come to my mind again.*

But it did.

She vividly imagined stuffing little Will, her own baby, face-first into the roaring hell of the fireplace. Ignoring the frantic kicks. Ignoring his different kind of screams.

Then little Mary. Her precious baby's stubby legs would make perfect handles for dashing her soft head on the mantle.

Kelly imagined white marble blotched with red marmalade.

The camera went *click*. Kelly burst uncontrollably into tears.

She wept and wept. *There, there* cooed her baffled parents. *Get a grip, Kelly.*

Get away from me! Kelly screamed. *You don't understand!*

She bundled the twins, flew back to her apartment, locked the door.

Kelly fed them.

Her breasts. Her beautiful breasts. The brats chewed her, sucked, until blackness came.

Later, they did it again. Attacking like cruel pale sharks. Then again. And again.

They gave her no mercy.

—22—

Lago de Garda

Gianni Abati proudly lifted a silver lid, his starched white toque and apron mirrored in the gleaming metal. He introduced the dish with a flourish: polenta prosciutto.

"It is, in Alabama, how you call it? Ah ... bacon cornbread!"

The handsome young chef smiled winningly at Mr. Wood. The jowly American in the cowboy hat nodded.

"Have you other gentlemens visit America in the South?" Abati kissed his fingers and lifted them high. "The food!"

Four Epicureans shared the *al fresco* table with Mr. Wood. Two were Japanese, the fashionable couple from Nagasaki. One, Don Gaston, lived in Brazil, where he bought and sold weapons for international clients.

A fourth Epicurean, Tiziano Sacco, Italian like the chef, hosted the gathering. Signor Sacco wore a fine Milan suit the color of his platinum hair.

Appropriately, Signor Sacco had made his fortune in precious metals.

The Epicureans had gathered at Signor Sacco's request to scout a potential solstice chef at a *ristorante* on Lake Garda. Chef Abati's space seemed convivial, good olive oil and bottles of spring water and fresh-baked bread set on a candlelit table in deepening twilight.

The convocation invited controversy.

Mr. Wood would host this year's Epicurean gathering, the 25th annual winter solstice feast, in west Alabama. The planner-in-chief wanted to wholly, autonomously, control the menu.

Everything is set, he notified his colleagues through their discreet channels. *I've picked the courses. I've picked a chef. I've prepared you a place at my table.*

But Signor Sacco was so excited by discovering a young chef at Garda that he begged, bribed and finally prevailed on an Epicurean 'tasting committee' to convene for a test meal.

Uncharacteristically, Mr. Wood yielded.

In truth, the trip to Italy gave him a good excuse to roll his custom-built Dassault Falcon 900 out of a private hangar, check it down himself, then blast into the heavens for a few hours of transatlantic flight with barcaroles playing full volume on God's-own sound system. Mr. Wood stocked the luxurious cabin with guilty pleasures – bootlegged Madonna porn and peanut-butter crackers and spicy meat sticks and cold Pabst Blue Ribbon longnecks.

You can take the boy out of the country, mused Mr. Wood, *but you can't take the country out of the boy.*

The Alabamian set the sleek black bird down at 4 a.m. near Trento at a remote strip owned by Signor Sacco. (Mr. Wood avoided flying close to Vicenza, where surveillance equipment at the U.S. Air Force NATO base might possibly have detected the flight even with all its advanced radar-resistant features.)

Vito, a pleasant man in peasant clothing, met Mr. Wood. He worked personally for Signor Sacco. He would watch over Mr. Wood's jet for the next 48 hours.

Vito got brownie points. With a smile, the Italian handed over keys to a new Lamborghini.

So *this* was the "*molto bene, molto bene*" Signor Sacco promised Mr. Wood for saying yes to a tasting trip to Italy to witness the genius of young Chef Abati.

A nice surprise.

The sports car looked like a black wasp, a prototype with a pulsing engine.

On its butter-soft seats, Mr. Wood discovered more gifts – a bottle of excellent *pinot grigio*, an antique bronze Venetian dolphin with a corkscrew penis, and a steaming-hot bowl of fusilli with pesto Genovese, perfectly *al dente*. With utensils. Basil fragrance filled the car.

Also, folded in a red-and-white napkin, two handmade Italian *pizzelle* cookies in the shape of children greeted Mr. Wood.

The pasta and *pizzelle* would be a fine tide-me-over. Mr. Wood would refrain from eating again until twilight. Signor Sacco had strictly advised that a very big, very grand evening meal would emerge from Chef Abati's lakeside kitchen near Malcesine.

Mr. Wood drove his astonishing new automobile very fast for two hours on a twisting road through the southern Italian Alps. The sun rose, shining like a coin.

Italy appeared. Vineyards climbed slopes. Yellow pastures nestled farmhouses.

For the first time in many months, Mr. Wood felt a peculiar excitement rise. He felt free. Anonymous.

An old appetite rose.

The car threaded a narrow two-lane. On a long, isolated downward slope, maybe a mile between curves ahead and behind, a high, stony cliff plunged away to the left.

Mr. Wood slowed.

An old Italian *paisano* leading a white horse trudged along the road. The horse appeared lame, making one painful step out of every four. The farmer walked with his head down. He wore a tattered hat and a brown coat.

Mr. Wood cruised past, slowed, carefully checked his rearview mirror, then braked. The Lamborghini's tail lights flared as he silently, rapidly, backed up a hundred yards.

Mr. Wood climbed from the car. The mountain air smelled clean.

He waited for the old brown man and the lame white horse.

Clop, clop. Clop, clop.

Buongiorno, husked the man, weary, raising a hand. He had brown eyes like a hound and severe wrinkles, deep as scars, down his cheeks.

Without reply, Mr. Wood shot out a thick left arm and grabbed the man's windpipe.

With his right hand, Mr. Wood gave the old Italian's chin a sharp, violent twist. The gaunt traveler – far thinner than he first appeared – fell heavily to the road. The white horse reared, whinnied, and fled in terror. The steed limped visibly, dragging its short rope.

For a heart-pounding moment, Mr. Wood stood in a swell of glory over his victim. He felt primal elation. Triumph boiled through his being.

He might have savored his kill for a long time. But a distant glow hinted at headlights rounding the curve behind him.

Mr. Wood carried the dead man effortlessly to the guard rail. He tossed the body over the cliff like a bag of garbage.

He picked up a beaten old hat from the road, solemnly dusted it, then sailed it past the rail too.

The Lamborghini smelled like pesto when Mr. Wood opened its door.

Just another Italian suicide. Mr. Wood gunned the engine. *The lame leg of a faithful horse was old Pagliacci's last straw ...*

Mr. Wood blasted away into blue morning.

He sang aloud for the first time in many, many years. "'O sole mio". Then he invented something tuneless, operatic, melodramatically Italian.

Stefan placed grilled portions of polenta prosciutto on each plate.

Mr. Wood was struck, as always, by Stefan's huge hands, though delicate as a pair of silver serving tongs. Beyond the candlelight warming their table, Mr. Wood spotted Ronaldo, the black server, quietly exiting the restaurant with wine.

Tonight, a sign hung on the gate of Chef Abati's restaurant: *Closed. Private event.*

The five Epicureans dined so near Lake Garda they could hear the rhythmic crunch and slosh of waves on its pebble beach. Southward, Mount Baldo soared to a snowy top. Nine o'clock twilight purpled the Italian heavens around the great peak.

This special full day of June, the solstice, had almost passed. Mr. Wood had not eaten since the pre-dawn pesto and cookies. Other Epicureans had fasted too, heeding Signor Sacco's advice.

The feast came forward, dish by dish, bottle by bottle.

"I am in Tennessee and Alabama and Louisiana three months," Chef Abati announced. Ronaldo poured a red wine from Signor Sacco's personal Alto Adige stock.

Gianni Abati had piercing green eyes and a nose like the Caesars. He wore shining black hair tied back in a ponytail. He clearly took pride in his English, a certain marker of worldliness and sophistication.

"I am so happy in New Orleans more than any other place."

He waved a hand toward *Una Tavola Chiamata Desiderio*, his establishment. A Table Called Desire.

"I am eating in the New Orleans *ristorantes* all the time," Abati said. "And I am happy in waves and waves of jazz. All time, I am happy ... and writing down the dishes and recipe."

Mr. Wood plucked a last polenta morsel from his plate with his fingers, daring any to question his manners. Nobody in Alabama history had ever used silverware to eat cornbread.

"I have visited New Orleans fifty times," Don Gaston, the Brazilian, exclaimed in his own boastful English. He sat next to Signor Sacco, the head of their table. "New Orleans is a main reason I am so big in the waist."

Mr. Wood patted his jacket pocket, drew out a handsome long Cuban, lit it, held it up, and announced, "New Orleans is also the reason I am so big in the pants."

The Epicureans laughed. So did the chef. The polenta prosciutto, his *amuse-bouche*, held great promise for the evening.

"Good! Very good!" Abati's eyes shone bright. "I will serving you more recipes inspired by New Orleans in Louisiana and by Nashville in Tennessee and the South of the U.S. By the end, *amicos*, you will be more big in the waist and in the pants!"

The table erupted again, and a cheerful laugh echoed from the lake.

Church bells rang down the blue valley that held Lake Garda. Hell's bells, Mr. Wood thought. Church bells always ring in Italy. Every damn hour of the day and night. Even a saint with a perfect conscience couldn't sleep through all the clanging.

Lively swifts jittered overhead, free from roosts in steeples and chimneys, their flocks slightly darker than the darkening sky. Venus glimmered.

Chef Abati's culinary skill shone like that heavenly body. He cannily brought out small tastes, one after another. He amused The Epicureans, pulling off with his charm a series of cheeky "tongue lessons" that would have insulted any other serious culinary club.

"I ask you to think of meeting my creations," Chef Abati explained, "as if meeting a beautiful woman ... "

Mr. Wood cut a quick glance toward the Japanese men. A beautiful woman? Those cats were so far past queer that the English language needed a new word for them. Under Beatle haircuts, they blinked stoically at the chef through identical gold-rimmed TAG Heuers.

"The first taste," Gianni Abati went on, "is the moment you take a beautiful woman's hand and look into her eyes and say *piacere*, how please to meet you."

"Taste two? You thoughtfully appraise the beautiful woman. She invites your conversation, courts your analysis.

"And what do you talk all this time?" the chef passionately asked. "Love! Without calling it love, without saying out loud that word! But by that time ... both you know it!"

Abati instructed his guests to carefully weigh and consider the woman's unique brilliance, her beauty, her intrigue.

In your imagination, he told them, *you compare this beautiful woman to other lovers you have known, the taste of her, the smell of her, the memories that live on your tongue.*

"When she is just right for you," Chef Abati declared, "you think of her long after the sun rises."

Chef Abati stressed that the consummate taste should be ... no, *must* be ... a moment of pure sensation, exclusively an instant of pleasure. No judgment. No distracting comparisons.

"You are now ... ah ... making love, but you are not a human thing. You are simply ... a tongue."

"Simply a ... *cosa?*" asked Don Gaston. The Brazilian was deeply puzzled. "A tongue?"

The ebullient young chef bowed, and he bounded away to the kitchen.

Don Gaston stuck out his tongue and let it dangle.

The Epicureans loosed hysterical guffaws. Their laughter echoed off the lake again and through stone arcades that lined garden paths surrounding the restaurant.

"I love this young man, I truly do!" announced Signor Sacco.

His face shone with pleasure. His candidate for chef of The Epicurean solstice feast proved as charming and skillful in his Veneto courtyard under a starry sky as he had been the night Signor Sacco discovered his talents in Verona months ago.

"He is very charming!" purred the Japanese John.

"Very charming!" Paul agreed, running a hand through the gold streak in his jet hair.

"Now ... we will see if he is the artist he claims to be," challenged Signor Sacco, offering a happy wink to all. His face beamed.

Course two arrived.

Chef Abati personally ... tenderly ... set down a lovely 18-karat gold tureen.

Its finely wrought handles – twin seahorses – gave the two Japanese guests all the information needed to identify it absolutely, positively, as a Botticelli. (The Nagasaki couple collected art, of course, including a notable Van Gogh.) The tureen, donated by Signor Sacco from his own collection, brimmed with savory fish stew – eel and succulent Adriatic oysters and chunks of white perch caught this very morning in Lake Garda. Abati's savory red broth made the meal authentically Italian, without question.

Faithful Stefan ladled while silent Ronaldo held a libation swaddled in linen. Each Epicurean received ... and savored ... two ample spoonsful, every man now consciously imagining the seductions of a beautiful partner with each careful bite.

Mr. Wood studied the servers in the candlelight. How old would Stefan be? He could not tell by any physical sign – the waiter's face bore lines and fissures like Dolomite granite. He might have been 30 or he might have been 60.

Ronaldo? A black man raised in Alabama with that physique might be playing cornerback on Sundays in the NFL. Or cutting grass with a borrowed lawn mower for his next gut-rotting bottle of Four Roses.

"Stefan, you've gained weight since December," said Mr. Wood gruffly. "You ever think of making friends with a salad bar?"

The server's face did not change.

"Thank you, sir. Your opinion matters enormously to me, sir."

Mr. Wood actually chuckled. Now he knew Stefan could tell a lie.

The server replied to other comments or requests pleasantly, if absent emotion. Stefan never missed a beat in his duties. The gigantic hands that used a garrote so expertly six months ago tonight managed dishes and cutlery without the clink of a single utensil.

The gigantic hands
that used a garrote so
expertly six months ago
tonight managed dishes
and cutlery without the
clink of a single utensil.

Ronaldo, lustrously black, handsome as a movie star, stepped forward to pour a perfect white surprise, a *spumanti*, to complement the stew. This playful pairing deliciously cooled lips flecked by red pepper, and it deepened the ocean flavors.

With the prosciutto polenta, Chef Abati had also served a perfect champagne, a little fizzing shallow in five stone cups. Those stone cups, Signor Sacco explained, first belonged to a 16th-century Sacco forebear who made his way out of Venice with stolen textiles to create a great, enduring estate. The Sacco line did all sorts of things. Signor Sacco went into precious metals because as a child his mother had told him a bedtime story and at the end mentioned how much she would love a son who possessed a true Midas touch.

"*Molto bene! Molto bene, tutti!*"

Sparkling wine toasts went round. Abati reappeared, ghostly with his white toque in the clutching darkness.

The chef delivered his third presentation. It came on a small pine tray with a simple carved cedar lid.

"This dish," he announced with booming pride, "I learned from a small wooden house by the road in your place called Nashville. Mr. Wood, this kind of tiny house is call a … a shuck?"

"A shack."

The chef smiled.

"Yes! A shack! It was where they make one thing, just one thing. Hot chicken. That is, hot chicken to the tongue. Hot Nashville Chicken! So hot! It make me weep. I cry like the day my little puppy die when I am six."

Abati lifted the lid. One-inch squares, thin as a page from a Bible, glowed on the platter. Deep orange and purple-black, the geometric construct appeared to smolder like lava.

"I serve you NOT a hot crispy chicken skin, Nashville-style," Abati cried in a stage voice. "I treat you with hot crispy *hummingbird* skin! The skin of nectar-drinking *colibri!*"

The two Japanese blinked blankly at one another, impossible-to-read messages passing. The other Epicureans also exchanged glances.

By golly, this was something different …

Chef Abati nearly hovered in air with excitement.

"The orange pieces of the skin? I make it with Assam bhut jolokia, the ghost pepper. It is so very hot. The dark pieces of the skin … I season it with Hungarian black pepper, in my secret way. It is even *more* hot. *Hot like hell is hot!*"

The young chef eagerly scanned faces, watching reactions.

Now you're talking, Mr. Wood thought to himself.

Stefan plated Mr. Wood's tiny hallucinatory squares of bird skin using what appeared to be tweezers.

"Your tongues belong to ME … after this course," Abati boasted, a portrait of magnificent Italian confidence. "May you to weep like I did."

The Epicureans raised forks.

"Oh merde," Don Gaston moaned. "Oh holy mother of god."

Mr. Wood had never tasted anything like it. He prided himself on the insulation of his Deep South mouth, a connoisseur of capsicums, a fearless pepper-sauce man, a habañero breaker.

But … this …

The ghost pepper exploded sinuses like a napalm bomb. Liquids abandoned posts in every part of his head. Nerves screamed from his taste buds to the roots of his scalp.

Mr. Wood took long breaths. He slowly regained his aplomb. He blinked through a teary blur at his tablemates.

The two Japanese gentlemen were – what? Either kissing in a paralytic trance, or giving one another mouth-to-mouth resuscitation. Don Gaston clasped his hands in his lap and stared straight up at the sky. He gave hassling, whining breaths like some kind of Brazilian canine.

Signor Sacco sat unperturbed. The paired orange and evil-purple squares of hot hummingbird skin remained untouched on his plate.

A tear the size of a marble rolled down Mr. Wood's left cheek. His top lip shined with moisture. At first, he couldn't make his tongue and lips form words. Finally, after great effort, he pointed a fork at Signor Sacco's plate.

"You ... gonna eat that?" Mr. Wood managed to say.

The courses arrived with military precision – Italian military, not German.

Gianni Abati put on a show.

He showed tender mercy after his dragon-hot course. The searing proved him seer too – the taste buds of The Epicureans really did belong to Chef Abati now. Wholly. Outright.

Raw dishes, cool and welcome, came next.

Stefan served a platter of whimsical carved-cucumber sculptures – a bear, a lizard, a centaur, a grinning monkey. These roamed a fresh radicchio garden. The menagerie wore yellow yuzu jackets, their aromatic rinds out-fragrancing the lakeside garden's rosemary and summer roses for a few dizzy moments.

Next came a flight of small, artful, harvest-sheaves of clover and celery and dill, bound with a filament of edible Chinese silk. Roma tomato rounds followed with tiny shining eyes of tapenade from olives in Signor Sacco's groves on Ithaki. The Italian confessed he wanted to someday buy the island to develop an Odysseus Theme Park.

Chef Abati proudly placed down *strozzapreti* – literally, priest stranglers, commonly called gnocchi. The steaming potato dumplings rested so lightly in bowls they seemed about to float off into the thickening stars. Lavish dollops of edamame pesto held them earthbound.

A busy whispering erupted in the Nagasaki precinct across from Mr. Wood. The Alabamian glanced at Don Gaston and Signor Sacco. After a thoughtful pause, Sacco shrugged, dabbing pesto at one corner of his mouth with a rose-colored napkin.

"Mr. Wood," the Italian host suggested, "I don't speak Japanese well, but I believe these gentlemen are conducting business."

"True!" confirmed the Brazilian, who did speak Japanese. He spoke it well enough, in fact, to host Japanese military friends in São Paulo, who bought his weaponry. "They are discussing plans to market the green sauce on this dish."

Now that Mr. Wood understood, he could interpret the small, quick hands of John and Paul speaking a manual sign language of weights and measures, numbers, logistics.

For a time, the Japanese guests failed to realize all eyes watched them. Then John glanced up. Sheepishly.

"So very sorry," the Japanese gentleman explained. "Paul and I last month bought one of our country's most notable soy product manufacturers."

"John and I know a good idea," Paul added, pointing to his gnocchi, "when we taste one."

"If the Japanese don't like it," John smiled, "we'll sell it to Italians."

Another moment of laughter felt good. Straining stomachs welcomed a little jostling. Several courses along, the meal had fully commanded their attention. But The Epicureans wondered when things would, inevitably, hit a plateau in Abati's kitchen.

The chef dispelled their doubts.

Abati delivered five Waterford crystal shot glasses. Each sparkling vessel brimmed with warm golden nectar – honeysuckle liqueur, garnished with a mandarin orange twist.

"Where the hell did a joker from Italy get *honeysuckle?*" Mr. Wood marveled, not realizing he said it out loud.

"Honeysuckle ... is a jazz song?" Paul suggested, his Asian eyes big and brown in the candlelight. "Honeysuckle Rose?"

"Mr. Fats Waller!" declared John, perfectly pronouncing the double Ls ... and preening with self-congratulation after he did.

Showoff.

The man from Alabama found it hard to like the two showy Japanese.

Maybe, he thought privately, *it's because I spent several years shooting gooks in the jungle who looked like that. Then eating them.*

Mr. Wood tipped back the honeysuckle elixir.

His mind sailed back to boyhood in Lafayette, a time and place before the world intruded, before the molesting doctor and the Good Fridays that turned out so really bad for his dad and family, before the endless reveilles of military school, then the real military, and after that the endless reveilles of business.

Mr. Wood remembered a long-ago day.

He stood barefoot in a sandy ditch, the sun a nuclear blast, his eight-year-old body hugging the only cool shade on a stretch of country road. He recalled plucking white and yellow blossoms from massed honeysuckle vines, slapping bees away, carefully squeezing each soft petal for one single shining drop of nectar from the delicate stem.

That drop of honeysuckle juice tasted sweeter than any honey.

By God, Mr. Wood thought, thunderstruck, *by God this cat ... this Gianni Abati ... well, The Epicureans have surely run into a great chef here ...*

He lurched back from his reverie.

Abati's big laugh from the kitchen turned their heads.

A skinny feral cat scrambled wildly out the restaurant door, a stolen piece of hot hummingbird skin in its teeth.

That cat will be even skinnier tomorrow morning, Mr. Wood thought.

Presto! Stefan now appeared from the perfect soft night. He wafted down the newest enchantment.

The Epicureans marveled at porcini and formaggio 'cigars'. Five smoky rolled mushroom vessels bubbled aged gorgonzola cheese – the aroma alone pleased The Epicureans tremendously. It paired with a thrilling Riesling.

Clever chef.

The Epicureans understood Abati's subtle message. They devoured the sizzling 'cigars'. Then five tipsy gentlemen rose and repaired to soft Adirondack chairs under an arcade by the garden.

Ronaldo deftly offered cured Turkish cigars, long thin instruments of pleasure barely the width of a pinkie. The sweet, unusual tobacco might have been the softest in his mouth Mr. Wood ever tasted.

The arcade overlooked the black mirror of Lake Garda. Stars burned. The snowy top of Monte Baldo was black ice. Clusters of light mapped the lake shoreline where Malcesine and other villages quietly settled to sleep.

The Epicureans breathed good scents from strange mountains – fragrances of alpine cedar and wild oregano and pine. Palates freshened and appetites rejuvenated.

"These are cured," explained Signor Sacco, holding up his cigar, "in a cave with walls holding prehistoric paintings. The human figures are all red. The important ones appear to be smoking tobacco."

The Epicureans rested for some time. Three of the cohort, Japanese and Brazilian, eventually milled about the garden, too full of bonhomie and merry spirits to sit for long. Left to themselves, Mr. Wood and Signor Sacco rose too and made off to a solitary spot by marble steps.

The stair was historic, Roman, the stones possibly set under an emperor's direct supervision. (This same notorious emperor, Signor Sacco explained, invited senators who might challenge his power to his villa here ... then burned them alive in the house as they slept.) The great steps descended to Lake Garda, where boats now boarded and unboarded tourists.

The pale stairway glowed with captured daylight. Lost in their own thoughts, neither man spoke.

Finally a star fell, its fiery trail reflected.

"Make a wish, Sacco."

The Italian host remained quiet a moment.

"Do you know," he sighed, "what the eternally damned Mohammedans say?"

Mr. Wood waited.

"They say that whenever Satan appears on the earth, Allah hurls down a blazing star from heaven to drive him back down into Hell."

"Do you think," Mr. Wood asked after a pause, "we should go indoors?"

They both chuckled.

They shared great secrets.

What dish could possibly follow fire and fine tobacco?

Leave it to a gifted young chef.

Arctic char steamed on bone china. They swam in a nimbus of Irish clotted cream flavored with garlic and ... well, who knew what embellishments Abati threw in?

Paper-thin circles of freshly sliced Sorrento lemon scalloped the platter.

Mr. Wood found the next dish curious. Ramp vichyssoise, morseled with carrot and millet and miniature spring greens.

By now, Mr. Wood had assumed that Chef Abati's dishes would grow more robust, more entrée and less appetizer, less second plate.

Had genius stumbled?

Hardly. With the arrival of the very next dish, the ramp vichyssoise instantly made sense.

Stefan uncovered – *ta-da!* – a pan-roasted halibut.

Perfect, Mr. Wood realized. We go here at lakeside from arctic char, a strong seared fish, to another fish, more gentle, a deeper dive. The stepping stone down to this milder pelagic dish would naturally be liquid. Mr. Wood realized the vichyssoise served as a sort of sorbet of soups, cleansing palates to set up a fine-tasting surprise.

"Wonderful!" exclaimed Don Gaston, chewing the white flesh slowly. His knife and fork poised in an X over a flaky section. "We never get fresh fish so good in Brasília."

Abati overheard. He had popped from the kitchen, this time brandishing a glass eyedropper. He looked to Mr. Wood like a mad scientist with a test tube full of secret potion.

"With last taste of fish," the chef interrupted, "the beautiful woman deserves one special extra jewel!"

Exuberantly, kidlike, over the left shoulder of each guest, Abati tipped the eyedropper. He colored the white fish flesh with an infinitely small dark drop of ... what?

The Epicureans waited for explanation. Mr. Wood realized with more than a little amazement that the young chef was playing them all like five fine fiddles, five Stradivarii.

"Licorice!" Chef Abati announced, mischievously.

The young man in the white toque and black ponytail scuttled back to his glowing kitchen before questions peppered him.

"Licorice?" Paul asked this, his eyes the widest they'd been all night. "*Licorice?*"

It crossed Mr. Wood's mind yet again that the Asian had pronounced the word twice simply to show off again his English command of the letter 'L'.

"Licorice?" parroted John. "For halibut?"

Mr. Wood shrugged. "This kitchen magician hasn't taken a false step so far."

It came as a huge surprise. With the ramp vichyssoise and first clean bites of halibut, Chef Abati had transformed mouths into clean canvases. The taste buds were now perfectly prepared for the sweet, thick darkness of licorice, spiced ever-so-slightly with Aztec chocolate, married to the steaming white meat of an ocean fish.

"Unbelievable!" someone gasped.

It didn't matter who uttered the word. It might have been everyone at once.

Down the lake, bells tolled again.

Stefan shimmered up. He lifted yet another serving lid, silver like a bell itself and making a slight hum as it left the tray.

Mr. Wood almost burst out laughing. Fifteen small dark gnarled objects the size and appearance of cicadas lay before them.

What on earth? Snails? Exotic insects? Some unexpected something *en papier marron?*

Chef Abati cleared his throat behind them. He bit his lip, eyebrows arched, looking like he might absolutely pop with self-amusement. He glanced directly at Mr. Wood.

Another homage to the Deep South.

"Fried pork skins," Mr. Wood announced, looking at each Epicurean around the table. He then made light of his Alabama roots, adding, "Y'all slap me nekkid and hide my clothes!"

"*Si! Bene! Bene!*" exulted Abati, not understanding the sarcasm at all. "Chicharrones!"

Salty. Crunchy. Spiced just right with some laterite of red pepper. Sweet and oily and totally unexpected at this point in their meal.

Dish fourteen surprised them nearly as profoundly.

This time, Stefan and Ronaldo brought four serving platters from the kitchen. Chef Abati carried a fifth.

Servers set the dishes down as one, a gesture clearly choreographed for maximum drama.

Presto!

Each plate held fourteen perfect loose pearls of Israeli couscous, these carefully arranged on the plate to form actual numerals: 14.

Around these couscous globes, glabrous as the wax dripping down the table candles, spread fourteen separate daubs of pure color, red to green to blue, a rainbow array. Stefan produced tiny skewers, little devil pitchforks. The Epicureans would spear the couscous orbs, dredge them through the palette of flavored hues, then transport fourteen separate and distinct oral pleasures to their waiting lips.

"I give you fourteen sauces made in summer Italian vegetables," Abati announced. "My palettes ...
for your palates."

Hilarious. Glorious.

English pea. Roasted red pepper, orange pepper, green pepper, purple pepper, white pepper. Roasted spiced cucumber, of all things, and pungent leek and some other pearl-colored onion-like root that Mr. Wood had never seen. Zucchini, two-toned, yellow with green, and corn puree and roasted eggplant and artichoke. And, as always, a surprise among the surprises: *foie gras*, the most delicious and distinct taste.

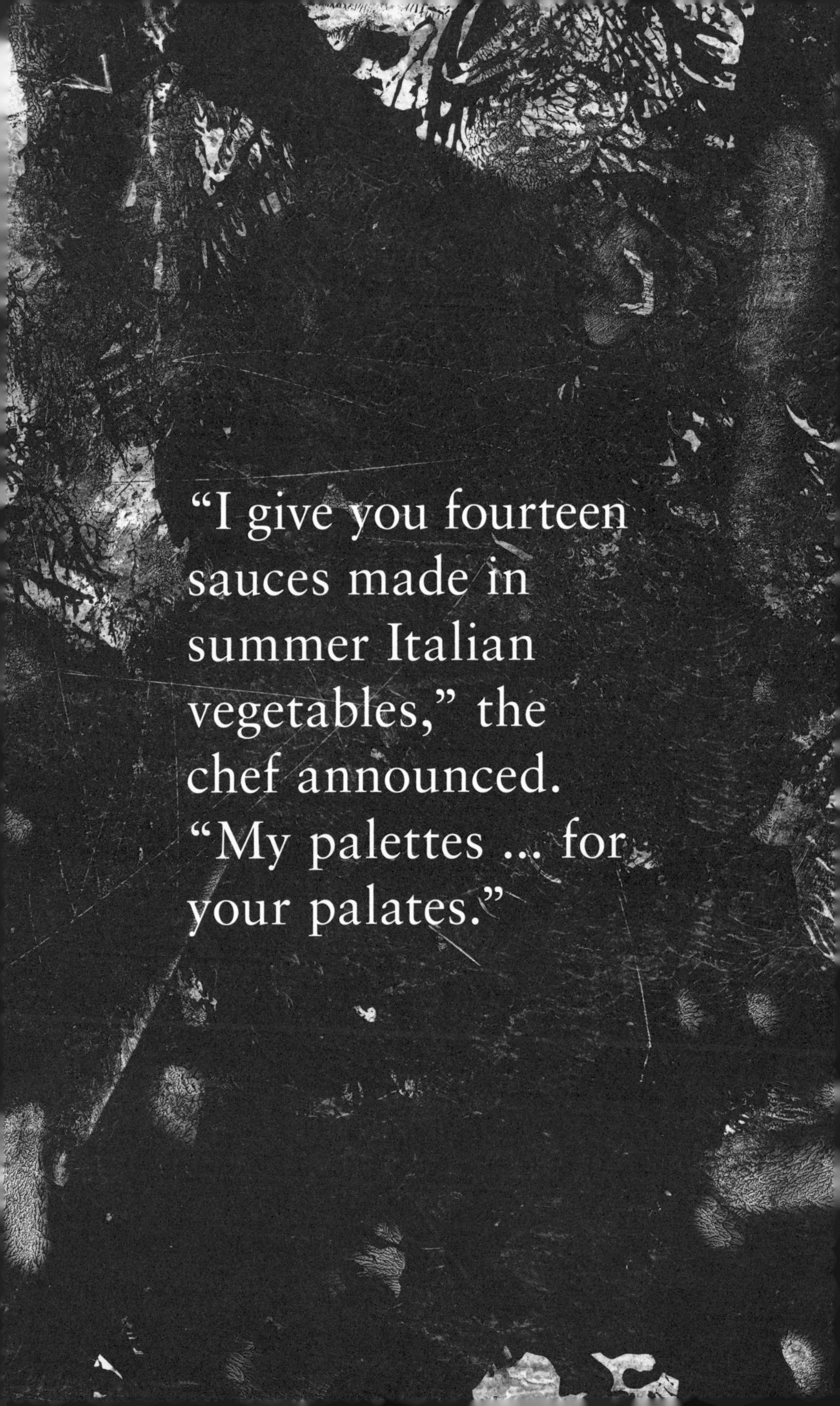

“I give you fourteen sauces made in summer Italian vegetables,” the chef announced. “My palettes ... for your palates.”

"I see you faces. You ask: Chef Abati, is goose liver a vegetable in Italy?" A roguish smile leaped to the cook's face again. "Tonight ... it *is!*"

The buttery texture and strong taste of the organ meat suggested to Mr. Wood, and all the other Epicureans, a hint of darkness, a winter solstice, a long, very memorable night to come.

"Holy smoke," sighed Mr. Wood.

"Jesu, Giuseppe, and Maria," nodded Don Gaston, eyes closed, chewing thoughtfully.

Signor Sacco watched in perfect silence, implacably pleased.

"Fucking ..." said John, pronouncing it like the name of a Japanese city.

"... A!" finished Paul.

The table cracked up. The Epicureans giggled like kids.

Chef Abati! Gianni Abati passed the test! He would cook a solstice meal!

"But not this year," emphasized Mr. Wood at that moment. He added, in a low voice. "This year, I've got a bigger surprise."

It hardly mattered what floated next from the magical Italian night onto the checkered tablecloth.

The baby swan came with an ambergris of mint jelly, like traditional roast lamb. (The two golden-skinned fowl artfully lay in a little nest of shredded carrot and fried ginger.)

The brandy-infused yogurt stopped conversation ... then sparked it again for a hearty discussion about a hidden layer of juniper salt. That very unusual taste pierced expectations, paving, yet again, a smooth path to the next plate.

For that, Abati burned, just right in a frying pan, a whole young mountain rabbit, with spring onions softened to translucence in its bubbling fat.

Stefan set down a roast elephant garlic, a little steaming mosque delicately balanced atop a weave of string-thin fried potatoes.

The roasted Sicilian wild boar piped with aromas – the chef served it with a stinging *salsa verde* of three wild forest greens.

Steamed spears of white asparagus arrived in a splay, bedded on soft red seaweed that the chef boiled exactly two seconds in the same water used to steam the phallic asparagus shafts.

Ronaldo paired different wines with every course. Sweet wine, tart wine, transparent wine, cheerful red wine.

After the asparagus-fern dish, The Epicureans traded glances again. Had the evening crested? What now?

Abati answered commandingly. Crusty ciabatta points spread with veal marrow arrived with three golden drops of edelweiss honey spooned on by fastidious Stefan.

Mr. Wood ate and ate. The portions and blends Abati presented dovetailed, blended, synchronized in the belly as beautifully as the mind. Mr. Wood felt roaringly eager for each next course, excited to feel the soft detonations of taste buds, the flood in his pleasure center.

His strange pleasure center.

Abati came from the kitchen again with neither platter nor plate. He wished simply to check progress, he said.

The two Japanese took this occasion to rise together and stand by their chairs with glasses raised. They sang, very tipsy now, in perfect harmony, in their Beatles suits and haircuts:

We love you ... yeah, yeah, yeah.
We love you ... yeah, yeah, yeah ...
... yeahhhhh!!!

John and Paul hit the famous closing seventh in perfect harmony. Amazing. *Especially from two nipping Nipponese*, Mr. Wood thought.

What next? Abati vaulted the table, nimble, quick, right over the candlesticks. He never made a flame flicker.

The young chef embraced both Japanese gentlemen in a bear hug and lifted both, legs wriggling, off the ground.

Signor Sacco leaned to Mr. Wood. He spoke *sotto voce*. "He played the beautiful sport. Striker, Italian national team. Our chef's the most eligible bachelor in northern Italy."

"Bravo!" cheered Signor Sacco. "Well done, John and Paul!"

The boys from Nagasaki blushed with pride and alcohol. Their boyish fun swept everyone up, raising the memorable pleasure of a night on Lake Garda.

The meal now turned to its final act: Cheeses. Desserts.

Chef Abati paired a brilliant and brilliantly named Brillat-Savarin cheese with an unholy Champagne, such a rascal in a bottle that even Stefan, with all his expertise, had trouble keeping bubbles from exploding over the lip of the flutes. The blocky server actually laughed, uncharacteristically, at his bumbling.

"Our French Champagne," remarked Don Sacco dryly, "seems quite excited to see us."

Another cheese appeared, a foul thing from Sardinia, a rotted milk block with maggots. It delighted the table. The Epicureans spread wiggling smears of Casu Marzu on fresh baguettes hot from the oven.

The party chewed blissfully for minutes, some with eyes closed.

Death odor fumed from their nostrils.

Champagne fixed that. The liquid transcended the filth of the world, wiped corruption clean. It purified, sanctified. Why not serve Champagne like this in churches, for communion?

Had he ever had a meal so good? Mr. Wood asked himself. *No. Except maybe one hand-prepared, in the Adirondacks long ago …*

Mr. Wood made a vow. He slipped his hand into his pocket, felt the key to the Lamborghini. He would hand that key to Chef Abati at the end of the night.

The young chef could enjoy this blazing-fast gift all his blazing-fast life.

The Epicureans took the next course, a communal bowl of toasted walnut, mint leaf, and puffed wild rice. The fresh herb and nutty savors gently pleased their mouths – mouths that had gone through a hard day's night with scores of flavors, spices, heats, and sauces. A wormy cheese. A late cool bath of Champagne.

One of the party stood now, glass raised.

"We happy few! We band of diners!"

John? Or Paul? Who the hell could tell? Quoting poetry?

"Shakespeare!" Don Gaston announced happily, raising his own glass. "Henry five."

Mr. Wood rose and raised his own glass. He gave a toast.

Shakespeare!
Kick 'im in the rear!
Hit 'im in the head with a bottle of beer!

The Epicureans laughed so hard they knocked things off the table.

From nowhere, a white terrier puppy appeared, barking madly, astonished by the uproar and all the strangers. The dog danced on its hind legs, howling, mixing in with the merrymaking. Even Signor Sacco's great mantel of dignity finally fell away – he brayed like a mountain donkey, his rose-silk napkin clapped over his mouth.

Hilarity threatened to kill them altogether when the little terrier found a big chunk of the Sardinian maggot cheese that Don Gaston accidentally elbowed off the table. The dancing white dog delightedly rolled in the crumbling, smelly mess, howling with happiness like the humans.

"Shakespeare! Kick 'im in the rear!"

The toast, perfectly parroted by Paul, sent partner John seismic again. He shot his last sip of expensive Champagne straight out his nose. It misted Mr. Wood.

Oh, the gales of Garda! The howls of a summer solstice night!

Woof! Woof! Woof woof!

The terrier barked fiercely at the cheese now. It just seemed to realize that it swarmed with tiny white worms.

At last, after many minutes, the table settled, exhausted.

The kitchen looked like the warm lights of home a traveler sees in the distance. Inside, Abati's head briefly vanished into a black oven. He emerged straining, pads protecting both hands. He held a clay roasting container with a plain orange lid and charred base.

"*La ultima!*" Abati called, this time in Spanish.

The last. Maybe, hell, the ultimate too, thought Mr. Wood.

Abati approached.

He carried the heavy clay pot alone.

Behind him, gliding slowly forward like ghosts, came two hooded figures

Leftover laughter stopped cold.

A church bell tolled.

Don't those hunchbacks ever stop pulling the damn ropes? Mr. Wood wondered.

Mr. Wood also heard a new sound.

It came from baskets of scarlet begonias hung in the arcades.

Peeping. Baby birds.

Why are baby birds awake at night? Mr. Wood wondered. *What woke them? Laughter? That barking dog? That goddamned church bell?*

The baby birds cried.

The terrier trotted to a spot directly beneath a basket. The puppy fixed a keen eye on the begonias, once standing on hind legs. It looked like a white monkey.

Abati reached the table.

The lid of the roaster allowed a plume of steam to escape. The clay pot itself glowed with heat, dull red.

Behind Chef Abati, the two shrouded figures stood back from the table, beyond the candlelight. They were fearsomely mute.

They wore hoods, The Epicureans could now see. White cloth. These had the shape of macabre birds, pale combs on top, long proboscises. Large and solemn eyes stared.

Peep! Peep!

The baby birds seemed desperate.

Mr. Wood felt strange.

"As my *amicos* Stefan and Ronaldo demonstrate us," Abati announced, now gesturing to the maskers, "it is tradition that our last course be eaten under hood or veil."

He let suspense build.

"This is so God cannot witness our indescribable earthly pleasure as we taste this dish."

Signor Sacco, so impassive and restrained all night, suddenly sat forward.

"Ortolan?" he stammered. "This is ortolan?"

Chef Abati smiled a most charitable smile. He placed one pad atop the clay roaster.

"Si, Signor Sacco! *Ortolan.*"

Abati announced it simply, the way a priest says *amen* at the end of a prayer.

Curiosity traveled from one Epicurean to the next. *Ortolan? What was ortolan?*

Signor Sacco turned his lean, handsome face to the candlelight.

"Such a tiny bird," he whispered, his eyes far away. "A warbler. A little song maker. The length of – let me see your hand, Don Gaston – yes, the length of our Brazilian friend's thumb. Only so big. But ..."

Signor Sacco grasped for words.

"... the ortolan has grown very rare now," he said. "That is because, some say, the ortolan is the most delicious food on earth. They say it is the last meal a dying man should ever eat, since nothing else will ever taste so good."

Except our winter solstice feast ... thought Mr. Wood.

"Stefan? Ronaldo? You will do the honor?"

Abati beckoned his servers forward. Now Mr. Wood could see that the bird men carried other white cloth hoods in their hands, big baggy soft things like shed skins. Eyeless.

Ronaldo handed a simple hood not much different from a white flour sack to Mr. Wood.

"Your instructions," Chef Abati announced.

Every eye turned.

"You each will be serve one ortolan. You eat in one bite. When you put it in mouth, under mask, hold head with you fingers and bite it off and place head back on plate. You slow, thoughtful, with great respect, taste the whole rest of ortolan. Taste the bone. Taste the juice. Taste the organs. Chew and chew. You will taste flavors, good flavors, bursting out from places in a magic bird as long as you chew. That ... is ortolan."

Signor Sacco leaned forward, hood dangling from his right hand.

"One more word, Maestro Abati?"

The chef nodded, a blush of color in his young cheeks.

"The ortolan can only be caught by net," Signor Sacco told The Epicureans. "It does not touch the ground."

The Italian host paused for a moment, and Mr. Wood saw that his eyes searched for something far away in his memory.

"When I was a boy, I saw the ortolan fly with others of its kind, so many in the flocks they would fill up the bare almond trees like leaves. Singing leaves."

Signor Sacco took a breath.

"After hunters capture them in nets," he said, "they put the ortolan in a clean cage ... under a hood or a blanket. They don't know night from day. That way, they eat oats and millet constantly, many kilograms, day after day. Until they grow very fat and succulent."

Don Sacco paused, turned to Abati.

"In old times, the chefs put out their eyes. The ortolan. We are more civilized, *e vero?*"

"*Si, Signor Sacco. E vero.*"

"When the ortolan is plump," resumed Signor Sacco, "it is drowned. In Armagnac. That fragrant brandy fills the bird's lungs and its insides. It is a wonderful flavor, they say. I have never had ortolan until this night."

Mr. Wood watched Paul, across from him, scribbling notes on his palm with a gold pen.

Chef Abati smiled broadly. Everyone looked his way, though he hadn't spoken a word.

"These ortolan," he said, "I catch with my own hand. I fed and soaked and plucked and roasted them. I have tried my best to make them sing their ultimate song for you tonight."

He opened the clay roaster.

The birds lay like plump little school children in dormitory beds, snug, forever safe.

The Epicureans donned white silk hoods.

Mr. Wood felt the shuffle of Stefan and Ronaldo as they moved about serving the final course. The hood muffled sounds, though not entirely.

"You are served," Chef Abati announced. "You must use only your hands for this course. It will be followed by one more taste – a sorbet made with Signor Sacco's own blood oranges. *Buon appetito.*"

The hoods were white, but the darkness inside them was total. Nothing existed but smell and taste. Purity.

Mr. Wood lifted the little aromatic bird from his plate – it had just the weight and size of an Ajwa date wrapped in bacon – and brought the bite underneath his billowy hood.

He saw a flash of light. He felt a caress of cool air.

He suddenly remembered a story he read in some long-ago book, back in a childhood when reading and stories seemed more real than the real world.

On some shelf in his elementary-school library, he found the tale of that lost traveler, Odysseus. He remembered a Cyclops in a cave, blinded by a hot poker, forever hungry, groping around with gigantic fingers in the darkness to catch and eat savory little Greeks, one by one.

Mr. Wood waited, delaying gratification.

He heard the surprised sounds of his party putting ortolans into their mouths.

Gasps. Small cries.

Don Gaston distinctly moaned. Mr. Wood wasn't sure, but … was Signor Sacco sobbing under his hood?

He heard one other sound.

The baby birds. In the dark arches of the villa.

Their cries grew weaker.

Mr. Wood shut one eye and opened his mouth like a giant.

He ate.

—23—

Faded Photographs

Elmore looked in on Will and Mary, two distinct lumps under a thin bedsheet. The children could have been sleeping storybook figures covered by snow.

They liked to get in the same bed, and Elmore didn't make it a big deal. Let the twins be twins another year or two. They slept nine months together inside Kelly, after all.

Kelly.

Elmore had the news.

Dan Neeley called Elmore privately from a pay phone. Elmore had no clue why. Blaring traffic twice interrupted their talk.

Elmore had hung up the phone in shock.

On the counter, two paper plates covered in crumbs sat by an open picnic basket.

No gingerbread men had survived.

The news jammed Elmore's head. Constant loop: *Hospital. Attempted suicide. Intensive care. Constant monitoring.* Neeley's report sounded clinical, legal.

Elmore sorted through feelings at the kitchen table.

He hated that he still loved Kelly so.

He should have spoken kindly.

At The Milky Way, Will and Mary stared at their mom with such love in their eyes. Kelly looked … haunted. Terrible and beautiful.

Why didn't he give Will and Mary time with her? Instead, he spoke cruelly. He made Kelly fly recklessly into the night in that green piece of junk.

Then the Lafayette High School class beauty, the All-American girl next door … Mrs. Kelly Bellisle Rogers … jumped off the Black Warrior trestle.

Elmore hurt Kelly so bad she wanted to … *die.*

He could barely make himself think the word. He squeezed his eyes.

Kelly wanted to die.

Thank God she lived. Thank God.

Elmore entertained an impulsive thought of rousing the kids and driving the old panel truck, fast, to Lafayette General. The kids would save Kelly.

Then he remembered Neeley's admonition. No one would see Kelly "until the danger passed". Not legal authorities. Not Elmore. Not mother, father, children, preacher, friend. No one but doctors.

Until the danger passed.

Kelly wanted to die.

Elmore couldn't stand it.

Kelly jumped off a bridge.

All those struggling years, Kelly with terrible depression, mad with colicky babies and a blown-up bitter husband, everyone in diapers but her, she never jumped off a bridge.

Elmore vividly imagined, complete with vertigo, a final step off a trestle into thin air. A terrifying fall through blackness. To more blackness.

Elmore felt despair.

Oh, God help her!

He wanted whiskey. Now.

For a goddamned reason.

Elmore broke. He sobbed, gasped air, sobbed louder. He hung his head and bitterly wept, thumping the table with a helpless hand.

He once saw Kelly weep this way.

He'd landed from Iraq, with other walking wounded. Crab-wise, first one good leg forward, then the other in a full plaster cast, he stumped down a ramp on a military plane.

He wore his dress uniform. Dressing in it was the most painful thing he'd ever done.

She waited in the sun, black hair blowing, at the end of the ramp with other military wives.

A bundle flailed in each arm.

Kelly had come to welcome Elmore home.

Broken. Ruined.

He hobbled. Kelly hoisted the babies. She seemed to smother them against her breast. Tears streamed down her face.

The twins cried too. His Will and his Mary.

Hurrying, Elmore stumbled. A G.I. escort flanked him for support, but Kelly had distracted them. Her storybook face.

Elmore fell. The steel ramp rose, sickeningly fast. Three small gifts in white paper and red bows scattered.

Kelly screamed.

Elmore's face banged hard, and he went to sleep.

He never delivered his gifts.

They disappeared, like so much else.

Elmore rose from his sad seat in the kitchen. He went back to his bedroom closet.

A squeaky wooden chair became a ladder. Elmore grimaced – his ribs still hurt sometimes, all these months after Christmas Eve.

From the closet's top shelf, Elmore brought down two items – a sloshing half bottle of Ezra Brooks and a small blue shoebox. Elmore studied the bottle carefully to see if cloudy algae grew in it after so many years.

He stepped carefully to the floor. His knee popped. He left the chair in place, worried he might wake the twins by moving it again.

At the kitchen table, he sat for a very long time with the lights off and the cap unscrewed from the whiskey bottle. The smell of alcohol made his head swim.

Kelly jumped off a bridge.

He lit a white candle the Rogers family kept for nights they lost power.

He opened the shoebox.

A wedding photo of Kelly Bellisle smiled up at him.

Oh. That face. Those eyes.

Without taking his eyes from Kelly, Elmore reached for the bottle and raised it in one motion to his lips.

He drank, deep and long.

The liquor burned his tongue, burned his throat. It burned his insides too, and it burned still more as the alcohol spread in his gut.

Elmore burned.

The white candle burned.

Whiskey changed the room.

Changed time.

Elmore lay on a bed in the apartment behind Kelly's parents' home. He couldn't remember what happened to his wedding band after the roadside explosion.

He opened his left hand again and again, trying to remember, trying to forget.

When he wet and dirtied himself, Kelly changed him. She sat on Elmore's bed and fed him with a baby spoon, opening her mouth *ahh* when Elmore opened his for bites.

As Kelly fed Elmore, Will and Mary cried in their bassinets. Cried and cried.

Elmore slept, wounded dreams. The babies cried and cried.

Elmore woke sometimes in terrible pain. He anxiously wondered where Kelly had gone. He called. Kelly hurried in, her eyes tired.

Elmore tried to make sense of her words, shaking his head to clear it.

What did she mean? *Postpartum depression?* What was lithium?

Kelly cried, laying her head on Elmore's bandaged torso. She sobbed medical words: *Psychosis. Side-effects of birth trauma. Electro-cerebral shock therapy*. She moaned other words: *Sad. Tired. Overwhelmed.*

She never said the babies' names.

Elmore tried to understand with a wheel of fire in his head and a dripping bag hung from his gut and a cast to his waist. He tried.

The twins cried and cried.

The liquor burned Elmore's tongue, burned his throat. It burned his insides too, and it burned still more as the alcohol spread in his gut. Elmore burned.

Elmore ate drugs too. White pills. Blue pills. Red and orange and green and black pills. They made him go to sleep, at least. Thank God he could sleep. Sometimes, he lay wide awake. Scared to death of the next explosion.

Kelly never slept at all.

The twins cried and cried.

Kelly came to hold Elmore, tried to make love to him.

It hurt him so bad.

She flipped her black hair back, wiped her mouth. Elmore could see disappointment in her eyes.

He felt like screaming. Maybe he did scream.

You don't know how it is! Did you ever see your own guts hang out! Did you ever see your bone stick through your skin! It hurts me, Kelly! I HURT!

Kelly chewed the ends of her hair like a scolded little girl. The twins cried in the next room.

She told Elmore something. Important. But the military machinery and the pain and the drugs in his goddamn aching head roared too loud.

Did Kelly say, '*I hurt too, Elmore*'?

He took another long pull from the bottle.

Kelly brought the twins to injured Elmore.

They cried and cried.

He took them clumsily in his bandaged arms. He tried to feel what fathers feel. As they howled, he only felt pain and a wheel of fire in his head.

Kelly watched him cluck and try. He couldn't bend his neck enough to kiss the tops of their soft little heads.

Kelly burst into tears, like the babies.

What was the matter with her? Why couldn't Kelly get her shit together? He needed her now. Couldn't Kelly see the fear he felt? The pain? The terrible trouble he faced?

Elmore stared at the white candle on the kitchen table.

He tipped the whiskey bottle again. He gasped. Tears burned his eyes again.

He felt stinging now in his right side. The liver. A million vengeful vultures. The whiskey had reached his bad spots. It would only get worse.

To hell with it.

Elmore took another hard swallow. The candle flame flared very bright.

From the shoebox, Elmore lifted another thing. Private.

Her panties smelled like perfume. The fancy French kind. And like Kelly.

She sent the lacy thing a week after Elmore reached Iraq.

Kelly jumped off a bridge.

Elmore drew breath, a sudden sob. He knotted the dainty underthing in one fist and held it to his nose and cried so hard he had trouble keeping quiet.

He couldn't wake the twins like this.

Elmore got up, swaying, and lurched to the back door. He fumbled with the knob – he saw two knobs now.

He clumsily stumbled out into the hot night.

A big buck deer was in the yard. It stared straight at him. Head raised. A huge rack.

The magnificent animal stood stock still. It stared for a long time at Elmore, then bolted, vanishing into the night.

Elmore took a quick step to race after it. Go with it.

The world lurched. Elmore fell.

Kelly jumped off a bridge.

Dan Neeley, Lafayette's newest police officer, stood close to Elmore, speaking confidentially.

Elmore couldn't believe the words.

She left them in the car, Elmore. Three-years-old, locked in the back seat. A car can get hotter than a stove. It's lucky somebody saw 'em. They're getting fluids at Lafayette General. We'll take you there in a few minutes. You'll see they're okay. Mostly okay.

Elmore stood thunderstruck.

Outraged.

He and Kelly had split a miserable year after he came marching home.

Limping home.

Elmore took the twins some weekends, though he wasn't very good at it. Little babies need a mommy.

Kelly stayed with the Bellisles. People hardly saw her.

Officer Neeley continued talking to Elmore.

We've got her in custody. Found her in back of the dime store with the stuffed toys. Bears and rabbits and monkeys, all kinds. She had 'em down off the shelves, sitting around her like in a classroom or something. Talking to 'em. Tellin' 'em not to cry, not to cry. When we took her, she resisted. Yelled about the stuffed toys. We had to put her in cuffs.

Elmore and Dan Neeley stood on the sidewalk in front of Woolworths. Downtown Lafayette. Blazing hot.

Kelly needs help pretty bad. You just go home and get the house ready. You're the father. You'll be the one taking care of the twins now. That's the way the law works.

Kelly's green VW rested at the curb, doors wide open. Yellow police tape fenced it off.

Neeley spoke again.

There will be criminal charges. Leaving kids in a hot car is attempted murder, by the law. The district attorney's on this already.

Elmore had no words.

She's in bad trouble, Elmore. She walked away from this car and went in the dime store and left two little babies in the back seat. Her life just changed. Not for the better, I'm sad to tell you. And yours changed too.

"How do I take care of two babies?" Elmore stammered. "Danny, I barely can take care of myself right now."

Neeley had no answer at first, then he cleared his throat. "You'll figure it out, buddy."

From the Woolworths windows, people stared at the policeman and the other man and the VW.

"What about her car?" Elmore knew it sounded stupid as soon as he said it.

The car is evidence, Officer Neeley said. *It will be exhibit A.*

Elmore felt the blazing sun.

Exhibit A?

Elmore, do us both a favor? All three of us a favor?

Elmore nodded. His head hurt. Like always.

Whatever you do ... do NOT look in the back seat of that car ...

Elmore turned immediately.

On the window glass, he saw a child's perfect handprint. In puke. A tress of red hair stuck in it.

Enough, El. Don't look any closer. The little things got sick in there, and pulled out all their hair, suffering so. Don't be shocked when you see 'em at General. Come on now.

What? What did Neeley say?

The policeman took Elmore by one arm, like an old man. He guided him from the green Volkswagen toward the police cruiser.

Elmore didn't open his eyes on the drive to the hospital.

Elmore woke on his back.

The sun had climbed high in a Sunday sky. A pair of blue jays nagged from a pine tree. Elmore felt ... or imagined ... ants crawling under his clothes.

He summoned the willpower to turn over – *god, his insides hurt* – and then raise himself to his hands and knees. His head hung like a sick dog's.

Elmore puked out his guts. Loudly. Violently.

"Daddy?"

Will and Mary stood side by side in the back door. They watched their daddy, eyes huge.

Elmore wanted to speak, but no words came. Instead, he puked again until everything inside him lay splattered in the pine straw.

"Daddy, you need some medicine," Will said bravely.

"Don't be sick, Daddy," Mary said. "We don't know what to do if you get sick."

Elmore caught his breath. He managed to speak, finally.

"Everything's gonna be fine," he said. "I just got a little bug is all."

—24—

The Rock 'n' Roll Regiment

Elmore woke on top of the bedsheets, sweating. He'd slept till afternoon.

It took a while to sort things. He finally recognized two finger-paintings, Will's spider named Boris, and Mary's flower ... also named Boris.

He swung stiff legs to the floor. The faded T-shirt smelled of vomit. The house felt unpleasantly hot under his bare feet.

He remained motionless for a moment, temples pounding. He made out faraway sounds from Snake Creek, the cries of Indians on the warpath. Fort Rogers was lively.

With a grunt – pain stabbed his right side – Elmore heaved to his feet.

He made it as far as the bedroom door, gripping it until the ship righted. He could see the kitchen table. To his surprise, Will and Mary had cleared away ruins of the past night – whiskey bottle, melted candle, even the little Shoney's match book.

Jesus. Elmore hated that his kids saw that.

Over the commode, he wobbled. Burned. More than just his head wasn't right.

Elmore loosed a painful stream of urine, red as ketchup. Bloody. His damaged liver and kidneys were paying him back for the whiskey.

The sight of his own blood locked Elmore's knees. His head swam. He closed his eyes and clutched a towel rack.

When he flushed, the psychedelic swirl made him grab the rack a second time.

He breathed. He breathed.

He'd be okay. He'd been worse.

He'd died on a battlefield.

Clothing. Food. Shelter.

Elmore changed his shirt, cleaned up. He needed things normal. Uncomplicated. Simple.

An empty Sunbeam bread bag, an open jar of peanut butter and a sticky knife lay on the kitchen counter. Elmore checked the refrigerator, frowned. The empty whiskey bottle rested on one side on a rack. A mostly melted candle and Shoney's match book sat by it.

Elmore closed the door, hoping to trap inside it a guilty conscience.

He shook six aspirin into his palm, drank water from the sink faucet.

Elmore finally called the kids. In a few minutes, Will and Mary, racing bikes, burst through a cloud of butterflies.

Timmy Wragg trailed, the happiest rotten egg on earth.

Elmore resolved to be a better father than the one his twins found in the yard at 7 a.m.

The bike brigade rattled up.

"Will and Mary," Elmore ordered, like any normal day of life, "y'all run yonder and ask Mr. and Mrs. Wragg if Timmy can go to town with us. Tell 'em I'll feed everybody Colonel Sanders."

"Daddy and Mama ain't home," Timmy answered, breathless. "He's went to the National Guard. It's the Service for Servicemen day."

Elmore dimly remembered a piece of mail, a flyer he found weeks ago in the roadside mailbox. It mentioned some big politician and some big preacher and Miss Alabama visiting the Rock 'n' Roll Regiment to keep patriotic spirits high.

In a rare moment, Elmore felt a pang of nostalgia for his Guard buddies.

"Saddle up," Elmore ordered. "We're going to town."

The headquarters of the 44th Regiment of the Alabama National Guard shared a parking lot with a new Piggly Wiggly. As Elmore and the kids rumbled in, they saw scores of cars and pickups, and a display of mothballed tanks.

Elmore squeezed the panel truck into a space between two oversized SUVs decked out with American flag decals.

Soldiers streamed from the Quonset hut headquarters of the National Guard. The day's dignitaries were just departing, rotund men in suits and a woman in a green gown and silver crown. The trio boarded a white stretch limousine.

Hickory smoke flavored the air.

"Come on, y'all. It's late. Let's see if there's any food left."

They found a Champions BBQ food trailer. The broad-faced proprietor smiled from the window and flashed his gold tooth.

"Jus' closing up, folks. No ribs. Ain't but two chickens. No light bread neither."

Elmore handed over seven dollars.

"Those chickens, please. One for these young'uns of mine and one for Timmy Wragg."

Timmy beamed. *Lord*, Elmore thought, *this kid craves attention.*

Champion handed out two brown paper sacks, grease already darkening the sides.

"You keep that change," Elmore said.

"Every nickel counts," answered big Champion, smiling again. "Don't let them young'uns choke on a wishbone."

Elmore flashed his first smile of the day. “These ones chew right through bones, Mr. Champion. I think they were alligators in a past life.”

“Good-lookin’ kids,” Champion observed. “That red hair from they mama?”

Kelly. Kelly jumped off a bridge.

Elmore felt a punch in the gut.

“Our mama’s got black hair!” Will yelled. “We got red hair from vikings!”

“Real vikings!” Mary answered proudly.

Timmy took in this new revelation from Will and Mary with absolute awe.

“Y’all thank Mr. Champion for the chicken,” Elmore said. His insides throbbed.

They reached the front of the armory. Open doors let in the twilight cool, such as it was. Guardsmen from over at Aliceville came through, talking too loud for Elmore’s headache.

They ran face-to-face into Major Plum in a crisp starched uniform. Elmore didn’t recognize him at first. Plum looked different without a stub pencil behind his ear and a roll of house plans. He’d been foreman on Wood Castle.

“Elmore Rogers!” Plum remembered his first casualty of the Iraq deployment. “And the famous Rogers twins, Will and Mary. Timmy Wragg too.”

“Evening, Plum.”

“How you keeping, Elmore? Able-bodied?” Plum’s keen blue eyes x-rayed the wounded warrior up and down.

“Mostly. I work for Rankin now. Making ends meet.” Elmore lifted two sacks of barbecued chicken as proof.

“Glad to see you back here …”

Will interrupted.

“Daddy! A bazooka!”

Elmore turned to scold Will for rudeness, but Plum gave him a look. He wanted to talk.

“You young’uns go see that bazooka,” Elmore said, patting heads. “But … Will, you do not touch it. And Mary, you do not SHOOT it!”

They scrambled, Timmy too.

"Fine-lookin' kids," Plum commented.

"That ain't what you got to say."

Plum's blue eyes scanned Elmore again. He lowered his voice.

"Elmore, news is all over about Kelly. I want you to know I'm sorry."

Elmore looked down, nodded. He took a deep breath, said nothing.

"And Elmore, I want to apologize for what happened. Last Christmas. I tried to get you back with the crew. I went to Mr. Wood in person."

Elmore didn't answer.

"*Nobody* goes to Mr. Wood, Elmore."

"Well, Plum, I'm much obliged. That was a bad day for me."

"He's a hard man."

"I reckon."

Plum hesitated.

"I don't know why Mr. Wood has it in for you, Elmore. He knows a ton of personal stuff. Like ... everything. Kids. Kelly. Your dad's sick, right?"

"VA Hospital in Mobile."

"Well, Mr. Wood knows. Talking to him was like reading the Elmore Rogers encyclopedia."

Elmore took in the unsettling revelation. Now his head really hurt.

"Mr. Wood has a lot of secrets, Elmore," Plum said. "He built a mystery room in that castle. I've heard there's a secret hangar at Moundville where he keeps a jet."

Plum and Elmore saw guard buddies approach.

"Mr. Wood knows all about you, Elmore. I can't say why. But I thought you'd want to know."

He nodded thanks, but Elmore didn't know what to say.

"Oh ... and you never heard all that from me," finished Plum, his eyes narrowed. "Not a word. You and me only talk soldier stuff. Okay?"

"Yes SIR," said Elmore, and he gave a sharp salute. The motion hurt his side.

Then six or seven men of the old company mobbed Elmore, fist-bumping, pounding his back. The rowdy physical greeting hurt, but made him oddly happy.

"Elmore, you been AWOL!" shouted Bert Napoli. "You shoulda been here earlier for the preaching! You coulda been saved!"

"He got saved!" Tack Cornelius yelled. "Neeley did that! And the sawbones!"

The band of brothers told crazy stories. Hoke Perkins, the scrappy corporal, told about shooting a buzzard with a pistol in a Mosul firefight. Their tales happened months after Elmore went home, those days when he was nearly dying and Kelly was nearly dying and the twins squalled with colic like they were nearly dying.

War seemed like a pretty good adventure when you weren't in the middle of it, Elmore thought. Even if it left men ruined inside.

Eventually, folks drifted, one by one, back to peacetime life. Elmore felt a pang when he shook hands with Shawn Butler, who somehow got to rural Alabama by way of New Jersey. He remembered Shawn had learned to call square dances. A friend.

Time passed. The armory lights flicked. The facility would close to visitors in ten minutes.

The children returned. Timmy hadn't found his folks. The Wraggs had come and gone.

"Y'all hold these?"

Elmore handed over Champion's chicken. The kids sniffed the sacks like hungry wolves.

"El! Yo!"

Dan Neeley.

Elmore hadn't seen Neeley in his National Guard green for ages.

"Hey buddy!" Neeley said with a low whistle. "Look what the cat drug in. You okay?"

"If I was any better," Elmore lied, "you'd have to arrest me."

Neeley kneeled to kid level.

"How are you, Mr. Will? And Miss Mary? Y'all stayin' in trouble?"

The twins were confused. Sheriff Neeley didn't look the same as he had in the police car on Christmas Eve. Different uniform.

The band of brothers
told crazy stories.
Hoke Perkins, the
scrappy corporal,
told about shooting a
buzzard with a pistol in
a Mosul firefight.

"Those bicycles working out? Your daddy told me Santa surprised you last year. They still got wheels?"

"Yes sir!" answered Will.

"Yes sir!" Mary repeated.

"I got a bicycle too!" announced Timmy, his little face earnest.

"I know you do, Tim," said Neeley. "I'm Sheriff of Lafayette County, and my deputy and my spies tell me every time you ride those bikes on the wrong side of the road. Or break other rules. So DON'T!"

Neeley's voice thunderclapped. Elmore hid a smile. He couldn't remember the last time he saw Will intimidated. Clearly, uniformed authority carried great weight with him.

Neeley stood.

"A word with you, Elmore? Over here?"

Elmore sent the kids off to eat chicken. He and Neeley stepped over to the sheriff's civilian car, a restored Toronado. Conspicuous for a policeman, even off-duty.

"What's up, Danny?"

"A little further."

Weird, Elmore thought.

They strolled another moment.

"Listen, Elmore," Neeley finally said.

Elmore waited.

"Kelly's going to make a full recovery. I'll keep you up to date on her."

Elmore, surprised and hung over, told the truth.

"No doctor can fix what's wrong with Kelly. We know that by now."

"Time." Neeley spoke to the air, not Elmore. "Time might."

"Right. And love. And peace. And herbal tea. You're still sweet on her, Danny."

Neeley didn't react. He weighed his words instead.

"Look at those young'uns, El. They need a mama ... AND a daddy. You don't want 'em, when they grow up, to be broke inside like the rest of us."

Elmore felt his blood surge. "The rest of us? How the hell are you broke, Danny? You don't walk with a hitch. You ain't got pieces of sharp steel hurting inside you!"

"El, I work for Mr. Wood, right? I don't really work for the city of Lafayette. No use pretending."

"Uh-huh. Let me guess. You feel compromised?"

"Maybe."

"You ought to." Elmore couldn't hold it back. "You work for a bad man."

A thick silence passed.

"I been in two meetings in the last month with Mr. Wood," Neeley said. "Both times, he brought you up, Elmore. By name."

This second news bulletin of the night made Elmore's hairs stand.

"Why on earth?"

"El, he knows about everything and everybody in Lafayette. Shit – maybe the world. He knew about Kelly going to the Black Warrior trestle all those nights for years. He's the one who ordered Turnipseed to stand duty out there. Kelly would be drowned and dead otherwise."

Elmore asked the obvious.

"Well ... why? What's his interest in me, Danny? What does it mean?"

They shared a long look. Old friends. Old rivals.

"Hell if I know," Neeley said. "But you can bet your hide it ain't good, Elmore."

End of talk. Neeley clapped Elmore's back – *ouch!* – and hopped into the Toronado. The engine fired. Tires screamed. A stinking blue burned-rubber cloud blew off.

"Hey!" hollered Will at the departing car. "That's against the law!"

Elmore headed for the panel truck. The kids gnawed drumsticks in the cab.

Overhead, unseen, a surveillance camera atop the armory slowly swiveled to track Elmore Rogers.

—25—

Snake Creek

Elmore cruised home from work the next afternoon. Another day, another ration of sawdust. He never let on to the Rankin crew about searing pains on either side of his spine. He kept his eyes shut tight on bathroom breaks.

The kids rowdied in the cab, dripping red popsicles. Mrs. Mock put those in their hands as they burst out her front door. After Elmore accepted his stepmother's childcare offer for fall Fridays, she surprised him. She offered weekday childcare all summer too.

Elmore couldn't turn down free kiddy care. Mrs. Mock seemed to be trying her best too. Popsicles were proof.

Almost home now. Mary sang along with Dolly Parton on the radio, "9 to 5". Will held his head out the open truck window and happily closed his eyes.

Elmore would surely never pass muster as a religious man, but he did believe in Something.

He felt thankful for this truck and popsicles and his children and ... for poor Kelly. Kelly in the hospital.

He hurt to think of her, suffering.

Elmore loved her.

He felt grateful for everything that led to this moment of his life. Pain and all.

The kids scrambled, whooping, from the cab. Elmore eased his achy-breaky self down more slowly – *ouch, ouch, ouch*. He gimped through the front door the exact moment the back door flew open.

"Fort Rogers!" Will yelled urgently over his shoulder. He and Mary mounted bikes and pedaled furiously toward Snake Creek. "Indians on the warpath!"

"We're gonna KILL 'em!" Mary hollered.

Elmore didn't believe his ears. His little girl said *that*?

The twins disappeared into the woods in a flashing instant.

Elmore turned on the bathroom sink, splashing sawdust down a thirsty drain. He changed his T-shirt for a clean one. He felt better, if vaguely troubled by Mary's war cry.

How could a single dad raise a little girl into a civilized young lady?

Elmore stared into the vanity mirror at a hard fact.

He wasn't a mother.

Kelly is their mother.

Elmore actually said the name aloud.

Embarrassed, he dropped his eyes. Then he whispered again.

Kelly. What happened, Kelly?

He heard faraway whoops. The bobwhites. The wild children.

Kelly jumped off a bridge.

Elmore softly swore at himself under his breath.

She left them in a car. Will and Mary in a hot car. She tried to kill the twins, and she tried to kill herself. She'll kill you too, Elmore.

But Elmore looked in the mirror again, and the man staring back had hollow eyes.

Elmore needed company today.

He would visit Fort Rogers.

He made peanut-butter-and-jelly sandwiches. He remembered how Kelly always put the peanut butter and jelly on the same side, then patted the other piece of bread on top like a crown.

Kelly.

He set off for Fort Rogers with four sandwiches. He stopped abruptly to go back and close the back door. He'd left it standing wide open.

He needed to get a grip.

A jingling came up behind. Elmore turned to see Timmy Wragg tearing down the path on his gleaming fine Spyder bike, bound for Fort Rogers too. Bright plastic tassels fluttered from Timmy's handlebars, and baseball cards buzzed in his bicycle spokes.

He copied everything Will and Mary did.

"Hey, Mister Elmore!" Timmy yelled. He flew past, his face cherry red. "Come on! Indians are on the warpath!"

Timmy disappeared ahead, flashing in the sun.

The Indians would have a bad day today.

Elmore felt a lift. He saw white summer clouds in the blue sky. The air danced with insects. He could hear Snake Creek splashing ahead.

Elmore caught sight of the handsome, well-kept outpost. Fort Rogers stood under tall pines. Past it, the creek dashed between overgrown banks.

Nature called. Elmore rested the sandwiches on a blown-over oak trunk.

This would only take a minute.

He stepped into a thicket and unzipped. He fixed his gaze resolutely toward the creek and the woods beyond. He didn't want to see bloody urine again.

Ouch. It stung.

Then Elmore spotted something so strange that he forgot the pain.

If he'd never served in the military, Elmore might not have noticed a figure in the trees across the creek.

Literally, in the trees.

A stranger skillfully descended the lowest branches of a pine. The climber suspended his body, then nimbly kicked back from the trunk and dropped. A shower of pine bark followed.

He landed catlike, soundlessly.

The figure wore camouflage, same as a hunter wears in deer season. The jungle-warfare clothing covered arms, legs, hands. The climber even wore green-and-black camo paint.

What the hell?

In midsummer, the only thing a man in the woods of Alabama legally hunted was a patch of cool shade. A fellow had to be crazy out in the woods dressed like that.

Or up to something.

The property across the creek belonged to Mr. Wood. What didn't? Folks referred to timberland all around Lafayette as "Wood National Forest".

Elmore didn't care what happened on Wood property. Men worked there some days – marking timber, cutting fire lanes, control burning.

But the military gear.

Elmore heard laughter from Fort Rogers.

Was that guy ... *watching the fort? The kids?*

Elmore zipped. Not a breath of wind stirred the fading afternoon. Three crows passed over, identical black shadows on the ground.

Elmore could hear himself sweat. He crept through the trees, hidden in shadows.

This is ... crazy. Why would some guy be up a tree watching Will and Mary?

A deer fly suddenly came out of nowhere. It lit aggressively on Elmore's cheek. *Little bastard.* The sting left a vivid red cut.

The insect's crushed body, killed by a slap, fell from his palm.

Elmore took another step toward the creek.

The watcher in the woods was gone.

Elmore put one hand on his brow, Indian style, shading his eyes from the low June sun.

He worried now.

Where'd you go, camo man? Who are you?

No sign.

Elmore studied the pine the man had descended. He saw something astonishing: A metal box. Camouflage green. Mounted to the trunk thirty feet up.

It looked like a surveillance camera. Pointed directly at Fort Rogers.

Elmore felt a sudden shock.

What did Neeley warn? And Plum's caution? He hadn't really processed it all.

Had a man mounted a camera to watch where Will and Mary played?

Elmore studied the pine the man had descended. He saw something astonishing: A metal box. Camouflage green. Mounted to the trunk thirty feet up.

Elmore felt rising anger. He slogged across the creek. Cold water over-rushed his boots. He mounted the bank and struck a beeline for the pine tree. He clearly saw a camera now.

Son of a bitch, Elmore realized. *Is Mr. Wood watching my kids? What the devil?*

Elmore heard sudden noises behind him.

He spun, on the defensive.

Will and Mary, pedaling madly, headed for the creek. Sunlight sparkled on chrome handlebars. Timmy Wragg wobbled after.

Elmore raised a hand … a greeting? A warning?

The three bikes hit the creek almost all at once. Sprays of water shot to the sides, and so did squeals of happiness.

"Pedal! Hard! Don't stop!"

Commander Will led his mounted soldiers through fast water.

"Yi! Yi! Giddyup!"

Elmore stood directly under the pine now.

He studied the surveillance device. A video camera. Camouflaged. Its swivel collar could sweep side to side, up and down. Beneath the tree, small metal and plastic pieces lay abandoned but inconspicuous. Broken bark covered the ground.

The kids rattled near, whooping.

Elmore saw a path. Someone leaving in a hurry had kicked over fleshy white mushrooms and knocked a few poke plants sideways.

It will be easy to follow that trail.

Elmore moved away from the pine. He didn't want the kids asking questions.

"Daaaaddy! Wait!"

Sweet little Mary's voice. The hurble-burble boy voices followed.

"*Chaaarge!* C'mon, y'all!"

Then … a horror. With no warning.

No rattle.

An eastern diamondback shot an ugly head out of the weeds. The snake struck Mary on the thin part of her shin just above the ankle.

Its fangs stuck in her leg. Mary screamed in pain. She frantically pedaled, and the reptile dangled from her like a fat tail.

"Help me, Daddy!"

Elmore would never forget his daughter's heart-piercing plea.

It was Will, brave Will, who first hurled himself forward, bike and all, at the flailing reptile.

Then Elmore swung a pine branch with a violent whoosh. He broke the snake's back. But he did not break its grip. The rattler remained clamped fast to Mary, its sticky gape stretched halfway around her little leg. Each time she pedaled, the snake's head went round, and its body circled and snapped, a terrible whip.

Christ, was the horrible thing chewing her?

Mary's panic overcame her. She crashed down on the bike, a bundle in the weeds.

The snake's unblinking eyes fixed Elmore. Enraged, he ripped the snake away and flung its doughy body high into the trees.

Elmore gathered Mary to him just as shock took her small body. A convulsion passed through her, another kind of rattle.

Elmore clutched his trembling beautiful child against his chest. He sobbed hard – violently – like he might inhale the world with a great gasp.

"Mary, sweetie," Elmore told her, "you're gonna be okay. You're gonna be fine, I promise you."

Get to the hospital, Elmore. Get to the hospital. Nothing else matters.

Mary felt light as a kitten as Elmore took off in a sprint, splashing back through the creek. She rocked side to side in the cradle of his arms.

"Will! Leave! Hurry!"

Elmore's throat broke, cracked by anguish.

Oh Mary, oh God. What will I do? Oh dear Jesus, can I save you?

Elmore ran as fast as human bones and muscles can run. Past Fort Rogers. Past the bobwhite field. Up the curving woodland path.

The house in the late gold afternoon bounced closer, closer, the truck parked just there.

It took so long to reach it.

—26—

Lafayette General

Mary lay on a hospital cot, small as a doll. A pulse beat in her neck, a little blue wink.

Elmore fretted in a metal chair at the bedside. He rolled and unrolled a hospital form. Two hours had passed since admission.

The longest two hours in history.

Mary had stabilized, doctors said. They waited on antivenin.

A nurse entered. Another day, she'd be pretty. Blonde hair under a blue cap. Blue eyes.

"Mr. Rogers, can I bring you something? Coke? Cup of coffee?"

Elmore barely heard. He dealt with a distraction – a dark figure seemed to pace the room between him and his daughter, sometimes blocking her from view.

Once, the figure stopped and stared at Mary with lidless yellow eyes.

Eyes like the rattlesnake.

The nurse asked a second time, softly.

"Mr. Rogers?"

She placed a hand on his arm. Why did a nurse's touch always feel cool and clean?

Elmore smelled Juicy Fruit and lipstick.

Some water, Elmore attempted to say. He failed, shook his head, frowned. He hadn't stopped sweating since he hustled Mary in his embrace through the emergency-room door.

"Water, miss," he croaked. "Please."

She spoke in a sweet voice. "Be right back with a couple of cups."

"Thanks."

"Sir, don't you worry. Your daughter will be fine. We'll get ... is it ... Mary?"

"Mary."

"We'll get Miss Mary well in no time. She'll be singing. You'll see."

Elmore nodded. But the nurse's reassuring words kindled an ominous memory.

In Mosul, a medic shared a little inside baseball with him.

The off-duty soldiers slumped over cold beers in a camp canteen, the one place that ever got cool in that whole godforsaken country. Elmore sat in shock. He'd seen a black private from Moundville blow a hadji's head off with a sniper rifle on an ordinary Sunday morning.

"Want to know what I tell wounded soldiers?"

The medic stared slightly above Elmore's head, avoiding eye contact.

Elmore had both hands on his cold beer.

"I tell 'em the same thing. Everyone. You're gonna be fine. You just hang in there, son. I've seen plenty worse. Just hang on."

Elmore peeled the Pabst label. "Every soldier? Even the goners?"

"Every last one. Especially the ones I know don't have a frickin' prayer. Legs blown off. Holes right through 'em. Every time. Every soldier. *You gonna be fine. You just hang in there, son.*

"What else can I say?"

The nurse went away. Without her white uniform, the room felt darker suddenly.

Elmore leaned, touched Mary's pallid cheek.

The black shadow, agitated, rose from its corner of the room. It prowled, back and forth, back and forth, strange crooked feet clicking on the tile.

Elmore forced himself to look again at Mary's terrible ankle.

Ugly twin punctures oozed a colorless liquid. How was it possible that two tiny holes like that threatened his little girl's life?

The suppurating wound gave the room a weird odor. The doctors who huddled in white jackets and talked in low voices agreed it would be best to leave the wound uncovered. Some venom would seep out, they said.

Lafayette General waited on antivenin to arrive from … where?

Mary had cold packs on either side of her leg. The ice bags looked like what trainers pressed to the battered faces of prize fighters.

Elmore studied Mary's ankle, the delicate blue web-work of blood vessels. (She had smaller blue webs on her closed eyelids.) Those mattered very much to Elmore right now – certain veins coursing up Mary's leg from the snake bite gleamed like black seams of coal in a road cut. Ominous black.

The doctors made marks on Mary's pale leg with a Sharpie, a new line every twenty minutes or so. These tracked the steady progress of the snake poison toward her beating heart.

Where was the antivenin? The black poison in Mary's leg had risen a half inch, maybe more, past the last pen mark. Elmore thought of mercury rising in a deadly thermometer.

He wanted to yell. *Mary's in danger! Can't you help?*

It broke Elmore's heart.

He was glad Will couldn't see his sister. Lafayette General had a strict rule prohibiting children under age twelve in any room but the lobby. The volunteer candy-stripers who greeted hospital visitors had taken Will and Timmy Wragg into their supervision. Elmore imagined the boys of Fort Apache sucking chocolate milk through straws. They'd be watching TV, probably *Beavis and Butt-Head* or something else Elmore didn't like them to see.

They'd be fine till Daddy came down the corridor with good news about Mary.

Please, God.

What kind of Alabama hospital didn't keep snake serum on hand in the summer? What kind of hospital made a little girl wait for two hours counting on life-saving treatment? How top-notch could such a facility really be?

It made no sense. Here in Alabama, some unlucky soul with a cane pole sat down on a cottonmouth on some creek bank once a week. Snake bites in Alabama were a natural fact.

Why had the hospital been out of antivenin?

Doctors assured Elmore a helicopter from Camp Shelby in Mississippi would soon bring the serum. *Forty-five minutes after take-off. Absolutely.*

Elmore bit back frustrated anger.

At Lafayette General Medical Center, staff in the lobby gave red lollipops to every visitor – man, woman and child. Endless lollipops.

But doctors couldn't find a drop of antivenin for snakebite?

Elmore just shook his head.

Okay ... he, Elmore Rogers, was to blame. No one else. He wandered out into the woods where his kids would follow him, foolishly trying to see why somebody would put a video camera in a pine tree.

How crazy was he?

Why hadn't the rattlesnake struck him instead of poor Mary?

Her whole leg, propped on pillows, had turned greenish-yellow. It looked like spoiled chicken meat. Elmore wished her wound were only a bruise, a twisted ankle.

The coal vein had climbed Mary's leg another half inch.

Mary's leg. His little girl's.

The dark intruder in the room passed between Elmore and the lamp, dimming the room.

Elmore hated that thing. It hung around for months in his convalescence, laughing when Elmore told visitors he felt fine, growling when he whispered to Kelly how he hurt.

"Daddy?"

Elmore was on his feet so fast he saw spots. He steadied, palms on the cot.

Why hadn't the rattlesnake struck him instead of poor Mary? Her whole leg, propped on pillows, had turned greenish-yellow. Like spoiled chicken meat.

"Daddy ... my leg hurts."

Elmore stretched a hand, snatched it quickly back. That simple motion, horrifically, made him think of the snake striking.

"I love you, sweetie. I'm right here."

A soft voice. "Did Will, Daddy?"

Elmore leaned. "Did Will what, honey?"

"Did Will get snaked?"

Mary turned her head. Her little face, so beautiful. Elmore felt a surge of heartbreak. Of love. Something exactly the opposite of snake venom.

Little girl, I've seen worse. You just hang in there.

Elmore's eyes filled with tears, hot and unexpected.

It didn't seem to be Mary in front of him now.

He didn't recognize the strange, bright eyes.

Kelly Rogers woke with a start.

She felt hands touch her.

The blue light from medical devices illuminated a nurse's silhouette. She quietly checked, in sequence, the Velcro restraints on Kelly's wrists and ankles, the tube snaking into her arm, the monitor readings. The nurse had a kind face. Her name tag: Eva.

Eva silently adjusted Kelly's bedclothes and gown, fussed with a setting on a device, scribbled on a clipboard knotted to the gurney.

Help ...

Kelly meant to say *hello*. A notification. Of life. Of feeling, consciousness. Awareness.

A tube ran down Kelly's nose into her lungs. She could feel it, uncomfortable and invasive. Was it there to suck stuff out? Pump stuff in?

Lithium. That's what. Lithium and friends.

"Miz Rogers? How you feeling?" Kelly heard care in the voice.

She grunted once. Truly, she felt like death warmed over.

"I know that tube is a bother," the nurse said, consolingly. "But it's gonna get you well. And you know what?"

Kelly grunted again.

Nurse Eva smiled. "It's the most beautiful day out there. You get better, and we'll go see the summer. Soon."

Not even lithium could stop a memory.

Kelly was a little girl. Her family posed for photographs in front of purple azaleas. Kelly wore a white summer dress, and her new patent-leather shoes glowed. Good old Frankie Bellisle, her dad, set a timer, and his camera ticked atop a shiny tripod. Dad scrambled, hilariously, to pose with Kelly and Mom. Everybody said cheese.

It was the most beautiful day.

Time jumbled.

Kelly raised a hand in bright sunlight.

Dad! Mom! Wait! We don't have Will and Mary in the picture!

Kelly heard a voice.

Clear as a bell. The clearest it ever spoke.

It's not what you did. It's what you will do.

Sleep slowly washed away the memories, the colors fading to black.

But Kelly remembered something else. Vividly.

Mary and Will.

The Milky Way.

They hugged her. They looked smart and healthy. So grown-up.

Maybe they would … somehow … forgive her?

In a high corner of intensive care, a surveillance camera silently recorded Kelly Rogers.

In suicide-watch rooms, cameras constantly monitored patients. The devices never slept.

Life and death depended on them … and on the unseen, anonymous figures behind the monitors.

—27—

The Black Helicopter

Mary died at 1:57 a.m.

Her heart stopped. Her breathing ceased. In seconds, her lips and eyelids and fingers turned the blue of ice.

Cyanosis.

Her death changed the temperature of the whole room. It woke Elmore in his chair by the bed with a start, like war nightmares.

It only took a moment for him to understand.

The small huddled shape on the gurney lay deathly still. Instrument lights glowed red. Lines on monitors ran flat. All numbers were zeroes.

It looked so normal. Mary had died.

Elmore leaped wildly from his chair. A thin alarm, like a tea-kettle whistle, wheezed from one instrument.

Elmore already knew.

This day in June, his beautiful little girl died of a rattlesnake bite. Mary passed away in a hospital with no antivenin.

She'd been waiting seven hours.

Elmore screamed.

He screamed again for doctors, nurses. To reach Mary, he ripped away a tangle of plastic tubing. By God, he'd carry her back to the emergency room right now!

"Help! Dr. Busbee! Nurse! Help! Mary's not breathing!"

The nurse appeared from thin air, flying into the room so fast it startled Elmore.

"Mr. Rogers! Stand back!" she yelled. "Back from the bed, mister!"

Her voice leapt out with startling volume.

"Mary – "

"Put yourself IN THAT CHAIR, mister! Do it NOW!"

The nurse stepped between Elmore and Mary and shoved hard.

Elmore tottered, lost his balance, flailed his arms among the dangling tentacles of the IV rack.

"Room 25! Dr. Busbee! Code seven! We've got a seven!"

The nurse seemed to simply babble into thin air, but Elmore then saw her left index finger on a gurney call button. Simultaneously, she probed with her right hand for a sign of life in Mary's wrist.

The little-girl arm looked like a doll arm.

"Security! Room 25! Urgent!"

It took Elmore a second.

Security.

"She's my little girl!" Elmore yelled. "You're not taking me from Mary!"

Not one, but two doctors skated into the room, almost comically colliding as they entered from opposite ends of the corridor.

Dr. Busbee had come at a run, stethoscope bouncing behind his back, the instrument flipped to the wrong side as he hustled into Room 25.

The second doctor wore green dress pants, a brick-red jacket – his church dress from services at Rose Lake Baptist Church earlier that evening. The kindly retired pediatrician moonlighted as organist for the Rose Lake choir, fifty strong. Dr. Thomson happened to be at Lafayette General to see a choir member, felled by a stroke.

"Gloves," Dr. Thomson ordered the nurse, moving straight to Mary's bed.

"What's he done to the child? What's he *done?*" Dr. Busbee, red-eyed and gaunt, pointed a ball-point pen at Elmore. The physician had brown rabbit eyes and a faint moustache. Papers slipped from his clipboard to the floor.

"He removed her IVs," Dr. Thomson stated in a voice of spooky control. The physician was spectral, with straw-colored hair. His pale blue eyes grew large as he examined Mary.

"Help her!" Elmore yelled. "Just help her!"

Couldn't they see? Mary was gone to sleep! What were they waiting for? Did they want to save a little girl's life?

"No pulse," Dr. Thomson grimly announced. He gave up on the little doll arm and searched Mary's jugular for the faintest sign of a heartbeat. His index finger plunged to the second joint.

Elmore saw Mary's poor leg exposed. Black to the knee now. The discoloration had out-climbed the Sharpie marks at the ankle, the shin, then the knee.

Elmore screamed. A war cry. A cry of father's fury.

What kind of hospital let a little girl wait seven hours on treatment for a rattlesnake bite? Could such a thing really happen this day and age?

Mary's thin blue lips parted just a little, like she might breathe or whistle or blow a kiss.

"Give me room," Dr. Busbee said, calm as that.

Then he stabbed Mary.

His fist rose in the air. It held a knife. Only it wasn't a knife, but a sharp shining needle, drops of something clear streaming from its tip.

"Oh Jesus! What did you do?"

Elmore felt himself coming undone.

That moment, strong male arms encircled him. Two powerful bands of muscle and sinew gave a swift single jerk that forced the breath out of Elmore's lungs. He felt a rib crack. Again.

A boa constrictor, Elmore thought, surreally. *Another snake ...*

Elmore's head flopped. He saw heavy boots on someone's feet.

A snake has killed me too. Now I'm dead just like poor little Mary ...

Elmore felt Fire Chief Wragg drag him away, then drop him roughly on the cool hospital floor against the wall.

Elmore's cheek banged the floor. He lay motionless.

Then he felt a tiny thread of oxygen find its way back to his lungs.

One precious thread.

Another.

Life.

Elmore gasped and sucked in breath.

He saw events in the hospital room with intense clarity.

Down plunged Dr. Busbee's silver needle. It stabbed through Mary's bare breastbone into her dead heart.

Adrenaline.

Out the window of Room 25, a long white crack of fire opened in the heavens. A shock of thunder shook the hospital walls, and car alarms whooped.

Instantly, small hailstones like pea gravel pelted the window.

Elmore lay on his side on the polished floor – it smelled faintly of isopropyl alcohol and urine – and watched the hailstones bounce crazily off the window sill.

He thought of tiny fish struggling for their lives in a giant black net.

Another flash of lightning.

Mary's eyes flew wide, weirdly blue, like her fingernails. Her blue mouth formed an O.

Elmore heard her gasp.

Mary returned from the dead, like he had.

The antivenin arrived noisily.

At last.

It descended from the stormy night on a helicopter blacker than the inky rain. The Eurocopter dared a rooftop landing on the medical center helipad in tumultuous winds. (The windsock stood straight out, like an orange megaphone.) Risky. But a skilled hand at the controls settled the bird down sweetly.

Dragonfly on a lily pad.

"That's our serum," announced Dr. Busbee. "That's what we've been waiting for."

A fresh lightning bolt struck so near the hospital that Elmore heard the air hiss, a *vroom* in his gut at the speed of light.

Mary breathed. Mary had a pulse.

But lightning posed a new danger.

Mary's eyes flew wide, weirdly blue, like her fingernails. Her blue mouth formed an O. Elmore heard her gasp.

Lights flickered. Off. Briefly back on. Then the entire hospital went dark.

Cries fluttered down the corridors like spooked birds. A symphony of beeping instruments and warning bells joined banging thunder and howling car alarms.

Elmore couldn't believe his eyes, his ears. A power outage. In a modern hospital. Could a thunderstorm really put a hospital out of commission?

He blinked in dismay at flashlight halos in the hallway. An old woman passed in a shapeless white gown, free of her bed. She carried a match, and its yellow light on her aged face made her look Chinese.

"MOMMY!" she bawled down the corridor. "I'm scared of the dark, Mommy!"

The two doctors and the nurse worked over Mary in the dark, reattaching tubes and drips.

With a great gasp of air, hospital auxiliary power sources kicked in.

Through the facility rolled a heavy thrum of engines – the kindling noises of air conditioning, respirators, fluorescent bulbs, all the refrigerators, freezers and heavy appliances that stored drugs and medical samples. The machines newly connected to Mary's body beeped, and her breathing tube gave a soft, steady hiss and inflated slightly.

Mary's pulse strengthened.

Where had Mary's heartbeat gone? Elmore abstractly wondered. What did the little ugly muscle do in those terrible minutes? Was it waiting to see how much Mary wanted to live again, black leg and all?

Her poor leg. Discolored above the knee now.

What if they had to amputate?

Lying on his hurt side against the wall, Elmore convulsed at the possibility.

Oh God. Thank God. At least she's alive.

Mary's bare birdlike chest rose and fell. A tiny spot of blood, red as a ruby, shone mid-sternum where the needle entered.

Elmore gathered his resolve and somehow pulled himself onto his feet. He glanced warily at Wragg. The ex-SEAL wore a Lafayette Fire Department black T-shirt. A holster with no gun wagged on his thigh for some reason.

"You stay right where you are, Elmore. The little girl's coming around now. These fine doctors don't need any more of your help."

Sure enough, Mary's pulse line on the monitors formed an endless row of green hills.

Elmore felt his own chest rise and fall.

Mary. Our little Mary is breathing.

Mary's lips took on color. Her soft cheeks grew pink before Elmore's eyes.

She coughed.

Mary turned her head to the side. The clear plastic nasal tubes moved. Elmore watched her tongue dart out to lick dry lips – a tongue the same black-green color as her poisoned leg.

The sight horrified Elmore. He felt like curling into a ball, screaming.

Instead, he breathed in, breathed out.

Mary breathed in, breathed out.

She moved a hand. A simple wave. Hello, not goodbye.

"Stay put, Rogers. Not one step closer."

Wragg poised like a linebacker on a fourth-and-goal snap.

Dr. Busbee raised his head. The rabbit face was triumphant.

"Mister Rogers ... we've got your daughter stabilized ..."

That moment, three rain-soaked soldiers in National Guard uniforms loudly burst into Room 25.

Every person in the room jumped in surprise. Even Mary jerked.

Gasping for breath, the rain-soaked soldiers stood at a sorry excuse for attention. One placed dripping hands on his knees, bent at the waist like a runner at the end of a marathon. Puddles collected like pee under his black boots.

In the corridor, a fourth figure approached. Slowly. A heavy, square man. He wore a white fringed jacket and a white cowboy hat.

The middle guardsman carried a Styrofoam cooler. Yellow tape secured the lid. The tape read "WARNING: HAZARDOUS MATERIAL".

It hit Elmore too fast. Too much.

The uniforms caused it. The three soldiers wore camouflage. Elmore's mind reeled, dizzily, like a camera on the head of a skydiver. He was freefalling, spinning, untethered. He saw a bright flash, heard an explosion. Lightning? Thunder? A roadside bomb?

His memory locked onto the image of a sinister figure in the woods. Climbing out of a tree. Camouflage clothing.

The soldier with the cooler spoke.

"Dr. Busbee? We … have orders to deliver this package to … whew … oh boy … is one of you Dr. Busbee?"

"I'm Dr. Busbee."

The doctor pointed a finger at the cooler.

"Soldier, that's the antivenin?"

"Yes, sir. I'm … I'm … Captain Tubbs. We've been … "

"It's freakin' TIME!" yelled Elmore. "It's freakin' TIME you got her medicine here!"

Wragg put a warning palm against Elmore's chest. But Dr. Busbee also chimed in.

"Where you boys been? We called for antivenin yesterday afternoon!"

An unprofessional lapse settled over the room.

"Look at this child!"

Dr. Busbee raised his voice, but Dr. Thomson leaned close and spoke to him, calmingly.

"We scrambled, sir," said Captain Tubbs. "We followed our orders!"

Tubbs stood stiffly at attention now, barking words as if he'd been busted to private on the spot.

Thunder. The lights flickered again.

Down the corridor, a lone figure shuffled closer.

"Captain Tubbs," Dr. Busbee said, more quietly. "I apologize. We just needed this treatment sooner."

Tubbs, earnest and pink with exertion, gave a momentary glance at Elmore.

Such a worried face would only belong to the stricken girl's father.

Tubbs gripped the Styrofoam cooler tighter.

"Dr. Busbee, sir, we've been trying to get a positive on a vial of antivenin since a call from command at exactly seventeen-hundred hours yesterday afternoon. We had a dozen men on this assignment and, sir, this batch of antivenin comes all the way from Memphis, Tennessee. We canvassed every hospital in a one-hundred-mile radius, sir. So either there's been a lot of snakes biting civilians these days ... or else medical planners have not been up to their task of keeping stockpiles in order."

The captain then barked a last word that might as well have been a curse.

"Sir."

Dr. Busbee glared, but Mary groaned from the gurney.

"Enough talk."

The doctor relieved Captain Tubbs of the cooler. He ripped away the yellow tape, prised off the lid with a painfully sharp squeak.

Dr. Busbee's head snapped up, his face a mask of irritation.

"It's frozen?"

The soldiers passed glances at one another.

"It's *frozen*, Captain?"

"Yes sir. We had orders to keep it frozen, sir."

The captain did not blink.

"It's *still* frozen?" Dr. Busbee's voice broke like a sob, and he trembled in frustration.

"Doctor, let me have it."

The blonde nurse stepped between the two men. As she took the cooler, it made a squeaking noise, like it held something small and alive trapped inside.

"Use the microwave in the doctors' break room, please." Dr. Busbee's face had turned a shade of purple. "We don't have time to take it to the lab."

"I'll hurry."

The nurse ran down the corridor.

"The little girl wants to talk!"

That was Dr. Thomson, working with poor Mary. He hadn't taken off his church jacket.

Mary's eyes opened.

She looked straight at Elmore.

An expression came to her face, a crinkle that made her resemble an old woman for a moment. Then she spoke.

Daddy.

And Elmore fell to the floor like a man stabbed in the heart.

A fit came on him.

The black shape roared out of the shadows. The thing's top and bottom jaws stretched wide and its mouth gaped. Like a great snake.

Elmore fought desperately.

"Christ Jesus! What's the MATTER with that dude?"

Captain Tubbs, frightened, leaped back. Privates Marco and Alvaro Castro, twin brothers, bolted into the corridor, Marco slipping in rainwater. The young soldiers had never witnessed a madly thrashing grown man with his eyes rolled back in his head and his legs kicking as if being electrocuted on the spot.

Even Dr. Busbee and Fire Chief Wragg leaped back in shock from Elmore.

Elmore flailed and jerked, fighting off the fearsome thing that rose from nowhere to attack him. He felt his boot connect with a device, heard a crash as plastic and aluminum catapulted into the wall.

"Grab his arms! It's a seizure!"

Dr. Thomson sounded far away, miles distant from the dark shape that dove onto Elmore, battering him to the floor, strangling him.

"He's swallowed his tongue!"

Not true. The beast had pressed its great forearm against Elmore's throat.

"Castro! You men! Get his legs! He's broken his hand! Come on!"

Elmore flailed and jerked, fighting off the fearsome thing that rose from nowhere to attack him. He felt his boot connect with a device, heard a crash.

Suddenly Elmore could no longer fight the beast. Someone threw weights heavy as sandbags across his legs, his arms. He fought them all desperately, the dark creature on his chest, the two soldiers, Wragg, even a doctor.

Someone pried Elmore's teeth apart, slipped something between them. A billfold?

He heard a voice, softer than any other sound in the room, but so loud it stopped the universe cold.

Daddy.

Mary.

Elmore was a powerful man. He had the physique of a center-fielder, a nail-driver, a ditch-digger, a cabinet-worker. His head and his rib and his wrist – what was wrong with his wrist? – hurt this second, but distractions didn't matter.

The power of a man's gathered rage, the superhuman strength of a father with a child in danger, infused him. He felt a godly flood of force through every vein and muscle and bone.

Elmore flexed. Simply flexed.

The black thing lay at his feet now, hurled away, the weird goblin face blinking up in surprise and maybe even fear.

The soldiers sprawled in separate corners, their camouflage clothes torn, one with a boot ripped off. Dr. Busbee lay against a huge dented metal panel on the climate control unit.

A little blood ran from Elmore's nose.

Daddy.

Elmore grabbed blankets, and he rolled his daughter, his Mary, into them. He held her swaddled in his arms as if she were still a little baby.

Elmore roared now, veins bursting in his neck, so loud Venetian blinds trembled.

A clap of thunder could not drown him out.

The nurse, hair flying, burst back into the room. She held a slushy, partly thawed vial of antivenin.

She blinked in complete surprise at the war zone.

But she knew what to do.

"Mr. Rogers, please put your daughter down," she said evenly. "Mary needs this treatment. Right now. This is life and death."

Elmore met her eyes. Blue. Unblinking.

"Please put her back on the bed, sir."

He heard her.

Elmore hoisted Mary for a better grip. He glanced at his wrist. It hung like a pocket pulled inside out. Useless. He saw a bloody tear in his skin.

He hugged Mary, a bundle of child in a blanket, closer to his chest.

Mary coughed. Her steady eyes remained open, on Elmore, watching.

Trusting.

"Okay." Elmore nodded to the nurse. "Please help her now. Please."

As gently as a man lowering a sinner into a river for baptism, Elmore settled Mary back on the white rumpled sheets of the gurney.

"Thank you, Elmore."

Behind the nurse, three soldiers and two doctors and Dick Wragg waited. In the corridor, a small mob of the curious had gathered. No one spoke.

A figure stepped forward.

The last time Elmore had seen Mr. Wood was from a rooftop. He looked tiny then. Such a little man to be such a big man.

What is that son of a bitch doing here now?

"Mr. Rogers," Mr. Wood said. Here stood a man who always gave orders. "Move away from that beautiful child of yours. If you don't, she will die. Or lose that leg."

Elmore knew it was true.

"Move away now."

Mr. Wood turned and whispered a few words to Wragg and the soldiers. The men nodded, never taking eyes off Elmore.

Elmore knew what would happen the moment he took his two hands ... one of them hurting ... off his little girl.

But Elmore smiled.

He lowered his lips to Mary's forehead. Her skin was cool as marble.

"I love you, Mary."

"I love you, Daddy ..."

Elmore stalled. He knew what would happen as soon as he took his hands off Mary.

"Mr. Wood, what brings you here? What's your business with Mary?"

The captain answered instead.

"*... Mr. Wood's private helicopter ... out of nowhere ... brought the serum all the way from Memphis ... on his own bird ... fastest damned machine ... saving a little girl's life ... not another drop from here to Timbuktu ... flew the damn thing himself ... lightning and thunder ...*"

Exactly that moment, Elmore whirled. Launched.

The hospital window crashed. Elmore left a gaping open hole through the glass.

The storm rushed in. Cheap Venetian blinds rattled violently in the burst of wind. Rain swirled. The air tasted of lightning.

"Go get that cracker bastard," snapped Mr. Wood. "We didn't bring that snakebite medicine all the way from St. Jude for this to happen."

The nurse pulled a blanket over Mary to keep off the blowing rain. The room quickly soaked. Papers gusted wildly off the doctors' clipboards, wilted in puddles. Some got sucked out into the corridor and whirled away.

Wragg and the soldiers disappeared just as quickly, racing to bring Elmore to justice.

Dr. Thomson stared out through the man-shaped hole in the window. Dr. Thomson was nearly eighty years old. He'd fought in World War II and stood at attention on the blistering deck of the U.S.S. Missouri the day Hirohito surrendered. He'd practiced medicine since the days of iron lungs.

He'd never witnessed a night like this in any hospital.

Dr. Thomson tried to hang a blanket over the blowing gash in the window.

In a lightning flash, Dr. Thomson saw Elmore Rogers, the broken fool, hobble free of a massive – and massively crushed – boxwood hedge that fringed the hospital. The thick greenery must have broken the man's fall from the second story. But look – Rogers trailed a length of bone-white Venetian blind, tangled around one ankle.

Rogers made it into the hospital parking lot. He limped badly, and his wrist dangled. He looked absurdly like a woman holding a purse. But with no purse.

Unexpectedly, the passenger door of a police car yawned wide.

Dr. Thomson saw Elmore Rogers stumble in surprise, then warily peer in.

He addressed someone in the police car.

A square little boy jumped from the vehicle in the rain and stood in front of Elmore. The kid seemed to be pleading.

Elmore first shook his head *no*. Then he shook his head *yes*.

He got into the police car with the little boy.

The light on top blazed blue. The siren howled. The squad car roared in a full-circle smoking turn, slinging rainwater.

"Jesus Christ!"

Dr. Busbee now stared out the window too, the left lens of his eyeglasses cracked.

"The world's gone crazy tonight!"

The squad car rocketed the length of the parking lot. It threw up a mighty spray of rainwater ... dousing three National Guard soldiers and Fire Chief Wragg, who burst onto the near sidewalk from a hospital door at just the wrong moment.

The squad car was still accelerating as it left the hospital parking lot and disappeared into Lafayette.

Dr. Thomson marveled. He'd never even learned to drive.

He turned back to the hospital room.

The blonde nurse and Mr. Wood sat on the gurney.

The nurse held Mary Rogers possessively. Madonna. Child.

Mr. Wood – the famous billionaire, Mr. Wood – stroked the child's soft hair.

The little girl's eyes fixed on him, wide.

Mr. Wood teased Mary's hair again. He cleared his throat.

"You get well, little girl," he gruffed. "The holidays will be here before you know it."

—28—

June 29

Sheriff Neeley and Deputy Turnipseed smoked cigars at their metal desks. The unglamorous cries of nighthawks eked through the open window of police headquarters. A breeze lifted one wing of a dead luna moth, rain-pasted to the screen like a scrap of green paper.

Sheriff Neeley squinted through smoke at a photo of this afternoon's traffic accident.

A log truck had tangled with a white Dodge Dart. Heavy pine logs blocked Lafayette's main street and entirely hid the crushed passenger side of the unlucky car. The Dart's driver, a middle-aged man in a white shirt and dark tie, stood miraculously unharmed. He held his hands to his temples, staring at the family vehicle.

"Video cam shows the log truck runs the light? You sure, Turnip?"

"Yes sir."

Neeley took a puff.

"Well ... that's one of Mr. Wood's haulers. Those trucks have diplomatic immunity."

Through steel bars, Elmore Rogers frowned. He stood by a cot with a ratty green army blanket, its foam-rubber pillow falling to pieces. He wore a wrap on his left wrist, badly sprained, not broken after all, and bandages down his whole right arm.

After a week, the steel bars had become as familiar to Elmore's hands as work tools.

"Hey, Dan. Tomorrow?"

Neeley put down the photo and answered without looking. "Tomorrow, El."

"Ten a.m.?"

Sheriff Neeley patiently answered the question yet again.

"Ten a.m. I'll send Turnip down to the courthouse first thing and get your walking papers. You'll catch the breakfast buffet at Shoney's."

Seven days a prisoner, Elmore licked cracked lips, felt beard stubble. He smelled his body, feral, sour. His mouth tasted bad, despite a taxpayer-supplied toothbrush and a tube of Pepsodent.

"Think I could clean up, Dan? Shave? Get my pants?"

"No sir. No blades for prisoners, Elmore. No belts. Those pants you got are fine this one last night."

Elmore hunched his shoulders between upraised arms. He stared at the bare cell floor. Globs of gum reminded him of a downtown sidewalk.

The most humiliating thing about a week in custody, Elmore decided, was simple – the jumpsuit. It had already been rank, unlaundered, when he put it on, and its particular shade of orange tortured Elmore's retinas. He would hate Halloween the rest of his life.

The rest of his life.

Elmore silently vowed for the thousandth time that when he stepped out of Lafayette city jail tomorrow morning, he would set straight his affairs with the world.

Things would change. Now.

He had time. Doctors told Elmore he'd miss work three more weeks, thanks to the cracked wrist and a concussion from his great leap forward out the window of Lafayette General.

Time.

Elmore would be a better dad for Will and Mary. He would find somebody special, try to love again. He would get his head examined – a war had raged inside it too long. He would be a model citizen of Lafayette.

He vowed to change his life as dramatically as his life changed him.

He would never wake up on the wrong side of jail bars again.

Elmore would never again spend seven days worried to death about Mary and Will, fretting, despairing over who cared for them, fed them.

Neeley reassured him about the twins every day. "The young'uns are fine, El. Just fine."

"Thank you, Danny."

"Fine," Neeley went on, "but no thanks to you. What the hell got into you, anyway, El? Your little girl's down with a snake bite, and I find Will in the first floor cafeteria, eatin' somebody's leftover Jell-O, just waiting all by himself ... and you're upstairs punching out the fire chief and doctors and National Guard? Well, your wild ass got slapped behind bars this time, Elmore, and you were lucky the judge said just a week. Plus you owe two-thousand bucks to Lafayette General ... not counting your disturbing the peace and vandalism fines ... and four or five people still might slap civil suits on you for bodily harm ..."

Enough.

Elmore would stop being a loser.

He didn't really remember the first days in jail.

Elmore blamed it on the fog that rolled in after Dick Wragg banged his head on the hospital floor. It got thicker after a haymaker in the brawl with the Thing in the room and the soldiers in camouflage and whoever else got close.

Or maybe Elmore fogged himself to forgetfulness by jumping through a hospital window and crashing down into a boxwood hedge two stories down.

Whatever, for the first days, Elmore saw wheels of fire and heard screams like people trapped on burning Ferris wheels. He jerked his head up, more than once, at the imaginary sounds of snarling dogs. He came back to his senses in fits and starts.

The soft brace hurt Elmore's wrist. Or maybe his wrist hurt inside the brace.

The face in the city jail's mirror ... a Barbie mirror fixed to the wall with black duct tape ... looked like a man Elmore didn't know.

From the fog, faces swam into focus, disappeared.

Dick Wragg. Elmore couldn't remember his neighbor saying a single word. He simply leered down through the steel cell bars at Elmore, spread out in orange on the rusted cot. Was Wragg gloating? Elmore wondered why – the fire chief sported a huge purple eye. His arm hung in a sling. What did he have to gloat about?

Sheriff Neeley appeared out of the smoke too. His messages didn't make sense at first, but they slowly took on clearer meaning as the jungle howls faded in Elmore's head.

Mary got out of the hospital, Neeley said, *the very next day after the snake charm came on Mr. Wood's helicopter. All better. She had a sore leg and felt tired a few days, but El you wouldn't know today she'd ever been struck by that evil thing.*

Neeley again, later.

Mrs. Mock keeps Mary fed and watered. Look ... I felt like it was better if we had a grown lady to look after our little girl. Mary asks about you every night when I stop by to see her, a stuck record, where's my daddy, where's my daddy. But I swear, Elmore, I'm not bringing that little girl or Will through these doors to see their old man in an orange jumpsuit in a jail cell. They just don't need to grow up with that memory.

They got enough memories, don't they?

Neeley once more.

Yeah, old Will. I got Lion Boy staying with me at night. He's enjoying a top bunk with an antique 'Wanted' poster of Jesse James on the ceiling. 'Dead or Alive', it says, and Will's been goin' around squawkin' 'Dead or alive, dead or alive', like a stuck record. And he's worrying me to death to shoot a pistol. I'm thinking about it. He's forever asking about you too. Like Mary. I been telling him how good you got it here, with ice-cold Coca-Cola bubblin' right out of the faucets and peanut-butter toothpaste ...

"I swear, Elmore, I'm not bringing that little girl or Will through these doors to see their old man in an orange jumpsuit in a jail cell."

Dan Neeley ghosted away in the fog.

Elmore, buddy, next time you do something stupid, we gonna keep you in here till Will hits puberty and Mary's a movie star with her own cosmetics line. I'll guarantee you that personally. Those young'uns deserve a daddy better'n this one sitting here behind bars lookin' like an orange crash test dummy ...

Dan Neeley was right.

Mr. Rankin came out of the mist. Elmore's boss.

He sat on a gray folding chair opposite the cell bars. Elmore thought of a movie gladiator, the brawny arms and thick neck. Rankin's Roman nose had been broken once upon a time, who knows how?

The boss was known to be a man of few words, but he had some for Elmore.

What did you ever do to get on the wrong side of Mr. Wood? he asked.

Elmore couldn't remember his answer.

Wood told me to fire you. Ordered me. Like I reported to him.

The revelation brought Elmore up off his cot.

Mr. Rankin ...

The big face with the statue's nose spoke from the mist.

Nobody, not even Mr. Wood, tells me who to hire and fire, Rankin told him. *He might be richer than God, but that don't make him better than God.*

I'm holding a place on the crews for you, Elmore. I been through a war myself, and maybe I know something about what it's like to come home busted up, with little chillun and a wife to feed. You been a good worker for us. Once that wrist is doin' right, you'll have a steady paycheck again ...

Sheriff Neeley eavesdropped. He listened in on *all* jailhouse conversations – Neeley never let a soul talk to Elmore without standing by, watching like a hawk.

Dr. Thomson, organ player and diviner of internal organs, doctored Lafayette's city prisoners. He also attended the Methodist orphan home and handled sometimes-unsettling duties at the women's shelter.

He appeared, thin and ghostly, in Elmore's cell. He wore a green plaid jacket and white shoes. With Elmore's orange jumpsuit, the cell turned tropical.

Dr. Thomson checked Elmore's cuts and stitches, examined the wrist. He put the popsicle stick on Elmore's tongue. He shined the painful light into Elmore's eyes and listened to Elmore's heart with a stethoscope.

He pushed fingers into Elmore's right side. The pain took Elmore's breath away.

Hurt you. The doctor stated the fact. *Sorry.*

Finally, Doctor Thomson drew blood. He used a needle Elmore didn't even feel. But Elmore *did* feel a familiar panic. He didn't make himself look at his own bodily fluid as it darkened the vial.

"Mr. Rogers, your records from the hospitalization after your fall last Christmas tell us you're blood type B." Dr. Thomson focused on drawing the sample and spoke flatly without looking directly at Elmore. "This sample will confirm that."

Elmore nodded wearily. In the last few years, he'd had a million needles stuck in him. Permanent scar tissue marred the crooks of both elbows.

"I keep a picture of a porcupine," he told Dr. Thomson. "To help me sleep."

By the fifth night, Elmore felt like himself again. He deplored the orange jumpsuit, but the fog had lifted, his headache cleared, the cuts and aches diminished.

Then Kelly Rogers walked into police headquarters.

She didn't knock. She didn't ring the bell.

She wore a simple black shift, flat shoes. She had chopped her hair, badly, so it barely touched her collar. She looked very thin.

She looked startlingly beautiful.

She surprised Sheriff Neeley, and Dan actually reached one hand instinctively for his pistol. Deputy Turnipseed's wet cigar plopped into his lap.

"You," Dan Neeley said firmly, "are not allowed here."

"Yes I am."

Kelly's voice held a challenge.

The room grew very quiet. A clock ticked. Out in the night, a driver blew a horn.

"Kelly, go home," Dan Neeley said. "What good will this do?"

"We'll see," she answered. Not a hint of emotion showed in her remarkable face.

She went to Elmore's cell. He struggled off the cot in his bright orange jumpsuit. His cheeks burned.

"KELLY!"

Sheriff Neeley's voice held a sharp warning.

She ignored old high-school Danny and held something out to Elmore, something in her hand, something in a wrinkled white paper Milky Way sack.

Elmore felt a million things. The headache slammed back into place between his temples. His heart hurled itself against his ribcage.

"Go on, Elmore. Take it." Kelly's voice sounded hoarse, like she didn't use it often.

Her beautiful eyes made Elmore want to die.

And to live.

"Go on, El," she whispered. "It's for Mary and Will. And you."

The sparkling glint of tears appeared in her eyes.

"I heard you fell off the …" Elmore managed to stammer.

He didn't finish.

"JUMPED!" Sheriff Dan Neeley yelled from across the room.

The officer stood now, finger pointing, shaking with anger.

"She *jumped*, Elmore! Off the old Black Warrior trestle. Turnip dragged her sorry carcass to shore, and she spent three days under a suicide watch, strapped to a bed so she wouldn't try that shit again …"

Elmore saw dark bruises on Kelly's wrists, livid red punctures up and down pale arms.

She turned to Neeley. Kelly's voice broke, but she kept her composure.

"Danny. Please. I'm out. Out. That's over."

The room grew quiet. Kelly turned to Elmore.

He couldn't look at her. He couldn't look away.

"Take it, Elmore," Kelly urged. She shook the white sack. "Put it in your house?"

Elmore reached through the metal bars. The bag wasn't heavy.

Kelly turned and walked to the police headquarters door and through without another word.

The room felt very empty as the door closed.

No one spoke for a time.

"Elmore," Sheriff Neeley finally said, "I need to see what's in that bag before I let you take it inside the cell."

Elmore's hand still clutched the sack in mid-air a foot beyond the bars.

Neeley gave a quick inspection.

He closed the paper sack. He walked back to his desk, avoiding eye contact with Elmore or Deputy Turnipseed. He briskly lifted his duty jacket off the back of his swivel seat. He snapped on his policeman's cap and wordlessly walked out the door without looking back, just as Kelly Rogers had done.

Deputy Turnipseed puttered another uncomfortable moment, then he made an exit too. He turned slightly sideways to ease himself through the door frame. He left an unfinished cigar on his desk.

Elmore drew the paper bag through the bars. He took a deep breath and opened it.

The black frame of the photograph held them all. Elmore and Kelly, hand-in-hand. Will and Mary, toddlers. The adults wore Sunday best. The kids wore new Easter clothes and looked oddly like a little bride and groom.

All smiled. The camera mercifully lied, showing not a trace of the Rogers family's troubles. Elmore's level gaze gave no hint of unrelenting pain and trauma. Kelly's Hollywood smile masked the crippling postpartum depression. The winning faces of the twins beamed.

Elmore fell asleep holding the picture to his chest.

—29—

A Trailer Home Companion

For weeks, Kelly had the nightmare.

She sank in blackness. The universe had no up, no down. Sounds came through skin. Clicks. Whistles. Groans of ship timbers shifting in currents. Cries of seagulls.

Cries of children.

Each night, a window appeared in darkness. Kelly peered through, apprehensive.

A shape swam from the blackness, drew close to the window. Blotchy. White. Hooded eyes. Thick lips.

Fish? Man?

It opened its mouth. A silver bubble streamed upward like a melting mirror.

Night after night, Kelly tried to beat the dream shape away. But night after night, she found her wrists bound tightly by her sides, her legs restrained by straps.

Plastic tubes violated her nose. Needles pierced her arms.

One night, the sinister shape spoke. Silver bubbles wobbled up through the ink.

I am everywhere. I know everything.

Kelly woke in panic. Kicking. Sweating.

It happened first in intensive care, that black room. Even masked by drugs, the heavy stone of lithium on her chest, it felt too real to be a dream.

It continued to happen later in the kind of private room where they parked people with special problems. Problems that caused falls from high trestles into cold, dark places.

She returned to the trailer home. Kelly kept having the dreams. Night after night, old Chessie leaped wildly off the bed, tripled in size by fear, hissing when Kelly woke up screaming.

Something in particular disturbed Kelly.

She distinctly felt the pale thing in the dream had touched her. Intimately. Thick, fat fingers.

Violation.

Everywhere. Everything.

Had someone come into the hospital room? A pervert doctor? Only medical staffers were granted access, Nurse Eva assured her time after time. Kelly tried to believe it.

But she had the dreams.

She created a mantra. A prayer of self-defense. To herself, to nothing else, no one else.

It's not what you did. It's what you will do.

It's not what you did. It's what you will do.

One Sunday morning, Kelly lay in bed, like always. Same clothes as yesterday. Same bedsheet as the month before. Same half-eaten canned beans by the pillow, same dirty spoon.

A knock startled her.

No one knocked. When Dan Neeley stopped by, he just opened the aluminum excuse for a door and entered. He removed his policeman's hat, and he always held it in both hands in front of him, nervously turning it like a little blue steering wheel.

"Who is it?" Kelly's voice, out of practice, barely carried.

Knock knock knock knock.

"Who is it? Who's THERE?"

She recognized Elmore's voice instantly. And the other two.

"It's me, Kelly. And Will. And Mary."

Mama! Mama!

Kelly remembered with a flash of horror and guilt another time she'd heard those cries.

This time, she called back their names. "Mary! Will!"

She called Elmore's too.

Kelly flung open the door.

Their little faces. She had never seen anything so beautiful.

Forgiving faces.

They rushed through the doorway. All of them.

Kelly's life started again.

Had someone come into the hospital room? Only medical staffers were granted access, Nurse Eva assured her. Kelly tried to believe it.

30

River Music

Kelly stared at the ridiculous panel truck. The whole shaggy yard around the trailer home smelled of gasoline as it erupted to life in the driveway, Elmore smiling down from behind the wheel.

The afternoon wind tossed her hair, frisked her skirt. Mary and Will, elevated like little courtroom judges, blinked from their places in the cab. They looked like they'd made a bet, and one was about to win.

A place waited for Kelly beside them, the passenger-side door wide open.

"Ouch! Mama, this seat's burnin' hot!"

Mary snatched her bare feet up from the floor and balanced on tiptoes to keep her thighs and butt off the cracked seat. Black strips of electrician's tape held the gray vinyl together beneath her.

"You're a sissy!" Will sneered. "You ain't tough!"

"Will," Elmore tiredly warned from behind the wheel. "What did I tell you?"

Kelly saw something Elmore didn't. Mary's little pink tongue stuck out, ever-so-briefly, quick as a little snake's. Take that, tough boy!

"Daddy!" Will crowed grievously. "She stuck her tongue out at me!"

"You're a sissy," Mary parroted. "You ain't tough!"

Elmore ignored the squabble, or pretended to. Kelly thought he looked like a man who had been walking through a hard pouring rain for a long time. *You ain't a Hollywood movie star anymore, El,* Kelly thought to herself. *And still …*

Elmore collected a few paper napkins off the dashboard and deftly flicked them into the shadow under Mary's hovering little self. He looked like a man dealing cards. After another moment on her perch, Mary settled down onto the napkin nest with a satisfied look.

"Kelly, all aboard. Truck needs your weight on that side."

Elmore didn't look straight at her, but Kelly saw his bottom lip tuck ever so slightly, the way it always did before he laughed.

She suddenly remembered Elmore's body underneath his clothes. Before the war. Then after the war.

"Damn!" she gasped, shocking even herself. "I mean, *ouch!*"

The seat really *was* hot. Scorching. So Kelly did just as Mary had done – she kicked off her shoes, tucked her long legs beneath her, and balanced on the balls of her feet atop the seat.

Everybody laughed. Kelly too, and a rush of hilarity and oxygen into her lungs left her slightly dizzy. How long had it been since she laughed? Kelly couldn't even remember. Maybe it was something Chessie did. A long time ago.

She slammed her door shut, then propped an elbow in the open window. The metal side of the truck felt scalding too, but she didn't flinch.

Mama's tough too, Will.

Some finger reached for a button, and a song crackled out of the truck's bad stereo speaker. An old country hit. Tammy Wynette. "Stand By Your Man".

Kelly rolled her eyes. Elmore still loved that crap country. And that song – did he have a spy at the radio station?

"Kelly! Listen!" Elmore sounded like an idiot. "They're playing our song!"

Elmore and the twins made small talk as he drove. Kelly could barely follow their shorthand, the inner-family references mysterious and intimate, sometimes just a single word or two. *Possum pizza. Ditch witch.* Kelly turned her head in amazement after she heard Mary say *rhombus*.

The little girl bounced in the cab next to Kelly, two ladies riding shotgun. Will kept busy by his dad, who let him work the panel truck's six-in-the floor stick shift.

"Every time you grind it," Elmore admonished, "you have to make a pancake for Mary and me."

"And Mama?" Will's face lifted with the earnest question.

The truck bounced over a pothole. A weird musical sound briefly came from the cargo.

"If she still likes pancakes."

Kelly couldn't help what she felt now. She turned her head once more to stare out the open window and to let the wind blow tears secretly away.

This family wouldn't give her any breaks.

As Elmore muscled the truck through a turn onto a bumpy unpaved road, the riders heard again a strange discordant sound from the cargo hold. Kelly had her mouth open to ask what-on-earth, but Elmore had an announcement.

"Kelly, we're going to one of the young'uns' favorite places," he said loudly and proudly.

"It's the Black Warrior River!" Will trumpeted. "Daddy lets us fish!"

The name of the river thundered in Kelly's head, chest, gut.

"I caught the biggest fish last time!" Mary looked imploringly at her mom for a sign of approval. "Mine was twice as big as Daddy's!"

"Daddy wasn't even trying," Will announced. "He was helping me tie worms together. Plus, I had a giant one, but it got my bait!"

"Your daddy took me fishing one time in high school," Kelly remembered, but the voice telling the story didn't sound like hers. Some Kelly from the past moved her lips and tongue.

"He showed me how to catch a cricket in a hollow in both hands and hold it ... really careful like it was in a little church ... and talk to it before I dropped it in the water."

Mary was exuberant. "Daddy taught me to hock up and spit on the bait for luck!"

"Did y'all know," Elmore interrupted quickly, "that your mama caught the most dangerous fish that ever swam in the Black Warrior River?"

"Whoa!" said Will, and he forgot the gear shift completely.

"She caught … the Largemouth Rogers!"

The children groaned at the same time. But Kelly spoke up.

"It just took the right bait," she said. "He didn't put up too much of a fight."

Elmore and Kelly remained in the cab of the truck, afternoon settling. Will and Mary ran in the golden light toward the Black Warrior, cane fishing poles bouncing. Will was in charge of the cricket cage, a marvelous aluminum thing that held two-dozen peculiar-smelling brown insects and the aging chunk of raw potato they ate and a miniature cork stopper.

So this was it.

Elmore and Kelly. Husband and wife. Broken and more broken. Sitting together, after so long.

"Those are ours," Elmore said, nodding at the twins.

Kelly heard a tone without retribution, without old blame. She wondered if Elmore could hear her heart beating so hard.

"Ours."

Kelly couldn't stop the break in her voice, a one-syllable word cracked in two. And then the tears came, without shame. A river of tears.

Elmore's grief spilled out too, to Kelly's amazement. They found themselves entwined, hair tangled, limbs clasped, faces close, tears mingled. They sobbed together, and they hurt as one, and they gasped for air between their uncontrollable outbursts.

Neither could speak. But what even needed to be said?

Kelly found Elmore's mouth and kissed him like it would save them all, all four of them. Their family. Save them from flame and water and shadow and light. Save them from one another. Save them from even death itself.

Far away by the noisy river, the voices of their children rose and fell. Echoes spanked back from the Black Warrior's far shore, happy and carefree.

Elmore spoke, his voice urgent.

"Kelly, follow me."

She found her hand in his. They climbed out of the cab and went to the back of the panel truck. Elmore used his free hand to roughly unlatch the squawking cargo door and shove it up. Kelly couldn't make out the curious glossy black shape inside the compartment.

Elmore struggled to climb up by himself into the hold of the truck – that leg of his – but he made it, then turned to hoist Kelly up too.

It was a most curious cargo.

An oversized ebony piano cabinet filled the entire floor of the vehicle, its metal frame and strings still attached, glowing with their own kind of light in one place where a cover cloth had not done its job. The enormous polished wing of the instrument leaned against one wall, secured with rope and padding. Three legs and the pedal apparatus of the grand lined the other side of the truck, looking curiously like the black stick legs of the crickets Will and Mary dropped into the river as they battled to catch the biggest fish of the day.

"It's a Steinway. It belongs to the music school in Tuscaloosa," Elmore explained. "I picked it up today to deliver to Rankin. We're going to refinish it ..."

"Elmore. Come."

Kelly already had her cotton summer skirt bunched in her right hand, pulled up high. With her free hand, she flipped back the padded cover cloth, exposing the fantastic and intricate string work inside the piano.

Elmore did not need to be told twice. He urgently yanked down the panel door with a squawk and a bang. For a moment, the interior of the truck turned as black as the aging finish on the old Steinway.

Light found a way, though. It sprang like bright water leaks through missing rivet holes and a jagged crack where a falling pecan limb had left some damage years ago.

"Do like this," Kelly said, and she coaxed Elmore to his knees, then gently tipped him back asprawl the surprised strings in the long piano bed. Elmore made a quiet hurt noise, shifting to get his thigh and kidneys in the right place.

The strings made a quiet hurt noise too.

Kelly urgently straddled him. He urgently answered. Cloth tore, but Kelly couldn't tell if it was her dress, her underclothes, or the piano's cover cloth. It didn't matter. They were one again, one, and she and Elmore moved together to fantastic dissonant primal chords sounded by their elbows, knees, heels, heads, hearts.

Neither would ever be able to say who claimed the biggest shining catch. Kelly only knew that all the pain, ever, went away for those few moments. Elmore arched in an ecstatic spasm and splayed out a chord no worldly instrument had ever played until that moment.

The passion sounds – the animal sounds – faded. The chord faded, traveling toward the end of the universe.

Kelly and Elmore lay without speaking. Bronze and steel wires pressed their backs and fronts. Their bodies stayed locked. Nothing else mattered.

No word of would-be-fatal trestle plunges or hot cars. No word of violent hallucinations or vomited pain pills or screaming nightmares.

They had passed, in the dim light, to some place beyond pain, sorrow, error, regret.

"El," Kelly whispered at last.

"My love?"

"I still love pancakes ..."

Little voices interrupted, broke the spell.

"Hey!" Will yelled, insistently beating the cargo door with his small palm. "Who's playing music?"

Kelly and Elmore lay without speaking. Their bodies stayed locked. They had passed, in the dim light, to some place beyond pain, sorrow, error, regret.

December

31

The Jolly Holiday

Three days before the winter solstice. Seven days till Christmas. Mr. Wood had his plan in place.

He was already awake, thinking, when the rising sun lit the highest windows of Sweet Comb. He lay under a 30-year-old army blanket.

An old excitement ran through his veins.

The Epicureans were on the way.

He would host them in the heart of the castle, a place of reckoning in its labyrinth of one hundred rooms. Meeting rooms and ballrooms. Bedrooms and smoking rooms. Grand rooms and intimate rooms. Secret rooms. Dozens of stairways and hallways and passageways connected levels and wings like a huge honeycomb.

A man could get lost.

Mr. Wood lived a solitary life in his monstrous home.

Except one Monday a month.

That day, for eight frenetic hours, cleaners and maintenance people and technicians and delivery folks and gardeners and anyone else tasked with serving the place worked all at once, getting in one another's way, bumbling, swarming like bees in and out of doorways.

Mr. Wood liked solitude 160 hours of the week.

He prepared and took his breakfast alone on a fifth-floor veranda with an eastern view. The bellies of morning clouds glowed pink. Winter grew close.

Mr. Wood thought of his Epicurean friends gathering far away at a designated rendezvous. Two days from now, they would board Mr. Wood's stealth jet for a long trip. A month ago, he had flown it, dropped it, and returned via Atlanta with Don Gaston, on his way home to Brazil after a deal with the Kazakhstan army.

Everything was ready. Guiding beams. Secret landing strip. The Room. All.

The big surprise was ready too.

Mr. Wood lifted his coffee. The wind caught his napkin, and it suddenly gusted out over the balcony and blew like a morning ghost over endless acres.

Mr. Wood remembered paratrooper training with the Airborne at Fort Benning, all those years ago. He daydreamed of floating under silk through the atmosphere again, setting his boots on some new world.

With thick fingers, Mr. Wood absent-mindedly peeled and ate six boiled eggs, then a ruby grapefruit. He tossed the shells and citrus peels over the balcony.

Blackbirds flew past, blown on the December wind like dead cinders.

Mr. Wood fantasized about the solstice.

Time to work.

Mr. Wood climbed down two stairways. The door to his private console room, by design, looked for all the world like an expensive paneled wall.

It opened silently under Mr. Wood's flat palm and spoken password.

A smell of overwarm wiring filled the air. Blue video light flickered.

Mr. Wood stood at the center of a circle of surveillance screens stacked six high. Scores of them beamed their black-and-white stories, some displaying small moving figures, drones of duty somewhere in Mr. Wood's empire.

He watched the concrete factory in Bangalore. The paper mill at Bangor. The Lafayette wood yards. Downtown San Francisco. Shanghai shipyards and Santiago copper mines. Lafayette City Square, where phone company crews in cherry-pickers hung giant red balls from light poles and draped lights on a huge evergreen.

The courthouse square now boasted Lafayette's first-ever Jolly Holiday tree.

One screen caught Jess Turnipseed dozing at his desk in police headquarters. Mr. Wood saw no sign of Sheriff Neeley.

He narrowed his eyes. The PD lacked supervision.

Another screen displayed Fire Chief Wragg. In his fire station office, the jowly ex-SEAL watched porn and dug his spoon into a huge bowl of Corn Flakes.

Mr. Wood was everywhere. He knew everything.

He watched nuclear plants and TV stations and slaughter houses and blazing foundries.

He also watched the cheap rental house of Elmore Rogers.

Mr. Wood clicked a small remote.

An image zoomed. It rewarded Mr. Wood with a spectacular scene of pure Americana.

Elmore Rogers left his front door. He opened the cab of that damned Rankin panel truck, then beckoned to the house, *come on, come on!*

Out scrambled Will and Mary, laughing. What a sight!

Each child held a gift in cheerful red paper. For a teacher? Today was the last day of school before Christmas holidays.

Husky Will.

Delicious Mary.

Mr. Wood described them last week on the annual conference call of The Epicureans.

Main course. Dessert.

Oh ... and look! A fourth figure entered the video.

She wore white pajamas, hair mussed. She leaned, softly smiling, against the open door frame. She crossed her arms over her breasts for warmth.

Elmore blew the horn cheerfully. The kids waved a crazy goodbye.

Even Mr. Wood begrudgingly admired the moment.

Kelly Rogers' raven hair blew in her face. She turned and her locks fluttered free.

Extraordinary, Mr. Wood had to admit.

She toodled fingers to the kids, and the panel truck chugged away.

Kelly stood in the doorway a long time after Elmore and the twins left, watching the place in the distance they disappeared.

Mr. Wood imagined something unholy.

—32—

A Star Among Stars

The Epicureans gathered in England. Mr. Wood's luxury jet would speed them by night from there across the Atlantic.

They would glow in the heavens, a star among the stars. A star falling on Alabama.

The Epicureans rendezvoused, as with each winter solstice for a quarter century, at an obscure staging area. The precaution mattered, of course. Twelve jets, even with stealth technology and exacting below-radar flight plans, would always be more trackable than one.

The closer The Epicureans drew to their plates and cutlery, the more care they took. They followed vectors from Japan, Brazil, Congo, Saudi Arabia, and other compass points to Albemarle. They met at a landing strip on the vast estate of the Duke and Duchess.

The aging nobles welcomed them, party by party. The Duke in tux and tails, she in sable, stood at the walkway leading to the hatch of Mr. Wood's thirty-seat jet.

Welcome! Welcome to the solstice!

The Duke's bear paw enclosed Epicurean hands; friendly kisses passed cheek to cheek.

All aboard! cried the Duke. *Pip! Pip! Next stop ... Alabama!*

The seats shone in gold-threaded silk, and Wagner flooded the cabin. The door soundlessly shut.

The Epicurean from Moscow, a big bear of a man who grew fantastically rich selling retired MIGs to the third world, piloted for Mr. Wood. He taxied in purring silence, made a smooth half-turn. The twin jet engines cleared throats, flexed steel muscles, waited in the English mist like a sprinter in the blocks.

The pilot stepped back into the cabin for a toast.

Standing before a real wood fire, the Duke raised a glass of Champagne to the cohort of elegant men and women. His voice thickened with emotion.

"Cheers!" he cried. "To The Epicureans! To twenty-five!"

Glasses of golden champagne rose, and a babble of languages.

"To the feast!" announced the Duchess, who always insisted on the last word. Her smile was a gash.

In a moment, the world fell away. England became a postage stamp, then the jet entered clouds of heaven.

The Epicureans drank down their Champagne, then another.

The great day of winter solstice would dawn as they flew.

The pilot stepped back into the cabin for a toast. Glasses of golden champagne rose, and a babble of languages. "To the feast!" announced the Duchess.

—33—

Yule Logs

Elmore entered bustling, green-and-gold downtown Lafayette. In his truck, among rattling cabinetry tools and padded blankets, ranged a herd of bewildered plywood reindeer.

Elmore had milled the little Rudolphs himself the past week at Rankin Cabinets. Each sported a battery-powered red nose that blinked. The deer cheered Elmore. He would drop them for Boy Scouts and other volunteer elves to distribute in city spaces for the big night ahead.

Elmore relished how Will and Mary would enjoy seeing reindeer he made with his own hands. He'd pick up the twins and Kelly after work, and the Rogers clan would ride together to witness the parade, carols on the square, and other merriments.

Elmore glanced at his speedometer and frowned. He'd just spotted Lafayette's flashing electronic population sign, the silly idea of a silly mayor and a silly city council. It reported Elmore's speed, plus other critical data:

47 MPH
Lafayette, Alabama
December 21
Population 8,369 (and growing!)
Elevation 390 feet (and stable!)
10:30 a.m.

Elmore eased the engine to 30 mph but still easily passed a John Deere in the slow lane. The tractor towed a cheerful peppermint-motif parade float. The chubby teenage driver wore a Lafayette Lions baseball cap, and he waved a corn dog on a stick at Elmore, *hello, howdy*.

He looked ... jolly.

And why not? Lafayette had gone all-out for The Jolly Holiday. Sidewalks bustled, and scores of merchants and store employees garnished the great gaudy Christmas tableau the town had become. Elmore reckoned all 8,369 residents, plus lots of guests, must be out and about.

Downtown's transformation had reached a grand finale. Christmas lights and tinsel garlands draped store windows, door frames, and overhead power lines. Sparkly Christmas balls, red and green and huge as Japanese lanterns, bobbed in the morning breeze of the official first day of winter. In store windows, waving plastic Santas resembled football linemen in padded red-and-white uniforms. A feathered-and-sequined group of little-girl angels flocked out of Ted Huddleston's music store, shedding fluff off artificial wings.

Elmore found good cheer welling inside him. He lifted the sun visor in his truck cab to savor the spectacular view of his Lafayette. A silly new idea by the mayor, for once, didn't turn out silly.

Will and Mary would love this so much.

And Kelly.

A first Christmas together since ... well ... since all that happened.

Elmore stopped the panel truck at a red light.

He felt thankful in this season of thanksgiving.

Kelly. The twins.

It had taken months. It had taken forgiveness. It took all four of the Rogers becoming something new.

A family.

That afternoon last summer when he took Will and Mary to Kelly's trailer, the twins stood shaking at the door. Literally shaking.

Kelly fell on her knees in the doorway and reached her arms to hug the kids. *Their* kids. The sobbing rose like one single voice.

That moment changed everything.

Elmore had vowed to change. He emerged from a jail cell and kept his promise.

The road back began at Kelly's front door.

RUUUUUMBLE!!!

Reverie ended. The teen to Elmore's right throttled up, and black smoke belched from the John Deere's smokestack. A driver behind the kid gently tapped his horn.

All the red lights in Elmore's life had changed to green.

He popped the gear in the floor, eased forward.

He saw a bright rush. He felt a bone-rattling jolt.

With pain.

Something happened.
Bad. Like a roadside bomb.
Things turned upside down.
Elmore looked up from the floorboard of the truck into a shattered windshield.
Glass glittered on the seat. He smelled rubber and steam. Torn steel.
A pain stabbed Elmore's right side, his right thigh.
He felt a shocking déjà vu.

Three blocks away, Fire Chief Wragg slowly cruised a line of parade floats colorfully queued in the staging area for the parade.
He spit Red Man at a hydrant.
"Damn, Neeley! I didn't know I could still be impressed by a parade. All those for Uncle Sam wore my ass out! God damn drums and bugles. But just look at this Jolly Holiday!"
Red-sequined majorettes practiced a twirling routine on one float.
"Damn! Baby Jesus gotta like that!"
Sheriff Neeley rode shotgun by Wragg, jaw set, eyes on another float. High-school students monkeyed in the rigging of a pirate ship, fastening ribbons and Christmas lights.
Sheriff Neeley didn't like the Scrooge feeling inside. But there it was.
Mostly, Neeley didn't like Wragg. He didn't like a fire department vehicle. He didn't like a chauffeur. But he was a man to follow orders, and Mr. Wood had handwritten meticulous instructions for The Jolly Holiday. Lafayette's police and fire departments clicked their heels.
They inspected the parade route in Wragg's official vehicle, as instructed. Wragg drove, as instructed. They drove one direction along the parade route from 9 a.m. to 9:30 a.m., as instructed. They cruised it again in the opposite direction from 10 to 10:30 a.m., as instructed.

The car felt overwarm, though the day outside dawned brisk. About every five minutes, Wragg gave a goofy grin and turned on the siren, scaring the daylights out of Lafayette.

"I wish you'd stop that redneck stuff," Sheriff Neeley finally said.

Wragg, with a vengeful expression, whooped the siren again, pure spite.

Neeley went back to staring out the passenger window.

Accident. Main and Foster. Accident. Main and Foster.

The hotline burst to life in the fire chief's car.

Accident. Main and Foster.

Wragg blared the siren. He gunned the car. Acceleration pressed Neeley into his seat.

The red cruiser ran a light in the first block and nearly hit a surprised shopper.

"Wragg? You're gonna kill somebody!"

The fire chief snorted.

"Been there, done that. You heard that message, Sheriff. We're headed to Main and Foster."

"Who the hell was on the radio?"

"The boss," Wragg said.

Wragg took the next corner with back tires smoking, like a vehicle in a movie chase. Neeley clutched the dash.

"Hey, Wragg! HEY!"

One traffic light ahead, they saw an entangled panel truck and a log truck, one of Mr. Wood's. Smoke rose. Pine logs had spilled onto the intersection. One came to rest blocking the doors to Klibanoff's Shoe Shop.

The crash had wrenched open the back door of the panel truck. Painted wooden reindeer with flashing red noses covered the street, many with broken legs and antlers.

Wragg's siren howled, then his brakes.

Sheriff Neeley scrambled out. He held up a palm to halt oncoming traffic in all directions. He stepped over a torn log reeking of turpentine. Broken glass crunched.

Sheriff Neeley could read the side of the panel truck, despite the damage:

Rankin Cabinets
Quality

He stopped.

Was Elmore Rogers in that crushed truck?

Neeley hustled to the battered cab. He yanked the passenger-side door handle. It opened, miraculously, with a groan.

Two groans. One from the floorboard.

Elmore gave Neeley the strangest look. His face asked, without a word, *again?*

"Elmore, can you move?"

His face was bloody, but he answered.

"It ain't as bad as last time."

Elmore eased onto his elbow in the bright glass. "Danny. I'm coming out."

Sheriff Neeley wheeled. Where the hell was the log truck driver? Screw Mr. Wood's precious pulp timber. This sad sack would pay for recklessness.

A twenty-something with a mud flap of hair stood on the street corner. He shook a Camel out of a pack. Absolutely calm.

A collision? All in a day's work.

The smell of spilled gasoline filled the air.

Sheriff Neeley stalked up.

He looked the log-truck driver in the eye.

"Put out that lighter, idiot."

The driver had a stray eye. It gave Neeley the impression he searched for an escape route.

"What's your name? Where's your license?"

The kid put the lighter away. Then he took a drag from his cigarette, and blew the smoke straight up over his head.

"Name's Einstein," he finally said. "Yourn?"

Neeley reached to his belt for a pair of handcuffs.

Wragg gave a yell.

"Whoa! Sheriff Neeley! Looka this!"

The fire chief pointed into the glove compartment of Elmore's panel truck. The container had been knocked cock-eyed by the crash. Its door dangled by a sinew of black duct tape.

"Lookee, lookee, Sheriff Neeley!" Wragg's voice practically sang. "Look what Elmore Rogers has been up to!"

A large tinfoil square rested jauntily among jumbled screwdrivers and grimy papers. It had been conveniently torn open.

The greenish-brown substance inside looked like putty.

"Sheriff Neeley," Wragg said. "That looks like hashish to me. Don't you think?

Neeley turned. Wragg met his gaze without blinking, snake-eyed, bad lip twitching.

"Looks like red Lebanese hashish," Wragg emphasized. "Red. Lebanese. Hash."

Dan Neeley, for once in his talkative Irish life, could find no words.

"Run him in, Chief Neeley. This Rogers character appears to be in unlawful possession. Mr. Wood warned us."

Elmore, very dazed, sat on his butt with his knees raised, his back against the front tire of his panel truck.

Sheriff Neeley stared down at him. A goose egg rose on the side of Elmore's head, but his friend seemed more concerned with a bleeding gash in his palm. Neeley remembered how Elmore freaked at the sight of his own blood.

"You know what to do, Sheriff." Wragg spoke with glee.

Yes. Dan Neeley knew exactly what to do.

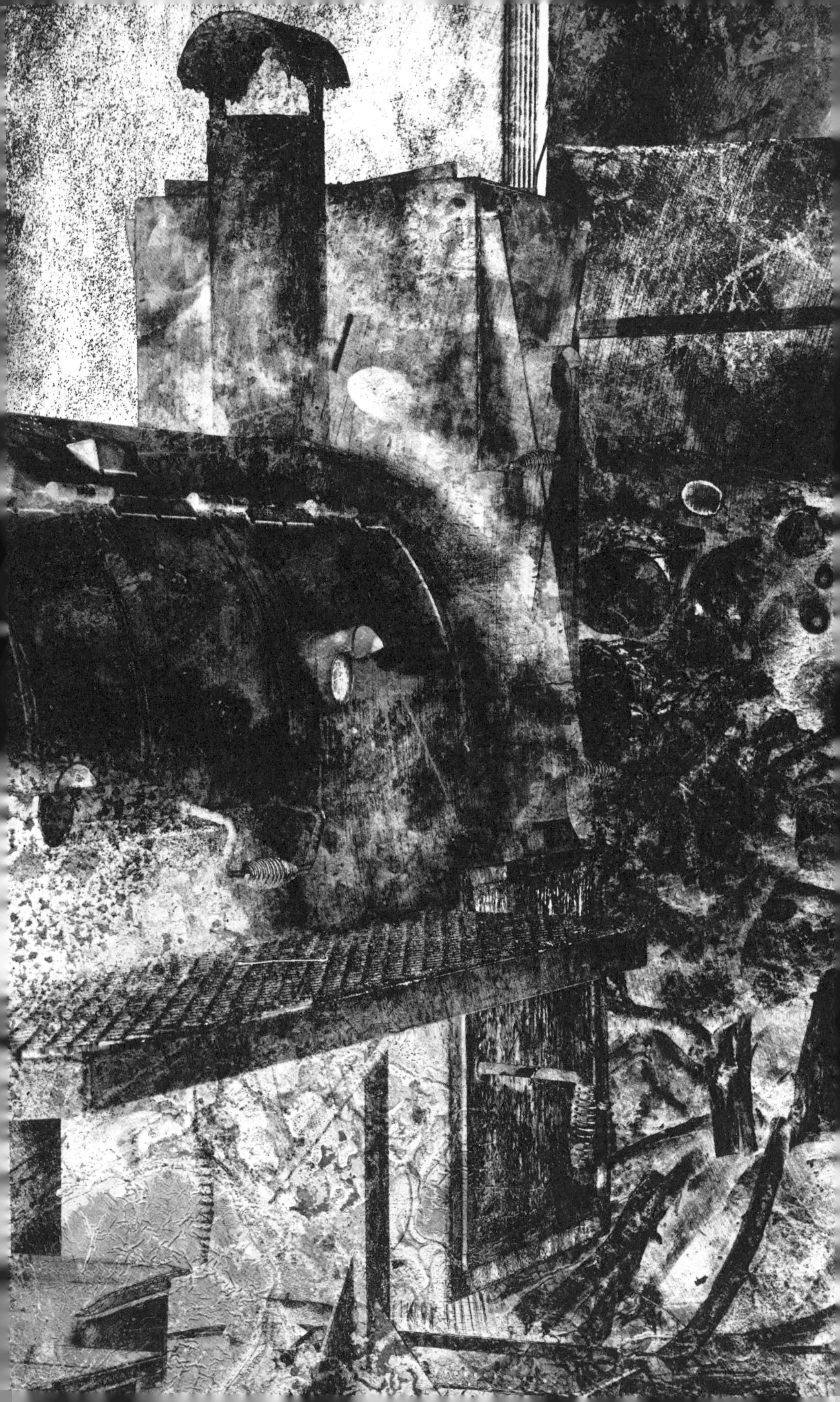

34
Order Up

Champion's BBQ shack smoked like a dragon. Slabs of ribs and roasted chickens went flying out the window as soon as Champion opened. Customers crunched the gravel lot a hundred times before lunch, and Champion's big arms ached from nursing the hot coals.

He made each sale a friendly ritual.

Welcome, y'all! Where you folks from? Butler County? Up here for The Jolly Holiday? Well, ho ho ho! Merry Christmas!

Vehicles sported reindeer antlers on top and holly wreaths on the tailgates and tinsel streamers. Bundled children stared from windows like runaway elves, many with the thin faces of kids who didn't get to town so often.

Ho ho ho! Champion waved a big cooking fork and channeled Santa.

The holiday money piled up in a Fuentes cigar box. Champion's son, Cleo, showed up twice to swap cash for coolers full of meat. Old Bill Perkins had killed hogs just yesterday, the first real cold snap in Lafayette. The fresh meat smelled wonderful on Champion's grill.

Through the day, Champion fed himself royally too. He tore apart slabs and cleaned the bones and tossed them into the dry blackberry patch in back of his shack. Years of bones lay in those weeds. This frosty morning, they gleamed like ivory in an elephant graveyard.

Red-eyed, Champion turned from the grill and got a surprise – the Sargent triplets, famously eccentric spinsters who lived in an antebellum mansion out past Aliceville. They had shown up for Lafayette's holiday party in identical dresses – *Gone with the Wind* gowns, heavy green velour. Fox furs draped their shoulders.

Champion had some fun.

"How do I know who ordered what?" he teased. "Y'all look just alike."

"Easy," said the middle Sargent. "I'm Mary. Like the Virgin."

A sister cackled.

"She's been a virgin several times now. Ask them boys from Gordo."

Proud Mary pursed haughty red lips.

"Well, at least I remember being a virgin. You were in kindergarten."

Sister three piped up.

"They're *both* sluts," she exhaled. "Just men with boobs."

Champion laughed, deep and hearty. He handed over three white cardboard boxes.

"Well, you fine ladies. Y'all enjoy these three French hens. They on the house."

The sisters walked off fussing like parakeets.

On his cloud nine of hickory smoke, Champion grinned all afternoon remembering the Sargent sisters.

The whole world looked bound for Lafayette. Champion watched tractors and brawny semis pull holiday floats along the road. Horse trailers rumbled by, and yellow school buses. More than once, Champion heard sousaphones and snare drums, blatting and beating.

Darkness came early this shortest day. Traffic waned. Champion couldn't remember a day when he worked so hard.

He knew one thing – the pig and chicken census of Lafayette was much reduced. He had sold a ton of meat. He'd lost maybe ten pounds sweating over the grill. He didn't have energy to drive to town and see all the hoopla. He would wait to hear the stories from his wife and Cleo.

He was scraping the grill and packing rubs away when he found the white envelope. It rested in the serving window.

He knew what it was without looking.

Champion slumped onto his folding chair for the first time all day. He fanned himself with the envelope. It was cold outside, but his shack felt like a boiler.

Champion looked out the window at the world.

Past the churned parking lot and over the dark serrated skyline of trees, a full moon rose.

Why is this night so still all of a sudden? Champion wondered. *This ain't natural.*

The night was cloudless, but Champion heard a low rumbling, like thunder.

It grew louder. Nearer.

A black airplane suddenly burst into view, very low, close to the treetops. It roared straight over Champion's shack, wheels already down, so loud every piece of biology in the cook's body stopped cold, scared to duck or shout or run.

The jet passed. Just that fast.

What the devil?

The hush settled back over Champion's shack. The oversized moon now had one bright star to keep it company.

Maybe that plane's bringing wise men to Lafayette, Champion thought.

He opened the white envelope.

It held ten Ben Franklins. A thousand dollars.

A paper clip clasped the bills and a note.

Champion read it twice to make sure his eyes weren't playing tricks. He couldn't have imagined an odder order.

He stuffed the bills into his right sock. Then, he turned to the barbecue pit. He was glad he hadn't already sprinkled water over the coals for the night.

Champion fed the note and empty envelope into the coals. It burst into terrible merry flames.

Then Champion picked up his cleaver and wiped its blade against his stained white apron. He threw new hickory on the coals.

Time to cook a most surprising solstice order.

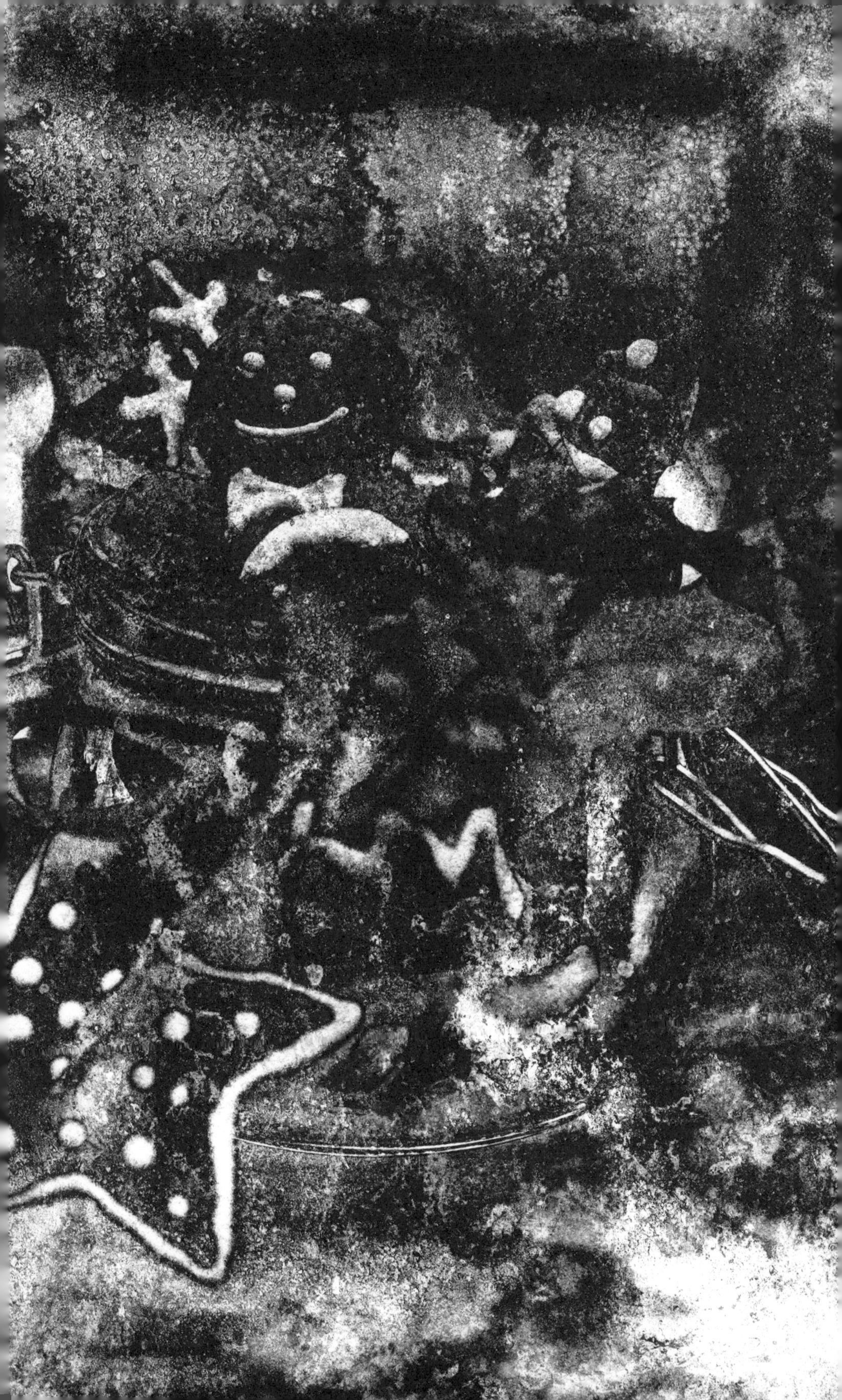

—35—

Nothing Like a Christmas Cookie

Mrs. Mock drew a quick breath in a blast of oven heat. Mitts shaped like puffy snowmen lifted an aluminum baking pan. The aroma of a holy trinity – butter, sugar, flour – filled her whole house.

"There's nothing like a Christmas cookie!" she warbled.

She dropped stars, reindeer, and holly leaves onto a green linen cloth in a picnic basket.

A plane screamed over outside, low and fast, rattling Mrs. Mock's windows.

"My goodness!" she said to herself again. "Jets for our Jolly Holiday! Just like at the Super Bowl!"

Lafayette, she thought proudly, was really getting to be something.

Mrs. Mock had made a million cookies before. Some society ladies declared that her Key-lime-and-ginger bites made them never want to bake again.

Still, she followed Mr. Wood's directions precisely. Into her mixing bowl, she mixed fresh butter, eggnog, and Mr. Wood's container of unknown powder – his "secret ingredient". She stirred. The pan baked in 15 minutes.

As Mr. Wood made her strictly promise, Mrs. Mock did not sample the cookies, not a single one. He wanted them all to be a generous gift to a certain family.

She didn't know what Mr. Wood had in mind for Elmore Rogers, the twins and that woman, but she would certainly help him spread holiday cheer.

He'd been good to her.

Off she traipsed to the car, cookie basket under her arm.

With school out for Christmas, Will and Mary returned to Fort Rogers. The weather was too cold for snakes, but the twins still stayed close to the little cabin, avoiding the creek.

Though a little overgrown after six months, their little wood-and-vine structure had held up pretty well. It pleased Will.

"That means we built it good," he told Mary, dragging a fallen pine branch off its top.

"I tied the sticks," Mary said proudly. She had stopped limping from her snakebite, and now two little white scars on her ankle were all she had to show for her grim experience.

Plus weird hospital memories.

The twins half expected Timmy Wragg to barrel up on his Spyder bike, but they played through the afternoon alone. Will bet that Timmy had gone to Lafayette to ride his dad's fire truck in the parade.

"Timmy better throw us some candy!" Mary declared. "And *not* licorice."

The afternoon passed dreamily. Mary spotted a hawk in that big pine tree. They tried to get up close. Will found something that looked like a little smashed TV camera.

"Look at this!" he announced. "It's a sure mystery!"

Mary seemed skeptical. "It coulda been a hunter, that hunted with a camera."

Will gave her a look, but after the snakebite he had stopped calling Mary 'igmo' and 'dumb bunny' and other names. He loved his sister.

"Maybe a hunter," he told her. "But it mighta been some important part of an Army airplane that fell off too. Let's keep it secret."

They played inside Fort Rogers, cozy under this season's leaf fall, the world red and gold as the day waned. Will grew hungry first, as ever, and he complained because Mary had forgotten to bring two banana sandwiches he made.

"Well, you coulda brought them as easy as me," Mary said.

"But I *made* them. I have to do everything?"

"You have to *tell* me you made them," Mary insisted. "Or I don't know."

"I put them on your blue sweater," Will said. "By the back door."

Mary looked confused. "That's Mama's blue sweater, Will. Mine ain't that big."

A sudden laugh on the other side of the fort wall scared them both.

Kelly Rogers stepped to the cabin door, the sun behind her. She wore a blue sweater.

"Mary's right. This is a big-girl sweater, Will."

"Mama! You scared us to death!"

Kelly looked very happy. She smiled so big. The sun shone in her hair.

"Well, y'all won't starve. Here you go."

She held out two banana sandwiches, each wrapped in a paper Milky Way napkin.

"Y'all eat these, then we'll go back to the house and get ready for the parade. Warm clothes – it's gonna be really cold. I haven't heard from daddy, but he'll be home any time."

Mary jumped up and down.

"Mama, where can we stand to catch the most candy?"

Kelly kissed Mary on top of her little red head.

"On the corner where the floats turn to head up to the courthouse. They slow down right there. I bet we can catch a ton of candy."

"But not licorice!" Mary made herself clear. "I'm giving the licorice to daddy."

Will, too hungry to talk, wolfed his sandwich in four bites. Mary carefully stripped the crusts off her sandwich and fed those to her brother too. She talked between thoughtful chews.

"Have you ever been in a parade, Mama? I mean, like riding on a float?"

Kelly briefly squinted into the sun. A late breeze blew a few colored leaves around her.

"Once upon a time," Kelly answered. "Before I even met your daddy."

Mrs. Mock's car glided to a stop. She turned off her headlights.

She pulled her dress seams straight, a Christmasy red wool dress with a warm mantle. She held her basket in the crook of one arm. The cookies smelled good.

She knocked on the door of the Rogers family. Feet thumped fast toward her.

"Daddy! Daddy!"

That beautiful little Mary flung the door wide. She had a dab of something white – banana? – at the corner of her mouth.

The child couldn't hide her disappointment.

"Hello there, Miss Mary," purred Mrs. Mock. "Merry Christmas!"

"Merry Christmas, Miz Mock."

Mary yelled back into the house.

"Maaammmmaaa!"

Will skated into view, one sock on, an old black cat skittering ahead of him in panic. Will took a quick look at the visitor and disappeared like a phantom.

Kelly switched on the porch light and spoke politely. She didn't invite Mrs. Mock inside.

"Happy holidays, Kelly! I brought over some Christmas goodies!"

The basket changed hands. Kelly smiled, showing Mary how to be polite.

"Merry Christmas to you too, Mrs. Mock. Do you have big plans for the holidays?"

Mrs. Mock did have plans. Exciting ones.

"I'm headed to downtown Lafayette tonight like everybody else in the world. Then I might just disappear for a while. Santa's been good to me this year. I could drive down to that Indian casino in Wetumpka and see if I get lucky!"

"I hope you do," said Kelly.

That was all.

"Well ..." Mrs. Mock waved an elegant red glove, "y'all have a jolly holiday!"

"We sure will," said Kelly evenly. "Thank you, and happy holidays."

"Enjoy those cookies! Don't they smell good?"

"Delicious," Kelly answered, sincerely.

Curious Mary peeked under the green cloth in the basket. Mrs. Mock winked approval.

She backed the Chrysler down the long Rogers driveway. She reached the end, but didn't go further. Instead, she turned off the ignition and headlights. And waited.

After ten minutes, she restarted the engine and flicked the defroster to high. With the sun down, she felt the first iron bite of winter cold.

She glided the car back up the drive, stopping with headlights directly on the Rogers front door. She left the car, the comfortable warmth of the heater, the cookie smell.

The doorknob rattled as it turned.

All three people inside lay still, as if fast asleep. Kelly's head lolled in the crook of her elbow at the kitchen table. Her hand held a half-eaten cookie.

Will and Mary lay side-by-side on a throw rug. Their shapes made Mrs. Mock think of dirty laundry dumped out of a hamper.

There's nothing like a Christmas cookie, Mrs. Mock thought.

She dragged Will first, hands under his armpits, all the way to her car. His feet, one sock off and one sock on, made two trails through the fallen leaves.

Mrs. Mock propped him upright in the back seat.

She caught her breath, then Mrs. Mock brought Mary out, a much lighter load.

"There," she said to herself. "That's that."

Through the open front door, Mrs. Mock caught a glimpse of Kelly slumped on the table. She fought back a sudden, impetuous desire.

Why, I'll search the house and find a butcher knife and whack off that thick black hair ...

There wasn't time. Elmore Rogers could drive up at any second.

She did dare go back in, though. For pure mischief.

She crammed a whole Christmas cookie, a star of Bethlehem, into Kelly's unconscious mouth and stuffed cookie crumbs tightly up her nose.

Mrs. Mock drove the children, smelling delicious as cookies, into the night.

Atop the utility pole by the Rogers driveway, a miniature camera swiveled.

Good girl. Mr. Wood smiled. *You've earned your final reward, Mrs. Mock.*

Deep inside Wood Castle, the magnate switched off the Rogers screen. He gloated a moment. He'd designed a Swiss watch of a plan. So far, it was flawless.

Mr. Wood lit a new screen. It bore a white superscript: *Lafayette.*

Downtown Lafayette looked festive as Mardi Gras. A throng had turned out – Mr. Wood guessed thirty-thousand people lined the parade route and jammed the courthouse square. Confetti flew, bottle rockets whistled skyward and popped.

He checked another screen: *Landing Strip.*

It looked for all the world like a long fairway on a private golf course. In seven minutes, a jet would scream out of the heavens onto it. A door would glide open, and The Epicureans would arrive.

Mr. Wood switched that screen off too.

It was time for a personal visit to pick up certain sleeping children.

Mr. Wood visualized The Epicureans stepping off the plane, sniffing Alabama. A paper mill. A vast turpentine sea of pine trees. He pictured their faces, the puzzlement in their eyes.

Mr. Wood glanced at one last screen. *Police Station.*

Ah. Déjà vu.

Elmore Rogers paced the same cell, in the same bright orange jumpsuit, as six months ago. He stopped, gripped steel bars with restless hands.

Tonight, Rogers had company – the hubbub of a downtown crowd and the blare of marching bands.

Mr. Wood smiled cruelly. *Who's watching the kids, Rogers? The big bad wolf?*

Mr. Wood didn't need audio to know Rogers was pleading with Sheriff Neeley. Pleading innocence, insisting that the hashish in his truck had been planted, that it belonged to someone else, that this was some weird plot.

Sheriff Neeley ignored his prisoner, focusing on paperwork.

Mr. Rogers' old buddy had turned out not to be such a buddy after all.

Amazing what a strong sense of duty could do to a man.

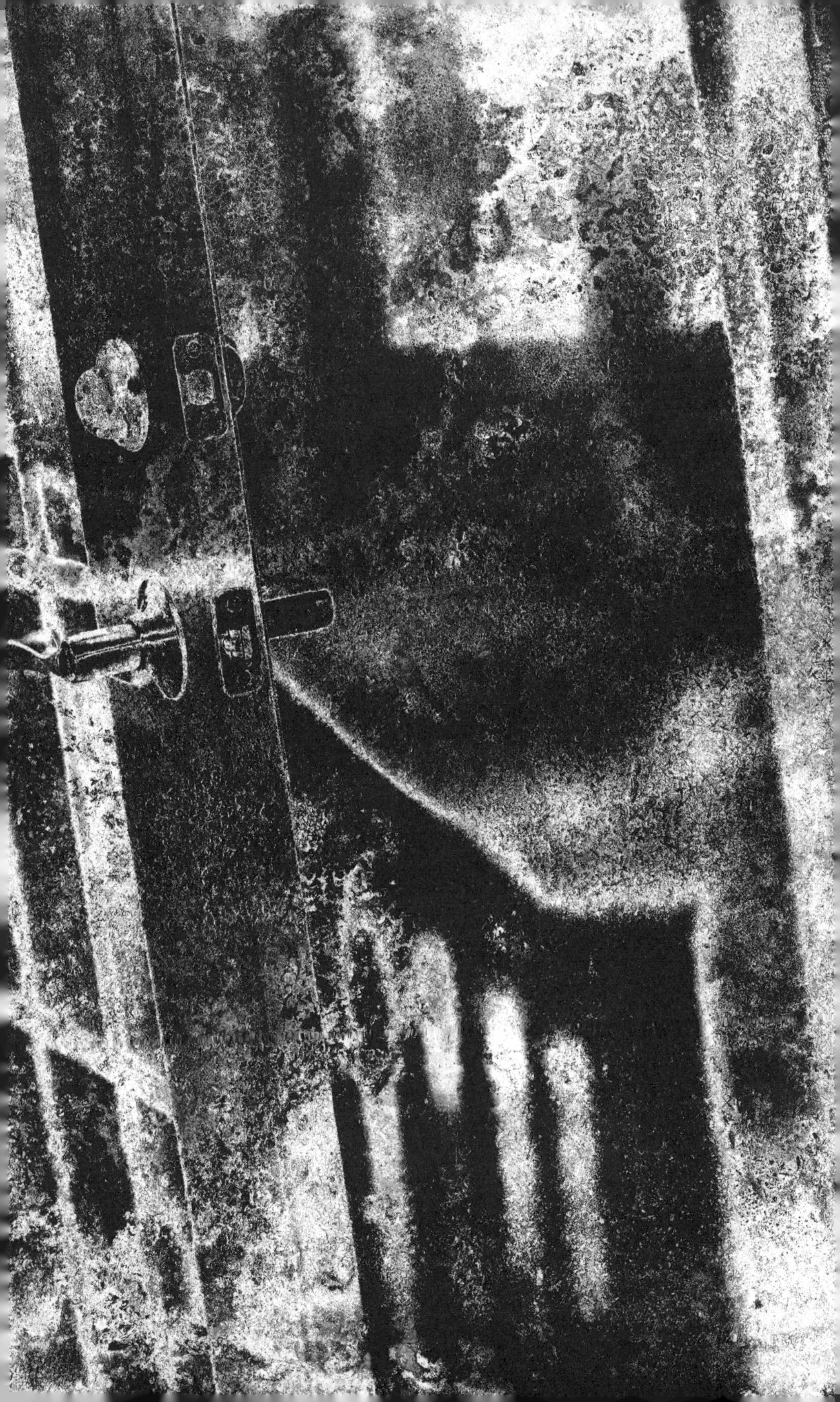

—36—

Waking Beauty

Ironically, postpartum had given Kelly Rogers one advantage. The cookie in her mouth contained a strong sleep agent, benzodiazepine class.

Kelly had used that drug for years.

First, in the depression nightmare after giving birth to the twins, she took a single sleeping pill, doctor's orders, to put her under, fast. Two hours of escape felt like heaven.

Soon one pill became two. Then Kelly took three, and finally dangerous handfuls.

After the Incident, she tore at the pill bottle lid on nights when her small twin demons screamed and screamed in her hot, guilty memory.

Each of Mrs. Mock's cookies carried enough drug to knock out a bull. But Kelly's body had fought a long war against that potion. Her resistance had mounted for years.

She woke with a start at the breakfast table, gagging, weeping, slick cookie dough extruding out her nostrils. The room spun giddily, cabinets, refrigerator, fresh Christmas tree from the woods, open front door ...

Open front door!

Jolted, Kelly attempted to stand. Saucers and uneaten pieces of cookie went flying.

She banged the floor. Her chair back splintered. Sparks danced around the Christmas tree. Wolves ... or something vicious ... howled, very near, surrounding the house.

If she didn't get off her floor, those terrible beasts, jaws dripping, eyes red, would come skulking right through the front door.

The open door.

Kelly struggled to her elbows. She felt a wet trickle down the back of her neck.

Mary and Will? Elmore! Where was Elmore?

She staggered across the room to the house phone, taking a knee only once.

Mary. Will.

Mama's coming. I'm coming.

For a horrible second, Kelly thought she'd gone deaf. The phone had no dial tone. The cold universe hissed in her ear.

The telephone cord was cut. A butcher knife lay on the kitchen counter, a severed cable to either side.

Kelly felt an implosion of deep fear now, mortal, dreadful.

Mary! Will! Elmore!

She didn't remember getting there, but Kelly stood in the dreamy solstice night by the green Volkswagen. A full moon poured silver. The winter evening, so cold, actually relieved her spinning head.

Then a new shock.

No keys.

They'd been snatched from the VW ignition.

Kelly flopped over the front seat.

Damn. Damn. Numb fingers rummaged glove compartment, searched dirty floorboard.

Someone had her keys. *Who? Why?*

Mrs. Mock?

A spasm shot through Kelly, an electric jolt. Panic.

Oh, sweet Jesus. What's happening to us? To me?

Kelly clambered from the cab, staggered. She fought back a scald of nausea.

Then she didn't fight, and a rope of vomit leaped out. Kelly desperately clutched her black hair, holding it back in one hand.

Kelly teetered, holding it together. She managed one spasmodic breath, a gasping deeper one.

She steadied, rallied.

Kelly stood on her own.

Now, she made out familiar sounds. A train. A farm dog barking far away.

Her head hurt. So badly.

But she gave her body a stern order. *Stop shaking.*

She ordered her left leg to take a step.

Dry leaves answered.

She took another. Then more, hobbling down the driveway in the cold night.

Stop swaying.

Kelly made it to the county road, silver as snow under the full moon.

She made herself trot, or what felt like it. She stumbled, but did not let her legs stop.

Kelly reached the Wraggs' house. Pitch black. No vehicle in the yard.

It took forever to reach the front door. She pounded and pounded with both fists. She tried to twist the doorknob.

Locked. No one home.

Kelly retreated back to the county road.

Seven miles to Lafayette, she recalled. *Once, I could run that far in forty-five minutes ...*

Kelly sought help at the next two farmhouses. She repeated a ritual. Pound the door. Pray. Try the door. Push it, shoulder it, slap it with desperate palms, sob against it.

No answers. No lights. No cars.

The whole world partied in Lafayette tonight. The Jolly Holiday could not be missed.

Kelly just ran.

She remembered high school, track, cheerleader training.

She stopped to puke again, wiping lips and chin on a dirty sleeve.

She forged on along the empty road. The stars shone too bright, like little explosions.

A V of birds crossed the moon.

Mary. Will.

Kelly ran.

Once, she stumbled off the road. Her feet punched through a thin skin of ice around dry cattails in a ditch. She needed a white stripe on the forlorn blacktop to guide her unsteady legs.

The icy ditch water chased more of the sleeping potion from her mind.

Kelly ran under the full moon.

She would find Danny ... Dan Neeley ... at the police station.

He would help her find her babies, and Elmore.

She knew she could count on Danny.

—37—

A Simple Twist of Face

The Lafayette radio station played "Silent Night". Will and Mary dozed peacefully in Mrs. Mock's back seat.

She left the motor running. Frozen children weren't part of the bargain with Mr. Wood. He counted on warm, toasty children. The twins were too gangly and too heavy, though, to drag through the back door into the house.

Mrs. Mock glanced at them.

Visions of sugar plums. The twins looked like holiday angels, even that little imp Will. He still clutched a crumbled cookie in his right hand. Greedy little boy.

Mrs. Mock quietly opened her car door. The overhead light flashed, and her hand darted to snap it off.

The cold of the solstice night knocked the breath out of her. Thank goodness Lafayette didn't have this curse more than a week or two every winter. How did people live in places like North Dakota?

Mrs. Mock flinched as she stood, grabbing her lower back.

The dead weight of two unconscious Rogers children had aggravated her condition. Mrs. Mock's sacroiliac would need hot water bottles. Maybe therapy. *I know*, she thought, brightly, *I can schedule that handsome Dr. Shack. He might do a woman a lot of good with a massage ...*

On the radio, "Silent Night" ended, and the local announcers breathlessly resumed chattering about The Jolly Holiday celebration. The giant tree! The thirty-Santa assembly! The floats and marching bands! Carved wooden Rudolphs, dozens of them, with blinking red noses!

Mrs. Mock shut the car door. She could make out the artillery roll of snare drums and the *oompah* of sousaphones across town. She heard an occasional wild cheer too, like at a fairground when a big Ferris wheel lunges earthward.

The Jolly Holiday, Mrs. Mock mused. *What a thing for Lafayette! I'll catch the parade if Mr. Wood arrives on time …*

She looked at her new wristwatch. Diamonds twinkled. A gift. From you-know-who.

Already pitch dark today at 6:30 p.m.

Why on earth did that man want Will and Mary Rogers brought to her home tonight? Kidnapped, practically. Why so secret?

Mrs. Mock entered her house through the patio. The fluorescent light she switched on showed off her prize African violets, artfully arranged on special display shelves.

She lit the kitchen too. Appliances and surfaces gleamed, spic-and-span. Beyond, in the parlor, Mrs. Mock's tri-color lamp changed her aluminum Christmas tree blue, yellow, red.

The empty house felt a little spooky tonight.

Mrs. Mock poured herself a sherry from a cut-glass decanter in her cherry china cabinet. The lovely glass changed to blue, yellow, red in winter wonder-light.

Mrs. Mock indulged herself. A fantasy.

After Mr. Wood stopped by, she would catch the parade, then drive straight to Atlanta. She had always wanted to stay in that famous hotel with the restaurant on top that revolved so diners could see the big shining city of Scarlett O'Hara in 360 degrees. Mrs. Mock would order a lobster, a whole one. And chocolate soufflé for dessert. She would buy a bottle of Champagne too, and drink the whole thing by herself.

She would sleep naked in a giant hotel bed with too many pillows. The next day, she would fly to Paris or Rome and live at a Ritz-Carlton for a month.

Mr. Wood had looked her in the eyes and promised that tonight he would change her life.

All she had to do was bundle two sleeping children into her car and wait.

She admired her watch again. The diamonds twinkled like stars of Bethlehem. Just a few more minutes.

Mrs. Mock knew above all else that Mr. Wood would be prompt. He always was.

This very afternoon, he opened his office door at the exact moment the cuckoo popped out four times. The appointed hour. He handed her the cookie basket and its ingredients to start their liaison. He gave her fastidious instructions. He made her repeat them twice.

Then he let her play Little Red Riding Hood.

Oh my, Mr. Wood. What big hands you have! What big teeth! What big ... everything!

A hot memory on a cold night. Mrs. Mock would never forget their latest adventure together.

She softly smiled. A sherry sip pleased her tongue. Her eyes watered just a little.

Blue. Yellow. Blood red.

Mr. Woods had dominated her. He could have eaten her up ...

Blue. Yellow ... Thump! Thumpbump!

What?

What was *that?*

A noise. In the basement.

Weird.

Mrs. Mock lowered the sherry glass. She squinted out through the picture window.

Empty driveway. Mr. Wood's car nowhere to be seen.

She thought maybe that noise ...

Mrs. Mock checked her watch a third time.

He was late? Mr. Wood? With his Christmas kids waiting?

She felt uneasy.

Something big made that noise under her floorboards. No mouse could be that size ...

It had *not* been her imagination. Mrs. Mock knew. Why, all her life she'd been told she didn't *have* any imagination ...

She went to the telephone.

She hesitated. Mr. Wood wouldn't be happy with a call, she knew. He had given her very strict orders … and stressed them dramatically, repeatedly … to never, ever, dial his number except on Friday. And only after she got his signal call.

Mrs. Mock drank more sherry, this time a gulp.

She calmed. Mr. Wood would pull up the driveway any second. He could take a quick look around the basement.

Mr. Wood was big, and very strong. He could handle any problem.

GRRRGGGGSSSSSSNNNNGGGGG!!

Mrs. Mock jumped, nearly gave a little yelp. Her heart pounded like the drums off in downtown Lafayette.

No mistaking it. Something big moved … or fell … in her basement.

A raccoon? She *hated* raccoons! A wharf rat? Even *worse!*

Mrs. Mock pulled open a kitchen drawer. She lifted out a 100-year-old butcher knife.

It came with a history.

The story had come down for generations. A great-great-grandmother mortally plunged the knife into a Yankee soldier who invaded the Mock family house in Greensboro, way back when. Every Mock woman made sure her husband heard that story.

She quietly placed the empty sherry glass on the kitchen counter – *clink!* – and moved down the hallway. The basement door was on her left. She adjusted the knife in her right hand, wanting the sure grip, the heft. If she had to use it, she would.

The floor furnace made a hissing sound when she stepped onto it.

Mrs. Mock stopped. She listened with all her might for new sounds below her feet.

The furnace light stared up her dress with its unblinking blue eye.

Mrs. Mock's skin crawled. She remembered making fun of Mary Rogers last year when that sickly little child asked if some scary old devil lived in the furnace.

The basement door was on her left. Mrs. Mock adjusted the butcher knife in her right hand. If she had to use it, she would.

BUMP! BUMP! CLATTER!

Oh my God! Mrs. Mock thought, terror soaring, the knife raised. *Something really is down there! Down the basement stairs! Something is moving ...*

Mrs. Mock felt her breath come in and out in quick pants. She clenched the knife handle so tightly it cut off circulation to her fingers.

The knife.

She held the knife. It protected her family in the war. It would protect her now.

BUMP BUMP BUMP.

She reached the basement door. On its far side, a shaky wooden stairway led down to darkness. An awful place. She couldn't remember the last time she set foot on those stairs. She always made the hired help carry boxes down and bring boxes back up.

Mrs. Mock put her trembling left hand on the doorknob. A cold draft licked her ankles. Her heart pounded so loud she could actually hear it, maniacal, inside her chest.

She readied the knife. She jerked the door handle. The hinges moaned.

No sound at all came from the darkness below.

Mrs. Mock yanked a hanging cotton string. It lit one bare bulb over the stairway. Dust floated in the gloom.

An enormous shape, something like a man, stood in shadows at the foot of the stairs. It moved slightly in the weak light, and Mrs. Mock could see a big hat and a pale, fringed jacket.

She spoke over a fearful lump in her throat.

"Mr. Wood?"

"Dolores," he answered calmly. "Step down here. I brought you something for Christmas."

Dolores!

Mr. Wood had never before used her first name. He said it like an incantation.

Do-lor-es.

Dolores Mock lowered the butcher knife. She issued a gush of relief.

Not a monster. It was Mr. Wood.

She put a red heel on the top step.

Mr. Wood ascended the stairs to meet her, wooden slats groaning under his weight. His face smiled warmly from under the brim of his hat. He spread his arms wide for an embrace.

He met Mrs. Mock on the third step down the stairs.

Mr. Wood's wide embrace gathered her. Then one massive hand clasped Mrs. Mock's face on the left side. The other hand clasped her face on the right.

Mrs. Mock felt sweet tenderness in his touch. She'd never felt that before, not once.

Tenderness.

Mr. Wood snapped her head to the right, one violent motion. Mrs. Mock's neck broke instantly. It sounded like a bone crunched in a hungry animal's mouth.

She went limp, and Mr. Wood let her body fall.

Mrs. Mock banged down the stairway, flopped six steps, rolled slightly sideways. She came to rest with her red dress hiked up.

"Those steep basement stairs," Mr. Wood breathed loudly, excitement musking his voice. "Certainly a safety hazard, aren't they, Dolores?"

Her lifeless body sprawled grotesquely, eyes wide. The rusty pipes and electric wires and cobwebs of the basement ceiling stared back at her.

Mr. Wood felt a swelling hardness in his pants.

Was there any feeling better than seeing the life disappear from a pair of human eyes, like dirty water down a drain?

Mr. Wood found the butcher knife. He hid it inside a cardboard box filled with fuzzy yellow chicks. Easter decorations. He chuckled out loud and tucked the box away in a corner far from the fallen body.

He left the basement where he'd entered – through the scuttle hole on the dark side of the house. Mr. Wood carefully closed the partly rotted wooden door. He emerged from a flower bed into the cold solstice night, brushing spider webs from his white jacket.

Though he wouldn't see it, Mr. Wood imagined *The Lafayette Legend* headline when someone finally noticed Mrs. Mock's absence and came to check on her:

Socialite Dolores Mock Found Dead After Fall in Home

She would smell horrible by then, Mr. Wood thought. *Just horrible.*

Mr. Wood's big white Chevy king cab waited on an empty side street. He stopped to pick up Will and Mary Rogers.

Literally.

He switched off the engine of Mrs. Mock's car. The heater and radio died simultaneously. Mr. Wood ignored an important announcement: *Our Jolly Holiday live coverage resumes after a brief word from Mayor Baker, generous sponsor of our city's inaugural holiday event ...*

He left the car keys swinging gently in the ignition, opened the back door, and effortlessly lifted Will and Mary, one child under each arm, like bags of sugar.

He lugged them through thirty yards of Mrs. Mock's landscaping, emerging in the lonely back alley. He snuggled the twins down in a new back seat, in his king cab. They rested with rosy faces close together.

Mr. Wood spread a warm blanket with a Christmas tree design over them.

As the white truck rumbled to life then pulled out into the long night of the winter solstice, Will and Mary slept in innocence.

Mr. Wood lifted Will and Mary, one child under each arm, like bags of sugar. He lugged them to his king cab and spread a warm blanket over them.

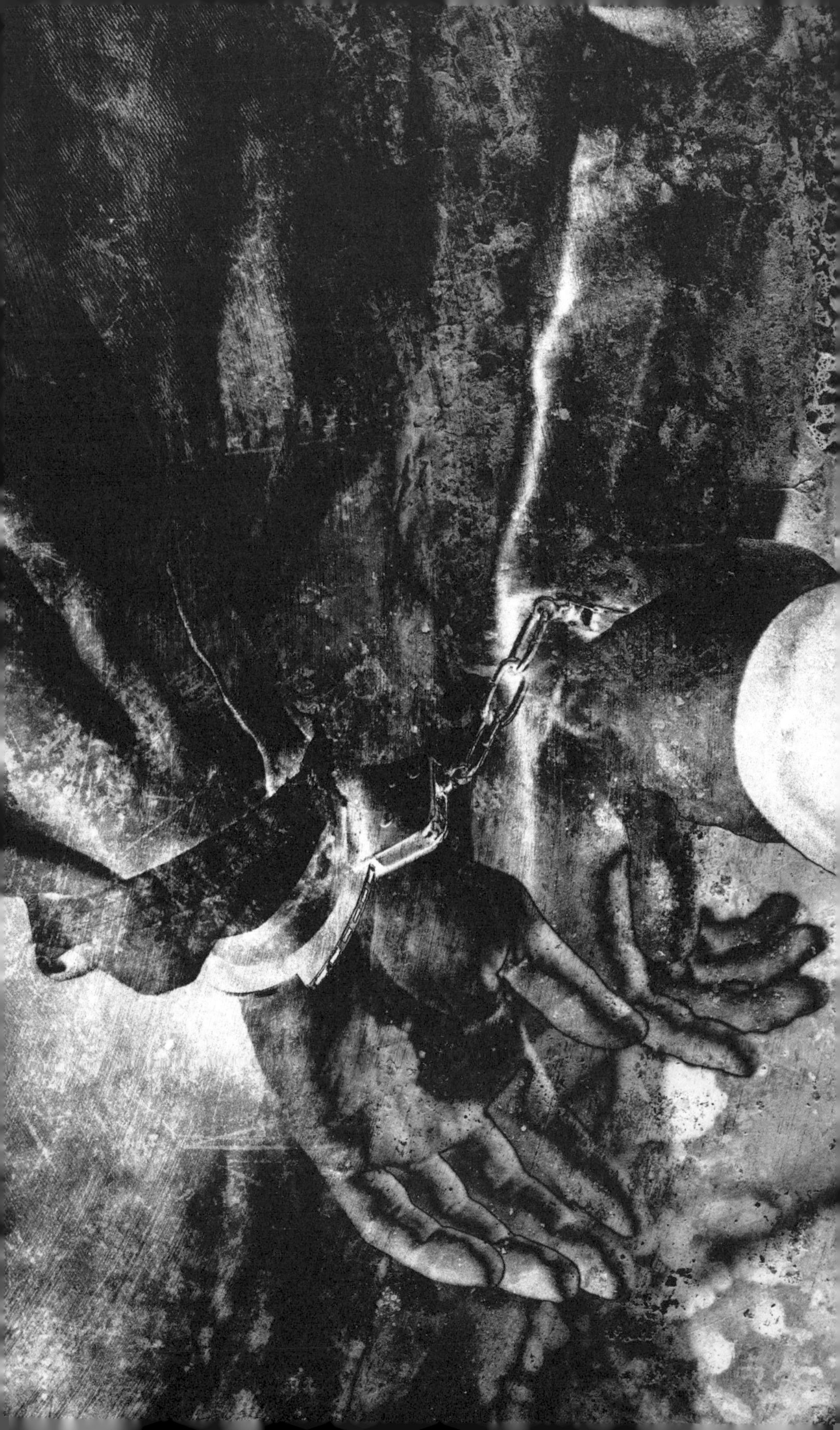

—38—

A Shot in the Dark

Elmore slumped on the same dirty cot in the same jail cell he'd hated last January.

He wore the same dejected-orange jumpsuit. It had the same sour-sweat smell. Last June's dented tin drinking cup lay on its side by the bed, and a yellow Juicy Fruit wrapper still hung in a corner spider web.

Just one thing was different – Elmore. This incarceration, he pressed a blood-soaked wad of brown paper towels to his nose.

He pulled off the soaked mess, examined it. Still bleeding.

Dan Neeley, I never thought you'd ever put a taser to me, he thought bitterly. *Never thought you'd tase your oldest friend in the world …*

Sheriff Neeley brought Elmore in the hard way.

Taser. Handcuffs. Physical force. A nasty steel cage in a squad car.

Elmore kicked the tin drinking cup in his cell and sent it clattering into the bars.

I smoked hash one time in my whole life, Danny. Over there, in the war. You tried it too. You sat right there at the end of the pipe with me. You remember how I didn't enjoy it. And you know in your goddamned guts that Elmore Rogers wasn't riding around Lafayette in Mr. Rankin's truck with a block of hashish in the glove compartment …

Elmore was stunned by the accident, but he loudly protested his innocence.

He raged at Dick Wragg, accusing him of planting the drug. (*I'll beat your Navy SEAL ass again, Wragg!*) Elmore had stalked Wragg through spilled logs and splintered Rudolphs until Sheriff Neeley stuck a taser to Elmore's belly, zapped him senseless, slapped cuffs on his wrists, and shoved his spasming body, bloody nose and all, into the cage of the squad car.

Things sure changed in a year.

Twelve months ago, Christmas Eve, Elmore and the twins sat at peace in that same sticky, smelly cage of the squad car. Officer Turnipseed played Santa and snuck a pair of shiny new bikes from the trunk into Elmore's kitchen.

One year.

Elmore applied pressure to his nose.

Who knew a taser caused nosebleed? Who knew a taser made a man's feet and hands feel like chunks of dead wood?

Taser or no, Elmore could hear just fine.

Outside police headquarters, big bass drums pounded past. Elmore imagined tonight even the dead up in Lafayette Lies Asleep Cemetery could hear the ruckus.

The Jolly Holiday parade passed the police station's front door. It was a thunderous pandemonium of drums and reed squawks and brass and whistles and rumbling tractor engines. Cheer after cheer rose for passing bands and floats, a stormy ocean of noise.

The police headquarters had no windows, but Elmore imagined perfect formations of musicians in red and blue and green school-band uniforms. He envisioned sequined majorettes showing off their legs and twirling batons. On ten-deep sidewalks, thousands of bundled-up Alabamians shouted for hard candies and lollipops and Moon Pies from dreamy passing floats.

Elmore thought of Will and Mary, leaping for sweets, a distracted Kelly minding them, her pretty face scanning left and right to spot Elmore when he finally bothered to show up.

Elmore Rogers, missing in action, just like old times.

Dammit!

Elmore savagely struck the solid-steel bars of his cell. The bars didn't even vibrate.

Wragg framed me, Danny! Set me up! You know I didn't cause that accident. And you know I don't mule drugs, or use 'em. Good Lord, Sheriff Dan – I don't even drink ...

Fresh blood welled from his knuckles. But Elmore didn't feel it. Only outrage.

Dick Wragg put Elmore behind bars. Why? What reason? What on earth was going on here? Why hadn't Neeley even given Elmore a chance to phone Kelly? Or call a lawyer?

The world passed by right outside tonight, and Elmore stared from a six-by-six jail cell.

He stared at a bag on Neeley's desk. His clothes. One leg of his blue jeans hung out.

Dammit, Neeley!

Outside, a new band passed, pouring hearts and souls into "Hit the Road Jack".

A cannon boomed, followed by a huge cheer.

Elmore gripped the cell bars with both hands. He could imagine a war was ending.

Or just beginning.

A block away, Sheriff Neeley watched the parade pass like a gaudy snake.

Neeley fidgeted in the shotgun seat of Wragg's official fire department cruiser. The big red Buick idled behind a line of orange-and-white barrels that blocked access from a side street. Wragg ran the defroster, but still had to lean forward to wipe the windshield clear with a glove every few minutes. The red cherry twirled atop the cruiser.

The emergency radio band crackled, but no instruction followed a single burst of static.

Neeley stared at Wragg, who clutched the radio receiver like a nugget of raw silver.

"Who the hell's using the emergency band tonight, Wragg?"

Frustration clouded his voice.

"I'm sitting here beside you. My police car's parked back of headquarters. Deputy Turnipseed's not authorized. Your firehouse ain't got a single authorized user. So who's on the horn here, Chief Dick? The National Guard? The governor of Alabama? Uh ... The Boss?"

Wragg waggled his peculiar top lip.

"Neeley," he sighed. "You never know who might be interested in our big parade."

Sheriff Neeley thought over the non-answer as a grandly decorated float passed, candy flying to both sides. A mob of townspeople jumped up and down, exhaling vapor.

Wragg's voice took on a snide note.

"Oh I know your problem, Neeley," he said. "Your old suck buddy Elmore got caught red-handed with twenty-five to thirty worth of contraband. And that don't count the wreck he caused, or the civil disturbance. Your buddy threatened me with bodily harm, Neeley. If you ask me, soldier boy was high as Stone Mountain and driving a heavy truck and causing a public nuisance. Plus, dealin' hash. Judge Childress is gonna throw the book at him, Sheriff. You watch."

Again, the radio sputtered, a giant clearing its throat.

"I need to get to work now, Fire Dick," Neeley said. "That's my hometown out there."

Sheriff Neeley tried the handle. Locked. Wragg operated the safety.

"We don't get out yet. We got orders. *You* got orders. From you-know-who."

Neeley felt his blood pressure rise.

Orders?

"We gonna sit side-by-side here together, like school chums on a Bluebird bus," Wragg said. "We are to remain at all times in *my* vehicle. We will monitor the radio. We will wait until we receive further orders ..."

Something got Neeley's attention, and Wragg's voice faded.

Kelly Rogers passed.

Female. Lovely. Familiar.

She picked her way along behind that surging, candy-crazy crowd. But what was wrong with her? Why did she walk that way? Where was her coat on this icy night?

Where were the twins?

What was going on here?

Sheriff Neeley turned to Wragg.

"You son of a bitch," Neeley growled.

Wragg turned in surprise.

"What the hell does it mean, you planting hash on Elmore? We both know where you got that shit. Elmore didn't drive up to that traffic light today with hash in his glove compartment."

Fire Chief Wragg raised his palms in protest.

"Sheriff! You the one who personally took that hash out of the cab. You seen it with your own eyes, confiscated it with your own hands. You, the police chief of Lafayette. Elmore Rogers been carrying on this bad business almost a year. Remember Mr. Wood talking about Elmore in our meeting last summer. Right? Elmore's guilty as sin on Saturday night."

Neeley felt something happen inside. Beyond his control.

"Wragg, by God, I'm not asking you again. Tell me what the hell is going on here."

The radio sputtered loudly. This time, a voice followed.

Both men recognized Mr. Wood.

Chief Wragg?

"Yes sir!"

Sheriff Neeley there with you?

Neeley waited one heartbeat to answer.

"I am, Mr. Wood."

Mr. Wood's cracker accent leaped from the radio.

Good. Alright. I'll say this once. Pay attention. It's my last instruction.

Neeley picked up the background noise of a truck engine. Mr. Wood was on the move, driving somewhere.

First, I remind you officers of the law to stay in the fire chief's car without leaving it for any reason, under any condition, for the next thirty minutes. This is my strictest order …

Neeley barely heard. He shifted in his seat, eyes searching the parade.

Kelly Rogers fell. She collided with a big country woman in an elf hat who was leaping, in her way, for sweets thrown off a Pocahontas float.

Kelly lay by a barricade barrel and didn't move.

The radio continued.

And you are certain you have Elmore Rogers in custody?

Now Neeley's attention riveted to the radio.

What did Mr. Wood just say? Why does Elmore Rogers matter to him?

"Yes sir, Mr. Rogers is in full custody," said Wragg confidently. "Just like you ordered."

A key turned in Sheriff Neeley's brain. A door swung open. He eyed Wragg.

The radio.

You keep it that way. And let me repeat: you two men will remain in the fire chief's vehicle exactly thirty minutes. You are then free to resume official duties with our Jolly Holiday. These are strict orders, and I want them followed. No matter what. Do you read?

"Yes sir," Wragg answered. "Mr. Wood."

He keyed the radio quiet.

Kelly Rogers lay crumpled like a heap of clothes by one of the orange barrels.

Screw all, Neeley told himself. *This is not right.*

The police chief furtively moved his right hand down to his belt.

"Listen, Chief Wragg," he began, conspiratorially. "I got a question."

"Shoot."

Sheriff Neeley checked his immediate thought. Then he spoke.

"Why, exactly, does Mr. Wood care that Elmore is locked up over yonder in my jail?"

Wragg smiled. Neeley thought of egg yolk oozing through a cracked shell.

Without another word, Neeley jammed his taser into the fire chief's sternum, right over the heart.

Full force. Twice.

Wragg flopped like a doll. Neeley saw the whites of his eyes, his bloody, chewed tongue.

The car smelled like burned shoes.

Neeley reached across the twitching body and pressed the cruiser's safety lock. He shouldered his door wide, and left it open.

"Kelly! Kelly! It's Danny!"

He rushed toward the fallen woman.

Elmore raised his head.

The front door of the police station burst wide open.

Dan Neeley, in full police-chief uniform, carried Kelly across the threshold cradled in his arms like a bride.

"Jesus, Danny! Not Kelly! What's happened to her? Where are my children?"

Neeley gave no answer. He eased Kelly down, her hair swinging, to a clear space on the headquarters floor.

Street noise, merrymaking squalled through the open door.

In a corner of the room, a video camera came silently to life. The device swiveled slightly to take in a panoramic view of Lafayette police headquarters.

Neeley placed his leather police jacket beneath Kelly's head. He briskly stepped over and kicked shut the front door. He fetched a big paper cup back from the water cooler and dashed it, every drop, directly into Kelly's bloodless face.

Her long eyelashes fluttered open, and the wonderful dark wells beneath showed life. She moaned.

"What's the matter with her, Dan?" Elmore's voice broke. "KELLY! Oh Jesus."

"She looks drugged, Elmore. Maybe overdosed on her pills. She fell down in the street up at Foster. Got knocked over, I mean, but she couldn't get up. I don't know about the twins."

Neeley took a pulse.

"Still, El. It ain't a good thing Kelly's here without Will and Mary."

Elmore stretched a hand through the bars to Dan Neeley. His old friend. His baseball and football buddy. The soldier who saved his life.

"Neeley! Let me out! Something terrible is going on. Look at Kelly! I got to find Will and Mary ..."

Kelly opened her mouth now, staring at the fluorescent lights of the ceiling. She spoke like a woman in a trance.

"Mrs. Mock." She whispered, licked her lips. "She brought cookies."

That was all.

Elmore watched Kelly's chest rise and fall, like a bird breathing.

Sheriff Neeley leaned directly over Kelly's face. His red buzz cut seemed to glow.

"Mrs. Mock brought cookies," he said, very slowly and clearly. "And what happened?"

Kelly gulped. Tears shone in her eyes.

"And Will and Mary ..." A hot drop slid fast down Kelly's right cheek. "Will and Mary ... gone."

Kelly fell to pieces. She cried like a woman burning, her fists grinding her face, her body curled into a fetal shape.

Elmore shook the cell door with all his might.

"Neeley! Let me out! This ain't right! Will and Mary are in danger!"

The police chief raised Kelly up by her shoulders, drew her to his chest. Tenderly. Her black hair covered the freckled hand against the small of her back.

"Kelly," he said, in the kindest voice Elmore had ever heard from his friend, "you got to get it together now. Come on, sweetheart. You got to be strong. We need you. Will and Mary need you. Right now, Kelly."

Her sobs subsided.

Hard-eyed, Neeley peered past her at Elmore.

"Here you go, El." He tossed a silver ring of keys. "It's the big one."

Elmore found the key, fit it to the lock. It clicked, and the door swung open.

"Let's sit her up in my chair, El," Neeley ordered. "We need a plan."

They lifted Kelly, fireman style, the way they learned to carry wounded buddies in the war. She felt light as paper. At Neeley's desk, the policeman swept an arm across the cluttered surface, hurling folders and manuals and law books and loose papers to the floor.

Elmore fetched more water, and this time it went to Kelly's lips.

Those lips.

She swallowed and swallowed, draining every drop.

"Kidnapped!" Kelly gasped. "Our babies!"

Sheriff Neeley knelt to meet her eyes.

"Mrs. Mock took them? They went with her?"

"I NEVER trusted her!" Elmore blurted. He was ripping off the orange jumpsuit. "She never cared for those kids or anything but herself ..."

Kelly spoke, huskily.

"They ate cookies. Will and Mary. She brought a picnic basket. Drug cookies."

"Come ON, Neeley!" Elmore shouted, jumping up and down. His nose still bled a little. "Let's GO! She's got Will and Mary!"

Outside, a huge cheer burst from the crowd. Something grand floated past in the dark. Songs from marching bands merged in a raucous cacophony. Earsplitting revelry drowned Neeley's answer.

"Right!" he repeated, yelling louder. "Let's go. All of us. I've got an idea. Help me, Elmore!"

They lifted Kelly to her feet, her pale arms draped over their shoulders. They walked comically for the door – tall, lean Elmore one side, short, blocky Dan Neeley the other.

Neeley yanked the knob, threw the door wide. A new blast of street noise entered.

Dan Neeley turned in the entrance to face Elmore and Kelly. His freckled expression was grave and earnest.

"Wragg's in on this, El. And Mr. Wood. For whatever reason, he wanted you locked up. And listen ..."

Over the parade, past the spectacle of music and cheering, Elmore saw a strange blink of light.

An instant later, a muffled pop.

A shot.

Dan Neeley's head disappeared. Like that.

Red mist, with globs of hair and specks of bone, covered Elmore and Kelly.

It speckled the desks and books and papers. It freckled the dirty wall in Elmore's cell.

The cell keys fell from Danny Neeley's hand, jangled on the floor.

Kelly screamed.

It was the loudest sound Elmore had ever heard.

Elmore screamed too.

Danny Neeley stood impossibly upright for a moment.

He collapsed in stages.

First, he dropped to his knees. Then Neeley leaned onto all-fours, palms flat on the ground. Third, he bowed like a man praying toward a distant holy city.

Finally, Sheriff Danny Neeley softly placed what was left of his face on the threshold of the headquarters door.

With a strange hurt sound from his chest, he died there.

Elmore and Neeley lifted Kelly, fireman style, the way they learned to carry wounded buddies in the war. She felt light as paper.

—39—

Showdown

"Maybe you shot the wrong son of a bitch, Wragg."

Mr. Wood growled from Wragg's cell phone. He placed this call himself. A rarity.

"I ain't done, boss."

Wragg placed his glowing phone on a dusty wooden floor. A voice in the speaker buzzed like a fly. Wragg ignored it to peer through the scope of a sniper rifle at the open doorway of Lafayette police headquarters across the street.

Elmore Rogers dragged the body of Sheriff Neeley out of view. It left a red smear.

Wragg wiped a sleeve across his own bloody nose. Sheriff Neeley's taser had kicked him like a mule.

Well, Sheriff Neeley paid for that.

Wragg lowered the rifle and thought to himself.

Mr. Wood, you're a billionaire and all. But for once, you are dead wrong. I didn't shoot the wrong son of a bitch. I shot the son of a bitch I wanted to shoot. Now I'll shoot the other ones. This is personal. A plum pleasure.

A dark drop fell from Wragg's nose onto the upstairs window sill of The Personality Shop. One pane displayed a bullet hole in a little spider web of broken glass.

Wragg readjusted the rifle, aiming it at the open door of the PD. Just like Lee Harvey Oswald, he thought. Trained military sniper. Just like in Dallas, a parade passing.

Any moment, Elmore or that woman would try to escape through the door. Then ...

Boom!

"Wragg? God damn you!"

The fire chief addressed the cell phone, not even looking.

"Yes sir, Mr. Wood. I'll take care of Rogers. You can count on it, Mr. Wood."

Behind Mr. Wood, two unconscious children lay on giant red pillows under a broad wall of video screens.

One screen showed a sleek black jet landing smoothly on a grass runway. Rows of lights blazed on either side. Those clicked off, one by one, and sank into the ground as the aircraft taxied past.

A yellow school bus waited at the end of the runway. That old-fashioned conveyance should be a hilarious novelty for passengers climbing off a ritzy plane after so many hours.

Mr. Wood would man the wheel of the bus when The Epicureans deplaned in seven minutes.

Will and Mary didn't move a muscle.

Mr. Wood turned to a new screen, the surveillance camera in police headquarters.

Elmore Rogers and Kelly, that gorgeous ghost, bent over the body of Sheriff Neeley, foolishly pressing his chest. Abruptly, Rogers got to his feet after the useless try at resuscitation. He unsnapped Neeley's holster and yanked out the service .45.

Mr. Wood leaned to the mic again. "Wragg?"

"Here, boss."

"Elmore Rogers got Neeley's pistol. He's coming after you."

Then, a surprise.

Elmore Rogers slowly pivoted. He took dead aim at the surveillance camera in the corner.

The first shot missed. But with the second, Mr. Wood's surveillance screen went dark.

A speaker sputtered.

"Rogers? Coming for me? Ha! My boy Timmy could handle him. Bring it on!"

Mr. Wood clicked a button.

Main Street zoomed to full screen. This surveillance camera mounted atop the police department recorded the parade.

An inspired distraction, thought Mr. Wood. *Merry Christmas, Lafayette.*

He checked the camera's time code. Five minutes before The Epicureans stepped off his jet.

Mr. Wood looked at the twins.

Mary lay with pale lips slightly apart, her thin chest rapidly rising, falling. She was very much the same small child Mr. Wood found in the hospital last summer, still with snakebite, eyes watery, but heart-stopping in her beauty. The little girl's red hair looked like frosting.

Will looked delicious too.

The Rogers children. Ripening. But not yet ripe.

Mr. Wood's tastes ran to teens. He discovered this in the isolated Hmong village in the war. He confirmed it with the Asian girl who skated away with his heart, his wildest appetites, in the Adirondacks.

It was a treat to anticipate, sumptuous Will and Mary. What a future Mr. Wood had in store ...

Sudden feedback pierced the control room. Wragg's phone. Mr. Wood spun to the video screen.

Elmore Rogers burst headlong, like a running back, out the door of the police station.

"I got him, Mr. Wood," said Dick Wragg, cool as that.

On video, Mr. Wood saw the heavy black pistol in Elmore Rogers' hand suddenly disintegrate, an explosion of black pieces.

"Now," Wragg said, "Rogers can't hurt anybody but himself."

Mr. Wood gave a grudging nod. He'd expect a Navy SEAL to be an excellent shot. He didn't expect a Navy SEAL to play with his prey before a kill.

The time code read 8:56 p.m.

Four minutes. Time to move.

Mr. Wood lifted his white hat from its peg on the door. To square it up just the way he liked, he eyed himself in the black mirror of a dead video screen.

He carefully locked the control room door behind him.

The Rogers children would probably keep sleeping. But why take any risk?

Everything in the world would change in the next thirty minutes.

Elmore fell when the sniper bullet shattered his pistol. The round left him with a handful of stinging bees and junk metal.

The sousaphone section of the Lafayette High School marching band passed in front of Elmore. Their puffing, pimply cheeks glowed cherry red in the cold. The musicians swung instruments side to side and proudly high-stepped, only a block from the mayor's viewing stand, the climax of the huge parade.

Elmore heard a bright ping, and a shot-away brass shard from a sousaphone bell stung his cheek. Wragg wouldn't let a crowd of innocent teens deter him. But another distraction did. Elmore caught a glimpse of Kelly bolting from the doorway of the police headquarters.

Wragg's hasty shot exploded the doorframe – head level – into flying white splinters.

Elmore exploded too, onto his feet.

He made a head-down sprint straight toward The Personality Shop. He pushed through the band, sprawling trombonists, scattering the flutes, bearskin hats toppling. Another shot ricocheted sharply off pavement.

Wragg is shooting straight down, Elmore thought. *How in the world can he miss the broad back of a man?*

But he missed.

And Elmore drove madly through the red sea of band uniforms, popping out beyond the dismayed shouts and curses and chaos. Then he careened into the crowd on the

Elmore fell when the sniper bullet shattered his pistol. The round left him with a handful of stinging bees and junk metal.

sidewalk like a cannonball, knocking people off their feet.

He made it to a sheltered spot under the awning of the building where Wragg waited.

The parade had been totally disrupted, like red ants when a finger blurs a scent trail.

Students dragged instruments on the pavement. Some of the kids held scraped arms or knees, faces in tears. Abandoned trombones and glockenspiels littered Main.

"Look out! Look out!"

A float decorated with a gigantic crepe-paper peanut lurched to avoid plowing into the crowd. The float veered clumsily onto the sidewalk. Crowns toppled off the heads of the beauty queens on board.

Under the awning of The Personality Shop, Elmore caught his breath. The shop's door hung open, left ajar by someone. Elmore stared through the opening into ominous darkness.

If you go in there, you'll die. Elmore heard an inner voice, an instinct. *Wragg's waiting.*

Someone in the crowd pointed in Elmore's direction.

That's him! He's the one that knocked us down!

Elmore scanned the crowd and helter-skelter marching band for Kelly. No sign.

His Kelly was free.

But Dan Neeley, his lifelong friend, lay dead across the street.

Elmore's heart froze in the cold.

And Will? Mary? Where were his children?

Wragg knew.

Elmore had to move.

If he didn't, Wragg would get him. Sooner or later. Then Kelly. Maybe the kids. All.

A new jingling band unit rounded a corner onto Main and struck up a tune – "Holly Jolly Christmas". Elmore saw another float in the distance, a giant set of praying hands that carried an entire church choir, men and women in red robes. They shined flashlights onto their music and sang "Holly Jolly Christmas" at the tops of their lungs.

Elmore felt desperate. The world, the beautiful world,

could end any instant.

He had to get to Wragg.

Elmore warily took a peek around one side of the awning. He could see straight up the front façade of the three-story building.

The Personality Shop had long been derelict, a downtown Lafayette eyesore. Dan Neeley had wanted it torn down – the sheriff just hated walking out of his office every day to confront a crumbling structure with one single window, a rotten Cyclops eye, staring down.

An iron fire escape still crawled the structure's side, its first rung eight feet off the sidewalk.

Elmore Rogers took a deep breath.

He knew what he had to do.

The first rung of the ladder snapped off in Elmore's hand.

He twisted awkwardly as he fell, but landed on his feet, shoulder against the thick glass showcase of the building. Old concert fliers rotted there, and Elmore accidentally ripped one down.

He eyed the second rung. It looked as rotted with rust as the first.

A brawny parent of a band member yelled at Elmore.

"You better climb, you creep! I'm about to whip your ass!"

Elmore leaped with all his athleticism.

The second rung held his weight. He pulled his body up, got his feet a purchase above the sidewalk.

Ominously, the bolts down one side of the entire ladder came loose.

Elmore hung on like a kid riding a rusty gate.

"Look!" someone yelled, and the crowd turned to watch some Jolly Holiday daredevil climb a building face.

Wragg will see the crowd, then he'll see me, Elmore thought. *Up, Elmore. Now or never.*

The next rusty rung snapped loose in his hand. Elmore

"Oh my God! He's falling!"

The new huzzah from the crowd panicked Elmore even more. Dangling, he looked down. A huge throng of people gawked up at him. Kids leaped with excitement like popcorn.

I'm entertainment, flashed Elmore's mind. *A Jolly Holiday sideshow.*

He climbed, spurred by fear.

A woman's familiar voice somehow cut through the cacophony of the street circus.

"El! In the window! He's ..."

Elmore heard the quiet pop of a rifle, some kind of silencer on it. A flash overhead. Crumbs of window glass sprinkled his head.

Kelly's voice went silent.

Elmore's next moments were a blur.

He scrambled skyward, adrenalized, desperate, for the window. The ladder yawed. Then, loudly, the top section of the fire escape came free of the wall and buckled backward toward the distant street.

Elmore made it to the third-floor window at the exact moment the ladder took its final tilt.

The deadly barrel of a sniper rifle aimed down, the focused face of Dick Wragg behind it, squinting through the scope, strange lip stretched in concentration.

The ladder convulsed. Elmore lunged for the wicked face behind the rifle. His hand grabbed collar, hair, skin of the neck.

Anything.

Elmore held on with all his might. The fire escape screeched like a dying animal, and it teetered further from the building's crumbling wall. The street screamed, a thousand voices, mass hysteria.

Hold on, Elmore prayed. *Don't let Wragg take another shot.*

The fire escape gave up its iron ghost. It fell away entirely, sudden and fast.

Elmore pulled Dick Wragg's head and shoulders through the upstairs window of The Personality Shop. Wragg fiercely flailed to catch a window mullion.

It was rotten. It gave way.

The sniper rifle tumbled end over end to the street.

Both men, one clutching a ruined fire escape, one kicking his legs in space, hurtled through icy air toward Lafayette.

Mr. Wood flipped away his cigar. It sparked in the wet grass, but went out immediately.

The yellow school bus looked cheerful in the moonlight, like a giant pumpkin on wheels.

The designer jet had taxied to a stop. Passengers of privilege waited to disembark.

In his recognizable white hat and fringed white jacket, Mr. Wood climbed aboard the school bus. He turned the key, rumbled the engine to life.

He flashed the bus's headlights three times.

A door slid magically open on one side of the jet. A stairway unfolded, the serrated leg of a hatching insect.

Down they bounced, free at last, laughing, hands waving, voices calling to Mr. Wood. Twenty-four of them. Twelve special couples.

The Epicureans.

"All aboard!" Mr. Wood called. "Welcome to Lafayette! My little town!"

The Epicureans acted very happy. The two Japanese businessmen danced jigs. Mr. Wood could smell alcohol on the whole bunch from ten feet away.

Good, he thought. *They'll catch right on.*

"Y'all take your seats. We'll head to Sweet Comb. Anybody hungry tonight?"

A cheer swept through the assembly.

"Good. Mighty good," Mr. Wood beamed.

He showed his fine teeth.

"Cause we're about to have ourselves one big barbecue."

—40—

One Big Barbecue

Last winter, Elmore Rogers fell three stories. He slammed violently onto the frozen red clay foundation of Mr. Wood's castle, still under construction.

This winter, Elmore fell thirty-five feet from the window of The Personality Shop. He crashed down onto a gigantic peanut atop a holiday float.

The chicken wire and crepe paper made a prickly cushion, but Elmore only had his breath knocked out. No teeth. No broken ribs.

He wasn't out of danger.

Four Lafayette beauty queens tumbled in a perfumed female avalanche onto Elmore.

One moment, he lay in a wire-and-painted paper crater, gasping to catch his breath. The next, four yowling Lafayette ladies caved in on him, scratching like cats in a sack.

"Lord we all gonna die! He's Satan!" wailed a beauty, lipstick smeared over her face.

Another beauty saved him.

Kelly's face appeared somewhere above. An angel of salvation.

"Keh … Keh …"

Elmore couldn't speak, even as Kelly grabbed his arms and pulled him, with all her might, toward the edge of the parade float.

One beauty queen rolled free of Elmore's chest. With shameless, noisy gasps, he filled his lungs. Those unearthly noises scared the Lafayette beauty queens even more. They fought with kicking high heels and slicing fingernails to climb out of the giant peanut and escape.

Kelly yanked Elmore again, mightily, and he found his feet on the pavement of Main Street.

The body of Dick Wragg, completely broken, stared him in the face. The fire chief's top lip oozed blood. So did his ears and nose and mouth. The man seemed to have exploded inside.

"Call the fire chief!" yelled someone.

He is the fire chief, Elmore thought bitterly.

The downtown crowd grew quiet now, a respectful distance from the dead man.

"Elmore," Kelly said. "He's not there anymore. Don't even touch him."

He turned to Kelly. Her eyes were different than Elmore had seen in forever.

Wragg might not be here, but Kelly Rogers was.

Kelly was home.

Elmore reached to touch a blood-red streak along her right cheek. Kelly caught his hand.

"Wragg?"

"He barely missed." Wryly, she added, "I guess I'm faster than a speeding bullet."

"Thank goodness, Kelly."

"Mary and Will," she said.

Elmore leaned over Wragg's body, avoiding the stare of open eyes.

"Hey!" a person yelled in the crowd. "That feller's robbing a dead man!"

Elmore ignored the shouts. He found the thing he wanted.

The cell phone case had totally shattered. Elmore pressed a black button anyhow.

The device's screen flickered to life.
Elmore saw Wragg's last call, ten minutes past.
Mr. Wood.
They ran.

The Epicureans had gathered.

Mr. Wood handed big Stefan and lithe Ronaldo two laden silver trays, and the gentlemen's gentlemen shimmered away to serve their masters.

Stefan's tray tinkled musically with elegant crystal. The flutes held a thick purple liquid. Ronaldo offered bite-sized wafers, white and round as full moons, artfully arranged.

The Epicureans stood happily before Mr. Wood's gigantic fireplace. Its stones fit precisely without mortar, the magic of master Irish stonemasons. Twin andirons wrought in the shape of gape-mouthed black serpents held a roaring fire on their backs.

The feasting room lay at the very heart of Mr. Wood's castle, a secret chamber far from distractions of the outside world. The Epicureans reached it by trooping down multiple stairways of ornately carved yew salvaged from an Irish abbey. On entry, guests passed single-file, like monks, through a long tunnel to a heavy wooden door.

They passed from moody darkness into a bright chamber. Mahogany walls gleamed with cozy warmth, and a dozen old-fashioned gas lights flickered nostalgically on the walls. A huge round mirror framed with ornate filigree reflected the whole room, doubling its light and warmth.

A wooden table, rough with age but made to last, ran the length of the fireplace. (Mr. Wood purchased the 700-year-old banquet board from a mead hall in Norway.) White butcher paper covered the table's rustic surface, and an anomaly – plump rolls of everyday white paper towels – rested every few feet, with white plastic baskets for hot sauces and condiments.

The stainless steel doors of a kitchen gleamed across the room. The porthole windows wore films of steam.

As Stefan and Ronaldo served each Epicurean libation and wafer, Mr. Wood cleared his throat. He wanted to project his voice now. He normally addressed only one or two men in a small room, confidentially, not two dozen in a banquet hall.

"Howdy again, folks. Welcome to Sweet Comb. And to re-repeat what you heard on the bus ride, we're gonna do things a little different this winter soltis ..."

Mr. Wood stopped.

"Dammit! Winter *solstice*. That's a hard word to say, ain't it?"

A row of sympathetic smiles flashed. The Epicureans glowed tonight with bonhomie.

Mr. Wood saw Dieter, last year's host, hug his *fräulein*. He took note of the big Russian, who always, every gathering, kept his heavy coat on. Mr. Wood noted the African warlord with filed teeth, the preening gold-haired lads from Nagasaki, Don Sacco and his stunning wife. The Brazilian arms merchant, the Argentinian soccer star, the Dutch art-dealer sisters, all the guests.

They wore the look of love, these Epicureans. Their faces shone, bright from the warmth of the room, the fireplace, the tall drinks on the long flight.

From mouth-watering anticipation.

"You are bloody well right, Wood! That word is deucedly hard to pronounce!" The tall, lion-headed British Duke spoke in a splendid baritone. "At Albemarle Abbey, we simply refer to it as ... Feast Night!"

A smile cracked the ghastly face of the Duchess, draped on his arm.

"My lovely man from Albemarle," she burbled, "always knows exactly what is meant when we speak of Feast Night."

Mr. Wood had a sudden mental image of the Duchess flossing human flesh from her teeth at the boozy end of the evening.

He hated these people.

All people. But especially these. These Epicureans.

They deserved what they had coming to them this evening.

"It's a very good home you have, Mr. Wood, very good." Dieter the German gave a slight bow with his compliment.

Mr. Wood recaptured his drifting thoughts and returned to the moment.

"My home tonight is your home," he said. "I trust y'all enjoyed our little bus ride?"

The Epicureans laughed.

"I didn't tell you on the ride," Mr. Wood shared in a conspiratorial voice, "but that yellow school bus once belonged to The Beatles. Ringo drove it in one of their movies."

It was a lie, but Mr. Wood knew it would get a certain response.

"Yeah, yeah, yeahhh!" chimed the two Japanese businessmen, together as if on cue. Their unexpected ... and excellent ... harmony on the last *yeah* brought a gale of laughter.

Stefan and Ronaldo served the last flute and wafer of the first course. Mr. Wood tipped his cowboy hat to say thanks, then raised his flute and lifted his white wafer.

"Tonight I'm gonna show y'all how we hold a warm special occasion here in this part of the world. Way down south in Dixie."

Here! Here! cried The Epicureans.

"First," announced Mr. Wood. "I want to offer a few brief words."

The Epicureans lifted high their glasses, engaged, listening.

"You have a rich and long tradition, you anthropophagites."

Mr. Wood watched every face. As expected, quizzical expressions appeared, brows knit, mouths closed. Not everyone spoke native English, or knew the technical term he'd used.

"You are *cannibals*," Mr. Wood clarified. "That's the common term."

The word shocked and offended, as Mr. Wood expected. It sounded ... vulgar.

The mood in the room changed instantly.

Mr. Wood didn't give a damn. He would enjoy the next few minutes so very much.

So very much would change. So many lives.

"Cannibals," he repeated. "Canny-bulls."

Several Epicureans flinched, and all the smiles disappeared.

"Yes, you cannibals can point to a long and rich tradition," continued Mr. Wood.

"You're embedded in the ages. Human mythology is engorged with cannibalism. You live in fairy tales and sagas and bedtime stories. Best of all, you have an actual, factual, timeline all through history.

"Did you know? Neanderthal caves littered with gnawed finger bones. The Donner Party. The chopping board of that Dahmer kid in Milwaukee. The effing Crusaders ... and Caribs ... and Aztecs ... and Jamestown colonists. The whale crew of the Essex. Japanese soldiers on New Guinea. The Andes plane crash. The list goes on and on, Epicureans. You are not alone."

Mr. Wood continued.

"And the way I see things, cannibalism is even at the foundation of a whole by-God religious faith."

Mr. Wood raised his wafer and glass.

"Here, my friends – this is my body. Eat. This is my blood. Drink. Remember me."

The roomful of faces stared at Mr. Wood like stones.

"Oh come on, brothers and sisters," Mr. Wood chided. "You folks play along here. It's our solstice, our twenty-fifth. We did things your way in the past, all those years. Let's do things Mr. Wood's way tonight."

He raised his glass higher. A challenge. Mr. Wood dared them.

"You're embedded in the ages. Human mythology is engorged with cannibalism. You live in fairy tales and sagas and bedtime stories."

"Cheers! Skol! Salud!" he spoke quite loudly now. "To your place in history. To your very special tastes!"

Mr. Wood placed a white wafer on his own tongue, grinned, tossed back his dark liquid.

Slowly, The Epicureans followed. All of them. Mr. Wood studied the room to make sure. Most made peculiar faces after the tasting.

The Epicureans waited now, deathly quiet.

Mr. Wood studied every Epicurean, going one by one, face by face. Then he greatly surprised his guests by noisily spitting out what he'd just ingested. Wafer and potion. An ugly purple mass plopped onto the varnished floor between his fine cowboy boots.

Now a new feeling, suspicion, filled the room. Mr. Wood could read their faces like twenty-four open books.

Good, he thought. *Fear is highly flammable.*

"Mr. Wood," said Don Sacco, who knew every nuance of English, "you are a ... cannibal ... too. One of us. Are you not?"

"Oh yes," the host agreed. "Most surely, I am. But, my friends, I'm much, much more than that ..."

Mr. Wood tossed his empty crystal into the roaring fireplace.

"Much more. And so ..." Mr. Wood resumed, "thank you tonight, this solstice, for your foolish trust. And while my 'body and blood' do their righteous work on all of you, I'll step out now for a breath. All the rest of my breaths, in fact."

Mr. Wood gave a lopsided smile, his face leering like a Halloween pumpkin.

"Did I mention we'll have a big barbecue tonight?"

Serendipitously, a giant hickory log in the fireplace popped out a burning ember. Mr. Wood strode right over the glowing coal on his way to what appeared to be a blank wooden wall.

He touched a spot, quietly spoke, and a doorway slid open.

Mr. Wood turned briefly back to The Epicureans. He gave a deadly baleful stare.

"In a few heartbeats," he announced, "you will begin to hallucinate. Violent, terrible hallucinations. The wafer … the host … you just consumed was made from my own human waste, and I served that, for your sipping pleasure, with a highly concentrated liquid psychedelic made from the mushrooms in our cattle fields here in Alabama. In the reeking shit of the cows you all eat when you're not busy chewing something more savory."

Mr. Wood waited to enjoy the utter consternation on the faces of The Epicureans.

"The truth about me? About Mr. Wood?"

He confessed.

"I love *murder*. More than feasts. More than flesh. More than money. More than anything you love or ever loved. So, tonight … I am giving myself, Mr. Wood, a solstice gift. I am taking the lives of each and every one of you in this room. Say your farewells, my dear goddamned Epicureans. You have exactly ten minutes."

The fringe shook on the back of Mr. Wood's western jacket as he disappeared through the secret opening.

The door slid shut behind him.

Kelly tore open the door of Sheriff Dan Neeley's police car. Elmore limped up and toppled into the passenger seat. Kelly somehow had keys. Elmore didn't want to think of her rifling Danny's pockets.

"Elmore," Kelly said. "We're gonna find them. We are."

"I love you, Kelly."

Elmore said it like a universal truth, a thing a man would tell about how he knew gravity existed or that the sun would rise the next morning.

Kelly pulled Elmore's face to hers. She kissed him and simultaneously twisted the key in the ignition.

The late Dan Neeley's squad car may have been ten years old, but a powerful engine still blasted energy to its four wheels. Kelly stomped the accelerator, and the cruiser screamed and slung parking-lot gravel like shrapnel.

Neither of them knew how to work the flashing light or wail the siren. The last thing they needed anyway was for Mr. Wood to see or hear them coming.

Did a billionaire hold Will and Mary hostage? Why?

What did Dan Neeley mean about Mr. Wood wanting Elmore put away?

Kelly hit 100 mph on the way to Mrs. Mock's. She screamed to a stop on the lawn. Elmore kicked in the front door after no one answered frantic knocks and doorbell rings.

He found the lights on, but no one in the house. No kids. No socialite.

Kelly topped 120 mph headed for Wood Castle.

Minutes passed like centuries. Eternities.

Elmore put his hand on Kelly's.

"Faster. Kelly, go faster."

Mr. Wood cracked ammonia capsules under the nostrils of the Rogers twins.

The children spasmed to life.

Mr. Wood chuckled. Will and Mary Rogers looked like frowsy roosting chickens hit with a bright light.

The magnate jerked them from their big red pillows to their feet. Dazed, the twins teetered as Mr. Wood spun them to stare through a round viewing space in one wall.

A hazy gaggle of well-dressed strangers, some searching, some waving arms, filled the window.

"You young'uns ever look through a one-way mirror before?" Mr. Wood asked amiably.

Too groggy and stunned to speak, the twins simply blinked.

"Didn't think so," said Mr. Wood. "Folks don't see many one-way mirrors in Lafayette."

"Mommy mirrors," mumbled Mary senselessly. Will still just blinked.

Ah. Mr. Wood now knew the twins could see and hear through their stupor.

Good. He wanted Will and Mary to remember the next fine moments. He wanted tonight burned into their memories.

Just for the hell of it.

The magnate indulged himself a moment, reaching out his heavy hand to squeeze Mary's little neck and Will's bicep. Her softness and his unexpected musculature at age ... what ... eight now? ... delighted Mr. Wood.

Their young lives pulsed in their bodies.

It filled him with anticipation. Like cheeses, these two would grow better with age.

They'd be ripe soon. Teens. Bursting.

Disgruntled noises sputtered through Mr. Wood's speakers. He turned to business.

The Epicureans had gathered.

His heart hammered.

He'd never murdered so many people at once, even in Vietnam. Seven or eight at one time there, maybe once a dozen. A blast of napalm. A booby trap with mines and grenades.

But twenty-six at one blow? Two dozen Epicureans, plus Stefan and Ronaldo?

It would be a solstice to remember.

"Don't think of me as evil or good," Mr. Wood told the twins in his fondest voice. "This is just what I do."

He glanced to find the twins watching him with dead eyes.

"Your parents will be coming for you," Mr. Wood reassured them. "And then I'll be coming for you. But lots will happen first."

On the far side of the one-way mirror, The Epicureans milled and moiled, clearly uncomfortable.

Atomized in little animated groups all over the banquet room, they searched for possible exits. A knot of men purposefully worked on opening the thick wooden door where they'd entered. Another three or four Epicureans explored the wall where Mr. Wood vanished. These folks ran their hands over the smooth mahogany, testing to find a hidden lever or button, and they chanted words they thought they heard Mr. Wood say to make the secret door open.

All moved very slowly, erratically, clearly now under the influence of the hallucinogen. Mr. Wood watched the big Russian flail at something invisible that flew in circles over his head. The ugly Duchess stood with her red shoes in one hand and the lifted hem of her designer dress in the other, afraid to wade into some fantasized pool she saw in front of her.

Mr. Wood made a tut-tut noise with his tongue.

"Barbecue," he whispered to the twins.

He pressed a red button.

The Epicureans didn't go to hell.

Hell came to them.

Twelve blue tongues of superheated flame spewed from nozzles set behind the antique gas lights along the banquet room walls.

Blasts of fire jetted out from massive burners inside the friendly hearth.

The sealed doors of the kitchen burst wide, and full-throated flamethrowers violently hosed plasma fires over The Epicureans.

Through the one-way mirror, Mr. Wood watched his privileged guests drift through an orange-and-white fantasyland.

He closely studied their deaths. They first walked resolutely, hair and shoulders and clothes on fire, then they slowed, and they finally stopped completely. Individuals then writhed and twisted and convulsed in agony until they dropped.

The African warlord's colorful dashiki became a gown of flame. The two Dutch sisters transformed into twin torches, feebly waving bejeweled arms. The two Japanese businessmen embraced.

The sealed doors of the kitchen burst wide, and full-throated flamethrowers violently hosed plasma fires over The Epicureans.

"Nagasaki," Mr. Wood said quietly.

The magnate's eyes reflected fire filled with small black silhouettes.

Will and Mary simply stared. Neither child spoke. Mr. Wood wasn't even sure they *could* speak yet.

"Look at 'em!" Mr. Wood urged, in a near sing-song. "Just look at that, would you!"

One stubborn Epicurean ghost-walked through the inferno all the way to the one-way mirror. Mr. Wood barely recognized Stefan, the bullish waiter. He somehow reached the glass and pressed his blazing face to it, as if trying his best to see who watched from the other side.

When Stefan fell, he left a smear of melting skin and oil down the glass. It bubbled away almost immediately.

Mr. Wood couldn't know, but Will and Mary did have their thoughts.

It's an aquarium, thought Will. *An aquarium full of burning people.*

Where are some water hoses? Mary thought. *We can put out the fire and save them if we get some water hoses ...*

The unlikely trio in the control room watched The Epicureans burn. They sat until the last body lying on the floor and leaning against the wall had charred completely black and its charcoal pieces had begun to crumble away in the sea of flames.

Satisfied, Mr. Wood now pressed other buttons.

Video cameras showed different rooms in vast Sweet Comb. All were on fire now, the whole mansion. Drapes danced, burning, writhing. Couches and chairs blackened. Beds in guest rooms and the master suite transformed into lakes of fire.

One video screen displayed a black-and-white car coming hard down a long thread of driveway. Smoke boiled from its engine. Was it on fire too? Around the police cruiser, the Sweet Comb grounds shone bright as daytime.

Mr. Wood smiled.

Good. All going just as planned.

Black smoke suddenly rose from the floor of the control room.

"Mary? Will? Seen enough? Hope so. This smoke means we need to move along."

Will and Mary remained in a spell, unable to move or speak.

Mr. Wood gave a belly laugh. "Cat got those tongues? Well, here. Take this."

He fished in a pocket of his western jacket. He drew out a paper napkin carefully folded around a surprise.

"How about another delicious cookie?" Mr. Wood asked.

They fell asleep again immediately, collapsed on the red pillows.

Mr. Wood easily lifted Will under one arm and Mary under the other. He made his way out of the control room and through underground passages toward the solstice night.

He didn't glance back. And when finally outside in the bracing cold, neither did Mr. Wood look back at the inferno spreading at the speed of fire through every floor of Sweet Comb and high over the roof.

He carried Will and Mary a safe distance from the conflagration. He stopped when he reached a backpack, carefully provisioned days before, and two brown paper sacks with grease stains showing through the sides.

The roar of the mansion in flames rivaled an erupting volcano now, and the fire sucked a rushing cold wind to feed it. Incandescent tongues and fingers leaped a hundred feet above the highest gables, and the solstice night in this part of Alabama turned to flickering day.

Mr. Wood kissed Mary on the mouth. He kissed Will on the mouth. Then he gently nestled the two sleeping children down in deep grass. He took a thermal blanket from the backpack, and he deftly spread it over the kids.

He left one of the grease-stained paper sacks by Will, one by Mary. They held Champion's special order for the winter solstice: two large grilled beef hearts. Blackened. Killer-hot with blazing peppers. Cajun-style.

"Bon appetit!" said Mr. Wood. "And see you later!"

He briskly strode away in the direction of the jet that brought The Epicureans to Lafayette.

He didn't look back at Will and Mary either.

—41—

Home Fire Burning

The night grew surreal as they sped up the long drive of Wood Castle. The sky brightened eerily. Orange fire fell down.

A big ember exploded against the windshield. Elmore ducked reflexively.

"What in the world, Kelly?"

The police cruiser raced beside a stone wall overgrown by kudzu in places, though the vine now lay winter-brown. Hot sparks glowered.

"Hold on, El. We're getting past that gate."

Ahead rose a formidable two-story guard house modeled on a medieval keep. It held a towering entrance gate with a twisted black wrought-iron Wood Enterprises corporate logo – a massive oak tree, roots covering … and squeezing … an entire globe.

Kelly accelerated. Elmore wrapped both arms around his head.

The black iron oak tree hurtled toward the windshield.

The car stopped cold. The impact stunned both passengers.

For a moment, Kelly and Elmore heard crickets – impossible sounds on this icy first night of winter.

Mr. Wood's heavy gate was designed to stop a siege machine. Yet, somehow, the sturdy police car banged the metal barrier off its hinge on one side.

Elmore and Kelly sat half through the cockeyed opening. Black smoke rose from the police car's hood. One headlight still worked.

"Ouch," said Kelly.

She felt moisture over her left eye. She flipped the rear-view mirror. It fell off into her lap. Kelly knew she had a fresh cut and a rising welt on her forehead. A nice match for the livid bullet wound down her right cheek.

Elmore was okay, just some small cuts on his forearms. Glass from the cruiser's shattered windshield covered his lap. He looked like a bleeding diamond thief.

Kelly twisted the key.

"Come on, car, come on!"

The engine fired, wheezed, belts screeching. The cruiser lurched forward, dragging its front bumper down one side.

Kelly rumbled once more down Mr. Wood's long drive. She rounded a blind turn behind mossy live oaks.

Kelly stopped.

"Oh my God," she whispered. "Tell me they're not in there, El!"

Disneyland burned.

The towers of Mr. Wood's castle blazed. The wings blazed. The mansion's brick façade and black steel skeleton blazed, melting into an inner blast furnace.

Please, dear God, please, Kelly prayed, biting the back of her hand. *Please don't let Will and Mary be in that hell ...*

The inferno stretched the length of the mansion, a spectacular view across the police cruiser's entire windshield – or the hole where its windshield had been. Kelly shielded her face even at this great distance from the heat.

Scores of castle windows glowed absurdly, white-orange rectangles in raging walls. Fingers of fire grabbed greedily at the moon. A dark mouth gaped where the wooden double front doors of the mansion once stood. Dragon breath shot through the opening.

Elmore and Kelly watched a high gable of the roof – the very one Elmore fell from a year ago – cave in with a splintering crunch and hiss. It sounded like a crashing tsunami. A solar flare of heat made both passengers duck down in the police car.

"What now, El?" Kelly's shoulders slumped. "How do we find them? Where?"

Elmore pointed.

"Look! Is that a plane, Kelly? Right there? An airplane?"

Elmore shouldered open his door – it groaned loudly – and raised one hand to shield the fire-lit side of his face.

The aircraft taxied briefly out of sight behind a stand of pines, then reappeared, spectral, a strange dark color for a jet.

"It's flying off, with the world burning down? Someone is trying to leave!"

"Get in, Elmore!"

Before he closed the door, Kelly had the police car clanking toward the apparition on the runway.

That moment, the entire south end of Wood Castle collapsed. A new heat wave billowed toward Kelly and Elmore. The fire-white field rippled ahead of them like ocean seagrass.

A scorching blast hit the car. Elmore and Kelly actually felt the vehicle rock on its axles.

Anything or anybody caught in such a fire would be destroyed. No living thing, germ to giant, could survive.

Will and Mary? Where?

Kelly gave up on Mr. Wood's paved road. Instead, she cut directly across the estate grounds, safari-style. She coaxed the damaged car over old field furrows and limestone chunks.

"Hurry, Kelly! Go!"

Elmore craned to keep the aircraft in sight.

"It's turning around in front of the woods!"

Kelly tried to press the accelerator completely through the floorboard. A broken tree limb dragged beneath the cruiser, ripping up deep grasses.

Then she saw them.

Like a miracle.

Two children lay under a pale blanket, a hurricane of wildfire over them.

The small bodies rested in tall grass just to the left of the passing police car. Red rags of flame fell around the little shapes under the blanket.

Kelly didn't need to see the faces. She knew it would be Will and Mary.

Dear God, please let them be alive. Please let them not be burned up ...

She slammed the brake. Elmore braced both arms.

The police cruiser slid, wrenched, twisted to a stop. It coughed once, a death rattle. The engine died. Twin smoking ruts stretched over the vast lawn for fifty yards.

Elmore, the center fielder, outraced Kelly to the twins.

He fell over them, covering their bodies with his as if that wracked physique could protect them, always, from falling walls, collapsing beams, chunks of fire from the sky.

Kelly tumbled on top of Elmore, weeping like her heart would break. Weeping like her tears could drown all the flames in a world made of fire.

Snug and warm in the cockpit, Mr. Wood saw Elmore and Kelly race to the twins and fall. He watched them desperately embrace the small bundles.

He brusquely switched off the video feed. Mr. Wood had seen enough of this whole Hollywood chase scene.

Of course, he'd looked on remotely as the City of Lafayette's police car crashed his gate. Yet another camera logged the damaged black-and-white rattletrap clunking through his estate and coming face-to-face with the great fire.

Mr. Wood touched a button, and the video image went away. He pressed a second button. It turned off and erased the memory of every surveillance camera in every location of Mr. Wood's estate and throughout his business empire. Little red camera lights extinguished all around the globe at the same instant.

Now, Mr. Wood could simply fly a plane for a while.

He considered briefly what he left behind.

Lafayette would have no fire chief, no sheriff. No official would be left to investigate the mansion fire ... and even if that happened, not one morsel of bone would remain from Epicurean bodies consumed ... yes, completely eaten ... by flames so hot, burning so many days.

Oh, Mr. Wood thought, *that slob Turnipseed might try something valiant.*

The deputy would never find a clue. Not one.

Mr. Wood's plan had worked perfectly.

He idly wondered how long a man as fat as Jess Turnipseed would burn before he melted down to nothing.

"Elmore?"

He lifted his ear from Will's chest.

"Alive. Our strong boy."

A moment later, he raised his head from Mary.

"Just sound asleep, Kelly. We made it."

Fresh tears burst from Kelly, and Elmore reached to pull her close and tight.

Tears overcame him too.

Freezing cold and roasting hot at once, Kelly prayed for thankfulness, prayed to be the mother
Will and Mary always deserved.

Elmore prayed for amnesia. Whatever the twins saw this night, he hoped with all his might they would never remember.

A spark landed in Kelly's black hair.

Elmore swatted it, and they laughed like crazy.

They laughed so loud, a father and mother embracing by their sleeping bundles. Then they wept again. Loudly. With no shame.

For relief. For sheer joy.

Mr. Wood checked gauges and dials one last time. He eased the throttle forward and sped smoothly down the runway in the full moonlight.

The g-forces pushed him back in his elegant seat.

The plane's nose lifted. It rose up, up ... and away. Burning Sweet Comb lay behind – a pyre, a fantastic signal fire, a vast burning dream.

Mr. Wood's new life took wing.

He would return, soon enough. Those Rogers twins would be just what the doctor ordered in a few short years.

Meanwhile, Mr. Wood had plans.

He would take a hunting trip.

A special kind of hunting. He'd learned to love the most dangerous game as that young lurp in southeast Asia. He'd never found anything to match the thrill. Not in business. Not in travel. Not in bed.

Certainly not in dining clubs.

The last Epicurean leveled the jet off at 150 feet, far below conventional radar.

A sudden thought struck Mr. Wood.

He was not an impulsive man, but this once, this memorable night, he acted on impulse.

He veered the jet over Alabama countryside, returning for one last look. He navigated not by onboard tech or bright stars, but by the distant signal tower of fire that used to be Sweet Comb.

Mr. Wood looped back to the burning spectacle, banking, banking more. He made out the toy figurines of the Rogers family down below, lit by the firelight, embracing, all of them standing now.

"See you," he said aloud, without feeling.

The airplane dropped to 100 feet, and Mr. Wood guided it straight toward the blazing mansion he'd painstakingly designed from day one as a perfect monstrous death trap for The Epicureans.

The plane entered a soaring borealis of flames over the north side of the castle. Mr. Wood could see glowing rooms and charred walls and scorched furniture and paintings and bodies ... yes, bodies. Those crisp blackened Epicurean corpses wouldn't even be corpses tomorrow, simply mere flakes of cremation, gases wafting through pine needles and Spanish moss.

Who, in their saddest dreams, would seek the missing Epicureans?

Go to Milan. Knock on the door of a troubled family and ask if they'd gotten word from Don Sacco.

Go to Moscow. Stand in the boardroom of the state-run oil conglomerate and ask its baffled directors for any word on Ivan.

Go to Nagasaki. In the bubble tea shop, ask the black-haired kids with smartphones and earbuds what on earth happened to The Golden Ones.

The Epicureans held pieces of the world together. Their passing would leave holes.

But they kept their secrets, The Epicureans. The solstice feast would be their deepest, darkest. So who would ever trace them? How? Where?

Tomorrow morning in Lafayette, a boy on a bicycle or a city worker on a loud truck or a girl with a ponytail out jogging the high-school track would take a deep breath. The air would be full of smoke and curious black flakes.

That's where you could find The Epicureans.

Mr. Wood's plane ripped through a last soaring curtain of orange flame then streaked south. A horizontal meteor.

He stayed at low altitude on a course he'd charted for months, a vector clear of any tall power lines and cell towers and even remarkable trees.

In one hour, he'd leave Alabama and pass over the Gulf of Mexico, spearing low winter clouds, fighting turbulence. The raised nets of a shrimp trawler would tremble with his passing. The men on brightly lit oil rigs he owned off Fort Morgan Peninsula would glance up from labors on the night shift, wondering what in the world could be noisier than their own work.

Mr. Wood would fly three hours further. He would first see land again over Cuba, next Jamaica, then Santa Marta, Colombia. Flying on, the spreading lights of Barranquilla and Cartagena would pass beneath his wings.

Finally, over the remote Pacific coast of that country where mad Spaniards once searched for El Dorado, a city of gold, Mr. Wood would briefly climb to 800 feet.

He would wrestle himself into a special parachute and a carefully provisioned jungle pack. He would program the jet's sophisticated auto-pilot to fly three more minutes at this altitude, then fall back again to 200 feet and follow a beeline out over the dark Pacific.

The jet would streak seaward four more hours. It would run out of fuel and plunge into black waves.

These next years would be just like old times, back when big green-bellied birds dropped him into the Vietnamese highlands behind enemy lines.

This trip, down to Colombia in the dark, he'd hunt again.

He'd mapped eight or ten villages, isolated pueblos. The world only knew them from accidental communication once or twice a year when a lost boat captain or a crazy scientist blundered into contact.

Soon, those villages would lose communication. Forever.

Soon.

At 4 a.m. on the day after the winter solstice, Mr. Wood walked calmly in his Special Forces parachute and pack to the rear of his jet. He had specially designed the hatch for sport chuting.

He stood in the jump door for a moment, exhilarated by the whipping wind, savoring the smell of a world outside the jet.

Mr. Wood recalled how Don Sacco had madly convulsed this night as the torches spewed out arcs of blue death in the banquet room.

Ultimate power, Mr. Wood thought to himself, *is making men dance and die.*

He felt happy.

His Sweet Comb plan had worked like a charm.

After his hunting trip, he still had three-billion dollars in Switzerland.

And a date with Will and Mary Rogers. All grown up.

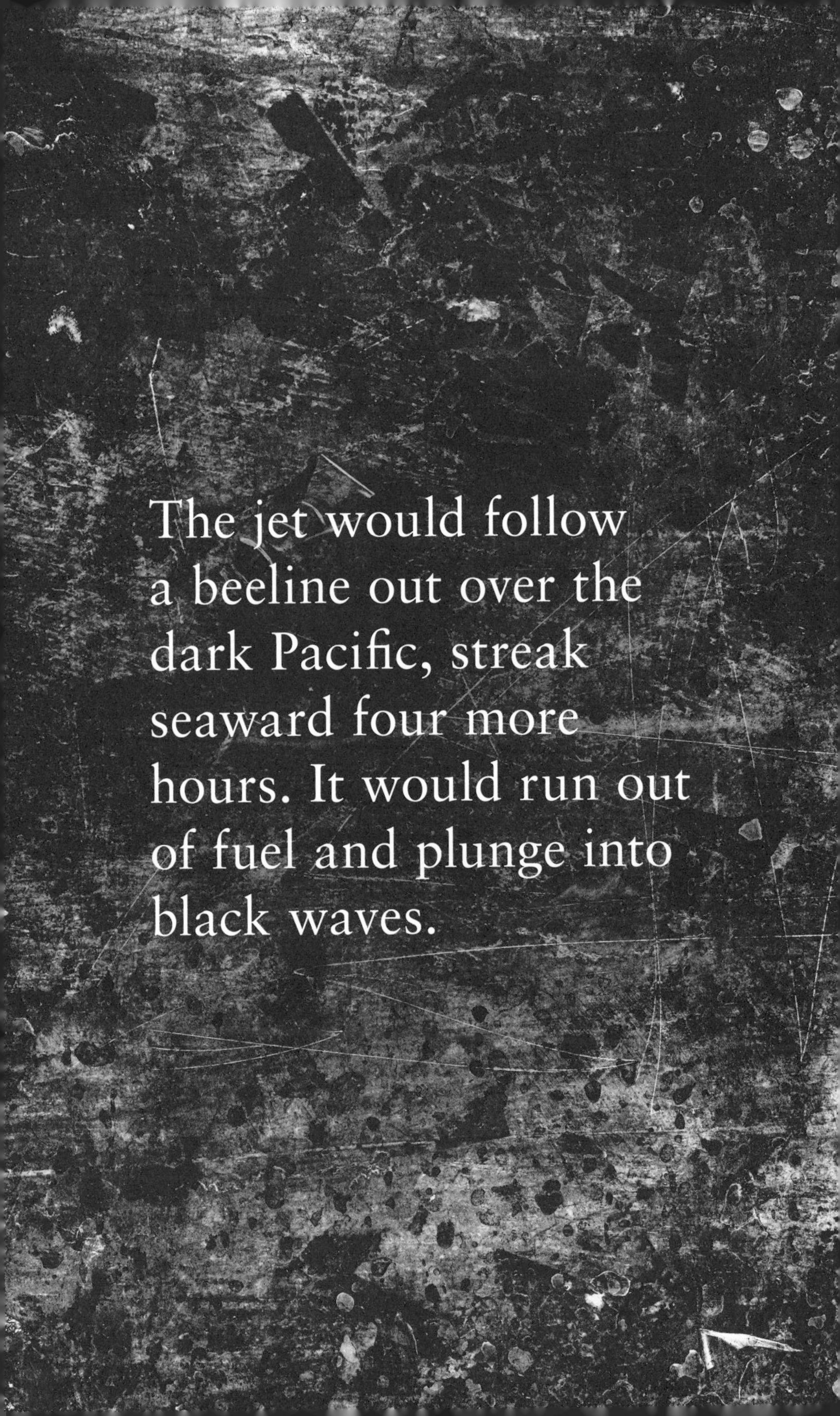

The jet would follow a beeline out over the dark Pacific, streak seaward four more hours. It would run out of fuel and plunge into black waves.

—Epilogue—

Eight Years After

It rained so hard, the day Elmore went away. A freezing downpour struck Lafayette Lies Asleep Cemetery just as mourners arrived. At graveside, twenty friends and family huddled miserably under a green tent awning. In back, people stood under umbrellas or sopping newspapers and did their best to ignore falling pellets of ice.

The service fell on his birthday, January 28. Elmore would have made it 37 years if he'd lived two more days.

Reverently by the coffin stood Kelly, in widow's black, and two red-haired teens. Kelly held a folded American flag.

Elmore didn't want a military funeral, but his National Guard buddies all turned out and made it seem like one. Tim Klein brought a flag flown over the Rock 'n' Roll Regiment somewhere in Iraq. Elmore's transport driver friends, Sharpe and Baxter, showed up in dress uniform. Elmore didn't know a preacher, but his old foreman, Plum – Colonel Plum on weekends and deployments – said a few words.

With Kelly's approval, Plum opened a Bible and read from Corinthians.

> *Love is patient, love is kind. It does not envy, it does not boast, it is not proud. It does not dishonor others, it is not self-seeking, it is not easily angered, it keeps no record of wrongs. Love does not delight in evil but rejoices with the truth. It always protects, always trusts, always hopes, always perseveres.*

Love, Kelly thought. *Oh, that boy could love.*

Tom and Johnny Lake, local boys who worked with Elmore on a Rankin crew the year he got sick, sang "Amazing Grace". Elmore liked to join their caterwauling in the panel truck on the way home from installations.

Two young Hispanic men who worked for Mr. Reece, owner of the funeral home, swung Elmore slowly down.

The hard rain washed red clay clods down one side of the grave onto the coffin.

Will Rogers, already a head taller than his mother, reached long arms around Kelly and Mary at the same time.

"I love you, Mama," whispered the striking young man, just turned sixteen like Mary. "Daddy loves you."

And now Daddy doesn't hurt anymore, Will thought. *He made it to that place with the lights.*

Elmore lived eight happy years after the kidnappings, the fire at Sweet Comb, the misfortune with Dick Wragg. After a kidney infection two years back, Elmore's compromised liver, the old war wound, stopped functioning normally. He got on a long VA Hospital waiting list for a transplant. It never came. The last months, Elmore watched reruns of *The Andy Griffith Show* and old episodes of *Gunsmoke* from a special bed.

Elmore spoke his last words at home, Kelly and the twins holding his work-roughened hands.

Gonna get some sleep now. I'll see you in a minute.

Those who braved the cold rain stepped forward to be received by Kelly and the twins. A line of doleful faces, male and female, offered sympathies.

Mr. Rankin, now hobbled by age, passed down the line. Elmore's old high-school ball coach, Mr. Inman, showed up with a cassette tape, a bootleg recording of Elmore and Dan Neeley singing "He Stopped Loving Her Today" in a locker room after practice. Kelly's classmate and rival for school beauty, Mona Lisa Flurry, couldn't stop crying long enough to even speak. She always had a thing for Elmore.

With dear friends, Kelly pulled back the veil for kisses on a cheek. The most beautiful face in Lafayette, rivaled more and more by young Mary's, nodded through pretty tears at one condolence after the next.

"I love you," Mary whispered, squeezing her mom's black glove. "And I'm freezing my butt off."

A young man, stick-thin, approached. A feeble moustache somehow clung to his top lip.

Timmy Wragg looked almost nothing like his burly dad, with the exception of the questionable facial hair. Skinny Timmy stooped, as if his head might be too heavy.

"Hey, Timmy," greeted Will and Mary at the same time. Will added, "Hey, thanks for coming."

It had been a while. The family history made things tough.

After all the ruckus, Elmore and Kelly and the twins moved from next door to the Wraggs farther out in the country, down the road to Tuscaloosa. Mrs. Wragg remained the same recluse after her husband's death. She died mysteriously about the time Elmore got sick with his liver. An aunt moved in to care for Timmy, and she kept the house.

Timmy carried his own Bible, red leather, bristling with bookmarks. Forgiveness was a mountain he would always have to climb in life.

"I'm really sorry, Mrs. Rogers." Timmy spoke in a rehearsed voice. "I admired your husband." Timmy turned to Mary. "Your dad."

Will felt a lump in his throat. Timmy offered a chilly, soft hand. Will shook it.

Kelly lifted her veil, leaned forward, kissed Timmy on the cheek. He blushed pink.

Mary, now a beautiful teenage girl, firmly shook Timmy's hand, and he turned even deeper pink and stumbled away.

Elmore's buddies from the Guard moved briskly, officially.

"A good man," Dee Langness announced.

"Fine soldier," said Fred Hardwick.

"Brave and a patriot," added Ed Morales.

Will and Mary and Kelly smiled politely. They knew Elmore's true feelings about his military service. He cautioned the twins about what happened to brave, patriotic country boys.

I'm Exhibit A, he told them more than once.

Sheriff Jess Turnipseed eased up. The funeral tent shrank.

"I'm so sorry, Miz Rogers," Turnip mumbled. He wasn't much for talking.

"You're so sweet," Kelly said.

"These young'uns look mighty grown up these days. I know their daddy was ... *is*, I mean, up there in Heaven ... he is mighty proud of 'em both."

Everybody liked Sheriff Turnipseed. He wore a gold badge. He had a heart of gold.

"Daddy was proud of *you*, Turnip," Will offered. "He always talked about how much you deserved to be sheriff."

Lafayette thought the same. The town cruised along under Turnipseed's watch. The slow-moving, slow-talking cop had a knack for keeping things calm.

People too.

After the Castle fire, Turnip spent days, then weeks, then months and years with state and national law enforcement officials, media, business associates of Mr. Wood, and curiosity seekers. Many arrived aggressive, seeking answers or bylines, prying into corners. Newly minted Sheriff Turnipseed gave them access to everything and anything they wanted to see. They poked through the ashes of Sweet Comb. They prowled Mr. Wood's estate and office at the idle wood yard. They combed through phone records and hospital files and interviewed dozens of Lafayette citizens. The FBI paid a visit, and then, soberingly, the CIA. The sign-in log at Lafayette Motor Lodge carried the signatures of foreign agents, investigators, government bureaucrats. They all descended on Lafayette to ask the same question.

What happened to Mr. Wood?

His empire had no direction, no head. He left no clue to his company strategies, his succession plans. His existence.

Visitors departed Lafayette with just about the same information they had when they first got out of their rental cars and climbed off their buses.

Nada. Niente. Nothing.

Not a clue on planet Earth existed about Mr. Wood.

When the files finally closed, Turnipseed's police report officially listed him a fatality in an accidental fire at his home.

"Turnip," Kelly whispered. "I'll always be grateful to you. You know that, don't you?"

She stood on her tiptoes in her black shoes to kiss his enormous cold cheek.

Ricky Kirkland, a teammate from Elmore's high-school baseball team, stepped forward.

"Elmore could hit a curveball," Ricky said, and that was all.

Will smiled, raised from grief. Will could hit a curveball too.

At the very end, among the last mourners, an elderly man hobbled up on a black cane. A hand or two in the dwindling crowd reached to steady Dr. Thomson as he deliberately picked his way around the red mound of dirt exhumed from Elmore's resting place.

"I'm so very sorry," Dr. Thomson told Kelly. "I'm sorry Mr. Rogers is gone."

His quiet voice had a distinguished, formal tone. Dr. Thomson always took great pride in being proper. His dignity had been a calming presence to patients nearly 70 years.

"Thank you so much, Dr. Thomson."

Kelly remembered that the physician had shown Mary tremendous kindness that terrible solstice when the snake struck her ankle. Kelly lay strapped to a gurney three floors below and couldn't see her own daughter. Dr. Thomson pulled rank on the intensive care staff and told Kelly what happened, and how Mary would come out of it okay.

"You didn't have to come out in this awful weather, you know. We would understand."

"We dang sure wouldn't be here," Will said, irreverently, "if we weren't burying Daddy."

Mary swatted Will's arm, but couldn't hold back a thin smile.

Dr. Thomson smiled too.

"Elmore was a better man than anybody knows," he said gently. "We have lost the kind of man I wish I'd been all my life."

The Rogers family lingered after the last car doors closed and the cemetery emptied.

It wasn't like Kelly to hang around. She despised funerals. She often told Will and Mary she didn't even want to go to her own.

But they silently said goodbye to Elmore. The wind whipped. The twins stood close to their mom with their arms hugging her.

They kept her warm. She kept them warm.

At last, shivering, Mary broke the spell.

"Won't a big cup of hot chocolate from The Milky Way be good?" Mary had restrained her tangle of red curls beneath a black scarf, but they looked ready to burst free any moment.

"Extra marshmallows for Mama," Will insisted.

"Extra for your daddy too," Kelly said. "He's the one who loved marshmallows."

Lafayette's newest widow managed the words without sobbing.

Now the rain, if anything, poured even harder. A cold front had pushed through. Breath turned to white vapor.

"Mama," Will said, "want to tell Sheriff Neeley that his old buddy Elmore is gone?"

Kelly smiled. That boy of hers. Just sixteen, but he had a heart like Elmore's.

"Let's do that," Kelly said. "But Danny already knows, I imagine. Those two are up in Heaven throwing a ball by now."

Will opened a huge black umbrella. It made a noise like a giant crow taking off. The twins flanked Kelly, and they said a short, silent graveside prayer, eyes closed. One last tear slipped from the corner of Kelly's eye and passed over her cheekbone and down the old scar from the sniper rifle.

"Bye, sweet Elmore," she said, and that was that.

Will opened a huge black umbrella. It made a noise like a giant crow taking off. The twins flanked Kelly, and they said a short, silent graveside prayer.

They moved among the headstones. The wind did its best to heist their umbrella, but Will maneuvered it just so and kept them sheltered, more or less, from needles of rain.

Dan Neeley's grave bore a simple headstone with his name, birth date, the day of his death – the winter solstice – and a few inspirational words chiseled in stone. The City of Lafayette had posthumously honored Sheriff Daniel Parker Neeley with a plaque that permanently displayed his silver badge. Encased in glass and surrounded by slightly sun-bleached plastic flowers, it made the grave look important.

The Rogers family didn't say much. They simply stood. Will and Mary ... and Kelly most of all ... knew how Elmore had loved Dan Neeley. How Dan Neeley saved his life overseas. What Dan Neeley meant to them all.

Will and Mary couldn't say why, but Sheriff Neeley's grave reminded both of a vivid, identical dream.

For years, the twins woke nights sweating, sometimes scared. In the same dream, they saw burning people, burning houses.

Somehow, in that way dreams have, the dream changed into a view out the window of a sweltering car.

For eight years, they kept their nightmares secret. They talked about them to one another, but no one else in the world. Neither twin understood the shocking dreams, but in time the terrible visions came less and less often in the night.

The grave reminded Kelly of something very different. Warm. Easy. Comfortable. A friend. And just when she met Elmore – before Elmore swept her away – more than a friend.

Kelly felt a surge of ... something. A thin veil between shame and fierce pride. A memory inappropriate for a funeral day, especially the day she buried a beloved husband.

Kelly remembered, unbidden, her fond farewell with Dan Neeley. His kind blue eyes. His freckled hands. His red hair cut in a new bristle to be like the policemen he admired.

Then Kelly helplessly remembered Elmore again. The passion of her life.

She turned to the twins.

They had come oh so soon in her life. Oh so difficult. At first, beautiful curses. Now beautiful gifts.

Kelly felt hot tears well up again. She pressed a black lace handkerchief to her eyes.

What happened to a life? Where did it go? How fast it passed, and what a blur the days, the nights, the strobe, the spinning carousel world ...

Danny. Elmore. Everybody. Everything.

A gust of wind, arctic cold, suddenly bulled into the mourners. The weather finally had its way and turned the umbrella inside out.

The Rogers family felt the stinging pain of the rain.

Do grieving people ever run at a funeral? Through a graveyard?

The Rogers family did. Will and Mary even raced.

They all laughed hysterically by the time they reached the car, emotions of every kind so near the surface.

Will claimed the wheel. He had grown into a man now, or almost. He'd gotten his license first, less than six weeks ago.

Mary put her arms around her mom and maternally pulled Kelly's beautiful conflicted face to her breast.

"Hot chocolate," Mary whispered, like a secret.

"Giddyup, Camry!"

Will kicked the car into gear. He drove a red import that Elmore had bought Kelly about a year before he got sick. It had a lot of hospital miles, but it could still go.

The Rogers family eased down a grass lane among headstones and plots, turned onto a paved cemetery road. It curved past a woodland, bare dogwood branches dripping onto the car.

From the corner of her eye, Mary saw something move in the trees.

A flash of white. A hat. A large shape.

She turned, saw nothing. One branch oddly twitching, up and down.

Mary's mind flashed back.

Something twitched in her memory. Up, down.

Winter, long ago. A rare snowfall. A snowman. A shotgun. Timmy Wragg's scared terrier.

A figure in the woods. White. Big. Watching. Then vanished.

A shiver surged up Mary's back.

It could have been just the wind.

One car remained at Lafayette Lies Asleep.

After the Rogers family departed, a door swung open on the black Oldsmobile. An umbrella popped out, also black, proper for the occasion. A black cane followed.

Dr. Thomson slowly emerged from the vehicle. Old doctors, he'd decided, could take their time doing everything.

The physician moved very deliberately for a second time that day toward Elmore Rogers' grave.

Most funerals in these times, Dr. Thomson lamented, a burial crew rushed to the grave with a front-end loader – a machine, for God's sake – before the bereaved family even got out of the cemetery. It shocked him. It seemed callous, so indifferent to those mourning loved ones.

But the bad weather today forced the gravediggers to wait a decent interval before pushing dirt over Elmore Rogers.

Dr. Thomson stepped under the green tent awning, wind ruffling, and he closed his umbrella. He looked down on the bare casket of Elmore Rogers.

He wrestled once again, for the millionth time, over one of the most difficult decisions of his life.

Dr. Thomson had a secret.

The doctor took a snow-white handkerchief from his pocket. He noticed the liver spots on the backs of his hands as he rubbed rain from the lenses of his bifocals. He often used this mannerism when he thought, pondered.

No one else in the world knew what he knew. And no one else in the world had been forced to wrestle, over and over, with it.

Dr. Thomson held the past and the future in his heart. His hands.

Years ago, a construction worker named Elmore Rogers fell off a roof. He showed up at Lafayette General in the flatbed of a pickup truck. The ER patched him up. The doctors took requisite blood samples.

Dr. Thomson had seen Elmore's charts, and he remembered the blood type: B. Type B, for baseball. For whatever reason, Elmore's blood type stayed in Dr. Thomson's memory.

The summer after Elmore's accident, Mary Rogers got bit on the ankle by a cottonmouth. She showed up at Lafayette General in the backseat of a car. In recovery, Dr. Thomson himself took requisite blood samples.

Mary Rogers had blood type A. Dr. Thomson knew her sample's integrity could not be in question.

Exactly that same time, by unfortunate, bewildering coincidence, Kelly Rogers tumbled off a trestle and nearly drowned. She showed up at Lafayette General in the back of Deputy Turnipseed's personal car. Intensive care doctors took requisite blood samples.

Dr. Thomson saw Kelly's chart too.

And so ... his secret.

Kelly Rogers had blood type O. Elmore Rogers had blood type B. B for baseball.

Mary Rogers had blood type A.

It was biologically impossible for a type O and a type B to produce a child with blood type A. It had never happened in the history of science.

Dr. Thomson had examined the science, the genetics. He had reexamined the science, for years now, and he'd closely followed breaking studies in the field.

He'd been left with absolutely no doubt.

Elmore Rogers could not be Will and Mary's father.

But Dr. Thomson had a hunch who might be.

He had lived a lot of years. He had heard a lot of stories. He had made a lot of diagnoses based on small clues.

Dr. Thomson reached beneath his dark funeral overcoat.

He took out a manila folder of medical records and slowly withdrew the paperwork. He considered for a long moment the name typed across the first page:

Elmore Rogers

Dr. Thomson took a short breath and said something like a prayer. Like Elmore, he wasn't really a praying man.

He dropped the medical records into Elmore's grave. They fluttered down like a shot dove and landed soddenly on the coffin.

Dr. Thomson ruined the shine on his black shoes by kicking in enough red clay to completely cover the medical charts. For all eternity.

Dr. Thomson felt relieved. His decision had taken a long time. Years. Now that it was made, a burden lifted from his mind.

He opened his British umbrella, an expensive model impervious to even gale-force winds, and edged out from under the dripline of the green awning.

The doctor slowly followed the exact route taken by the red-headed twins and Kelly Rogers through the cemetery just twenty minutes earlier.

Dr. Thomson stood reverently at the grave of Sheriff Dan Neeley. Its headstone bore name, birthdate, day of death – the winter solstice – and a few words:

Killed in the line of duty. Officer and gentleman. Rest in peace.

Dr. Thomson would rest in peace tonight too.

Dr. Thomson dropped the medical records into Elmore's grave. They fluttered down like a shot dove and landed soddenly on the coffin.

Acknowledgements

The Epicureans first appeared online in serialized form in *The Bitter Southerner*. That publication's founder, Chuck Reece, conjured Rumpelstiltskin skills, spinning my sentences of straw into shiny gold. Chuck and I learned that publishing a serial novel over 41 weeks is like building an airplane as it's flying. Thanks, Chuck, for your steady hand at the controls.

My gratitude runs deep for faithful friends and readers of all my books. *The Epicureans* makes three novels now, and I've also written a history. You inspire me to write.

Thank you, Adela, my brave and beautiful wife, and thank you Henry, my incredible son, and I thank the heavens for the love of Juan Manuel and Ana Maria, my stepson and stepdaughter. Endless thanks for the love of my sisters and my brother in Alabama (and my late brother too), and my family all over the U.S. South and elsewhere in the world.

I owe special gratitude to an exceptional writers group that sampled *The Epicureans* in progressive courses. The Verbalists – Chantal James, Tom Junod, Mel Konner and myself – invited the muse to a regular stop at my house on Seminole Avenue in Atlanta. (Ann Cale Kruger and the late Herb Perluck earn extra thanks for watching over our shoulders.)

I offer my lion-hearted friends David and Teresa Langness a thankful shout-out. You are always near my work.

Thank you to my beloved Alabama, home to all my novels. The stories I write come from my first 38 years of life and adventures in that hallowed, haunted, holy place.

I owe special thanks to two fellow Alabamians, Gene Elmore and Willie Rogers, who crewed my family's house-building business in Dothan a half-century ago. I blended their surnames to create my protagonist's name in *The Epicureans* – Elmore Rogers. I learned perseverance and endurance from these men; together, we drove a million nails and dug a thousand miles of ditches.

My thanks to all the writers who offered kind advance blurbs for *The Epicureans*: Tom Junod, Colum McCann, Melissa Pritchard, Brad Watson (we miss you, brother), Mel Konner, Chantal James, John Holman, Hank Klibanoff, Tom Mullen, Ben Montgomery, Josh Jackson and Jim Flannery. I revere your own works. Your glowing endorsements seem like treasures.

My eternal thanks to Jason Killingsworth, head of Dublin-based publisher Tune & Fairweather, and the talented designer Andrew Hind. Jason and I met in 2005 on staff at *Paste* magazine where I served as books editor for a decade. (Thanks to two of *Paste*'s founders, Josh Jackson and Nick Purdy, who found me too!) Jason moved with his wonderful wife Summer back to his birthplace in Ireland, and he chose to make *The Epicureans* Tune & Fairweather's first work of fiction, an honor that yet amazes me.

Thanks to all who supported *The Epicureans* Kickstarter campaign. Your underwriting gave gorgeous covers to a story I dreamed, and I consider us partners in publishing. Thank you from the bottom, top, inside and outside of my heart.

About the Author

Charles McNair is an Alabama-born writer now based in Bogotá, Colombia. His debut novel, *Land O' Goshen*, received a Pulitzer Prize nomination for Fiction. His second novel, *Pickett's Charge*, was nominated for the Townsend Prize for Fiction. *Play It Again, Sam*, a history of former Atlanta mayor Sam Massell, followed in 2017. His work has appeared in a variety of publications, including the *London Times Literary Supplement*, *USA Today*, *Paste*, *Atlanta Magazine*, *Southern Living*, and others.